W9-DGF-089

THE DROWNED VAULT

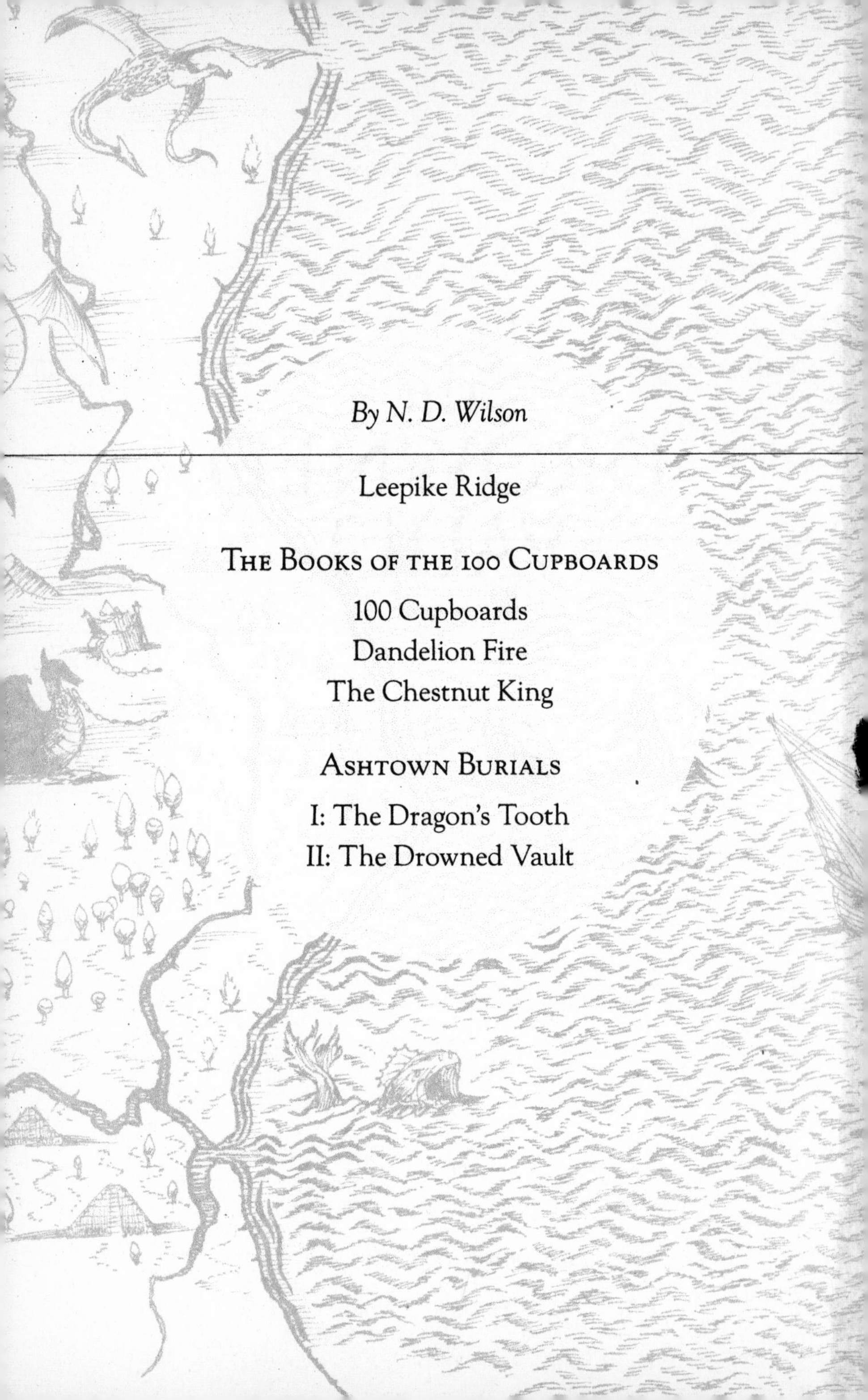

By N. D. Wilson

Leepike Ridge

THE BOOKS OF THE 100 CUPBOARDS

100 Cupboards
Dandelion Fire
The Chestnut King

ASHTOWN BURIALS

I: The Dragon's Tooth
II: The Drowned Vault

ASHTOWN BURIALS

BOOK II

THE DROWNED VAULT

N. D. WILSON

RANDOM HOUSE NEW YORK

Visit us on the Web! randomhouse.com/kids

Educators and librarians, for a variety of teaching tools,
visit us at RHTeachersLibrarians.com

Library of Congress Cataloging-in-Publication Data
Wilson, Nathan D.
The drowned vault / N.D. Wilson. — 1st ed.
p. cm. — (Ashtown burials ; bk. 2)
Summary: Cyrus and Antigone must track down Phoenix and the Dragon's Tooth while facing a threat from the transmortals.
ISBN 978-0-375-86440-7 (trade) — ISBN 978-0-375-96440-4 (lib. bdg.) —
ISBN 978-0-375-89573-9 (ebook)
[1. Secret societies—Fiction. 2. Supernatural—Fiction. 3. Brothers and sisters—Fiction. 4. Apprentices—Fiction. 5. Magic—Fiction.] I. Title.
PZ7.W69744Dsm 2012 [Fic]—dc23 2011051618

Printed in the United States of America

10 9 8 7 6 5 4 3 2 1

First Edition

Random House Children's Books supports
the First Amendment and celebrates the right to read.

For Lucia, Ameera, and Marisol,
three parts to my laughter

PROLOGUE

THE MAN IN THE PINK SHIRT stopped outside his house. Four steps forward and he could be out of the pouring Parisian rain, sheltered beneath his stone stoop. Instead, he took one step back. The wet paper grocery bag he carried was disintegrating in his hands. His shirt was plaster-pinking his shoulders. Miniature rivers burbled and swirled around the cobbles beneath his feet.

The man's eyes slid up his front door, up the stone wall, up past the gargoyles spewing rainwater, and settled on an attic window built into the roof.

In front of the glass, a broad spiderweb was bouncing and shivering in the rain. It hadn't been there when he'd left that morning. The spider had done her job—just like the girl had promised. Someone, some*thing* was inside his house.

Down one floor, a curtain moved.

For the past year, he'd been afraid of this moment. And now that it had come, he was frozen, weakly staring at the danger.

The man turned and tried to move casually up his street. Ten feet. Twenty. Then he dropped his grocery bag in the gutter and he ran.

Behind him, he heard his front door open.

For the first time in four centuries, Juan Ponce de León thought he might die.

He ran faster.

⁂ one ⁂

DASH

THERE IS ONLY ONE BEGINNING. There is only one place and one moment where the world, life, and time itself began. There is only one Story. It began in the dark. It has many middles and many ends. You and I could chase it for lifetimes and only make it longer by our living. It is too sprawling for these pages and too big for this mouth.

We begin in a middle. We trace a smaller arc.

This is a story about darkness. About lightness. About blood, and about family. About losing, about finding, about danger and dying, about what happens when the world remembers the oldest of its secret things (and what happens when the world forgets).

This is a story about Cyrus and Antigone Smith.

The sun dumped golden heat onto the flat back of Lake Michigan. It baked unwatered grass and persecuted Wisconsin cows. It sent men cursing back indoors and blistered unprotected skin beside a thousand swimming pools. Frogs, young and foolish, exploded while crossing sizzling asphalt streets. But the forests were happy.

Cyrus Smith was one year and one slice of summer taller than he had been when the Archer Motel had burned and he had first seen Ashtown's green lawns, its piece of the Great Lake, its airstrip, its mazes, its Burials, and its occasional hot-air-balloon battles. To Cyrus, one year ago was a different reality. One year ago, he hadn't known anything about the world. Now, well, he knew one or two things. But not enough for Rupert Greeves. Not enough to leave Ashtown on his own. Not even enough to travel with Rupert. He was stuck at Ashtown with hundreds of people who pretended they couldn't see him, dozens who truly hated him, and a very few he could call friends—and they were mostly staff.

Cyrus stood two miles from Ashtown, behind a rope laid on the ground, beside an old moss-covered stone marker, beneath a canopy of maple trees. He was sweating in the shade, waiting for someone official to arrive with a stopwatch. He sighed and rolled his head slowly on his shoulders, trying to ignore the heat. He handled it better than some, but this was beyond even his threshold—the last roar of summer. Fruit was ripe. Insects were fat—ready to lay their eggs and die. Soon the leaves would bake and brighten, but for now, hidden in the glowing green canopy, cicadas whirred and whined like distant weed-eaters. All around him, miniature droplets rained gently down from the maples as armies of gorging aphids ate and ate and ate. With his eyes closed, Cyrus could feel the sugary insect honeydew settling onto his face. With both hands, he swept it away in his sweat.

His bare arms were dark and lean from training. His bare feet curled impatiently in the grass. He'd shaved his head three weeks ago, but his thick hair was quickly shagging back in. In the center of his tight white tank top, a small black monkey was boxing inside a yellow shield. He reached up and felt the cool serpent body of Patricia, his patrik, the first of the strange creatures he had met in this new life. She was his invisible necklace, unseen whenever her tail was tucked firmly into her mouth, as it was now. Hanging from a ring around her body—made just as invisible as the snake—were two keys. Cyrus fingered them—one small and silver, one large and gold. Beside them on the ring was an empty silver sheath. Last year, when William Skelton had tossed the key ring to him, the sheath had held the Dragon's Tooth.

When he and Antigone had arrived at Ashtown, they had been heirs to the outlaw William Skelton. They had been Smiths, the last two members of a long and troublesome line. They had been swept away, disliked, ignored.

Now it was worse. Now they were the Smiths who had lost the Dragon's Tooth. At best, they were failures.

At worst, they were traitors. No matter what, they were the reason Phoenix had the tooth—the cause of Ashtown's fear.

Cyrus blinked sticky eyelids, lost in uncomfortable memory. He looked up into the maple branches and watched a red-winged blackbird hop along a twig. The bird was always there, always nearby. It chirped at him and he whistled back at her—*her*, even though he knew the bright splashes of red on the wings meant it was a *he*. But to him, it was a *she*. He didn't know why.

Stretched out on a bed of moss, Antigone groaned and stretched. The whistle had wakened her.

"Cy." Antigone stood slowly and leaned against a tree trunk. Cyrus ignored her; he knew she could not be ignored for long.

"Yoo-hoo. Cyrus. Rus-Rus!" Antigone's black hair was as long as it had been in years, actually reaching past her jaw. She tucked it back behind her ears, knuckled her eyes, and crossed her arms. Her skin was almost as dark as Cyrus's, and in the shade, her eyes glistened blackness. "You don't have to do this. And you know Rupe isn't going to like it one bit."

Cyrus squinted through the trees. In the distance, down a long, slow hill, he could just see the stone buildings of Ashtown. Beyond them, the glistering lake. A two-mile run to the shore. Two-mile swim to the buoy. Two-mile swim back from the buoy. Two-mile run back up the hill to the starting line. He could do it. Even in the heat. Maybe.

"Cyrus . . ."

Cyrus looked at his sister. She had leaf rubble clinging to her hair. "Rupe can tell me how much he doesn't like it when he gets back. It's not like he's been training us."

Antigone sighed and wiped her damp head with a forearm. "I don't get the hurry. We made Journeyman on time. We can go for more whenever. Or not. Who says you have to make Explorer at all? Rupe says it can take years. We don't have to rush."

Cyrus didn't answer. He could hear an old engine through the trees behind him. He turned as a rusted-out Jeep emerged between the trunks and stopped, weeds rustling against its bumper. Rupert Greeves was behind the wheel.

Cyrus held his breath and let his cheeks inflate. Rupert pushed scratched sunglasses up into a scruff of short hair on his head and locked eyes with Cyrus. Then the big black man slid out of his seat and moved slowly toward Cyrus. A lean and freckled passenger hopped out on the other side, but Cyrus didn't pay him any attention. He was waiting for a sign of Rupert's mood—a flicker of anger, a twinkle of approval. But the Order of Brendan's Avengel gave him nothing. The man's dark face was stone, if stone could have a swollen cheek beneath a small butterfly bandage. He was wearing tall canvas safari boots and worn shorts with bulging pockets. His white linen shirt was unbuttoned at the neck, revealing a tangled nest of scars on his chest, and his sleeves were rolled short, snug around his biceps. A short beard strengthened his already strong jaw.

Rupert stopped beside Cyrus and stared down toward Ashtown. Then he nudged the rope on the ground with his boot. Cyrus inhaled and waited. He could feel the big man's heat next to him.

"Hey, Rupe," Antigone said. "Welcome back."

"Hello, Antigone." He didn't sound angry. At least not at her.

"Any news about Phoenix?" Antigone asked.

Rupert shook his head. Cyrus clawed at the earth with his toes. The tall freckled kid—more of a man, actually—was stretching on the ground beside the Jeep. He hopped up and moved to the rope beside Cyrus.

Antigone pushed off her tree trunk and straightened. "Just in case you were wondering, this wasn't my idea."

Rupert waved her quiet. Then he thumped a heavy hand on Cyrus's back.

He looked down at Cyrus and raised his eyebrows. "No work on Cartography? Mazecraft? Navigation? Greek?" He sounded more amused than disappointed. Cyrus almost smiled. Rupert continued. "Sleep-fasting? Reliquary? No? Nothing?"

Cyrus raised his hands, relieved that he wasn't in

real trouble. "Rupe, you know I need someone to help me with that stuff. I hate being inside, and all the books Antigone reads make my head hurt."

"How could they make your head hurt?" Antigone asked. "I don't hit you with them."

Cyrus plowed on. "How am I supposed to study stuff on my own? I don't know how to do that. I'm supposed to have a Keeper. I mean, I do have one, but he's always gone."

Rupert's eyes sagged, suddenly tired. He raised a scabbed hand and scratched his short beard. "You want a new Keeper?"

"No!" Antigone jumped, shaking her head at her brother. "No, we don't! We're fine with you. We like you."

Cyrus shrugged. "I just want to come with you. At least sometimes. To, you know, help fix things. With Phoenix . . ." He looked up at Rupert. "We're always stuck here. But when I'm an Explorer, I can go where I want. So I train."

Laughter flashed across Rupert's face. "You train? Is that what this is called?" Rupert sighed and nodded at the man with the freckles. "Cy, Tigs, this is Jeb Boone. His first time back to Ashtown in two years. He's going to run with you, Cyrus."

"Boone?" Cyrus turned. "You're Diana's brother?"

Jeb grinned. He was a lot taller than Cyrus. His hair was even more strawberry than his sister Diana's, and his bare shoulders—as broad as Rupert's, though not as powerful—were swarming with an ant colony of freckles. "Yeah, Diana's my sis, and she's told me stories. I like what you're doing, little man, testing at the 1914 levels. It's gutsy. Hope you don't mind me joining you."

Cyrus was confused. "Aren't you already an Explorer? How old are you?"

Jeb glanced at Rupert, and then back at Cyrus, blue eyes sparkling. "I'm nineteen. And yeah, I've ranked up. So call this a retest. Curiosity, I guess."

Rupert laughed. "He's doing me a favor. I've asked him to pull you out if you drown."

"You know, Cyrus." Jeb cocked his head. "You *are* only thirteen. There's not much point in trying for this stuff until your body's ready."

"Don't bother yourself, Jeb." Rupert slapped Cyrus's shoulders. "The boy's a Smith. He'd walk on glass if you told him not to. He only learns one way—crash and burn, yeah? Now get loose . . . I don't have all day to sweat out here."

Cyrus watched Jeb bounce and stretch his legs.

Antigone glared at him. "Stretch, Cy."

"It's hot. I'm ready."

Jeb laughed and puffed a drop of sweat off his nose. "I know what you mean." He nodded at Rupert. "Anytime."

Rupert Greeves pulled a stopwatch out of one of his deep pockets.

Cyrus worked the ball of his left foot into the ground. He bent his knees and leaned forward, coiled, ready to spring. His limbs were long, and they loved to cover ground. Beside him, Jeb bounced in place.

Next to any thirteen-year-old in Ashtown—or in his old school in his old life—Cyrus would have been confident. But next to a nineteen-year-old named Boone? His nerves were tingling.

Breathing slowly, he looked down the hill between the trees and tried to focus on the distant water. He didn't have to beat him. Just beat the clock. It wasn't a race.

Cyrus tried to relax. *But if I do beat him . . .*

Just the thought, the mere possibility of triumph, tightened every muscle fiber in his legs. Somehow, Rupert knew.

"Your own pace, Cyrus Smith. Not his. Run your own pace."

Right.

"Marked in three," Rupert said. "Two . . . one . . . off!"

Cyrus sprang forward, legs straining, splayed toes grabbing at the ground. His long strides settled quickly into pace. Fast. Really fast for the distance. He tried to even out his breathing and relax his shoulders. He could hold it. He knew he could.

On his left, Jeb Boone swooped past.

Cyrus didn't have to tell his legs what to do. He was

already accelerating, fighting to match the faster pace. Grass and leaves flew up behind Jeb, and Cyrus sputtered and spat in the older boy's wake.

Antigone Smith winced. Her brother was nuts, and always had been. He was practically sprinting. He was going to kill himself. Beside her, Rupert Greeves, Avengel to the Ashtown Estate of the Order of Brendan, Keeper to Cyrus and Antigone Smith, sent a burst of laughter rattling through the trees.

"You know," Antigone said, "that was really mean."

Rupert looked at her, widening his eyes in innocence. "Mean? Antigone, I'm only doing what's best for him."

Antigone crossed her arms. "And you just had to get Diana's brother?"

Rupert grinned. "Cyrus wants to be trained? Today, I have arranged for him to run faster than he has ever run." He turned and watched the two shrinking shapes. "He'll find a new speed. I'm giving him that. And when he finally collapses in failure, he'll have found a little more wisdom. I'm giving him that as well."

Antigone watched for a moment. "He's going to die."

"He'll try to," Rupert said. He turned to the Jeep, knocking his sunglasses down over his eyes. "But Jeb won't let him. Come on. In this heat, the wise ones drive."

Antigone followed him, eyeing his battered cheek.

"What happened to your face? You had to have gotten close to Phoenix if you were getting your face smacked."

Rupert grunted as he slid back behind the wheel and fired the engine. He only fit because the Jeep had no doors and his left knee was jutting out the side. Antigone grabbed the roll bar and hopped in next to him. The Jeep was ancient. She could see grass through holes in the floor.

"Come on, Rupe." She smiled at the big man. "You'll feel way better if you tell someone. Was it animal, vegetable, or mineral?"

Rupert looked at her. "I approached a somewhat irritable transmortal who was yammering about a pair of kids named Smith and what he thinks they gave to a villain named Phoenix." He ground the Jeep into gear. Antigone's smile disappeared.

The red-winged blackbird watched the Jeep go. After a moment of indecision, she dropped out of the tree, wove her way around trunks beneath the canopy, and flew down the hill after Cyrus.

Cyrus's splitting ribs were breathing for him. His legs were on fire as they churned, and his shoulders were clenched as tight as wire knots. His throat was closing, his tongue swollen and dry, and still he needed to spit. And spit. And spit again. The heat was too much, the pace was too much, and the streaming sweat-salt in his eyes was too much to blink away.

Cyrus had switched off Time. It didn't matter how long he'd been going. It didn't matter how much longer he must go. There was only now—only these steps, and these, and these, and these, and no others. He set his mind to *ignore all pain* and struggled to keep it there. His body's screams grew distant and muffled, like nightmare residue after waking.

Somehow Jeb was only five strides in front of him, moving easily—shoulders gliding level with the ground, knotted calves driving feet that were casually chewing up yards at a time.

Ashtown was closer now—off to his right. Hulking buildings and statues and rooflines mounded out of the green lawns like a hand-carved mountain range. The sight no longer surprised Cyrus any more than watching planes drop onto the grassy airstrip outside the kitchen windows.

Running erased Cyrus's frustrations. The exertion overwhelmed thoughts of pale-faced Nolan and his ancient-language drills, along with all of Antigone's books and worries. The comments in the halls. The blank faces. The complete absence of tutors willing to work with anyone named Smith. Dennis Gilly—a porter—taught them sailing and navigation. Gunner—a driver—had started training them in marksmanship, but he had gone home to Texas months ago.

It should have been Rupert. It should all have been

Rupert. But he kept disappearing. And when he was at Ashtown, he just looked at Cyrus like he was hopeless.

A whimper from his side snapped Cyrus's mind back. He'd been running for at least . . . no, don't think about it. Too long.

He could see Rupert's Jeep a few hundred yards ahead, waiting by the lake. Antigone was standing on the hood, hands shielding her eyes, watching the runners come. Beside her, taller than she was, stood Diana, strawberry hair pulled back in a tight ponytail.

Darn it.

Cyrus looked away from the spectators, focusing only on Jeb, on his pace, on the rhythm his bare feet pounded out on the ground.

Jeb was accelerating.

How? Why? Cyrus didn't understand. He tried to push, to dig, to find another gear inside him. Mistake. His legs suddenly deadened. Acid surged through his veins, and his knees clipped against each other midstride. He was falling.

Cyrus threw up his hands and tucked his head to roll. He flipped too quickly, slammed onto his back, bounced up onto his knees, and fell forward onto his face.

Jackhammers thumped against his temples. His arms wobbled as he pushed himself up. He tried to find his feet, suddenly threw up in the grass, and then stepped in it as he managed to stand. He ignored the wetness between his toes, the foul taste, and the stringy cling on his chin.

He couldn't stop. Not now. He had to get to the water. Swimming was easy. It would be like resting. Cool water. He'd be fine.

At first, he couldn't control his direction. His legs carried him sideways. But the slope helped him steady his pace, and he accelerated slowly.

Jeb had reached the water. Cyrus heard Diana whoop and whistle and clap for her brother. He saw her ponytail swing. Jeb waved to her, bounced in a comic stride, and plunged in.

Two lifetimes later, Cyrus reached the Jeep. He saw Rupert check his stopwatch. Antigone was worried. Diana was smiling.

"Cy?" Antigone asked.

"Go, go, go!" Diana said.

Cyrus hit the water. High knees through the shallows. One foot worked; the other didn't. He collapsed forward, and his knees and toes and fingers banged against silty-skinned rocks on the bottom. He didn't care. He didn't feel the pain. He sank and felt the coolness surround him. He felt the relief of weightlessness. And then he needed to breathe.

On the shore, Antigone bit off her thumbnail while her brother splashed away. Diana watched next to her.

"He's a little crazy," Diana said. She looked at Rupert. "You're sure he'll be okay?"

Rupert shook his head. "I'm not sure of anything." He looked at Antigone. "That boy can run. I didn't think he'd even finish the first mile at that pace. He didn't run in school?"

Antigone snorted. "He hated coaches. Can we make him stop? Or just follow him in a boat or something?"

Stroke, stroke, stroke, stroke, breath. And again. Again. Two hundred *agains*. Three hundred. Or four. Or five. Cyrus didn't know. He knew that his strokes were growing shorter. His breaths were becoming gasps. Cyrus's dead, barely kicking legs slowly sank. His shoulders slowly petrified.

Cyrus hadn't seen Jeb since he'd hit the water. He couldn't see the buoy. He only knew that he was swimming. He hoped it was in the right direction.

His calves had already cramped twice, his toes felt permanently splayed, and his feet wouldn't bend. And finally, the next stroke simply didn't come and Cyrus's legs swung all the way down beneath him. Bobbing in place and spitting out sweet mouthfuls, he looked around. Ashtown's little harbor and its stone jetty were directly behind him. He had drifted well off course.

He shook his head and spat again. Water dribbled out

of his ears. He could hear something groaning—a machine. A boat?

Cyrus tried to kick up above the waves to scan the surface, but his legs had reached full paralysis. He could barely tread water. The groaning was growing. Engines, but above him. An airplane. He looked up.

A broad, fat-bellied seaplane the size of a small airliner was banking hard out over the lake. It turned, and turned, and turned until it was flying straight toward him. While he watched, it leveled its wings and dropped into a low approach, preparing to touch down. It was coming fast.

Panic erased Cyrus's weariness. His arms wheeled as he tried to crawl out of the way.

Too late. Fifty yards off, the fat belly hit the surface, blasting sheets of water up its sides. Two wing skis threw up huge rooster tails.

Grabbing one quick breath, Cyrus dove. He kicked and clawed himself down. And down.

Propellers dusted the surface. The white belly carved through the blue above him, and he felt himself being sucked back up. Covering his head, he slammed into metal. Riveted steel punched his back, rolling and spinning him into darkness. And then the plane was gone.

Cyrus was sinking.

Life became simple. Cyrus Smith was going to die.

His legs and his arms wanted to die. His back and his head and his lungs all wanted to die.

Fine, thought Cyrus. And then two arms slid beneath his.

They were not freckled arms. They were pale and thin and smooth. And strong. Cyrus looked at them, and then he looked into a girl's face made of moonlight and pearl, and haloed with long, swirling black hair.

The girl was pulling Cyrus toward the surface, and suddenly, his legs and his lungs and his head were willing to live again.

Fine, thought Cyrus.

two

ARACHNE AND . . .

THE WAVES IN THE FAT PLANE'S WAKE slapped together and died as rumbling propellers pulled the heavy metal body on toward Ashtown's harbor. The sun sorted through froth and foam and settled on a floating mat of brown and gray and black—a thousand tiny things with legs linked together, rocking on the waves. Bubbles rose up beneath them.

Gasping, Cyrus surfaced and spewed a mouthful of lake down his chin.

Across from him, the strange girl's head and shoulders slid up through the water without a splash. Cyrus sputtered and spat and blinked. The girl's wet black hair glinted in the sun like polished stone. Her eyes—set wide apart—were pale blue and full of light, but also worn and tired like ancient sea glass.

Cyrus shook his head. Droplets still clung to his face. And then one crawled onto his eyelid, and he slapped at it. They weren't droplets.

"Don't," the girl said. But Cyrus wasn't listening. The

things were all over his hands, his cheeks, his ears. All around him, the surface of the water was covered with a tangled mass of floating spiders.

Cyrus yelled. He clawed at his face and pulled at his ears. Spiders were on his lips, his nose, his eyes. Desperate, he grabbed a breath and dove.

Underwater, the spiders came off. While Cyrus sank, he scraped at his arms and neck and face and watched dozens of the tiny bodies float weightlessly through sunlight water-rays like an army of eight-legged astronauts. Above him, he could see the dark outline of the spider mat surrounding the strange girl.

The silhouette of a small boat with an outboard motor bounced into view.

Antigone leaned out over the prow of the boat, bracing herself against every bouncing wave and scanning the surface ahead. She'd spotted Cyrus just before the plane had landed, and then she'd seen the girl dive out of a side door behind the wing. But now . . . nothing.

She didn't like this. Not one little bit. She lifted her head just enough to let the wind snap her hair out of her face, and then she bit her lower lip hard. Last year, she'd been in the same boat, at night, in a thunderstorm, circling the burning wreckage of a plane, searching for both of her brothers and her mother.

"There!" she shouted. Two heads bobbed to her left.

She straightened and pointed and felt the boat veer beneath her as Rupert followed her hand. Diana Boone slid up into the prow beside Antigone, one hand above her eyes to block the sun, her strawberry ponytail whipping behind her like a flag.

A wave rose and, for a moment, Antigone lost sight of her targets. She caught her breath, waiting. There they were. No. There *one* was. Just the girl, calmly watching the boat come.

"Rupe!" Diana yelled.

"Got 'em!" Rupert throttled up and the boat surged forward, clipping across the rough water. A moment later, he killed the motor and let the boat drift toward the girl.

"Where's Cyrus?" Antigone yelled.

The girl didn't answer. With one easy backstroke, she pulled herself through an odd carpet of flotsam and grabbed on to the side of the boat.

Diana and Rupert each grabbed one of her hands and pulled her up out of the lake and set her on her feet inside the boat. She was Antigone's height, and she was wearing simple jeans and a black button-down shirt, but Antigone hardly noticed. She couldn't drag her eyes off the girl's strangely old and very perfect face. For a moment, Antigone even forgot Cyrus.

"Hello, Rupert," the girl said, pushing back her long, wet hair. "Not exactly how I was hoping to arrive."

Rupert nodded. "Arachne. Where's the boy?"

"Here!" Cyrus was treading water twenty feet off the other side. "Is the water clean? Is there anything floating on top?"

Antigone hopped across the boat and leaned out over the side. "Just us. I don't see anything. What do you mean? Are you okay? Anything broken?"

Cyrus shook his head and spat out another mouthful of lake water, then crawled slowly toward the boat. His arms felt like stone, but he managed to keep slapping at the water until he made it. Rupert grabbed Cyrus's wrists and heaved him up, his ribs cracking on the metal edge, and he tumbled inside. After a few panting breaths, he elbowed himself up and looked around.

Rupert's eyes were hidden behind sunglasses, but his mouth was almost smiling. Antigone looked worried. Diana grinned. The girl with the impossible eyes was staring at him. Behind her, the army of floating spiders was climbing into the boat.

Cyrus yelled, staggering to his feet.

Antigone and Diana turned, and then began backing toward Cyrus. Rupert simply watched the dripping rug of spiders slide in over the side.

"Arachne," Rupert said. "Meet Diana Boone, Antigone Smith, and Cyrus Smith. Di, Tigs, Cy, meet Arachne. The spiders are . . . hers."

Cyrus swallowed and wiped his eyes. The spiders were hers? What did that even mean?

Rupert scratched his jaw and focused on Arachne. "Who was flying that plane?"

Arachne looked down at the spiders swarming around her. A slight whisper trickled out between her lips, and the spiders began to herd themselves forward into the prow. She looked up. "Gil was flying. I saw the boy—Cyrus—early enough to pull up, but he still set it down. I thought we might have killed him." She stared at Cyrus for a moment. "If Gil had known who it was, he would have made sure of it. You're the one who lost the tooth?"

Bristling, Antigone stepped forward. "He didn't lose anything. It wasn't like that."

Arachne wasn't listening to Antigone, and she didn't look away from Cyrus's eyes. Cyrus couldn't have blinked even if he'd tried. His eyes were frozen by hers, trying to tell her every thought, every dream, every forgotten memory. He wanted to be strong, to seem carefree and confident to this spider girl, and then he knew it didn't matter. She saw him truly. There was nothing he could hide. He realized he'd been holding his breath, and he exhaled slowly.

"Yeah," he said. She released his eyes, and his head sagged. "I lost the tooth."

For the first time, Arachne smiled. "For what it's worth," she said, "I'm glad we didn't kill you. You were smart to dive. Are you okay?"

Cyrus hurt. His legs and lungs and shoulders. His head. His back.

"I'm fine," he said.

"No need to lie," Rupert said. "You'd almost killed yourself even before the plane. We'll get you to a nurse." He looked at Diana. "You spot Jeb?"

She nodded, shielding her eyes. "At the buoy and turning back. He'll stop if we make him, but he'll want to finish."

Of course he will, Cyrus thought. *Perfect.*

"Right," Rupert said. "The clock's still ticking. We can drop Cyrus off and be waiting for Jeb back at the line."

Most of the spider army seemed to have straggled into or onto the boat. Rupert Greeves jerked a pull cord, and the outboard motor roared to life.

With the boat racing toward the harbor, Cyrus sat and shut his eyes against the wind. Muscles in his thighs and bruised back shivered and quaked in tiny spasms of exhaustion. He felt someone sit beside him, and he opened his eyes wide enough to squint.

Antigone reached up and touched a lump on his scalp. Cyrus winced. His sister showed him her fingertips—blood. He didn't want to know what his back looked like.

Antigone leaned toward him.

"I thought you were dead," she said. "Again."

Cyrus forced a smile and shook his head. "Not yet."

His sister studied his face, and then looked at the strange girl in the prow, surrounded by huddling spiders. As the wind lashed and dried Arachne's black hair, it was beginning to curl.

"Cy, are we ever going to get used to this place?" Antigone asked.

Cyrus reached up and felt the keys hanging safely on cool, invisible Patricia. He stared at the spider girl. How much had he already gotten used to?

"Maybe," he said. "But I hope not."

The boat bounced on. After a moment, Antigone leaned her head against her bigger little brother's shoulder. A year ago, he would have shrugged her off.

"You did good, bruv," she said. "Better than Rupe thought you would, that's for sure."

Cyrus snorted. But he let the compliment settle in. He was grateful. He wouldn't have admitted it to anyone else, but he was even grateful for the plane. He wouldn't have finished the swim. At least now he had gotten out of the water with a shred of self-respect and one of the best excuses of his life—a plane had landed on him. But he wasn't any closer to making Explorer. He wasn't any closer to being able to set out from this place on his own.

He focused on the fat silver plane, now anchored just off the harbor jetty. Behind it, the green slope climbed up to the grassy airstrip and the underground hangars, and up again to the hulking stone building that was the heart of the Ashtown Estate, heart of the Order of Brendan. A crown of statues on the roofline posed against the blue sky, and sunlight sprayed off the tall windows Cyrus knew belonged to the kitchen. Last year, Big Ben Sterling had ruled that realm, walking on two metal legs with golden bells dangling from his ears. Now Cyrus only saw Ben in his dreams. Food in the O of B had been a lot better back when Sterling had been around. Even thinking about the crooked cook made Cyrus hungry, which was strange given that Sterling had ended his Ashtown career with a mass poisoning.

Antigone lifted her head from his shoulder. "Wanna go see Mom?"

Cyrus inhaled slowly. "Yeah," he said. "As soon as I eat something." He looked up, squinting against the sun. A small bird was flying fast above the boat, its dark outline moving in and out of the glare. As surely as he knew anything, Cyrus knew there were red feathers high on each wing.

Three hours passed before Cyrus opened a door in the hospital wing and stepped into his mother's room. He'd insisted first on returning to the starting line with Rupert to wait for Jeb—and to congratulate him on shattering an old Order record when he arrived. He'd scrounged for food in the kitchen. Finally, he'd gone to the hospital wing and been bandaged—one butterfly on his scalp, two on his back. Small cuts. He'd had worse from training with dulled sabers with Antigone. *Much* worse from training with knives against pale Nolan.

The hospital room was white and clean and fresh. A black ceiling fan whirled above the bed, and white curtains fluttered around a window. Bright photographs had been arranged on a small night table. Antigone was already seated beside their mother's bed, tipped back in her chair with her riding boots on a stool and a book in her hands. Her eyebrows shot up when Cy came in, and she glanced at a clock above the door.

"Sorry, Tigs," Cyrus said. "But I'm here now."

Antigone nodded toward the bed. "Tell her, not me."

"Oh, come on." Cyrus pulled a chair over from beside the window. "She's not mad at me. She doesn't even know I'm here."

Antigone slipped her feet off the stool and let them thump onto the floor. "Cyrus Smith!"

Cyrus dropped into his own chair, facing the bed. Leaning forward, he picked his mother's smooth, dark hand up off the white sheet. "Hey, Mom, I'm here." He shot a glance back at Antigone. "Now she knows," he whispered.

Antigone crossed her arms, but she smiled. "Cyrus was late again, Mom," she announced loudly. "Nothing's changed."

Cyrus looked at his mother's sleeping face. Her cinnamon skin was framed by the whiteness of her tight hair, surrounded by the bleached hospital whiteness of her pillow. She'd been asleep ever since she'd been pulled from the frigid waves in California, since Cyrus and Antigone and Dan had watched her plunge in after their father's distant, shattered boat three years ago.

Antigone had done their mother's hair in a braid, pulling it back from her face. Her breathing was steady and soft, her body relaxed, like she was well rested and ready for a new day, like she might suddenly yawn and stretch and smile at her waiting children. In some ways she seemed younger—three years without a smile to crease the corners of her eyes, without a laugh to seam her cheeks, without a son to give her worry.

Cyrus ignored the tightness in his throat. His thoughts were always a jumble beside his mother's bed. Words ran from him.

Something rapped on the window. Antigone stood and crossed the room to crank open the glass.

Cyrus kissed his mother's hand and pressed the back of it against his cheek.

"Love you, Mom." His voice was just above a whisper. "Lots."

Behind him, the red-winged blackbird hopped through the open window and perched on the sill. Antigone sat back down.

"Keep reading, Tigs," said Cyrus. "Whatever it was."

Antigone leaned back in her chair and picked up her book. She cleared her throat. " 'When one is attempting to reproduce a map or chart from memory, it is of the utmost importance to have first seen—truly seen—the original in the correct way, even if only for an instant.' "

Cyrus groaned. "Really, Tigs?"

Antigone continued. " 'One must learn to see things correctly at the first before one can recall things correctly at the second. For example, when looking at a map of an island, one might mentally overlay the shape of a twelve-pointed star on top of the chart and therefore see the unpredictable coastline in terms of the more regular, but still unpredictable—' "

"Tigs!" Cyrus yelled. "You're torturing her."

Antigone looked over her book. "She likes it."

"You're torturing *me*."

"Yeah?" Antigone smiled. "Well, I'm okay with that." She tapped the page. "This works, by the way. I don't use an imaginary twelve-pointed star, but it works."

"Well, you and your imaginary shapes can have fun together," Cyrus muttered. "Leave me out of it."

Antigone grew serious. "Listen up, Rus-Rus. You're the one who's insisting that we try for Explorer. At some point you need to realize that we can't do that just by running and shooting and fencing and swimming, okay? Are you listening to me? At some point, you are going to have to read an actual book. And Nolan can't force-feed you your languages, either. You have to want to learn . . . Cyrus?"

Cyrus dropped his mother's hand and straightened.

Antigone set her book down. "What is it?"

A woman's shout echoed in the hall. On the windowsill, the blackbird hopped in place.

"Run and fetch your precious Greeves!" boomed a male voice just outside the door. The knob turned and the door banged open, slammed against the wall, and bounced all the way shut again.

Cyrus and Antigone both jumped to their feet.

The knob turned again, and the door swung open again, slowly this time. A huge man ducked beneath the lintel. He was wearing white pants, white patent-leather shoes, and a white patent-leather belt. A bright turquoise polo shirt barely contained his massive torso. A carpet of chest hair crawled up from his open collar, and the same hair, though not as thick, coated his tree-trunk arms. His face had been recently shaved, but his dark beard was visible all the way up his cheekbones. His sparking eyeballs would have been big for a bull, and the thick curly hair on his head had been oiled.

"Doors can be tricky," Cyrus said.

The man's purplish lips were as thick as young snakes, and he spread them into a smile. His teeth were factory-perfect.

"Who are you?" Antigone said. "You shouldn't be in here."

The man gripped the door with a huge hairy hand and shut it quietly behind him. Cyrus blinked. He had six fingers, each the size of a cucumber. Cyrus looked at the other hand. Six.

"People call me Gil." His voice was oddly smooth and soft coming from such a big face. "And I have flown a very long way to meet the two of you." He looked at Cyrus. "But especially you."

"You were the one in the plane?" Antigone asked. "You're the idiot who landed on my brother?"

"Yes," Gil said. "I landed on your brother. And if I had known—"

"Right," said Cyrus. "Whatever. Arachne already told us. You would have made sure to kill me."

Gil smiled.

"What's your problem?" Cyrus asked. "What do you want?"

"My problem?" Gil's knuckle-size nostrils puffed out a breeze. "I have many problems. My home in France has been burned. My golf has become terrible. My money has become gone. My life has nearly ended. A friend's life—a life that should have been unending—*has* ended. Another friend is missing. I have retraced my problems, and my problems begin with this . . . place." He looked around the hospital room, and his big lips curled. Then he looked back at Cyrus. "But especially with you."

"Now, hold on," Antigone said. "Cyrus didn't do anything."

"Seriously." Cyrus shook his head. "I didn't give the tooth away, even when I could have. I tried to keep it safe."

"Keep it!" Gil's shout rattled through the room. The blackbird shrieked. "Safe! No man should keep it! There is no safe for such a thing!"

Cyrus and Antigone backed away slowly. Antigone pointed at the big man.

"You listen," she said. "Cyrus didn't do anything wrong. I'm sorry about whatever happened to you. We both are. Okay? But we didn't do those things."

Gil began to move forward. "No. The man-devil who now holds the tooth did those things. He is using it to do more things. He will not stop doing things. And why does the man-devil have the dark tooth?" Looming over Cyrus and Antigone, he waved his timber arms, smacking his knuckles against the ceiling. Another step forward and the black fan would kiss his scalp. His hair was already rustling. "No need to answer. Because *you* chose to keep it. Safe! Ha!" Twelve thick fingers curled and cracked. "Fools must be dealt with before villains."

Behind the big man, the door swung open quietly.

Cyrus watched Rupert slip into the room and off to the side. Jeb Boone slipped through and to the other side. Arachne stood framed in the doorway. Both men were carrying triple-tipped spear guns. Large spools of wire were coiled beneath each stock.

"Gil," Rupert said quietly. "You shouldn't be in here. Please step back."

Gil didn't turn, and he didn't step back. He locked eyes with Cyrus and grinned. "Or what?" he asked. "Little Rupert will hurt me?"

Rupert flipped a switch on the side of his gun, and Cyrus heard it begin to hum. Jeb did the same. A moment later, tiny electrical arcs trickled between the trident tips.

"Gilgamesh of Uruk," Rupert said. "Stand down. You are in violation of your treaty with the Order of Brendan."

"Violation?" Gilgamesh spun around, ribs heaving beneath his turquoise shirt. "The Order is nothing. Less than nothing." His fists clenched, and his huge shoulders flexed. "I should break your neck, Avengel."

"Gil, please," Arachne said.

"Fair warning, Gil," said Rupert quietly. "Stand down or I will bring you down. This will be your third violation. If the Order uses force on you now, you will be eligible for Burial." Rupert's eyes darted to Cyrus's, and his head twitched slightly to the side.

Cyrus grabbed Antigone and slid toward the window.

Still in the doorway, Arachne looked stunned. "Burial?" Her voice wavered. "Mr. Greeves, you wouldn't."

Gil began to laugh. "Of course he wouldn't. This place would be torn down around his ears first. I could hand him a sack of Smithling corpses, and he still wouldn't dare Bury me!"

"I can," Rupert said. "If needed, I will."

In a flash, the huge man lunged for Jeb. One six-fingered hand snatched the spear gun, and the other slammed Jeb against the wall.

Cyrus jerked in surprise as Antigone swallowed back a scream. Gil was much too quick for his size. While Jeb sank to the floor, Gil grinned, pointing the crackling spear gun at the ceiling. Rupert's was trained on Gil's chest. When Gil spoke, his voice was low.

"Do not threaten me, Rupert Greeves. I am harming no one. And neither are you. See?" Swinging his gun around toward the window, Gil fired. The electrical trident snapped a crackling web of blue through the air and blasted out through the glass as Cyrus and Antigone dropped to the floor.

Gil let his gun clatter down beside his tremendous feet. Rupert, still tense, nodded at the door. Arachne backed out into the hall.

"The Order will make this right, Rupert Greeves," Gil said, and he ducked out the door and disappeared down the hall.

"I won't play football again!" Gil shouted. "I won't!"

Arachne leaned back into the room. "Rupe?"

"Keep eyes on him." Rupert sighed. He flipped his gun off and let it dangle by his side. "Please." He was sweating.

Arachne nodded and reached into a canvas satchel slung over her shoulder. Three long-legged brown spiders climbed out of the bag onto her arm. She lowered them to the floor. Cyrus watched them race away after Gil.

Arachne straightened. "If there's anything else . . ."

"There is," said Rupert. "But we'll speak about it later."

Arachne nodded and hurried away.

Jeb was trying to stand. Instead, he sank groaning back down the floor, clutching his ribs.

"I'm sorry," he mumbled. "Rupe, I'm—"

Rupert shook his head. "Forget it. Stay still. Nurse!" He turned to Cyrus and Antigone. "We need to talk. Right now. Both of you Smiths come with me."

He picked up Jeb's empty gun and turned toward the door. "Nurse!"

"Coming, coming!" Two women bustled over to Jeb as Rupert strode out of the room. Cyrus and Antigone looked at their mother, then hurried after their Keeper.

When the nurses had taken Jeb away, only the red-winged blackbird remained in the room. After a moment, she dropped off the sill, fluttered toward the bed, and perched on the back of Antigone's chair. Cocking her head, she eyed the sleeper in the bed. Then she let out a low musical call—the kind heard all summer in the cattails beside ten thousand ponds.

Katie Smith's eyes fluttered. But only for a moment. And then they were still.

three

THE POLYGONERS

CYRUS AND ANTIGONE TURNED sideways to squeeze through an oncoming group of men. All of them were in safari boots and shorts; all of them were fit and hard with sun-browned skin. Cyrus had never seen any of them before—they'd either been on an extended trek, or they were from another of the O of B's Estates. The men were talking seriously, but every eye followed the Smiths as they passed.

They knew who Cyrus was, and they knew what he'd lost.

Antigone and Cyrus quickened their steps. The halls were crowded with the late rush to the dining hall.

"New people everywhere," Antigone said quietly. "Where are they coming from?"

Cyrus watched a group of five teens approaching. Three of them he knew—Sean, Chris, and Francis—typical boring, rich-kid Journeymen who disliked the Smiths and always seemed to be vacationing with family somewhere incredibly obscure. The three of them were clustered around and chattering at two blond brothers who Cyrus didn't know. Both of the brothers were shorter than Cyrus, but had broader, heavier shoulders and long, thick arms. They were wearing tight black T-shirts and pocketed fatigue shorts. A simple white design had been stenciled on the center of each shirt—an elephant skull with large curving tusks above crossed telescopes.

Cyrus stared at the strange Jolly Roger and then looked into the boys' faces. Tan skin, square jaws, and very blond hair. One of them had traded half of his right eyebrow for a lump of white scar tissue. Cyrus could still see a faint crisscross where the wound had been stitched.

The boy with the scar saw Cyrus and Antigone as they tried to pass, and shouldered his way free of his fans.

"You're the Smiths?" he asked. His voice was accented, almost British, but Cyrus knew that wasn't right. Australian? That was wrong, too.

Cyrus nodded. Antigone looked down the hall, where Rupert had stopped and was waiting for them.

"I'm Silas Livingstone," the boy said. He pointed at his brother. "This is my little brother George."

"Hey," said George. "You two are why we're here."

"Great," said Antigone, glancing at the three other Journeymen. They all looked like they smelled something unpleasant. "Nice to meet you. Cy, we should keep going."

"Wait." Silas cocked his head, raising one and a half eyebrows. He was looking at the emblem on Antigone's shirt. Then he looked at Cyrus's. "What is that? A boxing monkey? I've never seen that before."

South African accent, Cyrus thought. Or something close.

George pointed at it. "Is it your family's crest?"

Silas laughed. "George, that's not the sign of the Smiths."

"Right." George looked embarrassed, like he'd forgotten something obvious. "Well, it's not a Continental crest or an Estate crest or an Expeditionary Badge. Is it a new trainer's?"

Cyrus looked at Antigone, and back at the two brothers. He shrugged. "I have no idea what most of that meant."

Antigone tucked back her hair and smiled. "It's the sign of the Polygoners," she said. "We got it off a World War One flight jacket. Now it's our symbol."

"Smiths!" Rupert yelled. "Now!"

"What *is* the sign of the Smiths?" Cyrus asked.

Silas cocked his half-eyebrow in surprise. "The three heads?"

"Heads?" Antigone asked. "Of what?"

"Of men," said Silas, confused. He seemed to think he was missing a joke. "Grand to meet you both. And no hard feelings, I hope."

Cyrus and Antigone continued down the hall and rejoined Rupert. Antigone glanced at her brother.

"Heads? That's a little weird," she said. "And no hard feelings? What was that about? Why would there be hard feelings?"

"They'd like their father to be named Brendan instead of your trusty Keeper. Some would take that personally, but I share their hope, as unlikely as it is," Rupert turned and continued down the hall. "Stay close and keep moving."

"Where are we going?" Cyrus asked. "I thought you wanted to talk."

"We'll talk in your rooms," Rupert said. "Not before."

"Our rooms?" Cyrus said. "What about dinner?"

Rupert laughed. "Cyrus Smith, we'll talk when we get there."

Rupert carved his way through the crowded halls. Even side by side, Cyrus and Antigone fit easily in his wake.

Three heads. Living heads? Dead heads? Cyrus liked the boxing monkey better. He watched the mapped mosaic floors slide past under his feet. He stepped over a tile street map of Rome. And then what he thought was the Grund of Luxembourg—but only because someone had told him once. He still wasn't sure what a Grund was, but by now he was probably supposed to.

He and Tigs had been walking over these mapped floors for a year now, and in that time Cyrus had come to genuinely like their new home. A lot. Even though the rich Skelton inheritance promised to them by the little lawyer John Horace Lawney VII had been a wash, and even though they were surrounded by people who always seemed to be giving them the stink-eye, this was the place where Cyrus had learned to fight and shoot and fly. He could wander halls lined with relics and artifacts that would have been beyond his collector's imagination only a year ago. He knew what it was like to ride a bull shark and how its muscled sandpaper skin felt against his hands. There had been days when he had done nothing but search through faded old photographs of explorers, wondering which faces belonged to Smiths. But for all of that, he also felt stuck, almost more stuck than he had at the Archer Motel. He and Antigone weren't allowed to leave the Estate without the permission of their Keeper, and Rupert was never around to take them anywhere off grounds. He certainly wasn't about to let them go anywhere on their own.

There were no classes and no real structure. Every time he looked at a book, he suddenly wanted to go for a run, or find a sparring partner, or ask Diana to take him up in one of her planes. But he was going to have to start making himself do the studying if he ever wanted to leave this place and hunt for Phoenix himself.

Cyrus grimaced. Yeah, there was plenty he didn't like. The looks in the dining hall. The muttered comments in the halls and the collections and even in the armory. And the fact that almost no one would train with him. That made him angry—even angrier because, on some level, the people who hated him were right. He, Cyrus Smith, had come to Ashtown carrying the Dragon's Tooth—a dangerous relic given to him by an outlaw. And he had lost it.

Next time . . . he didn't even finish the thought. Even now, Cyrus could picture Phoenix's face and see the beast he became without his white coat. He could feel those powerful hands, and even more powerful eyes, eyes that could close a throat and choke out breath.

Cyrus shivered. He had to do something, had been trying to do something. But even he could see that his efforts to qualify for Explorer were usually distractions when he felt penned in. Would Phoenix really be any more frightened of Cyrus the Explorer than he had been of Cyrus the Acolyte? Phoenix wasn't even frightened of Rupert.

Cyrus hopped over a complicated tile map-tangle in the floor labeled *Sub Aquagium Parisii.* Aquagium? It didn't ring a bell.

"Tigs?"

"Sewers of Paris," she said simply. "You've scraped through one level of Latin. You should know that."

"You should know that I wouldn't."

The three of them passed the loud dining hall and wound their way through the hallways. They passed photographs and strange animal heads and maps and guns and swords and battered wooden propellers until the hallway broadened and they finally reached the ancient leather boat of Brendan on its pedestal and the long dragon skin on the wall. Rupert strode past them to the great doors—the huge wooden doors that opened onto the courtyard lawn of Ashtown. Rupert opened a small wicket door on the right side and ducked out.

Cyrus and Antigone hopped through after him, and a moment later, they were both blinking in the smoldering heat.

The sun was already low, but the humid air held the warmth like . . . like a baked potato, Cyrus thought. A potato he had to live in. He groaned and shut his eyes. His skin already felt greasy.

"I don't mind it," Antigone said. "Better than the cold."

Cyrus watched Rupert move down the stone stairs toward the huge courtyard lawn flanked by hulking stone buildings. In the center of the lawn, the towering fountain was steaming as it churned. All over the lawn, in tight regimented rows, Acolytes were erecting canvas tents.

"What's going on?" Cyrus asked. "Did I miss something?"

"Preparations," a voice said behind Cyrus. He wheeled around. Dennis Gilly stood beside the big wooden doors, sweating in his porter's suit and the bowler hat he had tied on with a ribbon beneath his chin. He wasn't nearly as pimply as when they'd first met him, but he'd hardly grown in the last year. "Mr. Greeves has ordered all Acolytes out of quarters. The staff are expecting a great number of guests who require quarters in isolation."

"Smiths!" Rupert shouted. He was already striding away along a gravel walk.

"See ya, Dennis," Antigone said. Dennis nodded and touched his sweat-slick nose.

Cyrus and Antigone jogged down the stairs and ran to catch up to Rupert. Two Acolytes shrieked past, laughing and wrestling over an old bloated football.

"Rupe," said Cyrus. "When Gil was storming out of Mom's room, he said he wouldn't play football again. What did he mean? Why would he have to play football?"

Rupert smiled. They were nearing the shade of a covered stone walkway. "After that whole scene, that's what you're wondering about?"

"No," said Cyrus. "I want to know why the courtyard is all of a sudden a huge campground, and I want to know if more Gils are going to show up, and I want to know what Arachne's deal is, and I want to talk you into taking me on your next trek. But if I bring any of that up, you'll probably just tell me to shut up and wait till we're in our rooms."

Rupert laughed. "All right, then. Money is complicated for a transmortal. Think about it. They tend to have the needs of mortals, but without the mortality. Just because they don't die doesn't mean they're wealthy enough to feed themselves and clothe themselves and shelter themselves *forever.* Mortals retire when they think they have enough money to care for themselves until death. But when there is no death, there's never enough money. Gil recently lost a great deal of his worth, and in the recent past, whenever he's run out of money—all the way out of money—he's made up a new identity and played professional football. He's actually in the Hall of Fame under two different names. Apparently he doesn't want to do it again. It's usually best if he waits a decade or so between careers."

"Bizarre," Cyrus said.

Rupert laughed. "You have no idea."

Their three sets of feet stopped crunching gravel and began scuffing along paving stones. The shade wasn't any cooler than the sun.

"I don't care about football," Antigone said. "And I don't care about Gil, as long as he stays away from us and from Mom. I want to know why the sign of the Smiths is three heads."

Rupert stopped at a battered door set into a rough stone wall. For Cyrus, opening that door always took two hands and a braced foot. Rupert jerked on an iron ring with one hand and the door squealed open. "The three severed heads?" Rupert asked. "Who told you about them? Did you see it in a book?"

"Severed?" Antigone grimaced. "That's disgusting."

Inside the doorway, stairs curled up in a spiral. "Yes, severed," said Rupert, smiling. "It's a grim crest and a famous one. The Order expunged it almost a century ago, but it's still in all the books and stories. Expunging history is harder than some committees might think." Rupert gestured for Antigone to go first, and she began to climb. Cyrus followed. The stairs were as dank as ever, but beautifully cool once the door banged shut behind them. Rupert's voice echoed in the stairwell.

"For the last forty years or so, crests and seals haven't mattered much in Ashtown. There were fewer great expeditions to be had and less pride in Expeditionary Badges, less pride in what remained of the old families, and less rivalry between Continent and Continent, Estate and Estate. Now one tends to see the symbol of the Order—the ship of Brendan—or the crests of trainers on the chests of paying pupils. But there are those who still keep the old crests close."

Cyrus reached the top and stopped in the long narrow hall that led to their rooms. There were windows, but only the size of arrow slits. The walls were cool bare stone. Antigone was waiting.

"What was the point?" she asked when Rupert reached the top. "And why did we have three severed heads?"

Rupert followed her down the hall. Cyrus trailed behind. "The point," he said, "was pride in one's family, in one's Estate and Continent and achievements, et cetera. People who understood could look at your badges and crests and they would know who you were, where you were from, what you had done, and—frequently—what your ancestors had done. Your three severed heads became the Smith crest four centuries ago as a result of John Smith and his . . . achievements."

At the end of the hall, Antigone pushed open a little door.

Rupert laughed. "You don't keep it locked?"

Cyrus shook his head. "Not usually. There's nothing in there worth taking."

Antigone stopped in the doorway and looked up at Rupert. "What is the crest of the Greeveses? Is your family old, too?"

Rupert looked from Antigone to Cyrus. After a moment, he sighed. Then he began to unbutton his worn safari shirt.

"You two," he said, "and only you two, get me to yammering like an old nan on her front porch."

Cyrus stared, confused, as the big man stripped off his shirt. The tangled web of scars on his muscled chest was beyond sorting out. His left shoulder was dotted with what looked like bullet wounds—or maybe teeth marks—and his right side had a large old-looking T scar just above his hip.

"Wow," said Antigone. "What are those—"

"No," said Rupert. "No questions." He jerked his safari shirt inside out, and then slid his arms back through the sleeves. Now there were patches on both shoulders—three on his right and one on his left. He slapped his right shoulder. At the top, there was a black medieval ship in a yellow circle.

"The Order of Brendan," he said. Then he tapped another round patch below it—silver chains knotted into the shape of a Celtic cross inside a green circle. "The old emblem of the Ashtown Estate." Beneath the two circles, there was a long, thin red band. Inside it, a golden dragon with six wings was roaring. Rupert traced it with his finger. "That tells you that I am the Blood Avenger for my Estate—First Avengel for the Order of Brendan." He turned and tapped the lone patch on his left shoulder—a silver chess knight with eagle wings, flying inside a dark blue shield. "The symbol my great-grandfather adopted as the sign of Greeves." He tugged his shirt back off, inverting it again. Then he slipped it on with the patches against his skin and began to button it up. Cyrus and Antigone were staring at him. He smiled and nodded at the doorway. "Get in there."

When William Skelton died in the firefight at the Archer Motel, he had already made Cyrus and Antigone his Acolytes and heirs. But they hadn't been allowed to move right into his old rooms. They'd been stowed in the Polygon until they'd made Journeyman, and that hadn't happened until the New Year. Anything would have been an upgrade from sleeping in a crypt and walking on planks above hungry Whip Spiders, but they'd expected something more from the rooms of the notorious and wealthy outlaw.

There were five rooms in all. The largest was a long central room with a stone fireplace at the end, two windows, and a moth-eaten Persian rug on the floor. The walls had been decorated with black-and-white photographs of Skelton's bone tattoos, all of which Antigone had quickly shoved into a small closet—only because Cyrus hadn't let her throw them away. There had also been one threadbare armchair. Now there was one threadbare armchair and a wooden chair stolen from the dining hall.

Every corner of the tiny bathroom was covered with tiny white tile, and every white tile had been covered with a filthy gray sedimentary skin. Antigone had scrubbed the place with bleach every day for a week. Now the tiles glistened like fresh false teeth, but the grout between them was a crumbly and rotten set of gums. The shower occasionally drooled a chilly trickle and occasionally blasted a fleet of sizzling liquid lasers that could blister skin. And the toilet sang like a dying bullfrog in the night. But it was all still better than the Polygon.

Off the central room, there had been one empty bedroom with one window, a moldy curtain, and absolutely nothing else. Now the room held two hammocks, slung in opposite corners. Cyrus had wanted a hammock. Antigone had wanted to sleep anywhere that wasn't the floor. Beneath each hammock, there were cardboard boxes that held what little the two had been able to salvage from the Archer. Cyrus's clothes were piled into another box. Antigone's were hanging in the little closet.

The remaining three rooms were unusable. The first was an active volcano of old boxes. Crates and cartons and chests and bins had at one time been stacked from floor to ceiling, but those stacks had slumped into each other and become a monolithic heap of dust. They called it Dump Number One and never bothered with it. The next room held a pile of exactly the same size and shape, but made entirely of books. Cyrus called it the library or Dump Number Two. Antigone called it the Book Dump.

They didn't know what was in the last room, because they had never been able to open the door. Cyrus's silver Solomon Key had released the lock, and the knob had turned easily. But the door had merely wiggled in place. And it was a completely interior room, so there was no chance of using a ladder to break in through a window.

Rupert Greeves stepped into the long central room and looked around. On the timber mantel above the fireplace, there was a small ebony box, left to the Smiths by William Skelton. Leaning against it was a battered book titled *How to Breed Your Leatherbacks.* Hanging by a string from the ceiling was a spherical rice paper Chinese lantern with a map of the world inked onto it, and oceans full of scrawls written in a language Cyrus and Antigone had not been able to identify.

"And the two of you," Rupert said, "have done half a notch more than nothing."

"Hey!" Antigone stepped forward. "Look in the bathroom and you won't say that." She crossed her arms. "Besides, what were we supposed to do?"

Rupert looked around at the bare walls. "Furniture? Art? Lamps wouldn't hurt a bit."

Cyrus looked at his sister. He knew she hated the rooms. He knew she desperately wanted to overhaul everything. Antigone sniffed and tucked back her hair.

"How?" she asked. "Rupe, how? We don't have a car. And if we did, we wouldn't be allowed to leave. We don't have money—Horace says there's barely enough still in the estate to cover our Order dues. You've been gone forever. Dan's in California. How would we do anything?"

Antigone's eyes were actually wet. She wiped them quickly. Rupert looked stunned.

"Do you think we want to live in a place like this?"

Antigone asked. "'Cause we don't. We don't come in till we have to sleep, and we leave as soon as we wake up."

"You do," said Cyrus quietly. "Sometimes I do, too. It depends on what the shower is doing."

Rupert's big shoulders sagged. "Antigone, I'm sorry."

Antigone wiped her eyes again. "I can fly an airplane, but I can't drive to a furniture store. And if I did, I would have to rob it."

Rupert stepped forward and cautiously slid his arm around Antigone's shoulders, patting awkwardly. She was tiny next to him.

"I'm sorry," Rupert said again. He looked at Cyrus. "I haven't been a good Keeper to either of you."

Cyrus shrugged. The whole scene was too uncomfortable for him.

"It's stupid," Antigone said, stepping back. "It's not your fault. You're not our dad. And you're not Dan. And chasing Phoenix is a lot more important than helping us. I'm still not used to having no one, you know, in charge of us."

"Forgive me," Rupert said. "Truly. And forgive me again, because I'm about to make things much worse."

"What?" Cyrus said. "What do you mean?"

Rupert dropped onto the ratty rug and crossed his legs. "Sit. There are unpleasant things you need to know."

Antigone silently lowered herself to the floor. Cyrus thumped down beside her.

"First," Rupert said, "I haven't found Phoenix. I haven't come close, not in a long while. The transmortals have become the more immediate problem. They're always difficult, but they tend to live in small enough pods to keep them manageable. Now they're fast becoming a bloody great herd. And that herd is coming here." He raised his hands defensively. "Please know that I was already sorry to do this, and even sorrier now, but for the foreseeable future, you are not to leave these rooms unless you are with me."

"What?" Antigone's mouth hung open. "You're joking. Why?"

"What do you mean 'foreseeable'?" Cyrus said.

"I mean foreseeable," said Rupert. "Indefinite. For the time being. Until further notice. In addition to the transmortals, members of the O of B are flying into Ashtown from all over the globe to remember the last Brendan and elect a new one. When they have, he will name a new Avengel."

"That's why there's a campout in the courtyard?" Cyrus asked.

Rupert nodded. "Right. And that's why you'll be in here."

"That all sounds like craziness," Antigone said. "But I don't see what it has to do with us getting locked up."

Rupert exhaled. His eyes drifted up to the window. Cyrus turned, glancing back at the age-rippled glass panes behind him. Then he looked back at Rupert. The Avengel's dark eyes locked with his own. Cyrus didn't need to be told. It was obvious.

"The transmortals," Cyrus said, thinking of Gil. "You're worried because they're unhappy about the tooth."

Rupert scratched his jaw. When he spoke, his voice was slow and cautious. "I worry because your name is Smith. Because you were the first person in generations to kill one of the transmortals—something they disapprove of in even the most extreme cases, and something that your family has an historical habit of doing. I worry because you are the one who held the tooth and lost it to Phoenix, who has now done some transmortal killing of his own. I am worried because the transmortals are more than unhappy. They are angry—with me, with the Order, and especially with you. Those who have treaties with the Order will hope to influence the election of the Brendan and the selection of the next Avengel. They do not forget, and they do not forgive."

Antigone groaned. "I'm so tired of everyone only blaming Cyrus. If it weren't for Cyrus, do you know how many people would be dead in this place?"

"Yes," Rupert said. "I do. But the transmortals blame me as well, and they are right to. The responsibility for all that happened lies with me." He knuckled his swollen cheek. "Phoenix has begun hunting them. You asked where I was? Egypt, Greece, and then France. Dozens of transmortals are missing—on the run, taken, or killed. We only found three bodies, but three is enough to start the stampede." He looked from Cyrus to Antigone. "Mortals like us live with fear, with the certainty of our own eventual deaths—some more boldly than others. Not so the transmortals. The undying live with boredom, with apathy, with love or anger or hate, any number of emotions. But never fear. Fear and death are two sides of the same coin, and death has been well behind them for centuries. To have the Reaper's Blade reemerge now, and in the hand of an enemy? To have friends struck down? Fear roars and they cannot control it. It rules over them like so many hunted animals. And men like Gilgamesh are *very* dangerous when afraid."

Cyrus exhaled slowly. "So what are we going to do?"

Rupert smiled grimly. "*We* are going to keep *you* in your rooms as long as *we* can. *I* am going to do what I can to calm the coming herd."

Antigone looked around the dingy room. "Does it have to be in here? I hate it like this. Could you at least get me some paint?"

Rupert stood slowly. Cyrus scrambled up beside him, but Antigone stayed on the floor.

"I'll come when I can," Rupert said. "Phoenix has been even more fox-cunning than I'd expected. He's diverted me and managed to threaten Ashtown even while he hides. And my own Acolytes are woefully unprepared." He shook his head. "I'd hoped there'd be time this fall for a stronger traditional training regimen for my two Smiths, but immediate danger creates immediate needs, and soon enough the two of you may be fighting to survive outside of these walls." Suddenly, he smiled. "But I have a card to play, no longer hidden in my sleeve. Arachne will be staying with you and working with you in ways that only she can. Some Keepers might object—fallaciously—to her unique skills, but I'm in no mood to care. You will do as she says without question. After dark tonight, if she thinks it's safe, you can walk the green with her. Tomorrow morning, the planes will really begin to arrive and you'll be locked in tight. I'll be by when I can."

"The spider girl's our babysitter?" Antigone grimaced. "Seriously?"

"The 'spider girl' has chosen her side," Rupert said. "She's betting on Smiths. As am I . . ." Rupert paused, focusing on Cyrus. "One last thing. Hopefully you'll be out of sight, but if you are in public, try not to use the word *transmortal.* It's accurate, but some of them are quite sensitive about ever having been mortal at all. They insist on *immortal.* Food will be delivered, and I'll send along some paint as well."

"Really?" Antigone jumped to her feet. "Something warm, please. Yellow. Orange. I don't know. Just bright. Please make it bright."

Rupert smiled. "Bright it is." He crossed toward the door. "And Skelton's estate wasn't that anemic. You should have *some* money. I'll talk to that dirty little lawyer of yours."

The door opened, and the door shut. Rupert was gone.

Antigone dropped into the armchair and laughed. "Hey, hey, Rus-Rus, you'll have to help me clean. There's a lot to do if we're going to paint this place."

Cyrus looked at his sister, laced his fingers through his short dark hair, and groaned. His cage had just gotten smaller.

"What?" Antigone said. "We'll be stuck, but it's better than being dead or beaten to a pulp by some transmortal, and at least the walls will be bright."

"I don't care about bright walls," said Cyrus. He dropped onto the old rug and flopped onto his back. "Maybe I'll run away to California."

"Good plan," a voice said from beneath the floor. A grate rattled, and the rug shook beneath Cyrus, thumping him in the back. "If you don't mind, I'd like to come up now."

At the same time, the front door opened and Diana Boone slipped in, followed by Dennis Gilly in his bowler hat, and pretty little Hillary Drake, who was wearing an apron loaded with cleaning supplies. Her curly hair was knotted in a fountain on top of her head.

"Are we on for Polygoners tonight?" Diana asked. "I wasn't sure when I saw you come in with Rupe. Thought you might be busy."

Hillary focused her green eyes on Cyrus and fidgeted with her apron. "I only have about thirty minutes till they notice that I'm missing."

"Yeah," said Antigone. "We're on. Cy, get off of Nolan."

Cyrus rolled off the rug, and then kicked it toward the wall. A pale face looked up through a heating grate in the floor. The grate rattled again.

"Some idiot locked it," said Nolan. "Now let me in."

four

THREE HEADS

In the beginning, Polygoners had been a self-imposed nickname, a point of upside-down pride, the only way Cyrus and Antigone could make exile in the Polygon seem like a cool thing. Neither of them could say when it had become something more. In a tight moment, they had promised membership to Dennis in order to keep him motivated and unafraid. He had invited Hillary Drake, no doubt in an attempt to impress the pretty, wide-eyed girl and prove that he wasn't simply a washed-out Acolyte-turned-porter.

James Axelrotter, the incredibly young zookeeper—Jax to anyone who really knew him—was officially included, even though he hardly ever made the meetings. The Crypto wing of the zoo seemed to be in a perpetual state of emergency, and little Jax was the only one willing to set foot inside it.

Diana Boone had been included because Diana was somehow always included, even though she had already achieved the rank of Explorer within the O of B. She simply liked the Smiths. Nolan had been included because, even though he had no interest in the Order and was an antisocial transmortal who sloughed off his skin like a snake, he had been the Smiths' first roommate, he had helped them stay alive, and he was the only member who still lived in the Polygon.

Gunner, the tall driver who had first raced the Smiths to Ashtown, had come to the meetings until he'd been sent back to Texas. And Antigone had insisted that they include the perpetually lonely Oliver Laughlin, grandson to the now-dead Brendan. Somehow she'd found a way to actually feel bad for the boy responsible for sticking them under the 1914 standards when they'd first arrived. If he hadn't, they never would have been sent down to live in the Polygon in the first place.

Oliver had not attended long. He hadn't liked being in a club with members of "the understaff," and Cyrus hadn't really liked being in a club with Oliver and his perpetually curling lip. Once the Brendan died, Oliver had announced his plans to leave Ashtown and the O of B completely. And he had. No one had seen him in months.

Cyrus looked around the room and yawned. As crazy as his day had been, and for all that was happening around Ashtown, the meeting wasn't amounting to much. Jax hadn't come, and Hillary was already gone, not that she ever really said anything. She would be cleaning out Acolyte rooms all night, preparing for the anticipated flood of arrivals tomorrow. Nolan was lying on his back with his hands folded on his stomach and his eyes closed. He was wearing his typical oversize fatigue trousers, belted with a rope, and a tight ashen tank that left his knotted paper-pale arms bare. His hair was cropped tight and uneven, and his smooth face looked strangely young when he wasn't angry and his eyes were closed. But when his eyes opened, smooth and ancient, worn by the years like two rocks tossed in the riverbed of centuries, then his age filled the room. Looking in his eyes was like looking into a pair of forgotten tombs, dark and unlit and impossible to explore or understand.

Beside Nolan, Dennis sat with his legs crossed neatly in front of him. His bowler hat was on his right knee but had left its creased imprint on his hair and forehead. Antigone and Diana were up, examining the walls and talking about paint color and how to get furniture.

Cyrus looked at Dennis and then at Nolan. His back hurt. His head was drumming, and his limbs all felt like splitting rubber bands. What was the point of all of this? Why had he even bothered to try to train if he was just going to be locked up in his rooms? And now Rupert had said they might have to survive on their own outside the walls. That's what Cyrus had wanted, but he didn't like how it sounded—*survive.* There was only one way to make it all stop, to make this strange world slow down and find a place for him that wasn't a cage and wasn't a motel and didn't involve undying people trying to kill him.

"We need to get the tooth back." Cyrus said it quietly, but Diana heard and glanced back at him over her shoulder.

"And . . . there it is," said Nolan. He stretched out his arms. "It has to be said once a meeting. The Polygoners exist for one reason and one reason only."

"Getting the tooth back is a good reason," Cyrus said.

"But that's not the reason." Nolan let half of his mouth grin. "We don't gather together to hunt the tooth. We gather together to hear you say that we should. The Polygoners are tooth talkers, not tooth hunters."

Cyrus bit his tongue. He wanted to hit Nolan, but he knew things wouldn't go well if he did. The ancient boy could outgrapple, outbox, and outbrawl Cyrus even at his angriest—*especially* at his angriest. And he was right. They weren't tooth hunters. And they couldn't be. And even if they snuck off and were booted from the O of B, Phoenix wouldn't be easily found. And if found, not easily beaten.

If Rupert Greeves, Blood Avenger, couldn't find the villain, what chance did Cyrus and the Polygoners have?

"So . . . ," Dennis said. The porter was nervous, eyes darting between Cyrus and Nolan. "Was there anything else for tonight? Anything you might need me to do before next week's meeting? Anything you might need me to bring since you'll be stuck in here?"

Cyrus watched Diana laugh. She had recommended green for something, and now Antigone was sneering. He looked back into Dennis Gilly's eager face.

Nolan stretched his arms above his head. "Bring Gilgamesh's head. I think our little society would appreciate that."

"It's not a society," Dennis said. "Private societies within the O of B are strictly prohibited."

Nolan sat up. A smile twitched at the corners of his mouth. "Our *secret* society would like you to decapitate Gilgamesh of Uruk. He's a prig and a pig and a killer. Can you handle that, Mr. Gilly?"

"I'm sorry," said Dennis. "It really is important that we not use the word *society.* Or *order.* We can't be those things."

Nolan pursed his lips and scratched at his smooth white cheek. "Will you do it if we're a club?"

Dennis squirmed. "Maybe. A club is better, but we would need to file a form and name a Keeper to oversee us."

Cyrus wasn't listening anymore. Something like this happened at every meeting. Dennis was so serious and literal, and Nolan was usually bored enough to needle him.

Cyrus was bored, too. Or maybe just tired and beaten up and feeling defeated. He wondered when Arachne would come and what her unique gifts were—a girl with a million spider pets didn't exactly seem like an ideal trainer.

Arachne was betting on the Smiths. That's what Rupert had said. The rest of the transmortals all hated the Smiths—except Nolan, but he pretty much hated everyone some of the time. Cyrus still didn't even know what it meant to be a Smith. To him, Smithness started with his own memories somewhere around the age of five. It was California and happiness, then heartbreak and the Archer Motel. And then Ashtown . . .

Even those blond brothers he and Tigs had met in the hall knew more about his family than he did. His father had cut all that history off when he'd defied the Order and married Cyrus's mother. But the history was still real, even if it was hidden. It was waiting. . . .

Antigone was saying something to Nolan, probably telling him to stop pestering Dennis. But that didn't matter. Nolan would do whatever he wanted. He always did.

"Hey!" said Cyrus. Everyone looked at him. "Dennis, there *is* something you could do to help. Do you think you could find some patches? I would do it, but I'm stuck."

"Patches?" Dennis asked. "More monkey patches? We already have extras, and I really don't think it's advisable to wear them publicly—your leather jacket is the exception, of course. That patch is historical, and predates the Polygoners' use of the—"

"No," Cyrus said. "A crest, I guess. A patch of a crest. I want the Smith family crest."

Nolan's eyes darkened. Cyrus thought he could feel dust and shadow creeping out of them. One more thing he couldn't get used to.

"You like trouble that much?" Nolan asked, his voice cold. He shrugged. "Of course, you'll be stuck in here. No one will see it."

"People will see it," Cyrus said. "Eventually. I'm a Smith. I mean, Captain John Smith? Jamestown? Pocahontas?" He looked at Antigone. "Tigs, we have a famous ancestor. You all are used to that around here, but we're not. I don't care how many greats away he is . . . it's our family, and I want to wear our crest."

Nolan chuckled. "He's not that far away, Cyrus Smith. He's buttoned up in one of the Burials. You have a famous ancestor turned transmortal villain. Take my word for it, Cyrus. He was not a nice man. No one liked him."

"Cy," Antigone said. "Three severed heads? It's gross."

Dennis, wide-eyed, looked from face to face and back to Cyrus, waiting for his decision.

Cyrus looked at Diana. She shrugged. "It's your crest. I have ours on some stuff, but I don't wear it often. Jeb was more into it than I was when we were little. Still, I'd be mad if people told me I couldn't wear it."

"Oh, I'm not saying that," said Nolan. He shot Cyrus half a smile. "But everyone has always loved the Boones. No one—except Pocahontas—loved John Smith. He was more brawler and pirate than Avengel. I never met him, and I made sure I didn't. The man was crazy." Nolan stretched back out on the floor. "Before you flash around that crest, know that you're waving the flag of a man who betrayed his own oaths and was Buried for it. Those three severed heads are his most famous kills—three severed transmortal heads. This isn't the week to make that popular."

Dennis sputtered to life. "Those men were evil. My grandmother told me those stories. Captain John did what he had to do."

Nolan yawned. "And Cyrus had to kill Maxi, but that doesn't matter to creatures like Gil. Cyrus had no authority to do what he did. We transmortals—sorry, *immortals,* if you ask the posh ones—are the superior race. You mortals must bow and scrape before us. Cap'n John killed more of us than anyone in history, before he pulled a switch and was Buried. Cyrus here has carried on the great killing tradition."

Cyrus looked at Dennis. "As many Smith patches as you can. And I need a couple Ashtown boat patches, too."

Antigone hopped over Nolan and sat down beside Cyrus. "Are there any books that would have the whole story?" she asked Dennis. "Could you find one? I want to know what John Smith really did before I'm going to let Cyrus march around with three heads on his shoulder."

Cyrus and Nolan both snorted.

"Before you let me?" Cyrus asked.

"A book?" Nolan asked. "You don't believe me, fine. But turning to a book? I was actually alive at the time, though I gave wild Virginia a wide berth." He nudged Dennis with his foot. "Make sure the author's last name is Smith. That way it will be fair."

Antigone rolled her eyes. "Whatever, Nolan. Like you're Mr. Honest." She smiled at Dennis. "Just do your best."

Dennis, blinking slowly, stood up and set his bowler hat on top of his head. The loose ribbon ties dangled against his cheeks.

"I'm not sure, I . . . understand what . . ." His voice trailed off.

"Just a book," Antigone said. "Whatever you can find about John Smith."

"Fine." Cyrus glared at his sister. "Tigs always knows best, doesn't she, Dennis?"

Diana stepped up beside Dennis. "I could get a book. Jeb used to eat that stuff up. He knows all the old Avengel stories."

Dennis sighed with relief. "I should go now." He began to tie his hat ribbons beneath his chin.

"Terrific," said Nolan, and he yawned and shut his eyes.

"I should go, too," Diana said. Her freckled face had gone serious. "This could be a pretty rough week for the Order. It really could. It's been fun, you know, the Polygoner thing, hanging out like this. But we—I—might have to stop." Diana stepped back toward the door. "Time to get serious. Anyway, I'll be around through tomorrow. Then I'll be wherever Jeb and Rupe tell me to be. Could be anywhere. I'm sorry you'll be stuck here. It would be great to have an honest-to-goodness trek together sometime."

Antigone's mouth fell open.

Dennis snuck out the door and shut it behind him.

Cyrus felt himself slumping. He straightened and met Diana's eyes. They were actually worried. Afraid of what he would think.

He cleared his throat. "Don't worry about it. It's not your fault we're stuck."

"Seriously," Antigone said. "Thanks for everything. We wouldn't be Journeymen without you. You taught us how to fly."

Diana laughed. "You would have been fine."

"No," Antigone said. "*I* wouldn't have."

Cyrus glanced around the room. "You're still a Polygoner. You know where we'll be."

Diana nodded. She opened the door behind her. "I'll try to come by before I leave."

Antigone's smile was a little too big. "See ya."

Diana wasn't looking at her. She was looking at Cyrus. He raised his right hand in a sloppy salute.

"See ya," he said.

The door closed behind Diana Boone.

"And thus," Nolan said from the floor, "the ancient Order of the Polygoners lost its most notable member."

Antigone groaned. "Shut up, Nolan. This is terrible. Where could they be sending her? She was the only one who helped us with anything."

Nolan rolled onto his side. "What ungratefulness is this? I taught you Latin."

"You know what I mean," Antigone said, and she dropped onto the floor. "Cy, what are we going to do?"

Cyrus walked to the window beside the fireplace. It was just high enough that he could rest his elbows on the sill. The sun was long down, but the horizon was still faintly glowing. Staring through the dusty, warped glass, he could just make out the army of lit tents that dotted the green. He didn't know what they were going to do. About anything. He wanted to leave his stupid rooms, and he wanted something to eat.

He wanted the tooth back. Sometimes he could still feel it and its power slipping from his grasp, being torn from his fingers. His body could remember the strength that had left him when the tooth had—the strength of an unbreakable bond between his soul and body, true deathlessness.

He understood why the transmortals were angry with him. It was hard to blame them. Not because he had killed Maxi; that was stupid. But because what they had could now be taken from them. He had tasted that loss, if only a little bit. Losing the tooth hadn't made him feel empty; it had made him realize that he had always been empty. There was a crack between his body and his soul that wasn't supposed to be there. He was meant to be whole—indivisible. But he wasn't. And in the end, like every mortal, his body and soul would split completely. He would die. Rupert had said mortals learned to face that fear. Maybe Rupert did, but Cyrus was pretty sure most people did the opposite—they just didn't think about it.

Cyrus's hand drifted up to his neck, and Patricia's cool body twitched at his touch. He fingered the silver sheath where the tooth had been. The tingle it used to give him was long gone. Skelton's two other charms were still on either side—the moon-colored pearl, gripped by the tiny silver claw, and the small reddish piece of wood, polished smooth by fingers and time. He didn't know what they were for, but they weren't the tooth. He moved on, fingering his shape-changing Solomon Keys—the longer gold one and the short silver one. Despite all the warnings—or maybe because of all the warnings—they hadn't turned him into a thief. Not yet. A trespasser, yes.

Constantly. And why not? When any door could be unlocked, curiosity was hard to kill.

"Cy! Hello?" Antigone elbowed up to the window beside him. "Arachne's here." She dropped her voice to a whisper. "You all right? Nolan left and you didn't even notice."

"What?" Cyrus looked around, startled. Nolan was gone. The rug was back over the grate. No doubt the pale transmortal boy was weaving his way through the heat tunnels, down to the Polygon.

Arachne, dressed all in black, stood in the center of the rug. Her midnight hair had been oiled and was pulled back into an explosion of curl. She had a backpack over one shoulder and a sagging, heavy satchel over the other. Her light blue eyes studied Cyrus and Antigone.

"Hey," said Cyrus. "I'm glad you're here. Rupe said we could head out if you were good with it."

"First things first," Arachne said, and she lowered her heavy satchel to the floor. As it touched ground, the bag sagged and deflated, spilling spiders like sand. Thousands poured out of its mouth and flooded across the floor, legs whispering like wind on a cactus.

Antigone screamed and jumped up onto the wooden dining chair. Cyrus lunged for the safety of the armchair, but his toe caught on the corner of the rug and he knocked the armchair over and crashed to the floor.

He twisted and tried to roll away.

Arachne jumped forward and put her hand on his head. "Be still," she said, and Cyrus felt cold pour through him. His skin was suddenly numb. There must have been things on him, all over him, but he couldn't feel them. He couldn't feel anything, not even the rough wool of the rug against his skin. Arachne was whispering, singing some strange and hushed spider song.

Then her hand rose off Cyrus's head, and warmth roared back through him. He scrambled to his feet and looked around.

Antigone was on her chair, biting the knuckle of her forefinger to keep from screaming. Her eyes were on the walls.

"Watch," said Arachne. "But be calm and silent. They need to hear me."

Cyrus did as he was told. He watched the spider storm begin to take a more ordered shape as the arachnid army scaled the walls and surrounded the windows, surrounded the mouth of the fireplace, surrounded the door behind him, and then became still.

Rows and rows of spiders had lined up on either side of the window. An even thicker regiment had lined up at the top. Not one sat on the sill beneath.

There were heavy spiders and tiny spiders. Fat-bodied garden spiders, and spiders built for jumping. Gray, brown, black, orange, green, and even white spiders, all still and ready and waiting for something.

Arachne dragged the wooden chair in front of the window, climbed up, and lightly touched four large spiders above the window. Immediately, they swung down on their lines and began to spin. Arachne moved to the fireplace, selected eight spiders, and then moved to the next window.

Cyrus studied the spinners in front of him. The four spiders were working on a single web unlike any normal spider construction. This was a grid. They were simply dropping vertical lines, attaching them to the windowsill, then climbing back up and doing it again.

Arachne stood between Cyrus and Antigone. After a moment, the spiders had finished and resumed their original spots.

"So . . . ," said Antigone. "They're just—"

Arachne raised a finger to her lips and then hummed a single note, long and low. The smallest spiders muscled forward on all three sides. She shifted her pitch up higher, and Cyrus shivered as the hair on his arms tingled.

Then, in unison, every spider marched forward, and every one was dragging a line. One row swept down, one left, one right. Keeping exact time and pace, they clambered across the web ladder and wove between each other, over each other, around each other. They tucked and ducked and braided and looped and twisted like a square-dancing militia. And then, when they had reached the other side, they regrouped, paused, and returned.

As Cyrus and Antigone watched, the loom of spiders wove the beginnings of a tight sheet of silver silk across the window. Cyrus looked around—across the other window as well. And the fireplace. He turned around. Nothing was happening at the door. The spiders there were waiting patiently.

"This will take them a while," Arachne said. She smiled. "If you'd like me to walk the grounds with you before your captivity, now's the time."

"It's . . ." Antigone shrugged, surprised by her own reaction. "Well, it's beautiful. And impossible."

Arachne smiled. "It is both. And when my weavers have finished, it will be stronger than steel and far lovelier than any worm silk." She laughed, as if worm silk was the most ridiculous thing in the world. Then she looked into Cyrus's eyes, and he blinked in surprise at her happiness. The pale ice in her blue irises was gone, replaced by the burning warmth of a summer sky or the blue of a . . . of a something really, really blue.

"Come," she said, and Cyrus followed her to the door. Antigone trailed behind him.

"Where are we going?" Antigone asked.

"For a walk on a hot summer evening," Arachne said. "Before your door is sealed behind you for the night."

The sky was dark above the Ashtown green. On one horizon, whispers of silver promised that the moon would soon rise above the trees. On the other, only the faintest blue glow was left behind the sleeping sun. All across the green and surrounding the tall fountain, hundreds of small canvas field tents had been pitched in tightly ordered rows. Lanterns hung on poles lit the rows within the tent town. More were hanging above tent flaps, and others were spreading their glow from within, lighting canvas walls like the sides of large lamp shades.

All around, Acolytes were racing, shouting, and laughing—like the coming wave of transmortal refugees and Order members was cause for a festival. Three boys were struggling to force a fourth into the fountain. In the distance, tent stakes were pulled and cries of revenge went up as canvas collapsed.

Cyrus, Antigone, and Arachne stood on the gravel path beside the green and watched. Antigone laughed.

"I'll follow you," Arachne said to Cyrus. "Go where you will."

Antigone stepped toward the main building. "Let's go down to the lake."

Cyrus turned the other way and began to walk.

"Okay, fine!" Antigone said, and she jogged up beside her brother. "Where are we going, fearless leader?"

"You can go to the lake," Cyrus said. "Go where you wanna go."

"Sorry," said Arachne from behind them. "You're staying together."

Cyrus watched the tents as they passed. A few Acolytes seemed to notice them, but not many. They were too preoccupied with their own comic turf wars.

He could hear an airplane landing, but he didn't look for it. He needed to get out of the courtyard gate, away from the green, and into the little street where Mrs. Eldridge had taken them a year ago to get their Order clothes when they'd first arrived. He hadn't ever been back, but he was sure the right building wouldn't be hard to find.

Antigone nudged him. "Cy? What's going on? Why so surly?"

"What do you mean?" asked Cyrus. "I'm not surly."

"Oh, come on," Antigone said, and she brushed back her hair. "Are you being a grouch because I bossed Dennis when you were bossing Dennis? Are we only allowed to boss one at a time now? Or is it because Diana is leaving and we can't? If I think about it, I start to get surly, too."

Cyrus shook his head. "Tigs, I'm not surly. Not at all. I'm just, well . . ." He trailed off. What was he? Not happy. Not unhappy. It wasn't like that. Worried? Unsure? The transmortals were afraid. And if they were . . . He felt like there was something dark creeping up behind him. Or something heavy hanging right above him that was about to fall. Phoenix was out there somewhere, using the tooth William Skelton had handed to Cyrus. The Acolytes could laugh and play and camp on the green, but something seriously unpleasant was brewing. And Cyrus could do what?

Antigone was watching him. "Well," she said, "you're either surly, or you're some synonym for surly."

Cyrus looked at his sister as they walked along the path, looping around the green toward the gate.

"I'm not exactly helpful to the Order, am I, Tigs?" Cyrus scattered a lump of gravel with his toe. "I lost the tooth. Phoenix is out there doing whatever he's doing while you and I prepare to be locked up with half the spiders on this planet."

Antigone opened her mouth, and then clicked it shut and scrunched her face. Cyrus watched her. He knew she wanted to argue him into being cheerful. But he also knew that *she* knew that arguing with him would only make him worse.

Suddenly, Cyrus laughed. "I am a little surly."

Antigone smiled. "Let's go with surlyish."

"I miss Dan." Cyrus sighed and glanced back at Arachne. Her eyes were down, focused on the sharp turf edge to the grass beside them. He could see faint shadows and whispers of tiny movement on the path behind her. Were all spiders her spiders? Did they really just find her anywhere?

A pack of giggling Acolytes raced by, weighed down with what had to be water balloons. It would have been nice to be one of them.

His eyes drifted up to the main building. The statues on the roofline carved black shadows against the dark sky. Four bulbous shapes were floating above them.

Cyrus turned Antigone around to see. Arachne stopped beside them.

"What are they?" Antigone asked. "What's going on?"

Arachne took them each by a wrist. Her grip was cool and calming on Cyrus's skin. Her voice was quiet.

"We should go back now," she said, and she pulled.

Cyrus resisted. "No, no, it's fine." He looked into his babysitter's face, and he grinned. "I know what they are. Really. Watch."

Four small football-shaped hot-air balloons with quiet rear propellers dropped down over the tented green. Each balloon was armed with a cannon for firing bread. While Cyrus and Antigone and Arachne stood and watched, the Journeymen in the balloons began their assault on the Acolytes below.

Loaves rained down and tents collapsed. Acolytes scattered, shouting in confusion. In mere moments, the tent-city neighborhoods had forgotten their feuds and had unified. From various corners, fast-moving teams with oversize slingshots began to launch water balloons as the floating fleet descended on every side.

A stale loaf thumped to the ground at Cyrus's feet. Laughing, he and Antigone began to run.

The battle was still loud and visible when they ducked through the gate and into the little road. The shouts still echoed and the belching bread cannons still *phoomphed* when they reached the door into the tall, narrow stone building Cyrus was looking for.

The door was locked, and on the ground floor, the windows were dark. They stayed dark for the first thirty seconds of Cyrus's banging.

When a light did flick on, Cyrus stopped. His sister studied him.

"And we're here why?" she asked. "You need another flight jacket?"

Arachne had stepped close to the wall and was looking up, studying the eaves.

The front door opened, and Cyrus felt cool air-conditioning rush out around him, carrying the smell of old leather and oil and mothballs and four generations of recollected clothes.

An old man glared at them from the doorway. His eyebrows were even more tremendous than Cyrus had remembered. He had a crumpled cigarette tucked above his hairy left ear, and another soggy, unlit, and thoroughly chewed cigarette dangling from his lips.

"Mr. Donald," Cyrus said, relieved that he could remember the man's name. "I'm sorry to bother—"

"Smiths," the man snorted. "Nineteen-fourteen guidelines. What do you want with Old Donald right now?"

Cyrus smiled and made sure he didn't look at his sister. "Patches," he said. "Some old patches."

Antigone moaned. "Cyrussel . . ."

"I *will* start calling you Tigger again," Cyrus said, still smiling. "Not you," he said to Donald. "Just her. And only when she's a total pain."

"Patches," Donald said. "Not many patches needed now."

"I know," said Cyrus. "But I also know that you keep everything. You have to have some patches."

Without answering, Donald turned and walked back into his shop. He hadn't invited Cyrus in, but he hadn't closed the door, either.

Cyrus followed him, and Antigone trickled along behind. Arachne stayed in the street.

The two of them tracked the man around and between the mountains of leather flight jackets and the ladders propped against them. They slid past a pyramid of riding boots and shelf after shelf of safari shirts and jodhpurs and fatigues. They pushed on, farther than they had gone before, to the very back of the shop. And there, the two of them stopped in front of a towering set of tiny drawers, like an ancient and oversize card catalog from a precomputer library. It was at least ten feet tall and fifteen wide. The wood was dark, but the stain was worn thin in places, revealing a light grain beneath. Each drawer was only a few inches across and had a little brass handle.

Donald sniffed and leaned against it. "Patches," he said. "What are you hoping for?"

Cyrus scanned the drawers. "Smiths," he said. "The old family crest. Do you have one?"

Donald's eyebrows collapsed down over his eyes. "I might. What will you be doing with it?"

Cyrus shrugged. "I just want one. Or a couple. I'm a Smith."

"Well, I don't have a couple," Donald said. "I have one. And it's not for sale. And not for display, especially right about now, with the transmor—with the immortals flowing in."

Cyrus cleared his throat. He had to sound confident. He had no experience negotiating for anything. "Everything's for sale," he said. That sounded right. "I know there's a price or something. Just tell me how much you want." That was wrong and he knew it. He was going to get gouged.

Donald's eyebrows climbed slightly and wobbled. He gnawed on his cigarette.

Be confident, Cyrus told himself. He felt Antigone's hand on his elbow and ignored it.

"Can you get it now?" Cyrus asked. "Please."

Donald fetched a short stepladder.

The little drawer he opened was in the very top row. From inside it, he pulled a small white cloth sleeve. Then he climbed back down, held it out to Cyrus, and chewed his cigarette.

While Antigone leaned in over his shoulder, Cyrus slid the patch out onto his palm.

The colors were old but still rich, and the patch's embroidery was incredibly intricate. It was a shield, but not a simple shield. Its curves were exaggerated and . . . Gothic? Medieval? Flowy? Cyrus searched for words briefly, and then focused on the design itself.

The shield was bloodred with a thin gold border. A thick gold diagonal stripe ran across it. Inside the gold stripe, there were three heads, shown in surprising detail. The upper head was the oldest and bearded. The center head had a long mustache that hung down past his jaw. The lowest head was young and clean-shaven. All of them had black hair. All of them had a stripe of red blood at the base of their necks, and all of them were wide-eyed and apparently conscious.

Above the shield, there was an unfurling scroll, embroidered with a Latin motto.

Sic Semper Draconis

Cyrus traced the old thread with his fingertip.

"Cy . . . ," Antigone said.

"I know," said Cyrus. "*Thus to all dragons.*"

Antigone sighed. "Close enough."

five

LOCKDOWN

CYRUS OPENED HIS EYES, yawned, and tried to stretch—something his hammock wouldn't allow. Frustrated, he kicked his one thin blanket onto the floor, swung over the side, and dropped onto his sleep-tender bare feet. Straining his arms toward the ceiling, muscles quivering back to life, he stared at his bedroom window.

The solid sheet of spider silk was backlit by the morning sun, and the whole room glowed silver. The weave was tight, complicated, and perfect. Cyrus stepped forward, squinting. There was a design in the center, the ghost of an image, embroidered with silk on silk—the shield and boxing monkey of the Polygoners.

Cyrus smiled. "Tigs, you see this?" He looked at the other hammock. Antigone was gone.

Once he was in the living room, Cyrus heard the rush and rattle of water through pipes in the floor. On the other side of the wall, he heard the shower bleat and hum. A muffled yelp told him that his sister was braving the water too soon.

Cyrus dropped into the armchair and looked at the windows and the fireplace. The weave of the silk was a little different on each one. And the embroidered image changed. In the first window, the monkey had shaken off his boxing gloves. Over the fireplace, he had stepped outside of his shield. In the next window, he was swinging away.

"Good morning," Arachne said.

Cyrus jolted in his chair. Arachne was stepping out from the Book Dump. She was in the same black clothes she'd worn the day before, but her hair was pulled into a tight braid. Her eyes were alive and bright.

"Did you sleep in there?" Cyrus asked.

Arachne nodded. "I did. Up at the top of the piles, near the ceiling."

Cyrus looked all around. Behind him, another sheet of silk covered the front door. He couldn't see if there were any extra images.

Arachne sat in the wooden dining chair across from him.

"Where are the spiders?" Cyrus asked.

"Eating," Arachne said. "Sleeping. Resting. They had a long night, but they're close if I need them."

Cyrus studied the girl's pale face. "How do you get them to do what you want?"

"Practice," Arachne said. "It used to be harder."

"When?"

Arachne smiled. "Centuries ago." She drummed thin fingers on her knees.

Cyrus closed his eyes and dragged his hands down his face. "Do you know how long we're going to be stuck in here?"

"That depends on the presence and behavior of my fellow transmortals," said Arachne. Cyrus didn't like how cheerful she sounded. "At least a week. And getting off on the right foot is important. We're going to divide our energies. Part of the time, we will overhaul and clean these rooms. Part of the time, we will study. And part of the time, we will train."

Cyrus looked at her. She was talking like she was a lot more *in charge* than he'd thought. In the other room, the shower turned off.

"Train?" he asked. "At what? There's not a lot of room in here."

"Rupert has given me a list." Arachne's eyes sparkled. He felt rude staring at them—into them—but he couldn't really help it. "I enjoy lists," she said. "There are very specific things he wants me to work on over the next few days."

Cyrus scratched at his head. His scalp was oily. He needed his own shower.

"A list?" he muttered. "Can I see it?"

Arachne shook her head. "The list is for me. Goals from my perspective. How would you like to begin? Cleaning, studying, or training?"

Cyrus slumped deeper into his chair. "Eating."

The bathroom door opened and Antigone stepped out, cinching her wet hair back with a toothed headband. She was in shorts and an old short-sleeved safari shirt. Her bare feet left damp tracks on the wood floor. Through the door behind her, Cyrus could see the shower spasming out the last of the water still in its gullet.

"Water's cold this morning," Antigone said. Cyrus caught her eyes and then rolled his own. "What?" Antigone glanced at Arachne and then her brother. "What's going on?"

Arachne straightened in her chair. "Rupert has given me a list of things to work on with you while you're locked in." She smiled. "And I'm going to help you clean and freshen this old place."

Antigone blinked in surprise.. She looked at her brother, confused by his obviously dark mood.

"That's terrific," she said. "Lists are terrific, and we could definitely use help in here."

"Oh, gosh . . ." Cyrus stood and moved past his sister toward the bathroom.

"It's cold!" Antigone said. "You might wanna wait."

Cyrus shut the bathroom door behind him.

A really cold shower isn't too terrible when you know that you're going to walk outside into frying-pan heat. Tight cool skin, tight cool muscles, and a near ice-cream headache were all solid preparation for a long morning in the sun. But Cyrus wasn't going to have a long morning in the sun. A long morning, yes. Sun, no. Air, no. Grass, no. Sky, no. Spiders, probably. Dust, for sure. Two girls talking about paint colors and decor or whatever they called it, almost certainly. And a list that sounded a whole lot like homework. Training wasn't supposed to be homework. Training was diving. Fencing. Running. Climbing. Sailing. Shooting.

Cyrus shut his eyes and ducked his chin to his chest. That was the only way he could fit under the low showerhead.

Water that had obviously been ice thirty seconds before, and would likely be ice again in another minute, splashed irregularly down his neck and back. Despite the loud pipes, Cyrus could hear the girls laughing.

His new boss was smaller than he was, and she had a face like an almost creepy doll. If almost creepy dolls could also be incredibly beautiful. Her eyes weren't real. They couldn't be. Looking into them was like . . . what? Falling? Tripping? Like taking an awkward extra step on stairs when the stairs have already run out. Her eyes—that's why she was in charge. Or at least why Cyrus didn't argue about it. Her eyes were the only part of her that said she wasn't just another pretty girl a few years older than him. Her eyes were all the way old.

Like the moon, Cyrus thought. They had craters, but

not literally. There was a lot of damage in there. Old hurt. But they were young eyes, too. Not like Nolan's. There was no anger in them, no hardness. They could sparkle like the sun on water. Like the sun through water.

Cyrus let his mind drift away, and he was back under the lake's surface, looking up at Arachne's silhouette, looking at the sun's golden rays slicing through the blue and the floating, weightless spider army all around. That's what her eyes were like.

He hadn't argued with her, but he had sulked. No one likes a sulker.

Cyrus bent his knees and tipped back his head, letting the glacier water tighten his face. The week was going to be awful, that much was obvious. But he wasn't going to sulk again.

The pipe shook in the wall. The showerhead quivered. Cyrus opened his eyes wide.

"No." He tried to jump back, but too late. Steam whistled at him. His bare feet skidded and he fell as the scalding water lashed across his skin. Yelling, he rolled on the tile and pinned himself into the corner, out of direct fire. But even the spattering drops were pure pain. Wincing, straining, he stretched his leg up through the lava lasers and grabbed at the handle with his toes.

Outside, overlooking the tented green, the red-winged blackbird was sitting on a windowsill in the sun. She heard the yells, and she knew the voice. She knew the sound of water in the pipes. She wasn't worried. She shut her eyes against the morning and nestled her head beneath her wing.

When Cyrus walked from the bathroom to his bedroom, most of the red stripes on his skin were hidden by his T-shirt. Antigone and Arachne were eating on the floor beside a pile of books. They smiled. He didn't. Books? And the pile wasn't small.

No sulking.

Cyrus stopped in the bedroom doorway.

"Water got a little warm," he said. "I feel bad for lobsters. Don't eat all of that."

While they laughed, he moved inside to root through his cardboard box for his cleanest clothes.

Day one: For Cyrus, it crept by like a snail parade. He could hear airplane after airplane descending, but he couldn't see the sky. He could hear Acolytes laughing on the green and training on the gravel paths, but he couldn't see the grass. For breakfast, he ate some cold bacon and a bowl of fiber flakes with what he was sure couldn't be more than two teaspoons of milk. There was no lunch. Arachne said they were in training. He ate some stale crackers that had been around for months.

And he cleaned. And cleaned. He scrubbed what he

was told, he swept where he was told, and he even dusted the ceiling, balancing on the back of the armchair. And for all of that, the rooms were only slightly less moldy and rotten—though now they reeked so much of lemon and pine that Cyrus's nostrils burned and he couldn't stop blinking his watering eyes.

The training was as uninteresting as it was grueling. Arachne said she was only testing their physical starting points, and she needed to see their bodies in motion. Which meant push-ups and sit-ups and lunges and planks and frozen poses.

Dinner was cold potatoes, sausage, and a pitcher of water.

Nolan delivered yellow paint up through the heat vent, Rupert never came by, and Cyrus climbed into his hammock early, trying not to listen to the girls talk about ancient Greek syntax while he bounced his foot against the wall.

Day two: Before breakfast, Cyrus did more push-ups and more sit-ups and more lunges while Arachne watched, hardly blinking. His legs burned with soreness from the day before, but he wasn't going to tell her. Nolan delivered three plates of cold, slippery eggs up through the heat vent, but left before Cyrus could talk to him.

After breakfast, Cyrus reslung his hammock. He resorted his cardboard box of clothes. He got the wobbly, clear Quick Water out of the wooden box on the mantel and played with it. Arachne pointed out particular books in the Book Dump and Cyrus carried them out in stacks and set them wherever she told him to. Antigone thought they looked interesting, but the titles made Cyrus's brain water.

The Seven Depletions of Bajan Voo. The Neverwhere Voyages of Timothy Maggot. Soils and Salts. Theses on Economic Inversion. Your Best Maps Now: A Cartographic Memoir. And more and more and more . . .

Finally, Cyrus got out his two new patches and sat in the armchair while Antigone and Arachne talked and planned and sorted through the books Arachne had selected.

Cyrus studied his patches. The basic circle patch of Ashtown with the black boat in the center—that hadn't cost him anything. But the crest of the Smiths, well, he'd made big promises before Old Donald had let him have it. Donald had said that he didn't think another Smith patch that old existed—at some point they'd all been burned. Some modern Smiths had worked up variations—all without the heads—but none of them had stuck around. The old Smith crest was too memorable, too rooted in the stories of grandmothers and thus in the imaginations of kids. Or so said Old Donald . . .

Sic Semper Draconis

Cyrus traced the motto, and then studied the three heads. Beard, mustache, and clean-shaven. *Thus to all dragons. Thus always to dragons*—that was the better translation, wasn't it? But he wasn't exactly sure what it meant. All dragons should be beheaded? But they weren't dragon heads. They were men.

Cyrus rubbed the red silky-smooth shield with his thumb. He wanted it on his jacket already.

His stomach rumbled, and he closed his eyes.

For a while, he was simply walking along the Northern California cliffs, listening to the seals bark, watching the white lines of surf roll in. For a while, he wandered the pastures of Wisconsin, searching for tires in the irrigation ditches. For a while, he walked along a country road looking for the Archer Motel. Cars would slow down with lowered windows and drivers would ask if he needed a ride. He told them he was heading to a place called Waffle.

And then it was night and he was sitting on a boulder on the side of a mountain. Beneath him, a thick pine forest rustled like the sea sucking at sand. Across from him, on another peak, there was a fortress. A needle-sharp crescent moon was rising behind it.

But the fortress didn't matter. Three men strode out of the pine forest and climbed up to his boulder. The oldest and heaviest man had a thick black beard, and he carried a long slender ax with a blade as thin and vicious as the moon. The second man was taller, with broad shoulders and long, lean arms. He had a mustache that dangled past his sharp chin, and in one hand he carried a long, slightly curved sword, like something between a saber and the weapon of a samurai. The moonlight danced across its blade, and Cyrus saw the long, twining image of a dragon etched into the steel. In his other hand, the man carried a long, sharpened wooden pole. The third man was the youngest and the slightest. His face was clean-shaven, and he carried only a bow, with arrows in a quiver on his belt. All three men wore thick silver chains around their necks, and thin silver crowns were nestled into their dark hair.

The man with the sword stepped forward.

"*Vos volo?*" His growling voice sounded distant, like he was speaking from a cave.

"Sorry," said Cyrus. "I need to sew your heads on my jacket."

The man lunged forward, slashing with his sword.

"Cy!"

Cyrus jerked awake as Antigone kicked him in the leg. Arachne was standing behind her.

"Tigs!" He grabbed at his shin. Both of his patches slid to the floor.

"Sorry," Antigone said. "You wouldn't wake up."

Arachne bent and picked up the patches. She tossed the Ashtown patch back onto Cyrus's lap, but she studied the Smith patch.

"A vivid dream," she said simply. "A wandering mind

can be a strength." She looked up from the patch at Cyrus. "The embroidery is good. I never understood the trouble about Smiths—apart from the treachery of your greatest grandfather. These three"—she tapped the heads—"earned their ends, though most of my kind will deny it."

"Who were they?" Cyrus asked. "Or are we not allowed to know?"

Arachne inhaled slowly. "It's on my list. Rupert said to tell you as much as I know. They were men that I—and the world—feared. The heart of *Ordo Draconis.* The Tri-Dracul. Sorcerers of a rare and bestial breed." Starting with the bearded one, she tapped all three. "Vlad the Second, Vlad the Third, Vlad the Fourth—each beheaded by Captain John Smith with their family's own heirloom sword." She handed back the patch.

Cyrus stared at her, waiting for more. But more wasn't coming. "Come on," he said. "You know more than that. Tell the whole story."

Arachne's blue eyes laughed, and she shook her head. "Train hard and I will tell you later." She looked at Antigone. "If you train harder, we may paint later."

Antigone smiled. Cyrus looked at the patch in his hands. "Will you help me sew this on my jacket?"

"Cy, no." Antigone crossed her arms. "Now that you have it, you should keep it somewhere safe."

Cyrus grinned at his sister. "Somewhere no one can see it, maybe?"

"Preferably, yeah," Antigone said.

Arachne looked from sister to brother. Then she nodded. "I may sew it on later. But now, both of you lie on the floor." She waved at the rug. "Facedown, please. You must learn to bend."

"Any chance of lunch soon?" Cyrus asked. His stomach roared at him as he slid out of his chair and onto his knees.

"No chance," Arachne said. "Not for a while. You need an empty stomach for this. Now flatten out on your face, arms at your sides, hands palms up."

Cyrus eased himself down. The rough wool rug scratched at his forehead and nose.

"What are we doing?" he asked. "What's the point?"

Arachne's cool hands closed around his right ankle. "Deep breath in," she said, and a second later, Cyrus's leg folded up into the small of his back. His toes splayed, his tendons screamed, and his mouth opened, but he couldn't even yell. His tongue clawed at the dirty rug, and in some other world, he could hear his sister laughing.

"Exhale," Arachne said, and electric ice shot through Cyrus's leg and rattled through his body. Pain and tension disappeared as he felt his leg bend farther and farther up into his back.

"What are you doing?" he heard Antigone ask. "You're going to break him! Cy, are you okay?"

Arachne pried Cyrus's other leg up into his back. His

face compressed into the rug, and an involuntary groan slid out of him as his lungs collapsed.

"I'm a weaver," Arachne said, and her voice was cheerful. She was enjoying herself. "To some, I am *the* weaver—the first and true spinster. And the human body is—like many things—woven. Rupert has asked me to rework and rearrange a few things in the two of you."

"y?" Cyrus licked the rug as he tried to speak. His teeth would have chattered if there weren't floor wedged in between them. The cold electrical current in his body was growing stronger. Even his eyelids were beginning to twitch.

"You could achieve this flexibility on your own over years—with the right training, of course. But Rupert cannot wait for years, and I am here now. He asks, and I comply. This will greatly improve your recovery after strain." Cyrus's legs dropped to the floor as limp as two sacks of liquid. Then his arms crossed behind his back.

"Oh, gosh . . . ," Antigone blurted.

Arachne continued talking, but Cyrus's brain was drifting away.

"Some muscle fibers will not change or be rewoven without dramatic assistance. Yours are strong already, but they need more endurance and more quickness. That means, well, you might call it braiding rather than weaving."

Cyrus's arms flopped back out to his sides.

"Lie down, Antigone. You'll catch up in a minute. Cyrus, this part is . . . uncomfortable," Arachne said. Her hand slid up to the back of Cyrus's head. "If you were awake, it would mean hours of prolonged cramping followed by the most intense itching and tickling you've ever felt. Like stinging ants beneath the skin." Cyrus tried to sputter an objection, but Arachne held his head still. "Which is why you'll be uncon—"

Darkness landed on Cyrus like a pile of quilts.

He looked around. There was nothing. No floor beneath him. No *him* to have a floor beneath. He'd been kicked out of his body and into . . . nowhere.

"Cyrus?" The voice was low and surprised and a little worried. It was a woman's voice, sweet and mellow, grown in tropical sun and tropical soil. It plucked thick unused strings in Cyrus's soul, playing a chord he'd forgotten. Shocked emotion roared through him.

"Mom?" He couldn't look for her. He couldn't search. He could only listen. Hours passed. Or years. And still he waited in the nowhere silence for his mother's voice.

"You should not be here, Cyrus. The sleep is long here. Go back. Stay with your sister."

"Mom?" Antigone's voice was louder, closer than their mother's. But Cyrus couldn't see her, either.

"Antigone? Take your brother and go. Before you are lost in the in-between."

"Mom, I want to see you," Antigone said. "Where are you?"

"You do see me," she said. "You braid my hair. You sit with me and sing to me and read to me. I listen and I feel. And, in my own way, I have seen you. I watch you run and sleep and study. I watched Cyrus race the bigger boy and sink beneath the plane. Cyrus has grown tall, like my lost brothers. And you, Antigone, your hair, your eyes, your face, they make me sing. Care for your brother. Cyrus, keep your sweet sister safe. Now go. Both of you. This is not a place for wandering."

"Wait," said Cyrus. "Mom, wait—"

They were being pushed, sliding away through the darkness. Antigone was gone. Cyrus was alone, alone without time, without thought, until even the darkness faded away. And then . . . he was incredibly hungry.

Cyrus opened his eyes. He was staring into the rug. He could taste thrown-up stale crackers in his mouth, and his body was shaking from somewhere deep inside. Sharp-bladed pain had sliced the inside of his gut, his smashed nose was running, and he could feel tears in his eyebrows.

He could hear Antigone crying.

"All right," Arachne said. "Antigone? Cyrus? You can stand up. Can you stand up?"

Cyrus didn't move. Beside him, he heard Antigone sob. He turned his head and looked at his sister. She sat up slowly beside him, and then wiped tears off the side of her nose. Cyrus could see the questions in her eyes. *Were you there? Was that real?*

Cyrus nodded slightly, feeling the wet rug grind against his cheek.

"Cy," Antigone said. "We were both there. But I woke up first. Cy, it was like you were dead."

"How long?" Cyrus mumbled.

"You both slept overnight," Arachne said.

That meant this was day three. Cyrus shut his eyes and tried to think. In that empty nothingness, he could have been gone for a year for all he knew. He was hungry enough.

Arachne's voice was low. "But, Cyrus, when the morning came, you fought with me as I tried to pull you back. You've been gone most of the day. My thread almost broke. What was in that place for you?"

Cyrus opened his eyes and stared at his sister. She knew. But he hadn't known that he was fighting. Antigone was wiping her face quickly on both shoulders. What had been there for him? His mother's voice had been there. And she'd know what Cyrus had been doing. Or maybe Cyrus had simply dreamed it all. He looked at Antigone. It couldn't be a dream if his sister had been there, too. Antigone shook her head at Cyrus, just a little. She didn't want him to tell Arachne. Not yet. Cyrus nodded, and his sister turned to their trainer.

"What now?" Antigone asked.

Cyrus sniffed hard, climbed to his knees, and wiped his nose on the hem of his T-shirt before he looked back at Arachne's curious face. He felt empty, and loose and taut at the same time. He felt like running. Alone. Until he dropped. Right after he ate something gigantic—like Leon, the car-size snapping turtle in the Crypto wing.

He wobbled, dizzy on his feet.

Arachne jumped forward and grabbed his arm, and her hand was midnight-cool. "You need to eat, Cyrus. And drink. Then we work."

Arachne didn't ask any more questions. It was obvious that whatever had happened, the Smiths weren't going to tell her. Cyrus ate a loaf of toast and a slab of cheese, and then he drained a quart jar full of room-temperature water and collapsed into the armchair, sweating like he'd spent an afternoon fencing in the sun. He dozed, and then he slept.

This was real sleep. Normal sleep. Sleep with dreams.

Cyrus dreamed of the three heads—the dark-haired men, bearded, mustached, and clean-shaven. They sat motionless in a cold stone room, and Cyrus stood before them, and the one with the long mustache had a sharp sword resting across his knees. He'd seen that sword in his first dream. The samurai-style blade had a long twining dragon etched into the steel.

Cyrus was pleading with the men. No, he was trying

to bully them. He was threatening them, promising their destruction. And then he was offering them protection, an alliance—but his voice wasn't really his. And he was speaking in Latin.

His dream jumped. The three men were standing, and they had ripped open their shirts. A circular bloodred dragon stood out on each of their chests, nestled in hair. Not tattoos, something more, something real, and alive, and trapped. Each man touched the tip of the sword to the dragon on his chest, and each dragon shivered and squirmed beneath the skin as a drop of blood ran down the blade.

And then the man with the long mustache handed the sword to him, and Cyrus realized that his own chest was bare. He was supposed to do the same. But as his hand closed around the hilt of the sword, he knew that he wouldn't. He knew that he would break his own Latin vows.

He knew that the dragon men in front of him were as good as dead.

The dream jumped again. He was back in Skelton's old rooms, and the place smelled of paint. The men were there, painting everything yellow with fat rollers . . . but they had forgotten their heads.

Cyrus stretched and opened his eyes.

Arachne and Antigone stood in front of him with arms crossed. They were both flecked with yellow paint.

The room behind them was completely yellow. Buckets and rollers were propped in the corner.

"You've had a harder time of it, but you've stopped sweating," Arachne said. "Stand up. If you don't throw up or pass out, it's time to test my weaving."

Cyrus stood slowly, and the dream fog slipped off him. He felt light and quick. His eyes were sharp, his breath slow and even. He couldn't stop the smile that spread across his face.

"You feel good, don't you?" Antigone asked. Her eyes were wide. "I feel great."

Arachne sighed with relief. "You worried me, Cyrus."

Cyrus grinned. "That's what I do." He glanced at the web-sealed windows. "What's been going on outside?"

"Nothing good," Arachne said. "But outside doesn't exist for us right now. Do you need more rest? More food? I doubt you feel ready for physical exertion."

Cyrus laughed and looked at his sister. "The way I feel right now, if I don't do something physical, I think I might explode. Tigs?"

Antigone nodded in agreement.

"Terrific," Arachne said. "To work, then. We're behind."

For the first few hours, she ran them through a grueling set of balance and endurance tests. Some less normal than others.

"We must see which gives out first," Arachne said.

"The body or the mind." And she gave no more explanation than that.

First, Cyrus and Antigone stood in the center of the room, with arms extended straight out from their sides—palms down, fingers spread.

Arachne balanced two books on the back of each hand. Over time, she added books to the shaking stacks. Cyrus couldn't help laughing, at least at first. The titles Arachne had picked out of the Book Dump hadn't been meant for study at all. She'd chosen them for size and weight.

With his burdened arms sticking out, Cyrus's shoulders burned and quaked, but he had no intention of losing to his smaller sister. And yet he did. They repeated the exercise again and again, and each time, Cyrus lost. But he was surprised that his shoulders seemed to get stronger—or he got better at ignoring their screams. Finally, Antigone's books toppled first.

Antigone smiled. "Throw the dog a bone," she said.

Cyrus snorted. "Yeah, right. Bring it, Tigger."

Arachne forced them to hold one-legged poses, balancing book stacks on their knees, on their feet, on their shoulders and heads. Books tumbled and tossed and cartwheeled across the floor so often, Cyrus actually felt a little guilty. A whole flock of pages flew out of *The Neverwhere Voyages of Timothy Maggot.* And *Soils and Salts* lost its back cover. But sometimes, usually right before they moved on to a new exercise, the books perched perfectly. They sat easily on his raised knee or foot or shin or shoulder or elbows, while his muscles shrieked and sweat dripped off his face and eternity passed. And then he heard the word *good,* spoken simply, the books were taken off, and he and his sister were molded into new positions. And in each of those new positions—seated on an invisible bench against the wall with one leg raised, or in a push-up position with the soles of their feet high on the wall, or leaning stiffly to one side with first one leg extended and then the other—they quivered and shook and fell to the floor. And then did it again and again and again, until Arachne was happy with how long they'd lasted.

Cyrus knew that nothing he was doing was actually required for him to move up to Explorer. But he didn't care. He was training, and he'd never enjoyed a burn in his muscles so much.

After too many failures and too little improvement, Arachne knocked Cyrus out again to rebraid something in his back. But this time, she didn't send his consciousness nearly as deep, and she didn't keep him gone for more than twenty minutes. When he came to, the muscles in his back were tingling and Antigone was waiting, eyes wide, curious. He shook his head. He'd seen nothing and heard nothing of their mother. It hadn't even felt like the same place.

Later, Arachne did the same thing to Antigone, focusing on her ankles and calves. Cyrus watched his unconscious sister shiver on the floor, her calves dancing and quaking beneath the skin under Arachne's slightest touch.

When Antigone rolled back over, he only needed to see her disappointed eyes to know that the same had been true for her.

Cyrus was flat on his back staring at the grubby ceiling. His arms were splayed out to his sides, and his feet were up on the armchair. Somewhere close by, he knew Antigone was doing something similar.

His empty stomach roared. He didn't know how long their break would be, but he knew it wouldn't be long enough. His exhaustion was total. He had no idea what time it was or even what day it was. He only knew that he was still in Skelton's old rooms, and Arachne wasn't done with them yet. He was starving to the point of dizziness, but if someone had set a plate of food just out of his reach, he didn't think he would be able to make himself roll over for it. He wouldn't want to.

"Cy," Antigone said.

"Yeah?" Cyrus asked. He didn't look for her. Water was running in the bathroom. Arachne was out of the room.

"Cy," Antigone said. "What's going on with Mom?"

Cyrus grunted. He hadn't had much time to think about it. They'd been doing this forever. He tried to breathe evenly. Muscle fibers throughout his body were still twitching—in his legs, his abs, his arms. He licked sweat off his lips while Antigone continued.

"I mean, she's in a coma. But Mom knew about us. She said she'd watched us. Do you think she's wandering around out of her body?"

"Maybe," said Cyrus. What else could he say?

"That scared me," Antigone said. "Hearing her talk, having her voice out of her body. Do you think she's dying?"

Cyrus didn't answer. He heard the bathroom door open, and a moment later, Arachne was standing over him holding two large plastic buckets full of water.

"You have done well," Arachne said. "Rupert will be pleased."

"I'm broken," Cyrus said. "Feed me something, and then bury me by the lake, please."

Antigone managed to snort out a pained laugh.

"I am serious," Arachne said. "Human musculature is incredibly intricate in its artistry and potential, but badly governed. Muscles are fired with imprecision, and people are rarely capable of using half, let alone all of their fibers at once. With my help, now you two are approaching that ability—your sinews and fibers are awake and obedient. I did a lot of weaving to prepare your bodies for these tests, but I know they still hurt. Fighting through hurt is all strength of mind. And there's little I can do to help you with that." She set her buckets down next to each other. "This is your last test. Finish this and we will eat."

Cyrus groaned. Through some strange magic, Antigone managed to sit up.

"This is about teamwork and controlling panic," Arachne said. She laughed a little. "And obviously strength and concentration and disorientation and blind balance."

"What is it?" Antigone asked.

Arachne's eyebrows climbed. "You're going to do handstands with your backs together and your heads over buckets of water." She seemed apologetic. "Rupert didn't think you'd even be able to try until the end of the day tomorrow. But you've gotten through everything else on the list."

Cyrus managed to sit up. He looked at the big plastic buckets next to him. "Back to back?" He looked at Antigone. "We can do it."

"How long?" Antigone asked.

"For ten minutes," Arachne said. "If one of you falls, the clock starts again."

"Ten minutes in a handstand?" Cyrus shook his head.

"Or a *head*stand," said Arachne. "But your heads go

in the buckets. And you'll need to move in unison or you'll fall."

Antigone laughed in disbelief.

Cyrus climbed to one knee, then both knees; one foot, then both feet. He reached down for his sister's hands, but when she pulled on him to stand up, he nearly fell onto her.

Cyrus wiped his forearm across his head. "Let's do it, Tigs."

At first, it seemed like getting into the back-to-back handstands would be the hard part. They fell sideways. And sideways. And sideways. Then Antigone fell on Cyrus, and Cyrus fell on Antigone. Finally, they were up, but they'd missed the buckets.

"Um, help?" Cyrus said. Blood was already pounding in his head. This couldn't be healthy.

Arachne slid the buckets under their heads and stepped back. The bucket's lip pressed against Cyrus's forehead, and he could feel the water tickling his scalp. Antigone's hair had to be all the way in the water.

"So . . . ," Antigone said. She was already wobbling against Cyrus's back. "Should we hook feet or something?"

Cyrus answered with his feet. They hooked bare ankle against bare ankle, and he suddenly felt a little more solid. Less than three minutes later, their arms were shaking.

"Cy?" Antigone said.

"Right," said Cyrus. "Try to hold your breath for two minutes, but I'll come up if you do. Ready? And . . . down . . ."

Cyrus felt the water flow into his ears and down his nostrils, flooding his sinuses. Wobbling slightly, he let his head rest on the bottom of the bucket, and he began to count. A sharp plastic bump on the bottom dug into his scalp, but he ignored it. He tried to pretend he was somewhere else, somewhere that wasn't dark and tight and wobbly and upside down, someplace where he had decided to hold his breath and count slowly to one hundred and twenty just because he wanted to.

The darkness made him dizzy. The blood in his head made his pulse thunder. He was counting too slowly for some reason. He had to be. *Twenty* should have been a long time ago. He should be at *forty*.

He felt himself drifting away, but his sister's legs tugged him back. *Thirty-four . . . thirty-five . . .*

Antigone wobbled; she was tipping away from him. Cyrus adjusted his hands on the floor and leaned against her, pulling her legs with his.

Bubbles leaked out of his nostrils as he strained, but his pulling worked. They were vertical again.

His pulse had quickened. The pain in the top of his head was intense. He released the last of his air and knew, as the bubbles skidded up out of his nostrils, that that had been a mistake. He should have nursed that air, his lungs were empty now, and he'd completely lost count. How long did he have to last?

He started over, counting from one. His lungs wanted air—even old air. They wanted something, anything, maybe even water. They needed to expand, and because Cyrus wouldn't let them, they lit themselves on fire.

When his blood ran out of oxygen, then his brain would run out of oxygen and he would pass out. Then he would fall, and the buckets would spill. He wouldn't drown, but he would have to start over.

Antigone was tapping him with her heel. Then Cyrus felt her body begin to slide up.

Slowly, arms shaking, wrists and shoulders screaming, Cyrus pressed himself back up into a handstand. Wobbling, his chin rose out of the bucket, and then his mouth, his nose, his eyes.

Antigone was coughing, and her whole body shook.

Cyrus gulped a breath through his mouth. His sinuses were full of water; any breath through his nose would send him hacking like his sister. He blew hard out of his nose, sending snot and water fountaining around his face. He blinked, but the room was still out of focus. Too much blood in his eyes, in his head.

Arachne's blurry shape knelt in front of him.

"You're doing well," she said. "Halfway there."

Antigone coughed.

"Tigs?" Cyrus said. "You okay?"

"Wonder"—she hacked and spat—"ful."

"Lock your elbows," Cyrus said. "Let's not do that again."

He felt Antigone's height shift in his back.

"Have to," Antigone said. "I can't hold this for five more."

Rupert Greeves strode across the green, weaving through the tents. He was wearing long trousers tucked into high, glistening boots. A thick belt held a holster—and a long-barreled revolver—on one hip and a wide-bladed jungle sword on the other. At the small of his back, a small but heavy glass ball bounced in a pouch. He was carrying a dinner tray covered with a napkin.

The Acolytes were all eating and talking at their tent flaps. Some still laughed or sang, but most had quiet, somber faces, far more subdued than the previous nights. Having the transmortals around was like having a pride of lions as houseguests. And these kids were in tents. All eyes followed Rupert as he passed.

It hadn't been a good week, not for anyone. The hospital wing was filling up quickly. The injuries were small enough thus far—broken bones, concussions, damaged joints—and they had all been caused by inexplicable accidents. Oiled stairs, broken chains on flying bikes, bursting blimps—the causes were varied. But if things didn't improve around Ashtown, the injuries wouldn't remain small, and there wouldn't be accidents to blame.

And tonight's assembly wasn't likely to improve anything. Quite the opposite. Regardless, it was time to lean into the anger before it blew the Order over. It was time for the Smiths to be seen.

Rupert could hear two more airplanes circling, preparing for descent, late arrivals no doubt carrying two more loads of transmortal trouble.

"Mr. Greeves," a girl said, "how many of them are there? People are saying the treaties—"

"You'll hear more soon," Rupert said without slowing down. His night was just beginning.

Once again bubbling in the bucket, Cyrus felt Arachne tap his leg. He didn't bother to attempt a dignified dismount. Unhooking his ankle from his sister's, he fell to the floor. His legs and stomach slammed to the ground, and water sloshed down around his shoulders and soaked beneath him.

His head was still in the bucket, but the bucket was empty now. He could breathe.

"Impressive." Rupert's voice echoed through the plastic.

Cyrus knocked the bucket away and sat up. Antigone sat up beside him. Rupert Greeves stood above them, holding a dinner tray and wearing nicer clothes than he usually did—and weapons on his belt.

"With Arachne's touch, that's months of hard training done in three days." He smiled. "Lockdown is good for you. Now eat and change. We're due in the Galleria soon."

Cyrus, sitting in a puddle, leaned back against his wobbling arms. The blood was still draining from his head, and dizziness swirled around him.

"We're leaving?" he asked. "We get to go outside?"

"I think I'm going to be sick," Antigone said, and she fell back onto the floor.

"That's right," Rupert said. "You're coming outside."

Cyrus could feel water draining out of his sinuses and down the back of his throat. He spat on the carpet, rolled onto his face, and shut his eyes.

❧ six ❧

ORDO

Cyrus moved quickly through the narrow hallway, following close behind Antigone. Ahead of her, Rupert disappeared down the stairwell. Arachne had stayed behind with her spiders.

They had eaten—but only cheese and a dry brick of strange bread. It would have been too hard to chew if Cyrus hadn't dipped each bite in water. Rupert had said that it was fortified and would fortify. He'd also said that he needed to know how their bodies reacted to it while they were still in a controlled environment.

Cryptic, but Cyrus hadn't cared. He'd been hungry enough to eat anything, but a steaming pile of noodles from the dining hall would have come back up as quickly as he pushed it down.

Antigone shoved back her hair with a headband and put on a linen safari shirtdress that Diana had given her. She belted it at the waist and pulled on caramel-colored boots. Cyrus wore straight trousers, his own shorter boots, and a black cotton tee with the Polygoner monkey on the chest under his flight jacket. Once clothed, Rupert had them heading for the Galleria without much explanation.

Cyrus adjusted his leather flight jacket as they went. It would make him sweat soon enough, but while he'd been unconscious, Arachne had stitched on his two new patches. Rupert eyed them as they walked.

Antigone groaned. "Rupe?"

"He is a Smith," Rupert said. "Those who hate that crest already hate him, and they will not have forgotten who he is simply because he wears no label. The motto speaks truth, and Cyrus honored it when he killed Maximilien. Soon enough, he may honor it again."

Cyrus smiled, though he didn't care to think about fighting anyone else like Maxi. High on his right shoulder, above the boxing monkey in its yellow shield, he now had the white circle and black ship that signified the Ashtown Estate. On his left shoulder, Arachne had removed the French World War I tricolor and replaced it with the sign of the Smiths—the three heads. The tricolor was now on the inside of the jacket.

At the bottom of the stairs, Rupert paused by the door. "Ignore the dragonflies. They're expecting us and will stay with us across the green. And no matter what any transmortal says or does, do not flinch, do not respond, and do not show fear." He opened the door and stepped through. "Stay close."

The evening air was still and wet and warm. At the green, Cyrus noticed the change in the Acolyte tent city right away. There were no water fights. No bread wars. No games of tag, and no pranks. They were all at their tents—all but a small group on the gravel path, huddled together and talking.

"Quarters!" Rupert shouted, and the group scattered, racing toward the tents.

"What's going on?" Antigone asked. "What happened?"

"I have placed the Estate under Field Rules." He glanced back at Cyrus and Antigone. "Every member above Journeyman is to be armed at all times. Acolytes are under curfew, and every member above Acolyte has been assigned to a Field Unit and a Field Captain, to whom they report."

"We're not Acolytes," Cyrus said. "And we haven't been assigned to anyone."

Rupert laughed. "You two are mine. And you didn't need a special assignment to know that. The protocols we are following were designed for large explorations in hostile territory. As long as the transmortals are here, Ashtown has become hostile territory."

As they walked, Cyrus could hear the giant watchful dragonflies hum and rocket through the darkness above him as they circled. Massive wings and abdomens like baseball bats flashed shadows across distant lit windows.

Somewhere, he knew, Rupert would have men carrying little domed monitors, seeing what the dragonflies were seeing.

And then he heard the shriek of a bird.

Antigone grabbed her brother's arm. The red-winged blackbird shot past them, low to the ground, flapping frantically. Two three-and-a-half-foot dragonflies zipped after her, like jets after a crop duster.

"No!" Cyrus yelled. "Rupe! Make them stop!"

Confused, Rupert wheeled around, reaching for his gun. The blackbird twisted and wove its way through the tent city, lapping tents, twisting, doubling back, looping figure eights. But the dragonflies kept pace easily, and everywhere they went Acolytes ducked and yelled and dove for cover.

Antigone and Cyrus were sprinting, dodging tents and jumping Acolyte legs, trying to catch up. The bird saw them from down a long row. Veering quickly, she dropped low, and with wings battering blades of grass, she flapped frantically toward them.

Above her, the huge dragonflies closed in.

A moment later, the bird smacked into Antigone's stomach. Antigone dropped to the ground and curled around it as the dragonflies shot past and swung around.

Cyrus stood above his sister, fists clenched, but the dragonflies hovered just out of reach, their huge heads cocking and twisting, studying him.

Behind the insects, with gun drawn, Rupert strode between the tents. "What was that?" he asked. "Antigone, what are you protecting? Why was it following you?"

"Our blackbird," said Cyrus. "She always follows us, and she's not dangerous, no matter what the dragonflies think."

Antigone rose to her knees and held out her hands, fingers laced around the bird's body.

"She's terrified," Antigone said. "Her heart's racing."

The bird opened its beak and shrieked at the dragonflies. The big insects drifted forward, and the wind from their wings gusted warm, sticky air across Cyrus's face. Antigone pulled her hands back.

Rupert whistled short and sharp, and with a blast of air, the dragonflies were gone. He looked around at the startled Acolytes, and then back at Cyrus and Antigone.

"You do realize that bird is male?" He arched his brows, but Cyrus and Antigone didn't answer. Rupert shrugged and turned around. "Stay close."

By the time they reached the main building, Antigone had the bird perched on her shoulder. Rupert took the stairs two at a time, and Cyrus and Antigone quickstepped up behind him. At the top, just outside the tall doors, three shapes were waiting for them—four if Cyrus counted Dennis Gilly, playing porter off to one side.

George and Silas Livingstone stood on either side of

a huge blond man with a short, thick beard. The man wasn't as tall as Rupert, but his chest and shoulders looked like they belonged to a rhinoceros, and his bare woolly arms had been borrowed from a blond orangutan. He wore an old pocketed shirt cinched tight beneath a thick belt loaded with weapons. And he had a patch on each shoulder.

Rupert stopped, and Cyrus and Antigone stopped on either side of him. Rupert extended a hand, and the big blond man shook it with a stern face. Laughing suddenly, the blond man pulled Rupert into a bear hug, slapping his back with thick arms. Cyrus and Antigone watched in surprise, while George and Silas smiled.

"Ye stiff Brit," the man said. His accent was like the boys', but thicker. "Times are dark, but it's always good to slap eyes on an old tent mate. I searched for a glimpse of you all the day yesterday, but I knew where you'd be tonight. I laid my ambush."

Rupert pulled free, and when he turned around, he was smiling.

"Cy, Tigs, these are the Livingstones. Alan, Keeper from the Carthage Estate, and his sons, George and Silas—but you've met them already."

George, Silas, and Cyrus all nodded. Antigone smiled.

Big Alan stepped forward and dropped a ten-pound hand on Cyrus's shoulder. "It's a pleasure to meet you both—despite the storm clouds. I knew your old dad, though not as well as I would have liked.'' He shook his head sadly. ''I love the Order, but it did him wrong when it denied his bride—your lovely mother. I understood his leaving, and I grieved his passing. And when I heard two Smiths were back in the door, well, I laughed, and I'm not ashamed to say I wiped a tear or two—though you came in wearing the boots of an outlaw and I was sure you'd track in trouble.'' He winked, smiled at both of them, and then stepped back, suddenly serious. ''Can't say I knew just how much trouble, and I wouldn't have laughed if I had. But the blame rests on old dead Billy Bones, not on you.''

Antigone sighed. ''It's nice to meet you, too, Mr. Livingstone. And thanks. Most people seem to think everything is our fault.''

''My fault,'' Cyrus said. ''Usually.''

Alan Livingstone nodded, and then thumped his fist on Rupert's shoulder. ''Well, in we go,'' he said. ''Come what may.''

Dennis Gilly opened the wooden door, and Alan stepped aside. ''Smiths and their Keeper first,'' he said. ''The Livingstones will watch your back.''

The halls were crowded with people, but Cyrus and Antigone walked in an empty hollow, the space between Rupert Greeves and Alan Livingstone. They moved easily past the ship on its pedestal and reached the wide-open doors of the Galleria. George and Silas followed close behind them.

Inside the Galleria, a narrow path to the front was all that was still empty of bodies. The mezzanines were overburdened on every side, and the scaled stone columns rose to the vaulted ceiling like pylons holding up a pier above a sea of heads.

Cyrus could feel his sister's tension. The blackbird hopped in place on her shoulder. They had walked through a smaller version of this crowd when they'd first arrived at Ashtown. He'd felt like a curiosity then. Now it was hard not to feel like the condemned.

They passed the Brendanites in their monastic robes and sandals. They passed men and women they had never seen before—Asian faces and African faces, Russian faces and Spanish faces, pale faces and faces as brown as and browner than their own. Some wore khakis and boots and linen, and some seemed to be in understated uniforms. Some wore patches, and some wore shirts as empty as the expressions they ladled onto Cyrus and Antigone.

As Cyrus and Antigone moved forward, the crowd on their left changed. Cyrus saw Gilgamesh scratching at his bearded cheeks, and he saw men even taller and broader than Gil. He saw men sleek and shiny and well oiled, and men who looked like heroes. He passed two identical pale women with almost entirely white eyes and tangled hair bound back loosely and hanging down to their waists. He saw women who were lean towers and men as small and slight as his sister.

As Cyrus passed them all, Patricia's sleek body grew colder and tighter around his neck. If his snake was nervous, he had to be. These were the transmortals. Every eye was angry, and Cyrus could feel their hate. He tried to keep his own eyes forward, to stare at Rupert's back. But he couldn't.

His eyes darted left and collided with a tall, beautiful woman's. Her skin was olive, and her black eyes searched his before they slid down to his shoulder—his left shoulder, his patch.

Up front, Rupert pointed at empty chairs to the right of the aisle. Cyrus sat. Antigone sat beside him, and the Livingstones beside her. Rupert walked to the front of the room and turned around beneath the towering wall of portraits.

Rupert cleared his throat, and his ribs expanded. When he spoke, his voice boomed in the vaults.

"Journeymen, Explorers, Keepers, Sages—sons and daughters of the Voyager, sink."

Rupert dropped to his knees. With a tremendous scuffling of feet, the crowd of mortals followed his lead. Cyrus and Antigone lowered themselves to the stone floor. Cyrus glanced back at the mob of transmortals, some still standing, some still in their seats. There had to be more than a hundred of them. Maybe two hundred.

Rupert closed his eyes and let his chin drop. "The fallen Brendan!"

"Hail!" With one voice, in one moment, the crowd cried out that single word, and Cyrus felt his bones shiver.

"Life—" Rupert cried.

"Vapor!" the crowd roared.

"Glory—"

"Dust!"

Rupert opened his eyes and looked up. "The voyage—"

"Done!" the crowd shouted.

"The race—"

"Run!"

"The fallen Brendan!"

"Hail!" Cyrus and Antigone finally added their voices to the crowd. The echoes died and silence fell. No one moved.

From above the roof, a heavy bell rang. Once. Twice. Thrice.

Rupert rose to his feet. "Sons and daughters of the Voyager, rise."

The mortals rose.

Rupert's arms were behind his back, his chin up, his eyes glistening. "Do you hear the bells?"

"We hear the bells!" the crowd roared.

"Where is our captain?"

"He has reached the shore."

"What has he found?"

"Haven."

Rupert took one step forward. "Shall we join him?"

"No!"

He took another step forward. "Shall we join him?"

"We face the storm!" The crowd's roar washed around Cyrus, and chills ran down his back, from his scalp to his heels.

Rupert took a final step forward, and this time, his voice was lower.

"Shall we join him?"

"Soon," the crowd said. "We shall join him."

Rupert seemed to relax, but he wasn't finished. Cyrus watched his Keeper—broad-shouldered, long-legged, sharp-eyed, dark-skinned, exuding pride and strength—pace in front of the crowd.

"Sages," Rupert said, "Keepers, Explorers, Journeymen in the Order of Brendan." He stopped in front of the transmortals. "Allies and Tributaries, name one to lead us."

In one rumbling motion throughout the crowd, on both sides of the aisle, those who had chairs sat down.

The process, as Cyrus and Antigone discovered, was a long one. A name was called out and seconded, and then the person named—the oldest ones first, both men and women—made their way to the front and faced the crowd. Rupert asked if they would stand in the Order for Brendan. Most of them said they would not, and then returned to their seats. But every now and then, someone would say yes. That person would then speak about the Order, about difficulties, about mistakes, about the future, and men and women would stand up in the crowd and shout questions, and the old woman or old man would answer, and people would shout affirmations, and people would shout denunciations and boo and hiss and whistle. And when the speaker and the crowd had both grown tired, Rupert would step in and ask who wanted the person to stand for Brendan, and people would shout "We do!" all at once, and then Rupert would ask who denied them the right to stand for Brendan, and other people would shout "We do!" And the second group of shouters was always much, much bigger and much, much louder, and they shook the high windows and skylights with their whoops as the person sat back down.

Eventually, the people named grew younger. They were able to walk to the front without canes, and they stood up straight beneath the towering wall of oil portraits. They talked about the need for fresh leadership, and they talked about the Smiths, and the tooth, and its loss. They never looked at Cyrus when they spoke, but he still squirmed in his seat, and Antigone's hand would clench his knee.

Throughout the proceedings, Cyrus would glance over at the transmortals, and every time, he would see faces studying him—simmering eyes and jaws of cold stone. He realized quickly that they weren't voting. Occasionally, one of them would shout a question—always about the tooth or Phoenix or him—and they would boo or cheer, but they never raised their voices when Rupert called for a vote.

And then a man strode to the front whom Cyrus had never seen. He was tall and thin, and his movements were fluid and relaxed. When he turned, he rested one hand on the holstered butt of a revolver and the other on the hilt of a sheathed machete. To Cyrus, he looked like a coiled whip or a compressed spring—maybe a cocked gun.

The man was wearing a battered pale-khaki suit. His mud-colored hair was slicked straight back, his creased skin was tan, and his face was unshaven. Gray whiskers dotted his jaw, and he turned sharp eyes straight onto Cyrus.

Rupert addressed him from the side. "Will you stand in the Order for Brendan?"

The man smiled at Rupert, and then looked back at Cyrus. His voice was Australian. "My name is Bellamy Cook, Keeper from the Barrier Estate. I will stand in the Order for Brendan."

Cyrus was relieved when the man broke eye contact and slowly—with brows hooded low and creases at the corners of his eyes—scanned the silent crowd.

"Edwin Laughlin," he said, "now known as Phoenix, brother to our fallen Brendan, was raised and trained in this, the Ashtown Estate. William Skelton, the late outlaw known as Billy Bones, was a Keeper in the Ashtown Estate. His Acolytes who carried and lost the Dragon's Tooth brought it here, to the Ashtown Estate. Now Phoenix is hunting immortals and somehow"—he paused, looking out at the transmortals—"somehow, he knows where to find you." He sighed, glancing back at Rupert and adjusting his belt. "Something only the Avengel of this Ashtown Estate should know."

Cyrus heard the crowd shift and rustle behind him. He could feel undying eyes staring at the back of his head.

Bellamy Cook grinned and began to pace silently. After a moment, he scratched his scruffy jaw thoughtfully and then continued, doling out his words slowly like spoonfuls of ice cream.

"The world has changed. The Order needs cleaning. Old rules need erasing." He stopped and pointed at the transmortals. "We have tributaries among us, immortal men and women forced into treaties centuries ago. They had their own worries to attend to, and their own Order. But we destroyed it." He shrugged, still pacing. "Of course, by *we*, I mean . . ." He held out his hand for the crowd to finish his sentence.

Gil jumped to his feet. "Smith!"

"Right." Bellamy Cook paused again, nodding. "Captain John Smith, onetime Avengel to this Ashtown Estate. Hater of all immortals, and rather ironically—for a man who betrayed his own mortality—now the occupant of one of his own infamous Ashtown Burials."

He stopped pacing directly in front of Cyrus and Antigone.

"What's even more ironic—strangely coincidental, in fact—is that the two Acolytes with the tooth were both Smiths. This girl and this boy with the three severed heads so proudly sewn onto his sleeve are descendants of the last man before them to bloody the immortals. And now, thanks to them, Phoenix is carrying on that work and more."

A rumble washed through the Galleria. Cyrus flushed. Antigone's fingers dug into his knee.

Bellamy Cook raised both hands and waited until the room was silent.

"Sons and daughters of the Voyager, you must hear me. The immortals are dying. Can we protect them as the treaties require? No. But do we allow them to protect themselves? No, the treaties prohibit it." He studied the room. "Dissolve the treaties. Make our tributaries equals and allies, accountable to their own Order. Sweep Ash-town clean of its corruptions!"

The room exploded with noise. Scattered cheers and shocked boos swept forward from the mortals. Chairs scattered and clattered as the transmortals jumped to their feet.

With a startled shriek, the blackbird flapped up off Antigone's shoulder and wheeled toward the ceiling.

Cyrus's mouth hung open. Rupert strode toward Bellamy.

Bellamy cocked a wry smile and looked at Rupert. "Call my vote."

Gil forced his way into the aisle and raised a hairy football-size fist. His huge voice plowed easily through every other noise.

"*Ordo Draconis!*"

Alan Livingstone jumped to his feet, as did dozens of others in the rows behind him—all with hands on weapons.

"*Ordo Draconis!*" the transmortals chanted. "*Ordo Draconis!*"

Cyrus and Antigone both stood as George and Silas grabbed on to them, pulling them away from the aisle.

"Open the Burials!" Gil shouted, and his followers roared approval.

Cyrus saw Jeb and Diana Boone racing down the

aisle, dragging little James Axelrotter, the zookeeper, between them.

Over their heads, three thrown wooden chairs flew into the mortal crowd. A fourth chair skipped off Diana's head and sent her sprawling.

The first guns fired.

seven

BRUISES

CYRUS GROANED AND TWISTED, trying to get back to sleep. His legs, his head, his back, his . . . everywhere . . . really hurt. He tried to open his eyes, but only his right eye was working. With it, he stared at the corner of his blanket, the edge of his hammock, and his spider-sealed window. The web had been replaced, and the charred original was dangling down the wall. A large burn mark ran up the wall into a smoke spot on the ceiling.

He shut his eye. He didn't understand. There had been dreams, too, he knew that. And they hadn't been fun ones. The three heads had been there, and Phoenix, and someone who wouldn't stop hitting Diana with a chair.

Somewhere, someone laughed—loud, merry, perfect. He knew that laugh. It sounded like it had freckles. Cyrus reopened his eye. Diana was somewhere close.

He tried to sit up and instead spilled out of his hammock, landing on all fours.

His head was a lot heavier than normal, and it felt

like some kind of dinosaur was trying to hatch out of his skull—a dinosaur with horns. He stood slowly, bracing himself against dizziness.

He reached up and felt for his left eye. Someone had strapped an eye patch on with a headband. Wincing, he tugged it off and dropped it onto the floor. His left eye was swollen and sticky from his eyebrow to his cheekbone.

He had a vague memory of Gil and some incredibly large woman with a thick blond braid chasing him. And Rupert and guns and a whole lot of electricity flying through the air. And fire. And falling glass.

His hands and arms and bare legs were dotted with tiny scabbed-over cuts, and someone had bandaged a large patch on his right calf. He staggered for the door and leaned against the jamb for support.

In the living room, the rug was gone and the armchair had been scorched, as had the fresh yellow walls by each window and around the door. Except for the door, the webs had all been thickly replaced.

Nine heads turned and looked at Cyrus. Cyrus lost focus, blinked, and then looked from face to face, forcing himself to recognize the shapes. Jax, Dennis Gilly, Hillary Drake, Antigone, George and Silas Livingstone, Nolan, Arachne, and Diana Boone.

Seven of them were seated in a circle. Nolan and Arachne stood by the door.

Little Jax stood up. He had a large bruise on his cheek but seemed fine otherwise. "Good morning, Cyrus. I'm glad you're alive. You looked dead last night."

Cyrus grunted and studied the others. Dennis had two black eyes and a possibly broken nose. Hillary seemed fine, but terrified. Antigone had small burn blisters on her left arm and a bandage on her right. George and Silas were polka-dotted with bruises. Nolan badly needed to shed—his skin was peeling off in large patches. As for Arachne, she looked as perfect as ever.

Diana Boone had three butterfly bandages on her forehead, up by her hairline. She smiled and waved for Cyrus to sit down. Cyrus eased himself off the doorjamb and shuffled forward.

"You okay, Cy?" Antigone sounded worried. "You can go back to sleep if you want."

Cyrus managed a smile. "Couldn't get back in the hammock. What's everyone doing?"

Antigone looked around the room. "They all slept here. Not much choice. The riot lasted for hours, and even when it was over, there were still transmortals lurking around. Nolan got everyone in through the heat vents."

"It wasn't a riot," Dennis said quietly. "It was a war. The hospital is overflowing."

"It would have been worse," Diana said. "But Rupe was ready for it—as ready as anyone could have been. The transmortals did have the right to be there, so he couldn't stop that. But Field Rule meant the O of B members were all armed. The bullets don't kill, but they slow 'em down a bit. Rupe also had half a hundred heavy charge guns with Keepers all through the crowd."

"You should see the kitchen," Hillary said. "And the dining hall. Everything is smashed, and they barely got the fires out."

Cyrus reached up and lightly touched his swollen eye.

Arachne stepped forward and smiled. "Believe it or not, it's actually looking better than it did last night. How does it feel?"

"Like someone slammed a baseball in there and it won't come out." He pointed at the charred walls. "What happened here?"

Nolan laughed. "What happened is that I nobly defended your stronghold while you slept."

Diana raised her eyebrows. "*You* did?"

Nolan shrugged. "Diana helped. As did the charge gun she brought. Unfortunately, despite the strength of the spinster's webs—Gil tried to tear through the door—they do burn." He looked at Arachne. "And I'm afraid he now knows which team she's chosen."

Arachne sighed, and her eyes seemed to pool with sadness. "Gil can be nice. He just doesn't react to fear very well."

Silas arched his one and a half eyebrows and looked at Cyrus. "We've seen some rough nights, but that was the roughest." George nodded as his brother continued: "I thought you were a goner for a little while. You got hit with a flying statue and dropped like a sack of mud. Mr. Greeves had a glass grenade in his belt that he threw into the mob as they were coming for you, and the electric arcs and the shards caught you a bit when it exploded. Barely missed us. We haven't seen our dad, but Diana said that she was in the hallways with him for a while and that he was fine—having fun, even."

Diana nodded. "When I left, he was with Jeb and yelling things in something that sounded pretty Zulu."

"I'm sure it was," George said. "It's his favorite language for fighting."

"So . . . ," said Cyrus. "What exactly happened? I don't remember much."

Antigone shook her head. "It wasn't fun, Cy. When Rupert tossed his grenade, they were trying to tear off your patch."

"Did they get it?" Cyrus looked around the room for his jacket. "Tell me they didn't get it."

"My stitches don't tear, Cyrus Smith." Arachne's voice was quiet. Cyrus didn't know if she sounded more exhausted or sad.

Antigone continued. "Rupe gave you to Nolan, and he dragged you into a vent."

Cyrus looked at Nolan. The pale, peeling boy smiled slightly.

"How'd it all end?" Cyrus asked the room.

Diana crossed her legs and leaned back against her arms. "People ran and people hid. Rupe and Big Alan and Jeb and the other Field Captains shocked and dropped and chained transmortals in the halls for hours—sometimes retreating, sometimes pushing forward. A lot of them came to and broke free, but a few didn't. They're locked up deep for now. Gil and the others eventually retreated into collection rooms and barricaded themselves in. That's when things got quiet."

"Footsteps." Nolan raised his hand. Peeling skin dangled from his fingers like paper flags. He jumped toward the door and picked up a charge gun leaning against the jamb. Arachne stepped back as Diana drew a revolver and followed Nolan.

Everyone else scrambled to their feet.

"Quiet," said Nolan, and he flipped a switch on the butt of his gun. The electric charge grew, whining in Cyrus's ears as he held his breath. He couldn't hear anything else. And then someone rapped quickly on the door.

"Unlock. It's Rupert."

Arachne stepped toward the door. "Password?" she asked. She crouched down and lowered her hand to the floor. A brown spider slipped out of her sleeve and darted beneath the door.

"What?" Rupert sounded confused. "I truly hope I didn't set a password."

The spider returned and climbed into Arachne's hand. She nodded, then stood and unlocked the door. Rupert Greeves came in, a charge gun dangling from a strap over his shoulder. He was wearing the same clothes as the night before, but his shirt was bloodstained, the top buttons were missing, and the collar had been torn halfway off.

He had bruises—or dirt, or smudged blood—on his neck, and the old scars on his chest were a sticky mess. His holster was empty, but his wide-bladed sword was still in its sheath.

Rupert shut the door and looked around at the clustered group. "Well, the Polygoners all seem to be alive." He managed half a smile. "Excepting Cyrus. Well done. Mr. Gilly, Miss Drake, you can return to your duties. Diana, your brother needs you at the airstrip."

Dennis and Hillary smiled at the group, and then hurried through the door. Rupert patted them each on the shoulder as they left.

Diana holstered her revolver, then mock-saluted Cyrus and Antigone. "Polygoners, ho!" she said.

"Hey, Di," Antigone said. "Thanks. Seriously."

Diana grinned back over her shoulder as she left. "We'll do it again sometime."

Rupert assessed George and Silas Livingstone.

"You're not mint in the box, but you don't look too terrible. Your father might be disappointed—he had to have a nostril stitched back on. He wants you in the dining hall."

"Right," Silas said. "He's okay, though?"

"He's more than okay," Rupert said. "He's spitting fury and battle cries into a stack of pancakes."

George laughed, and the two brothers nodded silent goodbyes and hurried out of the room.

Jax stepped forward. His cheeks were flushed. "Mr. Greeves, do I need to head back to the zoo?"

Rupert seemed surprised. "Don't you want to? I've never known you to want to be anywhere else."

The thirteen-year-old zookeeper shuffled his feet and pulled on his ear. Antigone was grinning. Cyrus saw his sister glance at Arachne, and then he understood. Arachne smiled slightly.

"Well, Mr. Greeves, I've always been interested in spiders. I collected thousands of webs for years and used them in the exoskeleton I wear for protection in the Crypto wing. It's incredibly bulky for me. But, Miss Arachne . . ." He glanced into Arachne's eyes, and then looked quickly back at his feet. His cheeks grew even redder. "The spiders do what she says. Do you know how strong a spider-woven sheet of silk could be? I want to learn."

"Jax," Rupert said softly. "You can't. Not any more

than you could watch a bird and then grow feathers. What Arachne does, she does by nature."

Arachne moved toward Jax, and her smile was genuine. "By second nature, at least." She touched Jax on the arm, and he looked like he might melt. "James, someday soon I will weave you a sheet and you can make what you will. I'm pleased you like my creatures."

Jax nodded, unable to speak, and then he made his way toward the door. He paused, looking at the burnt web tatters dangling against the wall.

"Take them," Arachne said.

Beaming, Jax snatched up the shreds and hurried out into the hall, leaving the door open behind him.

"Jax!" Rupert yelled after him. "I need two pairs of squid at the cube if you can!"

"Yessir, Mr. Greeves!" And the young zookeeper disappeared.

Rupert sighed, shut the door, and turned around. "I am left with two Smiths and two discontent immortals."

Nolan laughed and dropped into the armchair. "Oh, we hardly count as that."

"How bad is it out there?" Arachne asked. "What did they do?"

Rupert crossed to the window and looked at the charred walls. "They did enough. Gil, in particular. But they were smart, and now those I didn't lock up have retreated out of sight. The Estate is as smashed up as it's been since a similar night when I was a boy, and yet they didn't kill anyone." He glanced back. "And they could have killed many. That mob clearly had orders—rules of engagement from some authority. I think only Cyrus was really in danger of death. That riot was their shot across our bow. They want the O of B to fear them—to fear an uprising in which hundreds might die. But they didn't want our fear to become deep anger, as it would have if they'd given us a stack of bodies."

"Why not?" Cyrus asked. "I don't understand."

Rupert continued, now eyeing the ceiling. "Then our terror would work against them—strengthening our resolve, convincing us that we absolutely must not dissolve the treaties that bind their powers. Their goal is the resurrection of their own Order, not our destruction. For now."

Nolan leaned against the wall and crossed his pale, knotted arms. "And have they succeeded? What will happen to the transmortal treaties?"

Rupert studied him. "You want to be thrown to Gil without the Order's protection?"

"No," Nolan said. "I've had enough of Gil to last all my lifetimes, as you well know. I'm not interested for myself."

"Gil is not in charge," Arachne said quietly. "And the *Ordo Draconis* never died; it simply lowered its voice."

Rupert managed to swallow slowly before he spoke.

"What do you know, Arachne? What have you held back?"

Arachne said nothing. Rupert turned to Nolan.

"What do *you* know?" he asked.

Nolan shook his head. "I steer clear of my own kind. All I know is that Gil went romping with that mob in the Galleria. Cyrus wearing his gory badge around didn't quiet things any, but they would have rioted even if he'd arrived waving an *Ordo Draconis* banner." He looked at Rupert and nodded at Arachne. "Press her. She knows more than she says."

Arachne's cheeks flushed. "I have always honored my treaty." All around the room, spiders began to trickle out of cracks and corners as she continued. "Rupert Greeves, I have always told you what I know, but not what I guess. What I knew yesterday is not what I know today. All of my friends, the only family I have had for centuries, have always thought that I was foolish trusting a man like you. Now they call me a traitor to my own kind. Do not mistreat me."

Rupert studied the flowing puddles of spiders on the floor, all racing toward Arachne's feet. When he spoke, his voice had softened, though not much.

"What do you know today that was a mystery yesterday?"

Arachne was a statue. Spiders surrounded and covered her feet. They swirled around Rupert's legs, too, and up onto his boots. He didn't move. Cyrus and Antigone backed away.

"You need your army before you speak?" Rupert asked.

"Radu Bey," Arachne said quietly. "The last Dracul."

Rupert shook his head. "John Smith destroyed him after he sent those three heads on Cyrus's jacket rolling. Just before Smith was sent into his own Burial for breaking his vows and becoming a transmortal himself. I've read the account."

"Radu Bey is alive," Arachne said. "And the *Ordo* with him. He is behind the mob. And yes, the Smiths are to be killed."

"How do you know this?" Rupert asked. "You were in here all night."

Arachne nodded at her quietly rippling spiders. "You shouldn't have to ask."

"Okay," Cyrus said, inching forward carefully. "I'm really tired of not understanding any of this. Is this really all because they're angry about the tooth?"

Rupert sighed. "The tooth is resurrecting an old war and an older fear. I had wondered why Phoenix turned to hunting transmortals. But this is reason enough. The Order is in peril. We may be overthrown by our own tributaries."

"I don't get the treaties," Antigone said. "If the transmortals want out of them to go fight Phoenix, what's the problem? And what do the treaties even do? Couldn't Gil just ignore whatever old piece of paper he signed anyway?"

Rupert shook his head. "Centuries ago, the Order offered the nations of men their only possible protection from the transmortals. They were subdued one by one, some with great difficulty, others with no difficulty at all. With the transmortals functionally colonized and their behavior restricted, the Order assumed responsibility for their protection—from men who still hated and feared them, and from each other. Every transmortal has a unique treaty, though many are similar."

Nolan laughed. "Behavioral restrictions? Is that what you call it? It was a full powers ban—for those with powers. They didn't need to restrict me and my peeling skin, but Arachne's spinning is now limited to the natural order. She can spin tough stuff, but she can't spin anything with supernatural properties—not like she used to."

"I couldn't, and I don't want to," Arachne said. "No good ever came when I did."

"But what would happen if you did want to and you found a way?" Antigone asked. "What could the O of B do?"

Arachne's eyes grew wider. "Burial. Forever."

"The treaties may have been clumsy, but most were necessary," Rupert said. "Transmortals were captured and contained, or they submitted their powers to the authority of the Brendan and were bound to mortal laws in their registered nation of residence—no killing, no theft, that sort of thing."

"And no political office," Nolan said, smirking. "No more leading the nations of men. And more relevant to our moment in time—no self-governing orders or societies."

"The *Ordo Draconis,*" Antigone said.

Rupert nodded. "It was the most powerful of those societies, maintained by the Dracul family until John Smith . . . well, until he dealt with them in his own somewhat questionable way."

Nolan's cold, old eyes were amused. "What Rupert meant to say is that John Smith broke his oath as Avengel by becoming undying himself so that he might face the most dangerous of his undying enemies when they refused to submit to the treaties. The three Vlads—Vlad the Second, his son Vlad the Third, famously called the Impaler and Dracula in some tales, and *his* son Vlad the Fourth—were responsible for tens of thousands of deaths and were committed to the subjugation of mortals."

"They were beyond vile," Arachne said. "Blood sorcerers with dragon souls, they fed on their victims and mortal followers alike. Well done, John Smith."

"And amen," said Nolan. "Smith buried the heads and bodies separately—no one knows where—named his Avengel successor, had himself condemned for his oath-breaking, and then went cheerfully and more than a little drunkenly into his own Burial, knowing that he'd shattered the *Ordo Draconis.* Of course, he had time to make the Smiths a new family crest—*sic semper draconis.* Thus always to dragons. But as your Latin tutor, I'm confident you knew that already."

Antigone looked at Cyrus, then back at Rupert. "That's all true?"

"It is," Rupert said. "Nolan was there. And despite upheaval and complaints every other generation, the treaties have functioned."

"Until now," said Nolan. "This time, things are different."

Arachne crouched and lowered her palms to the floor. Spiders flowed over them and up her arms. "Now," she said quietly, "the immortals are dying and their *Ordo* is reborn. They follow Radu Bey."

Antigone looked around the room, clearly trying to avoid staring at the spiders. "But who is he?"

Arachne studied her spider herd. Nolan crossed and tensed his pale arms. Rupert massaged his jaw.

"Well?" Cyrus asked.

Rupert scratched his short beard. "Radu Bey was the brother of Vlad the Third, called the Impaler. If Arachne is correct and Radu Bey still breathes, he is a bloody nightmare emerging from centuries of shadow." He sighed, and then focused on Arachne. "After last night's mayhem, the Sages have waived any future gathering of the members. Sometime today, they will meet alone to name the new Brendan. Alan Livingstone should be their choice, but that would mean more riots and even war. They're more likely to name Bellamy Cook out of fear. And he's likely to immediately vacate the treaties. If that happens"—Rupert looked at Cyrus and Antigone, and then back to Arachne—"we'll be running. The Smiths are physically ready, but with your own treaty gone, would you be willing . . ." Rupert's question trailed away.

Arachne straightened. Her face was blank but her eyes were wide, searching Rupert's. "Angel Skin? It has been a long time. I will need to awaken old memories and taste the old words before I try."

"Angel Skin?" Antigone asked. "Do any of you feel like explaining?"

"No," said Rupert. "None of us do." He swung his charge gun out from under his arm and moved toward the door, stepping carefully over and around puddles of spiders. "Both of you come with me. You're going to have a strange day." He threw open the door and stepped out into the hall. "And an even stranger night."

At first, as Cyrus and Antigone scurried along behind Rupert, keeping up with his long, brisk strides, they'd tried to ask questions. Antigone wanted to know what Angel Skin was, and Cyrus wanted to hear more about Radu Bey and John Smith.

When they reached the green, the chatter stopped and Cyrus, even in his jacket, forgot the heat.

Tents were strewn everywhere. Quiet teams of Acolytes were sorting through them—collecting tatters, folding torn canvas, and piling the scraps that were black and still smoking. All around, the stone faces of buildings were charred. Windows were smashed. Four big statues had been thrown down from the roof of the main building. Now they jutted awkwardly from the green turf where they had landed, like stone carcasses hatching from the earth.

Cyrus looked around, stunned. "No one died? Really?" It seemed impossible.

"No one died," Rupert said. "Yet. And the Sages will want to keep it that way. Stay close."

Cyrus walked by Rupert's side as they circled the green. "Where are they now? The transmortals."

"We have two dozen in containment. The rest have kept to their rooms. They are angry, but quiet for the time being, waiting to hear the decision of the Sages. Our patrols are constant and heavily armed. Even so . . ."

"Gil?" Cyrus asked.

"Couldn't say," Rupert said. "And I really wish I

could." Cyrus and Antigone instinctively inched a little closer to their Keeper as they walked.

Inside the main building, Cyrus and Antigone remained silent as they passed through the rubble-strewn halls. Almost every display had been damaged. Tables had been tipped and snapped. Maps and paintings and photographs had been torn off the walls. Shattered glass was sprinkled across the mosaic floors.

The leather boat of Brendan himself had been thrown down off its pedestal, its sides slashed.

Somber Journeymen and tense Explorers worked in the rubble under the quiet instructions of Keepers. Every worker was armed, and the Keepers all carried heavy charge guns with electric coils humming quietly.

Every pair of eyes followed Cyrus and Antigone as they passed. Some were unfriendly, but Cyrus thought most simply looked sad. He didn't see any Sages. Not one old face. They would be off somewhere, naming a new Brendan.

"Cyrus," Antigone said quietly. "You should really ditch the patch."

Rupert glanced down at Cyrus while they walked, waiting for an answer.

"No way," said Cyrus. He looked at Rupert. "Not unless you tell me I have to."

"Keep it," Rupert said. "You've flown an ancient

battle flag. Don't strike your colors just because the guns begin to growl."

Antigone tucked back her hair and didn't look at her brother again until they began descending the stairs.

Cyrus knew the route well. He knew the statues under canvas tarps and the dusty rooms cluttered with forgotten storage. They were on their way to the Polygon. But they stopped short of the final stairs. Rupert led them into the long, low room with a glistening ceiling. Pillars held up the thick glass underbelly of the water cube—the three-dimensional liquid labyrinth. Cyrus had seen people train in it blindfolded, and simply watching had caused his throat to tighten and his heart to race. Swimming was fine. Holding his breath was fine. But swimming blind, with only one breath, through a tight, tangled maze cube?

They wouldn't have to do this. Rupe wouldn't make them. Technically, they didn't have to achieve anything difficult in the cube until they tested for Keeper. And they were only Journeymen. He might never even make Explorer.

Rupert was heading for the iron spiral stairs that climbed up beside the cube.

"What are we doing here?" Antigone asked. She had stopped. Cyrus stopped beside her, staring at the dark water above him. His first time here, a woman had been slithering on the other side.

"Training," Rupert said simply, and he began to climb the stairs.

"Rupe!" Antigone said. "You can't be serious. We don't have to do anything with this to get Explorer."

"I'm with her," Cyrus said. "Let's shoot or fence or something. I'm still not great with a saber."

Rupert stopped and looked back down the stairs, his face just below the ceiling. Then he laughed. "This has nothing to do with promotion."

"What then?" Antigone asked. "What are we training for?"

Rupert's smile didn't disappear, but it faded into something grim, more stoic than pleasant. "You are training for survival. And to be helpful to me in the tasks ahead. But we hardly have time to call it real training. We are bracing ourselves for a storm. We are doing what little we can before the hurricane swallows us. If you and I and we survive the summer, then we will talk about training for recognition."

He disappeared up the stairs.

Cyrus looked at his sister. Her brows were pinched. Her lips were tight. One of her legs was bouncing. It was her worried look, the look she used to wear when he got detention or skipped school or got too filthy scrambling in the pastures behind the motel, or when there wasn't enough food, or when he fought with their older brother, Dan.

Cyrus would have been thrilled to face any of those problems now. Rupert Greeves was not a man who over-estimated danger.

"Cy . . . ," Antigone began. She tucked her thumbnail between her teeth. "I thought we were done with this stuff. Things were almost . . . easy."

"I lost the tooth," Cyrus said. "And we're Smiths. Things never stay easy long."

"We were going to visit Dan in California in a few weeks. Surprise. It was supposed to be for your birthday. Diana was going to fly us. She was sure Rupe would say yes."

Cyrus inhaled slowly. He did miss Dan. Just thinking about his brother brought back the smell of the Archer and bad waffles. He'd spent the last few months wishing for excitement, hoping Rupert would take them—just him, actually—on one of his hunts for Phoenix. But now . . .

"Smiths!" Rupert's voice echoed above them.

The two of them jogged for the stairs.

The room above the water cube was big, with high ceilings and tile walls and the feel of an indoor swimming pool, even though the water was mostly contained beneath the huge glass slab in the floor that acted as a lid. In opposite corners, dark water shivered in small square openings—the entrance and exit to the liquid maze.

There were two locker-room doors on one wall and a

tall arched door on the other. Beside it, Jax was seated on a small bench and leaning back against the wall. His eyes were closed and his mouth was open. At his feet were two large plastic buckets. Rupert was standing above him, studying the buckets.

When Cyrus and Antigone stepped out of the stairs onto the tile floor, the big Keeper grabbed the buckets by the handles and carried them over to the nearer open square of water in the floor. Jax stirred, blinked, and went back to sleep.

"Shoes off," Rupert said. "And then a biology lesson before we swim."

Antigone grimaced. "Don't we get to change?" She looked down at her pocketed shorts and safari blouse. "I'm swimming in this?"

"You are," said Rupert. "But not yet."

Cyrus kicked off the permanently tied canvas shoes he wore when he didn't feel like buckling or strapping boots. He wasn't wearing socks. His shorts and shirt were rumpled and dirty. A swim could only help them. Antigone unlaced the light boots she was wearing, and then tugged them off along with her socks.

Rupert nodded at the buckets, and Cyrus and Antigone leaned in to take a look. A pair of small sleek rubbery shapes were squelching in tight circles at the bottom of each.

Cyrus laughed. "Squid? What for?"

Antigone scrunched her face and leaned back. "They're disgusting."

"Oh, c'mon, Tigs." Cyrus grinned. "Don't be such a girl. People eat these things."

"Not these, they don't," said Rupert. "Unless they want to die. These are Jet Squid, and the underflesh is toxic. But they are quite useful. Two are male." A cluster of bubbles broke the surface. "And two are female. The males are no good to you unless you want to make a bomb. They constantly separate the hydrogen from the oxygen in water, and they blow the hydrogen out of their beaks. The females do the same, but they exhale blasts of oxygen." He looked at Cyrus and Antigone, but especially Antigone. "You need to be able to identify the females, and then swim with one. Even the small ones—like these—can extend your dive length indefinitely, and without the negative effects of using pressurized air in tanks."

"You're not serious," Antigone said, squinting into the bucket. "That's disgusting."

"How?" Cyrus asked. "I don't understand."

Rupert plunged his hand into the bucket and pulled up a glistening black squid the size of a guinea pig. Tentacles lashed quickly around his wrist. Flipping it upside down, Rupert separated the tentacles, revealing the creature's sharp, clacking beak, shaped almost exactly like a parrot's. The beak was as black as its body with only one difference—the very tip of the beak had a cluster of tiny red spots.

"Red means dead," Rupert said. "This is currently male, though they can change. Remember that." He unpeeled it from his arm and dropped it back into its bucket. Then he grabbed the other squid in the bucket, just as black as the first. He sorted through the tentacles. Cyrus crouched and cocked his head, staring in the creature's wide eye as it searched the room.

"Cyrus?"

"Yeah," Cyrus said, straightening. Rupert held out the animal with its perfectly black beak exposed. It clicked open and shut like a bird's. Antigone had retreated with arms crossed.

"No red means female. When you put this in your mouth, make sure the beak rests on your tongue, opening up and down."

"No," Antigone said. "No way. Rupe, this isn't funny. Don't be disgusting."

Rupert looked at her. "If the beak goes in sideways, you're going to lose a chunk of your tongue." He raised the squid to his face. The beak went into his mouth.

Cyrus's eyes widened. His mouth fell open. The squid's tentacles wrapped around Rupert's face, gripping the back of his head. Chills raced down Cyrus's back, and then the squid suddenly released, dropping into Rupert's hands. He stuck it back in its bucket.

"When you want it off, just blow. A little puff and she'll drop. Her air will be irregular, so you have to be ready to grab the breath whenever she gives it. Exhale through your nose. Through your mouth, and she'll pop off."

Cyrus studied Rupert's face for any sign that he was joking. But the big man's face was stone. His eyes were sharp but understanding.

"Okay," Rupert said. He pointed down at the open square of water in the floor. "The goal here is maze memory. Once you've made it all the way through, you need to return in less than half the time. But first, let's just get you used to the squid."

Antigone choked. Her hands were over her face. Cyrus couldn't tell if she was crying or gagging.

Rupert put his hands on her shoulders. "Antigone, I'm not doing this for fun. I'm doing this because soon you and your brother will be out in the world with me. The dark world. The world your father hoped you would never know. Soon we will be hunters and we will be hunted. You can do this, because you can—and you will—do much harder things. All right?"

Antigone nodded and wiped her eyes. Cyrus was quiet.

"Okay," Rupert said. "Grab a squid and check the gender."

The big door banged open, and Jeb and Diana Boone

stepped into the room, breathing hard. Jax jerked awake and thumped his head on the wall.

"It's done," Jeb said. "The Sages named that bastard Bellamy Cook from the Barrier Estate. He's the new Brendan."

"The rite?" Rupert asked. "The anointing? Will they wait the full three days?"

Jeb shook his head. "No. It's happening right away. Tonight, maybe."

And then bells began to ring, raining down joyful peals through the skylights, echoing against the tile walls—a new man was standing in the Order for Brendan.

"They've done it already," Rupert said.

Diana stomped angrily and began to cry. "Rupe, I'm so sorry. It should have been you. Or Alan. Bellamy won't even keep you as Avengel."

"I wouldn't serve under him anyway," Rupert said. He looked at Cyrus and Antigone, and then pointed at the buckets. "I need to know if you two can do this. And I need to know now."

"Seriously?" Antigone asked. "It sounds like there's a lot going on."

"Right now," said Rupert, and he turned back to the Boones. "Find that lawyer, John Lawney, and get him to the Skelton rooms. Diana, I need you to file a trek for me before anything else happens—tag it as Avengel and selected others. He's unable to remove an Avengel in the field or the memberships of anyone with me. Not yet, at least. Destinations and return date undeclared. That's still my prerogative."

Antigone's eyes were on the bucket and her cheeks were puffed out wide. "I can't do this, Cy. I can't. I will absolutely puke up inside some poor squid."

Ignoring his sister, Cyrus got down on his knees and plunged his hand in the water. He'd expected the squid to be difficult to catch even in the confined space—they darted so easily, so smoothly in their circles—but as soon as his hand was in, he felt something latch on hard. The squid caught him.

The door banged shut as Jeb and Diana left. Rupert was talking to Jax.

Cyrus pulled his arm up and studied the soft black dripping creature with its bundle of suckered eel arms swathed around his fingers. The squid's head quivered and pulsed like a black heart, and its large fishy eye searched the room and settled on Cyrus's face.

"Cy?" Antigone asked. Cyrus began to unpeel tentacles until he found the beak. No red dots. Black. Sharp. Hard. But attached to soft rubbery tissue. Like a parrot crossed with a lung.

Cyrus raised it to his face.

Antigone gagged and turned around. Cyrus held his breath, pretended that he was dreaming, and slid the beak carefully into his mouth. It clicked open and shut—up and down—pressing against his tongue, banging against the roof of his mouth. Cold. Wet. Salty.

And then, in a flash, the squid latched on.

Tentacles lashed around the back of Cyrus's head and neck, pulling the body tight against his face. The squid's body covered his nose. Legs whipped up over his eyes, grabbing on to his forehead.

Cyrus flailed, panicking. Antigone was screaming.

"No! No! Calm down!" The voice belonged to Jax. He was slapping Cyrus's hands. "Be careful or you'll kill it!"

Cyrus couldn't breathe and he couldn't see. And then two hands carefully worked the tentacles off his eyes and parted them around his nose. Through his nostrils, he pulled in a long, slow, squid-smelling breath. Jax was smiling at him. Antigone stood behind him with her eyes wide and both hands over her mouth.

"Mr. Greeves asked me to help you for a minute. He'll be right back. Now get your face in the water or she'll die."

Jax snatched another squid out of the bucket, parted its tentacles, and turned to face Antigone.

Cyrus's heart was racing. Breathing through his nose, trying to ignore the oppressive living mask clinging to his face and the clicking parrot beak in his mouth, he sat next to the open square in the glass floor and lowered his bare legs into the water. It wasn't cold. He slid in up to his armpits.

Antigone was sobbing behind him. And then suddenly, the sobbing stopped.

Cyrus raised his arms, the water closed above him, and he dropped into the maze. The water burned his eyes a little. It was salted. Why did that surprise him? Immediately, the squid beak clacked out a cluster of bubbles in his mouth. They tasted like—well, like squid burp. He held them in his cheeks. How was this supposed to work? He exhaled a little from his nose, and then replaced the space in his lungs with the bubbles.

Blinking, he stretched out his hands and felt the glass sides of the square tunnel around him. He needed to get farther down, and there wasn't enough room to fold and dive now. He should have come in headfirst.

Antigone's feet clipped him on the head, and she shot in next to him, pinning him against the wall. She didn't seem too upset, but everything was water-blurry. They were tight enough together that their squids were touching.

Antigone pointed down, and then slid herself past him. Cyrus's squid trickled out another bubble belch. Then he pressed his hands against the walls and followed his sister deeper into the darker water.

Years ago, in the California house, when his father had been alive and his mother had been awake, Antigone had dared Cyrus to wriggle into a tight sleeping bag headfirst, turn around in the end, and come back out. She had raced him over and over again, and every single time, when the space had gotten tight and hot and sweaty, and he had gotten stuck half bent in the end, he had kicked the zipper open in panic, usually shouting.

Now Antigone had somehow twisted herself head down, and there was no way Cyrus could keep up with her unless he did, too. And he was inches taller and half as bendy.

She was already exploring side passages in the maze and there was very little light. He was losing sight of her.

He tucked his head and began to fold, scraping and scrabbling at the glass sides. With his chin tucked to his chest, his jaw dug into the keys dangling on Patricia around his neck. He hoped he wasn't crushing her. He wondered what she thought of the squid. If she thought the squid was trying to suffocate him, the little snake might get big and angry, and the squid would get dead. Cyrus would be stuck in the bottom of the cube with no burps to breathe.

Cyrus kicked and twisted and banged the back of his head. It was working. Unlike the inside of a sleeping bag, these sides were slick. And unlike the sleeping bag, he wouldn't be able to kick his way out if it didn't work.

With a sudden burst and two heels cracked against

a wall, Cyrus did it. He was head down. He kicked forward. Where was his sister?

Dark water. Thick glass walls and more dark water. Rupert could turn on lights if he wanted, but that would be less real. The deeper you dove, the darker it got. The squid bubbled and Cyrus swallowed the hand-me-down air instead of inhaling. Uncomfortable lumps sat in his chest.

And he still couldn't see a thing—not without goggles. The salt water was blinding. An opening passed by in the wall. He pushed backward and squinted into it. Blurry darkness. He pulled himself down. And down. Had she really turned off somewhere without making sure that he was behind her? He was starting to worry, and worrying made him angry. The beak in his mouth released a barrage of bubbles and then nipped at the inside of his cheek.

He didn't notice. His head thumped against glass. He was at the bottom of the cube. He had to turn, but he couldn't see anything. There should at least be a glow through the glass. The lights had been on in the room below the cube when Rupert had brought them through and climbed the stairs.

Patricia. He'd used his little undying snake for light before he'd known what else she could do. Cyrus reached up and slid his fingers beneath her soft body. Careful not to let his key ring drop off his living necklace, he slid her tail out of her mouth. Immediately, the water around him flickered silver. Patricia had become visible. He held her out, watching her strain to pop her tail back in her mouth and disappear. The key ring dangled from her middle. Her tiny green eyes sparked irritation as she snatched her tail and disappeared, but only for a moment. Cyrus wrangled her tail free again, the silver body appeared, and Cyrus popped his thumb in her mouth. Her body wound tight around his fist, pinning the key ring against the back of his hand. Then Cyrus looked around.

Down a tunnel to his left, Cyrus could see Antigone gliding toward him.

And on the other side of the thick glass, faintly cast in the silver light, he could see a face. Cyrus's heart stopped. The face was large, bearded, grinning. A huge six-fingered hand reached up and stuck a tiny red salamander onto the glass. It didn't move, but flames flickered around its body. The other six-fingered hand raised a huge sledgehammer.

Cyrus understood.

"No," he said. And with that word, the squid dropped off his face and slid away. Cyrus grabbed his sister and shoved her up the tunnel. He didn't need to push twice. Twisting, kicking off the bottom, he clawed up through the water after her.

The blast wasn't behind him. It was everywhere. The water jolted and compressed his ribs, his head. His heart skipped and twitched inside him. Half-conscious, ears ringing into deafness, Cyrus drifted into a wall. Something beneath him was cracking. Thick glass was grinding its teeth. And then everything around him fell.

He was inside a water volcano erupting straight down. He was in the middle of a falling lake. Water slammed him against stone. Existence unplugged.

eight

EXODUS

RUPERT GREEVES WAS RUNNING toward the bells. He was running toward the biggest fight of his life—a fight with Bellamy Cook of the Barrier Estate, duly named Brendan. Bellamy Cook, the transmortals' puppet. The Sages were old and timid, and Rupert had wasted his breath singing the praises of Alan Livingstone to them each in turn. They had chosen the path that would make tomorrow quiet. But Rupert knew the coming months would roar. Now he would have to fight with the Order itself. He was ready. It was long overdue. He should have fought years ago when Lawrence Smith was removed. He should have fought when corruption and rot first enabled Phoenix to riddle the O of B with his influence.

Rupert pushed open a door. Two more long hallways and he'd be outside the Galleria, facing the end of the life he had always known.

And then the ground shivered.

Rupert Greeves pressed his hand against the wall and froze. Something was very wrong.

The bells were forgotten. Rupert Greeves turned back and ran. His fight would wait.

When Rupert banged through the door into the room above the water cube, Jax was lying in a puddle, blinking.

"It just, something . . ." Jax sat up and pointed at the labyrinth glass in the floor. It was pale without the water beneath it, cloudy and cracked. "Water launched up the holes. Then it was all gone."

Rupert peered down through the empty dripping walls of the maze. A jagged hole gaped in the bottom at least four feet across. Turning quickly, Rupert raced for the spiral stairs.

"Wait!" Jax was on his feet. "What should I do?"

"Pray your friends are still alive!" Rupert said, one hand on the rail. "Grab what you need and get to Skelton's rooms as fast as you can."

Ducking his head, Rupert Greeves raced down and around the stairs until he stood in darkness at the bottom. Water lapped around his ankles. A current was pulling at his feet, sucking out into the hallway. It was draining into the lower levels.

"Cyrus! Antigone!"

Rupert drew his long revolver and splashed toward the door.

Cyrus opened his eyes. He was floating, staring up at low gray stone vaults. He knew that ceiling. He was in the Polygon.

Someone was holding him up by the shoulder, dragging him. Cyrus twisted, just glimpsing Nolan above him. Then his face bobbed underwater. Choking, he threw up salt water.

The hand on his shoulder became two hands, and he was suddenly pulled out of the water and thrown face-down onto a soiled mattress. He was on the rotten top bunk of one of the Polygon's old white metal beds.

Coughing and spewing, he pushed himself up. Nolan was splashing away. Antigone was on the mattress beside him, lying on her back with one arm flung out, skin white, chest heaving, a bloody goose egg on her forehead.

"Tigs," Cyrus said. He patted her cheek. "Antigone!" He glanced around the room.

The Polygon was under at least four feet of water. The plank walkways were floating. White Whip Spiders bobbed around the surface in mats. Nolan stood facing the door, up to his ribs in the water, his wet pale skin looking like the pearly flesh of some strange sea creature.

The wooden door to the Polygon was gone, blown off its hinges by the flood. Gil stood just inside the empty doorway. The skin on his face was charred as black as his beard. His shirt had burned away, revealing his massive chest and shoulders, carpeted with dark hair but tiger-striped with old bald scars.

He was carrying the sledgehammer, but the iron on one side was mushroomed, molten and steaming, reforged by the salamander explosion. His bull eyes were red and wild, and his thick purple lips were curled back in a snarl.

He waded into the room, the water lapping at his hips.

"Little thief! Serpent! Coiled in your hole! You will not steal from me again. Give them to me now or I will crush your brittle skull."

Nolan's shoulders tensed. Blue veins bulged and snaked on his bare arms. His voice was cold—blizzard quiet, blizzard angry, carrying a thousand years of edges. "Flood my home? Threaten my friends? Back away, Gilgamesh. You know this snake cannot die. I will strike. And strike. And strike. I saw Maxi die."

"Maxi was a fool," Gil said. He eyed the pillared vaults of the long, many-walled room, then turned and swung his hammer at the nearest dark stone pillar. The column shattered like a candy cane. Cyrus tucked his head as tiny, jagged rocks rattled through the vaults and skipped off his back.

Gilgamesh raised his arms toward the ceiling, his chest inflating.

"I am awake, little Nikales!" he bellowed. "Gilgamesh of Uruk is awake, and he will never sleep again!"

"Your treaty, Gil," Nolan said. "Rupert will still Bury you."

Gilgamesh laughed. "Even now, my treaty is in flames, and at long last. Contained by human law? No true power? That is not immortality." He pointed his hammer at Cyrus. "I will open myself to the ancient power and gorge on the sweet taste of battle rage. I will wear the children's skin like a Scythian king!"

While Cyrus watched, Gil's eyes rolled back in his head as his muscles seized and writhed beneath his carpeted skin. His jaw unhinged as his arms twisted against their joints, bending against his elbows, bones grinding and cartilage crunching.

Nolan plunged forward, a knife suddenly in his hand.

They had to get out. Now. Cyrus slapped his sister hard. "Tigs! Wake up!"

Nolan rose up and buried his knife in Gil's chest. Gil didn't notice, and his spasms didn't stop. Nolan pounded on the hilt, driving the knife all the way in between his ribs.

Antigone opened her eyes. She grimaced and sputtered her lips.

"Sick, sick, sick. I taste like squid."

"C'mon!" Cyrus started to drag her off the edge of the bed, then jerked back. A raft of Whip Spiders was bobbing around the bed, pincers and whips stretching toward the mattress, straining for dry land.

Nolan was wiggling the knife in Gil's chest. He looked back at Cyrus. "Jump!" he shouted. "Go! Now!"

Too late.

Gil's eyes snapped back down. The hammer swung

up. Nolan tried to jump away, but the iron head caught him in the chest. His body rose out of the water in a geyser, tumbled across the surface, and slammed into a wall.

Gil locked eyes with Cyrus, and he roared.

Antigone sat up, shocked. "Cy . . ."

Gil waded toward them, knife still in his chest, muscles still sliding and twisting unnaturally beneath his skin.

Behind him, Rupert Greeves splashed into the room carrying a revolver.

Gil spun around. In a flash, Rupert dove beneath the murky surface. Gil stared at the ripples and raised his hammer, waiting.

Against the wall, Nolan stood up, sputtering.

"Go!" Cyrus said. He and his sister jumped off the bed, away from Gil, clearing the island of Whip stings.

Dirty salt water swallowed them. Knees bent, not standing at full height, Cyrus popped just his face up out of the water. Antigone did the same next to him.

Gil was stomping through the flood. Raging through stinging Whip Spiders. Feeling for Rupert with his feet, hammer raised and ready. Nolan was sliding through the water around him, just out of hammer range.

"You're not immortal, Gil," Nolan said. "You'll die. You'll rot. Your hulk will be dust, a colony of worms."

Gil wheeled on him, spitting his words. "Thief. I will

knock your head from your body and bury it deep. Is that death enough, Nikales, fruit thief?"

Nolan stood up straight, arms extended from his sides. "So be it," he said.

Gil stepped toward him, cocking his sledge.

Behind him, Rupert exploded up out of the water. In one geysering motion, he was on Gil's back, an arm around Gil's neck, and the long barrel of the revolver in Gil's ear.

The gun fired.

The giant collapsed into the water.

Cyrus and Antigone stood up slowly.

Chest heaving, Rupert stood, dripping, above the huge floating body. His gun was still pointed at the back of Gil's head. He looked over at them. "The Smiths pass another test. Nolan, rope? Chains? Something? He won't be stunned long."

Nolan bounded through the water and ripped a length of rope off a floating plank.

"Rupe, he went through the rage-warp. A full spasm."

Rupert nodded. "Then we have even less time." He holstered his gun, grabbed Gil's huge floating arms, and pinned them at the small of his back. Nolan began to tie the thick wrists together. "Cy, Tigs, get out of the water. Watch the Whips. Get to the stairs."

Cyrus and Antigone splashed forward. Nolan and Rupert moved to Gil's ankles.

"Won't he drown?" Antigone asked.

Nolan snorted.

"No," said Rupert. "He won't."

Gil's floating body shivered. Arms tugged at the ropes. Tree-trunk legs shook as Nolan cinched the knots at his ankles. The huge back arched, but Gil's face remained submerged.

The yell rippled the water. Cyrus could feel it in his legs even as he reached the door.

"And now," said Rupert, "we run."

The four of them were silent in the halls and on the stairs—but for the sound of slapping wet feet and dripping water and occasional spitting and snorting. It wasn't long before Rupert was leading the strange train through the broad upper hallways. Nolan trailed behind. The damage from the riot was still strewn across the floor, but the cleanup crews were gone.

And the bells had stopped ringing.

Outside the Galleria, a large silent crowd was pressed in around the big doorway. Someone was speaking inside.

Rupert tapped shoulders, and a narrow alley formed for the wet train. A swarm of whispers surrounded them as they pressed through.

"Rupe, do something," a woman said. "The treaties gone . . . they can do anything they like!"

"He can't . . ."

". . . discharged as Avengel."

"No Avengels at all now . . ."

"*Ordo Draconis* an ally?"

". . . Hell's own daftness."

"Radu Bey . . ."

". . . Radu Bey."

"Radu . . ."

". . . Bey."

Rupert reached the doorway and stepped inside. Cyrus squeezed in next to him. Antigone hooked her arm in his and wedged herself forward. Nolan hung back.

"Bellamy Cook!" Rupert shouted.

Every head in the Galleria turned. The men and women standing in the aisle parted to the sides, leaving an empty path all the way to the dais where Bellamy Cook stood, draped in a long bright robe, intricately embroidered with maps. Old men and women were seated in a half circle behind him.

The wiry man had shaved, and his mud hair was oiled into curls. He smiled. "Mr. Greeves," he said. "You appear to be all wet."

"I have bound Gilgamesh of Uruk in the Polygon, after the attempted murder of two Journeymen of this Estate. It is his final violation. He is eligible for Burial."

A whisper danced through the crowd.

Bellamy Cook let his head drop, chin against his

embroidered chest as if lost in thought. When he spoke, it was to the floor, but his sharp voice filled the room.

"The Brendan will not consider Burial in any case. We no longer have authority over our immortal allies. Gilgamesh of Uruk is accountable to the laws of his own Order. As soon as they have a chance to establish themselves, I suggest that you notify them of your charges." Bellamy looked up. "As for you, Rupert Greeves, Keeper of the Ashtown Estate, we thank you for your service. Our allies in the *Ordo Draconis* now offer *us* protection, and all the strength we could ever need. The primitive office of Avengel—"

Rupert took another step forward, and his booming voice rattled the upper windows.

"I am the Avenger of Blood! Where my brothers fall, there I will be. Where my sisters stumble, there you will find me. My road is paved with shadow, and my bed is made of pain. I am the Keeper of unmarked graves and the walker of forgotten tombs. I am the point of Brendan's spear, and the hunter of Brendan's enemies, *wherever* they may be. So I have sworn, so it has been, so it shall be—till Death bend me and the ground take me."

For a long moment, the room was silent. And then Rupert was backing slowly away, pulling Cyrus and Antigone with him. Bellamy Cook nodded at the front row. Tall shapes began to stand, but the crowd was already closing, swallowing their Avengel and his Smiths.

◆ ◆ ◆

Outside, the heat haze suppressed the sun's glare, but not the sun itself. The fire orb sat high in the sky, pearly perfect without its flame halo. Cyrus would have normally given it more appreciation, but he was jogging to keep up with Rupert's long strides. They'd lost Nolan, but somewhere in the crowd Rupert had snagged Dennis Gilly by the back of the neck, and he was now dragging the porter alongside him, delivering a long string of instructions into the boy's ear.

Antigone looked at her brother as they ran. "What now?" she asked. Her wet hair was slicked straight back, and the blood on her forehead had dried. Her bare feet didn't flinch on the gravel path. As for Cyrus, his head was splitting, salt water was still draining out of his sinuses and down the back of his throat, and his whole body felt like he had fallen out of a tree. It was even hard to jog straight.

He snorted and spat on the gravel. "I think we're leaving," Cyrus said. "With Rupert."

Ahead of them, Rupert released Dennis with a whoop and slapped his backside. The porter raced away without a glance back. Rupert turned.

"Smiths!" He was almost cheerful. "No time for pain. Hurry now, hurry." Rupert's steps were long and quick, his thick arms arched away from his body like a gunfighter's, and his head was always moving, his eyes sweeping their surroundings. Even his nostrils were flared, like he was catching traces of some enemy in the air.

"Do you hear that?" Rupert asked, suddenly pausing on the path. "Too low and too fast."

Cyrus didn't hear anything. Antigone shook her head.

"Don't stop," Rupert said. "We need you in your rooms now."

Beyond the buildings that surrounded the courtyard, above the trees that lined the hills, the shape of a strange plane appeared. Rupert was right. It was too low and it was definitely too fast. A second later, the shape had become a roar; another second, and the roar had become the plane—olive green, part boomerang and part stingray, Cyrus had never see anything like it. It was like a single wing, but with two jet intakes crowded into the center like gaping nostrils beneath the cockpit.

The jet ripped through the air above Ashtown, tossing the canvas remnants of the Acolyte tent city like so many leaves. And then it was gone, banking hard and disappearing out over the lake. The roar faded.

In its wake, a blizzard of red paper rings fluttered and swirled quietly through the air.

People were flooding out the big main doors and down the steps into the courtyard. All of them watched the strange rings rain down, spinning as they fell, like the seeds of an unknown tree.

Rupert grabbed Cyrus and Antigone by the shoulders and pulled them back on course, faster this time. He didn't let go.

"What are they?" Antigone asked. She grabbed at one and missed.

"You'll know soon enough," said Rupert. "We can't be in the open right now."

Three steps later, the rings were coming down in clouds, rolling down their shoulders, scuffing along the path in front of them, gluing to their wet clothes and wet hair and damp skin as they moved.

Paper dragons. The head was on the right side of the ring, at three o'clock. The neck and body arched up over the top and then down into the tail. The tail formed the bottom of the ring, looping back up to the head where the tip was folded tight around the dragon's neck. A flame-shaped wing stuck up off the back, and two clawed legs dangled off the belly, sticking into the empty center of the ring.

Behind the three runners, the crowd was frozen, watching the red paper rain twist in the air and cover the ground.

Rupert forced them into the arched walkway that led to their stairs. He pushed them up the stairs first, but cut ahead and banged the door open with his gun drawn when they reached Skelton's old rooms.

When he lowered the gun, Cyrus and Antigone followed him in.

The webs on the windows had been tightened and thickened to the point of near darkness, and the spiders were still working. Jax was already inside, sitting in a corner, clutching an enormous backpack. He clambered to his feet when he saw the Smiths.

"You're alive! Are the squid okay? Did they make it?"

Cyrus snorted. "I don't know, man. Maybe if they like eating Whip Spiders."

Jax nodded and sat back down. "Good. They'll be fine for a while."

Arachne walked toward them. "Sorry, Rupe," she said. "I'm not ready for the skins." She clicked her teeth, and Cyrus heard a rustling behind him. He jumped away from the door as hundreds of spiders began to unroll a rippling silver sheet from above the jamb. It was smooth and light, but it looked tougher than steel wool.

"Fine," Rupert said. "Things are moving faster than I'd hoped. Lock this place down, but expect Nolan. He'll be playing shuttle service for some others through the vent. Antigone, do whatever Arachne tells you. Cyrus, you're coming with me."

Arachne plucked a paper dragon off Rupert's shoulder, her eyes wide. "Already? It's been years."

"Not years," Rupert said. "Centuries."

"Have you opened one?" she asked.

"Don't need to see what's in the belly to know what's

there." Rupert banged open the doors to Dump Number One and the Book Dump, and then grabbed the knob to the room Cyrus and Antigone had never managed to open. The knob turned, but the door didn't budge. He looked at Cyrus with eyebrows raised.

Cyrus shrugged. "It was like that when we showed up."

Arachne delicately unfolded the dragon's tail from around its neck while Antigone hovered at her elbow. The paper unfolded and uncreased easily in her weaver's hands—the claws disappeared, and the fiery wing splayed open and flattened into mere paper. Then the body opened and Arachne was holding nothing but a delicate red page with a bizarre outline.

"Well?" Rupert asked. Arachne exhaled slowly, and Cyrus leaned in to see.

In the center of the paper were three small, brightly colored crests arranged in a triangle. The bottom right corner of the triangle was a winged silver chess knight on a deep blue background. Beside it was a red shield with three severed heads. Above them both was a black shield with a scarlet taloned bird with wings spread. In one claw it held a flame; in the other, a skull.

"The crest of the Laughlins," Arachne said quietly. "That one is for Phoenix."

Behind them, Rupert spun and, with a huge booted kick, split the door to the locked room right down the middle. Then he attacked the shards, clearing a hole and shouldering his way through.

"Boarded up from the inside," Rupert said, flinging splintered scraps behind him. "Old wood. Get in here, Cyrus."

Cyrus lifted his bare feet carefully over the splintered wood and ducked through the hole. The dim room on the other side was not what he'd expected—not that he'd expected anything. But given the state of the rest of the rooms when they'd moved in—especially the library—he certainly hadn't expected tidiness.

There was a film of dust on everything, but even that wasn't too heavy. The floor was oiled and polished wood; a plush rug covered half of it. There was a small cot with a pillow and a folded blanket. Two slippers sat side by side beneath it. There was a hot plate and a tiny refrigerator, one tall, tightly packed bookshelf, and a two-drawer filing cabinet. The top drawer was labeled MAPS, and the bottom drawer was labeled LAWNEY. Rupert jerked the bottom drawer open and then kicked it shut again. It was empty.

There was also a desk with an old wooden chair behind it, and a small artist's table with a stool. On the artist's table were detailed drawings on strange, fragile paper. Cyrus immediately recognized it as rice paper. The same kind of paper that had been used to make the floating lantern globe Skelton had left them in his will, the globe that had been covered with indecipherable ink scrawling. Cyrus would have looked at the paper more closely, but Rupert whistled at him from the opposite corner of the room.

"All of this makes sense," Rupert said. "For years I knew Skelton had to be in and out of Ashtown. But I assumed his little lizard lawyer John Horace Lawney hid him."

"Rupert Greeves, you're in no position to be making slighting remarks."

Cyrus spun around and laughed. Bald and spectacled, the lawyer himself was sticking his head through the door. "Really, Rupert," Horace said. "I thought we were past all this suspicion and doubt."

"Horace!" Cyrus said. "We haven't seen you in forever."

"And that," Rupert said, "is just one of the reasons we haven't gotten 'past all this suspicion.' The so-called estate of William Skelton hasn't done much for his heirs."

The short lawyer stepped into the room. He was as stout and calmly pompous as the day Cyrus had first met him, sitting on Cyrus's bed in room 111 of the Archer Motel, surrounded by the debris of Cyrus's shattered wall. Now, like then, he was wearing tweed trousers and a tweed vest, but no jacket. And he was completely filthy, trailing hair snarls and cobwebs.

"Were you in the vents?" Cyrus asked.

Horace nodded briskly, adjusted his half-moon glasses, and squared off with Rupert. "You saw the will," he said. "You witnessed the unsealing. The estate has been sufficient financially, but I was as surprised as you were at the somewhat modest contents."

Rupert stepped toward the lawyer, towering above him—looking almost straight down. "No, Horace, I don't *know* that. What I *think* is that you were hiding Skelton's full holdings, because to reveal them would have been an admission that you maintained and controlled illegal assets for years."

Horace sniffed. "You are, of course, free to believe whatever nonsense you like."

"Um, why are we in here?" asked Cyrus.

Rupert looked at Cyrus, then turned back to Horace. "We are here to discover how the outlaw Skelton used to slip in and out of Ashtown."

Horace rolled his eyes. "And I would know that how?"

"Horace . . . ," Rupert said. "This is an opportunity for you to avoid a beating." His voice was low, but there was distant thunder in it.

"Fine." Horace pointed at the ceiling. "When Skelton did come, he came through there. He dropped in, as it were. Check the desk. There's a bottle opener on one of the drawer fronts. Lift it up."

Rupert holstered his gun and jumped around the desk as Cyrus studied the high ceiling. It was covered with dingy tin squares, each bent and shaped to look like plaster.

"Mr. Cyrus," the lawyer said, "I hope that you and your sister feel that I am above suspicion of any wrongdoing. I did get shot in the line of duty—serving as your Order solicitor."

Cyrus laughed. "And we saved your life." He glanced at the little lawyer. "Rupe is right. What you told us about Skelton's estate wasn't true. We got these rooms and just enough money to pay our Order dues and send Dan to college."

Horace sniffed, but before he could respond, four tin squares banged out of the ceiling, followed by a bundle of rope and boards. Wooden treads rattled and clattered down onto knots until finally the whole thing was swinging gently in place—a spiral staircase made of rope. The lowest tread was just a few inches above the floor.

Rupert eyed the swinging ropes and treads, then sat down on the desk, crossed his arms, and stared at Horace.

"What?" Horace said. "I was his lawyer. I couldn't have told you when he came and went. Not ethically."

"You realize," Rupert said, "that I am currently in a lot of trouble with our beloved O of B?"

"I do," said Horace. "And I'm sorry about that. If I thought I could help—"

"In fact," said Rupert, "it is likely that my relationship with the Order is nearing its end. You've heard this?"

Horace nodded.

"Then my question is this." Rupert pulled at his short beard. "Would I be in any more trouble if I shot you right now? Think about it. Don't answer too quickly. I want your legal opinion."

Horace laughed, but his eyes were jumpy. "You wouldn't. This is just cheap theater."

Rupert shrugged and set his gun on the desk. "You're right. I'm not going to shoot you. But when we've gone, I'm going to have a rumor sent Gil's way, a rumor that John Horace Lawney the seventh knows full well where we are, and that John Horace Lawney the seventh helped us leave." Rupert smiled. "How's that sound, mate? I don't want my threats to be cheap."

Horace had turned white. "He'll kill me," he said.

"Eventually," said Rupert. "But you're mortal. It was bound to happen sometime."

Horace sniffed and took off his glasses. He was polishing them on his vest when he finally spoke. "I'm not a thief. I was going to give them everything," he said. "Eventually."

Rupert's eyes narrowed. "Why the fraudulent will? Why the game?"

"You," said Horace. "Skelton made me swear never to reveal the contents of the estate to any officer of the

O of B. He thought you'd confiscate it and that the children would get nothing. The will was always going to be a fake—the will the Order saw. I was to communicate the rest directly to the Smiths—off the record, completely off book."

"Why didn't you?" Cyrus asked. "A little money would have been nice. We've been sleeping in hammocks."

Horace nodded at Rupert. "I was in the hospital. Eleanor Eldridge was killed, and then the Avengel himself became your Keeper. As long as that was the case, the full estate could wait."

Rupert stood. "Here's what you're going to do. Money, and a lot of it, needs to show up in traditional non-Order bank accounts in the names of Cyrus and Antigone Smith. And it needs to show up fast. When the storm has blown, you can tell them what else is theirs. I'll not probe—they can tell me about whatever they choose to. Is that clear?"

"Mr. Greeves," Horace said, cheerfully popping his glasses back on. "It is. I appreciate the—"

"Jeb!" Rupert bellowed.

Jeb Boone stuck his head in through the broken door.

Rupert nodded at Horace. "Keep an eye on him. Tie him up if you have to, but the lawyer doesn't leave until we're gone."

Jeb nodded.

"Has the herd arrived yet?" Rupert asked. "Who all is here?"

"Everyone, I think," said Jeb. "Diana, Antigone, Dennis the porter, Jax, Nolan, Arachne, and a little staffer named Hillary. Dennis brought her."

"Good. Get them ready and keep them calm. One pack per, if they have gear—and only if they can carry it themselves."

Rupert stepped cautiously on the lowest tread of the rope stairs, letting the whole structure swing for a moment before he began to climb. Jeb escorted Horace back to the broken door, but the little lawyer hesitated.

"Mr. Cyrus," Horace said, "I am sorry things have been so . . . complicated."

Cyrus rolled his eyes. "Things have been real simple on our end."

Cyrus stepped onto the spiral rope stairs. Using his hands on the treads in front of him like he was climbing a ladder, he scurried up.

Squatting in the darkness beneath attic rafters, Rupert was waiting for him, poking at an old electric coil gun that was strapped to a beam, pointed down the rope stairs.

"Crude but effective," Rupert said. "At least if it still held a charge." He stood as tall as he could under the low ceiling and began to weave his way down a narrow plank path. "Mind the route, Cyrus Smith. You'll have to retrace it." He glanced back as Cyrus scuffed along through the dust. "Maps and mazecraft have their uses. Remember that."

Cyrus followed Rupert as their attic met up with other attics—crossing or joining the hollow, dust-filled skulls of adjacent buildings. To Cyrus, the taste of the dust was old and familiar—he had eaten a lot of it in the barns and haylofts out in the pastures behind the Archer Motel. Even in the rafters of his school, the perches he had retreated into when teachers and classes and desks and chairs and the whole organized world became too much for him.

The planks in the attic paths were loose and uneven, balanced on the rafters wherever there was headroom beneath the sloping roves. Petrified tar hung down, and nail tips nicked his scalp when he stood too tall. Old insulation kicked up around his bare toes and floated in the slanting slices of light that slipped through the occasional roof vents.

The path turned left at an attic junction, and then left again. It led Rupert and Cyrus past a large camp of sleeping bats. Judging from the smell, the bats and all their bat friends had been camping there for quite some time.

The plank path dead-ended at a brick wall.

"Right there." Cyrus pointed at a rumpled-up pile of insulation between two rafters. An old ladder had been bedded down inside the pile.

The ladder was a rickety one, but it held Rupert easily enough. Cyrus followed his Keeper up over the brick wall and onto a long slope of fir planks that must have been above a vaulted ceiling. A path had been worn smooth by others—or perhaps only by Skelton over time. They disturbed a smaller camp of bats and discovered a deposit of brittle ancient carnage left over—most likely—when some cats had discovered a favorite pigeon roost.

They climbed and they slid, and they walked silently over precarious planks listening to muffled voices through the ceilings beneath them. And all the way, Cyrus watched as—one by one—the last of the red paper dragons that had clung to Rupert's wet clothes slipped off and settled in the dust among the rafters, where they would stay, perhaps for always.

"Rupe?" Cyrus asked. "What does the dragon mean? And the crests on it . . ."

Rupert ducked beneath another rafter. "Inside it. The crests were in the dragon's belly. It's a message, and an old one." He glanced back. "A death sentence. The *Ordo* has claimed us for its own. The Dracul decree. They would issue them to kings or popes or sultans when they intended to take one of their subjects." He laughed. "Or one of their cities. Or one of their nations. It was a warning to stand back—to expel the condemned and provide no aid or protection. And—with very few exceptions—it was obeyed."

"We were in the dragon's belly?"

"We *are*," said Rupert, and he cracked a dark smile. "'Shall I fear the dragon's inners, where it keeps no armor to turn my blade?' That from your famous ancestor, the Captain."

"Arachne said the other crest belonged to Phoenix."

Rupert grew serious again. "It belonged to the last Brendan—and to his twisted brother, Edwin Laughlin." He glanced back. "Phoenix. And to his grandnephew, Oliver Laughlin, wherever he may be."

Cyrus slipped along behind Rupert. The shrunken old Brendan had been nice enough, but Cyrus had only spoken to him once before he died. He'd actually interacted more with Phoenix. Just thinking about that man sent Cyrus's neck hair bristling—the singsong drawl; the limp; the wild all-seeing, all-sucking eyes; the ancient stained white coat; the electric tingle in his frigid touch; the voice that had probed into his mind. And Mr. Ashes—the snarling, rushing power he'd become when the coat had slipped off his shoulders.

And Oliver Laughlin. The boy. He had sat beneath the wall of portraits in the Galleria and decided Cyrus's fate with silent nods and silent shakes of his head. The Order had bowed to him as the rising successor. But he hadn't cared—not about anything. And he'd turned out to be the loneliest kid Cyrus had ever met. He hadn't hung out with the Polygoners for long. The Brendan had died, and Oliver had gone.

Now they were inside a dragon together.

Cyrus thumped into Rupert's back.

The path had terminated at a tremendously thick chimney. Bricks had been removed from one side and carefully stacked out of the way, leaving a black ragged arch behind. A rope ladder dangled inside.

Rupert squeezed himself in and began climbing. When the avalanche of ash and char finally slowed and stopped, Cyrus held his breath and ducked into the hole.

After fifteen feet of darkness, Cyrus reached the upper lip of the chimney and stuck his head out beneath the hazy sky. Rupert grabbed Cyrus's forearms and rocketed him out the chimney into the daylight.

They were standing on a copper roof—old and tarnished green. The roof sloped down past a row of mossy statues and stopped at a broad gutter. Another rope ladder had been attached to the chimney, and it ran down to the edge of the roof and disappeared into what looked like nothing but treetops and sprawling woods—the outer unkempt grounds of Ashtown. To their left, looking past the stone corners and higher roofs of the main building, they could just see the jetty, the crowded harbor, and a flock of anchored seaplanes. Gil's was the biggest, floating on its fat belly.

"Smart," Rupert said, squinting against the light. He

pointed at the closest corner of the main building. "No windows overlooking this spot, and the roof peak behind us keeps us invisible to the courtyard and the other buildings. Old Billy Bones could have kept this up for a long time. Probably did."

Cyrus looked around. "Yeah, but what do we do now?"

Rupert smiled. "A philosopher stood on one leg in the middle of a road, unsure of what to do. 'What is the best and wisest step? Where shall I put my foot?' he asked. A farmer passing with an ox gave him his answer. 'Put it down,' he said. And so the philosopher did, but his other leg rose up. 'Terrible advice!' he yelled. 'My predicament hasn't improved. Where shall I put this foot?' And again, the farmer told him, 'Put it down.' "

"And . . . ," said Cyrus.

"And this time when the philosopher put his foot down, he put it squarely in a pile of the ox's dung. Concluding that the farmer was either a trickster or a fool, he left his foot there and never moved again. As for the farmer, he walked on to Rome."

Rupert met Cyrus's eyes and laughed. "Your father loved that one."

Cyrus groaned. "So the joke is that philosophers are stupid and farmers aren't?" He blinked and shook his head, looking around at the rooftop. "Why are we even talking about this right now?"

Rupert grinned. "Two reasons, Cyrus Smith. First, the next step is always right in front of you. Pick your feet up and put your feet down. Second, we are most definitely standing in the dung right now. Your first trek starts now, and it's madness. Are you ready?"

Cyrus nodded.

Rupert pointed over the wood toward a small jagged peninsula sticking out into the lake. "You will go back and get everyone else, and you will have them gathered at the base of that peninsula in one hour. Keep them hidden in the trees." He looked back at the harbor. "As for me, I will go steal Gil's plane. It's the only one big enough for all of us, and the justice of it appeals to me. I'll pick you up on the peninsula." He slapped Cyrus's shoulder. "Can you find the way back?"

"Yeah," said Cyrus. "Can you steal the plane?"

"It's right in front of me," Rupert said. "I'm going to keep walking till we're through this patch of dung."

The return trip was easy enough for Cyrus, though he wished he wasn't barefoot. He would put on his boots when he got back to the room, but what he really wanted were his canvas shoes. They were probably sitting right where he'd left them, next to the entrance to the water cube.

When he finally was in the ceiling above Skelton's rooms, he knew he had time to spare. Not a lot, but enough to quickly pack his own bag.

"Tigs! We gotta go!" he shouted. He'd grab the Quick Water, and his boots, and Skelton's old rice paper globe.

He scurried onto the rope stairs and froze halfway down. The place was full of smoke. Dennis, Hillary, Jax, Antigone, and Diana were huddled on the floor with packs in their laps. Antigone raised a finger to her lips.

"Arachne! Demon spinstress!" Gil's voice boomed through the walls. Plaster smashed.

Arachne and Nolan appeared in the doorway. No Jeb. No Horace. Arachne had her sagging satchel of spiders slung over her shoulder. Her cheeks were streaked with tears. Nolan was carrying two packs. Cyrus's leather jacket was buckled onto one of them.

"Are you ready?" Arachne whispered. "Where's Rupert?"

"Ready or not," Nolan said quietly. He lobbed a pack at Cyrus. "That web in the door won't burn, and it might be hours before they get a flint knife sharp enough to slice through it, but I can't say the same for the stone walls—Gil's almost through."

Antigone was already on her feet. Diana Boone stood beside her. She looped her strawberry ponytail in half on top of her head, cinched it tight, and slung on her pack. Then she smiled through the smoke.

"Take us away, Cyrus Smith."

nine

DUNG PATCH

CYRUS WAS WORRIED. He kicked a lump of soft insulation off the path, ducked a rafter, and glanced back.

"The Quick Water . . ."

"Is in your pack," Nolan said from the back of the line. "Like I said already."

Antigone was right behind Cyrus. "It's in a little pouch, Cy. Don't worry."

But he wasn't really worried about the strange liquid fungus. He was worried because they had lost too much time trying to figure out how to get the stupid rope stairs to reel back up into the ceiling. Leaving them down for Gil to find would have been ridiculous, but he'd almost had to. How long had they spent on that? Five minutes? Ten? It didn't matter now. They'd gotten it done. Now they had to hurry.

He glanced back at the line trailing through the rafters behind him. With this many bodies on the old boards, the wood was visibly sagging. They were probably mysteriously cracking plaster ceilings everywhere.

Ahead, he spotted the chimney. "Okay," he said to Antigone, pointing. "You see that? We're almost through this part."

Antigone nodded. She wasn't used to seeing her brother stressed. She also wasn't used to seeing him responsible for anyone but himself.

"You're doing good, Cy," she said. "Seriously."

"Whatever," said Cyrus. "I'll be doing good if we make it."

Getting up the chimney took a lot longer when also head-shoving a pack up the hole. And Cyrus did it twice, once with his own pack and once with the ridiculously heavy and suspiciously sloshing pack that Jax had been carrying.

Finally, standing in a line with his friends on the roof, Cyrus realized that the rest of the way would be even harder. He didn't know if there were paths through the woods, and if there were, he didn't know where they led or if he could trust them. And once they were down inside the trees, even the general direction of the peninsula wouldn't be as obvious as it was from the roof.

At least Gil's plane was still anchored outside the harbor. Cyrus figured they had about twenty minutes to get down and get through the wood. He hoped.

"Okay," Cyrus said, wiping his forehead on the back of his arm. He'd missed lunch. Was it lunchtime? It had to be. His legs felt wobbly. And his temples throbbed like twin volcanoes. He looked at his sister. She was giving him her best worried look—eyebrows together and up. Cyrus managed a smile, but Antigone wasn't buying it. She brushed back her hair. For some reason, Cyrus focused on the scabbed gash on her forehead—that morning's gift from Gil.

Pick up your foot and put it down. Do the next thing. Even if you're standing in dung and stepping into more. Not a pleasant thought when barefoot. He'd been so worried about reeling up the rope stairs, he'd forgotten to grab his boots.

Nolan was studying the old rope ladder that dangled over the gutter edge. "This held Rupe?" he asked. "It's seen a lot of weather."

Cyrus pointed over the woods. "See that peninsula? We need to be there. Pretty much right now." He looked at Diana. "Can you get us there once we're on the ground?"

She nodded.

"Tell me if I go wrong. C'mon. Jax, you first." With that, he tossed Jax's pack down into a thick bush.

They made it safely to the ground, though it took longer than Cyrus was willing to think about. The ladder's rungs had been overgrown by ivy; finding them hadn't been easy, especially descending three stories of vertical stone wall.

Everyone slipped back into their packs. Cyrus handed his to Jax and took the bigger one.

"Okay," he said. "Now we have to run."

Picking a gap between trees, Cyrus began to jog.

Bare feet are great for running on grass. They can even be great in the woods—with a path. But ten strides in, Cyrus was once again wishing he'd grabbed his boots. Nettles. A hunk of granite. Branches. His toes refused to find soft earth. But he didn't slow down. He wove between trees and over mounds, trying to maintain a pace that he knew the others could maintain. With a lighter pack, little Jax was doing better than he had in the attics. Now it was Hillary Drake who lagged, and Dennis Gilly lagged with her. Nolan had Hillary's pack strapped to his chest, but she was still struggling.

A long branch took a swipe at Cyrus's face, and he kicked a root when he ducked it. Ahead, he had to choose a path over, between, or around two large moss-covered boulders.

"Cyrus!" Diana yelled behind him.

He stopped and looked back, expecting to see Dennis and Hillary leaning on a tree, panting. But they were right behind him—flushed and scratched and sweating, but still with the group. Hillary kept her wide green eyes on him, clearly waiting for his rebuke.

Nolan—pregnant with Hillary's pack, and with his own on his back—was breathing as easily as a sleeper, and his face was dry of sweat. Arachne stood beside him, somehow still seeming fresh and pale, wearing all black and carrying only her spider satchel. Jax staggered to a stop beside her, wheezing.

Diana and Antigone were both sweating, breathing hard but evenly. Antigone tucked back her hair and put her hands on her hips. Cyrus smiled, and his sister smiled back. Antigone might prefer the books, but she had been training.

"You're drifting east," Diana said. "Tick a few more degrees north."

Cyrus nodded and glanced back at the boulders. Around the left side, then.

Hillary staggered forward, gasping. Her cheeks were red, and her forehead shone. She had a habit of looking only at Cyrus—something Dennis obviously hoped to change. "Why are we going?"

Antigone looked at Cyrus with eyebrows raised. Then she turned to Hillary. "Did you want to stay?" Antigone asked gently.

"I'm just staff," Hillary said. She glanced at Dennis and Jax. "We don't go on treks."

"You're a Polygoner," Cyrus said. "We have to run, but you don't have to. If you'd like to stay, you can."

"Hillary!" Dennis practically stomped. "We talked about this! The O of B is changing. The treaties! The paper dragons! Gil is trying to kill them. We're going with Rupert."

"Mr. Greeves frightens me," she said simply.

Something fluttered through the leaves above them, landing on a branch above Antigone. Cyrus looked up at the red-winged blackbird.

"Cyrus?" Antigone asked, glancing at Hillary. Cyrus nodded.

Nolan slid Hillary's pack off his stomach and held it out to her.

"You can stay," Antigone said. "No one is trying to hurt you here. And we won't be angry. But don't tell anyone anything. You're still a Polygoner."

Hillary took her pack. "What about Jeb?"

Diana laughed. "You can talk to Jeb about anything."

"And Mr. Lawney?" Hillary asked.

"No," said Cyrus. "Let's leave him out of things."

Hillary nodded seriously and began to back away. Dennis was frantic.

"Hillary," he said, and his voice wobbled. "You really—"

Antigone cut him off. "Don't confuse it, D," she said. "Not right now."

Up in the tree, the blackbird shrieked, flapping and hopping in place. In the distance, they could hear plane engines rumble.

Trailing shouted farewells, the gang of seven scrambled up and around the boulders and raced off into the wood.

Hillary Drake and the blackbird watched them go.

After a moment, the blackbird dropped off its branch and glided through the trees.

Hillary turned and began to walk back to Ashtown. Walking was nicer than running. She stopped to pluck a lady's slipper, then slid it into her hair.

Sprinting through the trees, barely keeping pace with the Smiths, lashed by brush and beaten with branches, Dennis Gilly began to cry.

Bellamy Cook stood at the long row of windows in the Brendan's high quarters. He was looking out at the lake, past the statues that guarded the rooftop below him. His new rooms were nice enough—if he decided to keep the O of B's tradition and reside in Ashtown.

He heard the door bang open and the long heavy stride that could only belong to Gilgamesh. There were others with him.

"Where are they?" Gil demanded. "Bellamy, so help me, I'll snap you in two and fling you through the glass if you're hiding them. The dragons were a courtesy."

"A courtesy," Bellamy said quietly. The water below him was dark beneath the heat-hazy sky. "Right, mate. Is that what that was? Courtesy would have been waiting till I'd had the chance to formally remove Rupert bloody Greeves from his bloody office. There are protocols, you ox, and I've already trodden on as many of them as the Sages will allow. I'd rather the Order not regret their choice the day of my anointing. Courtesy would have been waiting two bleeding ticks before trying to kill the kids."

"I saw my chance," Gil said.

"And you missed it, Gilgamesh of Uruk." Bellamy glanced back. Gil's face was black with soot, and his eyes were wild and bloodshot. At least he had a shirt on again. He wasn't armed, but he didn't need to be. And he was flanked by three other male transmortals—brutes cut from the same mold as Gil, but on a smaller scale. Bellamy didn't like being alone with them, but transmortals were all the same in some ways—he couldn't show his fear. He stared straight into Gil's huge eyes. "Turns out living forever doesn't give one a brain, more's the pits."

Gil snarled. Bellamy turned back to the window, studying the harbor and the seaplanes clustered on the gray water. He knew how to fight. He could uncoil into bloodletting viciousness between two heartbeats, but he only had one gun, tucked into his belt, and a long knife in his boot. Neither would amount to much against Gil.

Maybe he would need an Avengel after all.

"The old Skelton rooms were empty," Gil said. "Looked as if they ducked into the vents. We tried to smoke them out."

"I heard," Bellamy said. "The whole wing had to be evacuated. Just the touch we needed after you destroyed the water cube."

"You've been helping them," Gil said. "For all your talk, you're just another slobbering mortal son of Brendan."

Bellamy sighed. "Tell Radu Bey that members of his *Ordo* are no longer welcome on the grounds of any holding or Estate of the O of B—but especially here. No treaties, no restrictions, but also no privileges. It's time you left Ashtown. You and yours, mate. All of you lot. This fight is yours. Leave us out of it."

Gil stepped up to the window beside Bellamy and looked straight down at the sun-leathered Australian. Bellamy sniffed. Gil's huge body reeked of smoke and sweat, part singed hair, part wet dog. His thick lips curled into a sneer.

"I'll leave when I've collected those three from you. Not before."

"Really?" Bellamy smiled and nodded down at the harbor. The biggest seaplane was taxiing away. "That is your plane, isn't it, mate?"

"There!" Diana yelled.

Through the staggered wall of tree trunks, Cyrus caught a glimpse of the sun reflecting off the water. They were a little off course for the peninsula, but not badly. And no plane yet—they weren't too late.

Cyrus adjusted and caught his heel on another log. Soft wood fragments flew as Cyrus plowed headfirst into a fern. Before he could even assess the pain, Antigone was pulling him up. She was flushed and breathing hard. The rest of the herd raced on.

"Almost there, Cy," she said. "You've done good." She looked down at his bare feet. "Oh, gosh."

Cyrus started to look, but his sister's hand smacked up into his jaw, holding his head up.

"Don't look," Antigone said. Her hair was moisture-glued down, and her eyes were wide. "Not yet. Just run."

The two began to jog.

"You run well," Cyrus said.

Antigone laughed. "I have shoes." As they picked up speed, she thumped his shoulder. "And I have the same genes you do, Rus-Rus. Why wouldn't I run well?"

Cyrus gave his sister a smirk and began to accelerate. "Same genes, different legs!"

"Cyrus!" Antigone yelled. "Look left."

As Cyrus hurdled a log and sidestepped a moss-covered boulder, he scanned the tree gaps on his left side. He could see flashes of Ashtown's harbor—bobbing, rocking sails. And then a glimpse of Gil's plane, turbo-props whirling, chugging through the waves toward them.

Antigone pulled even with Cyrus, straining to see through the trunks. "Anyone chasing it?"

"Not yet," said Cyrus. "Come on."

The two of them surged after the others. Cyrus whooped, and when Diana looked back, he pointed to the approaching plane. She nodded and started encouraging Dennis and Jax.

Leaping and crashing over driftwood, Cyrus and Antigone finally burst onto the rocky shore. The rest of the group was heading toward the bare peninsula.

The big seaplane was two hundred yards offshore. While Cyrus and Antigone hurried after the others, the plane turned in a slow loop, coming alongside the peninsula, pointed out toward the lake.

Cyrus glanced back toward Ashtown—three small aluminum-shell boats with outboard motors raced out of the distant harbor.

"Go!" Cyrus yelled. "They're coming!"

On the rocks, Antigone was easily faster than her barefoot brother. She raced ahead to the bigger group, already jogging out onto the peninsula—Diana in the lead, Nolan at the rear.

Cyrus's ankles rolled, his toes splayed around driftwood, and his skin ground on the rock. Hobbling and wincing, he felt like an old man trying to escape his wheelchair.

He was such an idiot. Boots, boots, boots. Never again without boots.

A rock shattered in front of Cyrus. Shards sprayed his shins and arms and face. A ricocheting bullet whined off into space.

In the bow of the closest boat, Cyrus saw a muzzle

flash—small enough to be nothing more than sunlight sparking on aluminum. Beside Cyrus, a driftwood limb exploded. Again, the bullet whined away.

Cyrus reached the water as another slug snapped through the air above his head. The cold water felt like heaven swallowing his feet and his branch-lashed shins and knees. He jumped into a dive, arms stretched above his head.

A bullet slammed into his pack, spinning him in the air. He splashed through the surface on his back and hit the shallow bottom. He turned and began pulling toward the throb of the plane's big engines. The pack slowed him down, but he'd make it as far as he could below the surface.

When he grabbed his first breath, the plane was much closer. Everyone else was either on board or climbing into the side door, behind the wing and the roaring propeller. The boats were closer, too. Another bullet skipped in front of him and he dove back underwater. Swimming with the pack on was like flying a flag—a shoot-here dorsal fin.

Another breath, and he decided to risk it. Humpback whale or not, he kicked into his fastest crawl stroke. In another moment, he felt the hurricane wind thrown back by the propeller, dusting the water's surface. He raised his head to find his sister at the side door, waiting for him with an extended arm.

She grabbed one hand, and Nolan grabbed the other. A second later, Cyrus swamped onto the floor inside the plane, and Nolan was slamming the door behind him.

Inside were several luxurious leather seats with glistening wooden tables between them. Back in the tail, there was a massive web-netted cargo space. In the opposite side door, Rupert was manning a huge gun hanging from the ceiling. A large glass shield was mounted around the barrel.

"Stay down!" Rupert yelled. Dennis, Jax, and Arachne were crawling into the tail. Diana was already there, pulling a long rifle out of the cargo space and slamming in a magazine.

Rupert was dripping wet. His wild eyes landed on Cyrus, and he nodded at the cockpit. "Get us out of here! Go!"

"Me?" Cyrus yelled. But Rupert didn't look back again. His gun was chewing through a belt of rounds. A bullet from the boats splattered on his shield, sending tiny cobweb cracks through the glass.

Cyrus shrugged off his pack, grabbed his sister, and dragged her up into the cockpit. As Antigone took the copilot's chair, Cyrus perched on the edge of the pilot's seat, which was set far back from the wheel. His bare feet found the pedals, and he grabbed the wheel and scanned the controls for the throttle.

He found it and jerked it to full. The left engine roared, and the plane began to turn, twisting toward the peninsula.

"Two engines!" Antigone yelled. "Cyrus, two engines!"

Two engines, two throttles! Cyrus thought. He reached down and pulled the second throttle.

The right engine kicked in, and the plane lunged forward—straight at the shore. Pressing down on the left foot pedal with all his strength, Cyrus fought to turn the plane. The pontoon under the right wing hopped out of the water as it scraped over a rock before splashing back down.

A bullet punched through Cyrus's window, and he ducked low in his seat.

"Okay!" Cyrus yelled. "We're okay."

He straightened the plane, moving toward the heart of the lake, and they began to pick up speed, bouncing over the choppy waves.

Cyrus watched his speed climb.

One of the boats was racing right in front of them, catching air off the waves. Gil was driving. A man with a rifle was bouncing too much to get a good shot.

Cyrus held his breath, bit his lip, and pulled back on the wheel. Nothing.

Antigone lunged forward and flipped two levers on the dash. "Wing flaps!" she screamed, and the plane nosed off the water. But Cyrus had already pushed the wheel in again.

The plane slammed down and plowed over Gil's little boat. Metal squealed and metal crunched. Antigone bounced into the dash, and Cyrus slammed his face into the wheel.

Bleeding out of both nostrils, Cyrus sat up and jerked the wheel toward his chest. The fat-bodied plane tore itself free of the water and slid up into the air with wings shivering, engines roaring as they climbed toward the sun.

Antigone was on the floor. "Ow," she mouthed. She climbed back into her seat and leaned toward Cyrus. She had to yell to be heard. "I think you just flattened Gil! And your face!" She laughed suddenly. "Go, Team Smith!"

Cyrus wiped his bloody nose on his arm and grinned. "*Sic semper draconis!*" he shouted.

A heavy hand landed on his shoulder and lifted him out of his seat. Rupert Greeves dropped him onto the floor halfway out the cockpit door and stepped over him to slide behind the wheel. He banked smoothly right and then leveled out, staying low over the lake.

Cyrus sat up slowly. "Sorry!" he yelled.

Rupert glanced back and curled half a smile. "Still alive, yeah? Test passed!"

ten

DIXIE MIST

Dixie sat in bed and stared at her alarm clock. The hands were in the right place—the little one past the four a ways, and the big almost to the six. And the clock was still ticking. She hadn't been sure it would be. She never was.

Scrunching her face impatiently, she looked around her tiny room. A diagonal slab of moonlight ran from her window down to the lemon oil polish on the plank floor. That chunk of moonlight looked as solid as a metal slide. It was all the humidity in the air. Light just sat on it like that. But Dixie wasn't turning on the air conditioner. That would mean turning on the generator, and she didn't know when she would get more gas for that old thing. Five big cans had been full when her daddy had left. Now she only had one, and it was half full.

People got nervous when an eleven-year-old tried to buy gas—especially when that eleven-year-old looked nine. And nervous people asked questions, and then made phone calls. Plus, she was miles from the nearest gas station. Closer if she headed back through the woods behind her house and crossed the swampy tail of Rodney Lake into Mississippi. But that came with its own troubles. Still, she'd do it when she had to.

"*If* I have to," Dixie said to herself. Her daddy might still come back and do it. She almost sighed, but instead, she sniffed the sigh away and glared at the moonlight, at the floor, at the clock.

It had been 189 days since Alfred Mist had kissed his daughter, told her he had a job to look into, and stepped out their homemade screen door. He'd even been careful not to let it bang behind him. He always was. Now that he was gone, Dixie was careful for him.

The big hand clicked onto the six. Dixie waited. She drummed her fingers on her bare knees. The windup alarm was sloppy. She refused to set the alarm for 4:29 a.m. just to trick the clock into ringing at 4:30 a.m. And when she set it for 4:30 a.m. and it actually rang at 4:31 a.m., she felt insulted. She didn't care that it was old. No excuses. The clock only had one job to do. She had as many jobs as she could think of.

The big hand clicked another spot, and the little hammer tried to rocket between the twin bells, but Dixie's hand slammed down before the noise had a chance to work itself up into a fit. She hated those bells. Why go to the trouble of making bells if you were going to make them off-key?

Dixie stood up and stretched in her long T-shirt. Then she stepped in front of her little mirror. Her mama's picture was tucked into the frame at the top, taken on the day she'd married big Freddie Mist. Dixie had her mother's deep-brown skin. She had the same wide-set eyes and loose hair. But she had her daddy's ears, and her daddy's square jaw that looked like it was made of brick. Of course, her square jaw was set on top of a long slender neck, not her daddy's oak stump.

According to her daddy, she had a little trace of just about every kind of blood in her. When she'd finally beaten him at chess, he'd said she oughta be grateful for his Russian grandpappy. When she'd cooked him something that made him groan with hunger just from the smell, he thanked God for her mama's French grandmammy. When she sang and when she smiled and sometimes when she was doing just about anything, he called her Dido, his Carthaginian queen. But mostly, he'd just called her Little Dixie, and sometimes Sweet Eve—mother of all.

Dixie didn't know she was beautiful. All she knew was that she was alone.

"I'll find him," Dixie told her mother's picture. "He'll be back." She glanced at the incompetent clock. Fifteen minutes to get where she needed to be and see what she needed to see. Plenty of time.

Five minutes later, wearing tight worn jeans tucked into her tall snakeproof boots, and a clean oversize black

T-shirt, she stepped out the screen door and closed it gently behind her. The house was tiny—one story with a front door and two windows—but it was tidy and crisply painted.

Moving along a beaten dirt path beneath big Louisiana trees, Dixie hurried through continents of moon shadow and seas of moon silver. While she went, she popped the last of her breakfast of orange slices into her cheek and threw a long corkscrewed peel into bushes. All around her, crickets sang to crickets, and frogs belched to frogs. She stepped over a beaten-down log and around the sprawling roots of an ancient cypress tree. Down the slope, smothered in moonlight, the Mississippi River slid slowly past on its belly. Tonight, with the moon being so social, it looked like a river of mercury.

Dixie dropped into a crouch and looked upstream. There it was—her father's dream. What he'd sold everything to buy. In the daylight, the old cigar factory looked like the beached and forgotten carcass of some creature from another time. A place to play in and explore, though Dixie hadn't managed to get inside since her father had gone. But at night, it looked like the place might still be alive. And, as she had discovered last week, at 4:50 a.m, well . . .

Keeping close to the shadowy tree line, Dixie began to jog. She only had half a mile to cover.

Moriah Cigars had mattered once. It had mattered

enough to build a factory on the banks of the Mississippi River—250 yards long and 75 yards deep. An army of old log pylons held its backside up over the ever-crawling water. Barges had brought in the tobacco leaf. Barges had brought in the workers. Barges had carried away boxes and boxes of cigars—enough boxes to build pyramids, to fill trains, to make men around the entire world feel wise and important, to make their mouths sour and their clothes stink.

Three stories balanced on top of beams on top of pylons. Paned windows and barn doors and pigeon roosts and brick smokestacks and forgetfulness. The river still rolled, kissing the pylons, willing to do its old work. But time had rolled further. No more barges. No more workers. Not for ninety-four years.

But Alfred Mist had made plans. Shops. A restaurant. The Big Muddy hotel. Swamp tours. River tours. Huckleberry Finn rafts for rent . . .

That factory had taken three more years from one more worker. It hadn't yet given anything back.

Dixie slowed as she reached the near end of the structure. The dead factory behemoth stretched away from her, bent in the middle to match the course of the river. She could see beneath the building, into the forest of pylons anchored in the mud. The water threw moon glare up at her as she backed into the long grass beneath the trees.

Frogs. And a lot more frogs. She couldn't even hear the crickets anymore. Something splashed. A small animal screamed in the darkness behind her, probably at a snake.

And then it happened. Lights. The old paned windows blazed, first at the near end, then marching down the length of the factory.

Dixie blinked, and her rib cage tightened. She could feel tears building—tears of fear, of worry, of anger.

With her eyes on the glowing windows, she began to jog along in front of the factory, toward the big new ramp her father had built in the middle. She could barely breathe, she could barely think, but she was absolutely-no-matter-what going to make herself look inside.

Smoke, or maybe steam, began to escape from the mouths of two of the tallest brick chimneys.

Dixie wasn't jogging anymore. She was running. It wouldn't be her father. It couldn't be. What could he say that would make sense?

The ramp was just ahead. At the top, a big barn door began to slide.

Dixie froze. A yellow slice of light. And then a little more. And suddenly, all at once, the door rattled open, banging against the end of its tracks.

A man limped out onto the ramp. Not Dixie's father. A white man. In a white coat. With one arm missing at the elbow. He leaned on a cane. Behind him, a tall, strong shadow stood beside the open door, ready to throw it shut again.

Dixie's eyes strained to capture anything, any promise, any hint that he might be . . . and then he moved. Not her father. He was shirtless—pale and blond.

Dr. Phoenix, once known as Edwin Laughlin, known as Mr. Ashes on his worse-than-bad days, let his weight rest on his bamboo cane. It bent beneath him. His burnt-off stump arm itched badly, and he ground it against his side. It always itched. His remaining hand gripped and regripped the silver knob at the top of his cane as he stared out into the bayou forest. His boat was late, but he didn't mind. It was worth the wait.

His lower eyelid spasmed and twitched. It did that now. Thirteen months, that's how long it had been. Far more difficult months than he had expected when he'd ripped the tooth out of that Smith brat's hand. But finally, he was making progress again. Rupert Greeves had sniffed out his buildings in Miami, but no matter. The factory was working well. Soon it wouldn't matter who sniffed him out, or how many men came with them.

He glanced back at the tall, blond body that stood at the door. The puckered bullet holes were still visible in its chest. The skin was white and blue, but of course it would be. He'd been dead for three years and kept in a freezer along with all the other sons and daughters of Brendan that Phoenix had managed to collect.

The man—of course, it wasn't really a man anymore, just the shell a man had once worn—was still on his feet. And he had been for almost four minutes. That was a huge improvement. He'd walked where he was told and opened the door when he was told, and all with his frozen eyes firmly closed.

Phoenix rolled his head slowly and stared at the face that had once belonged to Lawrence Smith—peaceful, handsome, undecayed. He wasn't really alive, and it was infuriating. He was supposed to be. That was the whole point of the tooth—power over life and death, even among the transmortals. The power was there; Phoenix could feel it. Always . . . feeling it . . . around him. In him. But handling it? The handles were slippery and hard to find. And now his eyes twitched, and his fingers never stopped moving.

Phoenix brushed his tangled and unwashed black hair back over his shoulders as he hobbled toward Lawrence. Not Lawrence. Puppet Lawrence manipulated into walking around—he might as well be hooked to strings. There was no soul in there, no human spirit, just the borrowed life force of a sleeping wild pig two walls away. And if the pig woke up in its pen, there would be problems. The man shape in front of Phoenix would collapse right where it stood. And if Phoenix kept playing with his puppet for much longer, the pig would never wake up at all. Which would be a shame. The pig was the most useful battery Phoenix had found. It had already outlasted three stray dogs and two big gators.

Phoenix stepped even closer to Lawrence, studying the man's gently closed bluish eyelids. He should walk him back into the freezer now, while he was still on his feet. But maybe the time had come for another risk.

Inhaling sharply through his teeth, Phoenix flipped open the silver knob on the top of his cane, revealing the extreme tip of a tooth that had once been as long as a sword. It was black, blacker than night's night, a light-empty triangle. He pressed the tip of the tooth to the lips of the body that had belonged to Lawrence Smith.

"Puppet," said Phoenix. "Open your eyes."

The eyelids didn't even flutter. Instead, all at once, the body went limp, collapsing to the ground in a tangled pile of limbs.

Through two walls, a pig squealed. Out in the darkness, a girl screamed.

Phoenix wheeled around, eyeing the black. Nothing. He stepped onto the ramp.

"Who's there, now?" he drawled loudly. He tapped his cane on the planks. "Ain't polite to spy, darling."

"Is it polite to kill people?" The young voice floated out of the darkness.

Phoenix laughed. "Oh, you've clearly misunderstood

the circumstances—not that I blame you, mind." He looked at the body. "These circumstances aren't the easiest to grab at a glance. For myself, sometimes I wish I had a little instruction manual."

"He's not dead? You didn't kill him?"

Phoenix grinned slowly. "Now, I can't lie to a sweet little thing like you, Dixie Mist-from-down-the-way. Wouldn't be neighborly. This man *is* dead, God rest him, but I didn't kill him. Leastways, I didn't do it myself. Some rough men did it for me, but that was just about three years ago now, and in another state."

Phoenix waited, smiling at the shadows that surrounded the base of the ramp. The girl, he knew, would be confused by every single thing he'd just said. And she wouldn't like that he knew who she was. How could he not notice such a close little neighbor? He'd been saving her for later, and she hadn't caused any trouble to speak of.

In the distance, he could hear a boat—his boat.

"Dixie," he said, "why don't you come on in and we can talk about all sorts of things. Behave yourself, and I might even let you see your daddy." He sighed. "But if you run . . . I'm afraid there'll be dogs on your heels. Dogs like you ain't never seen and never hope to see."

One second of silence. Two. Three. The boat was growing closer. And on that boat . . . Phoenix's smile became genuine, the smile of a child ready to open the only present he really wants, a present he's already peeked inside. The boat was bringing him his handles, an instruction manual of sorts. In a few days, he would truly know how to use the tooth, he was sure of it.

No more puppets. Soldiers would be better.

At the bottom of the ramp, Dixie Mist stepped into view. "You're a liar," she said.

"Sometimes," Phoenix said, nodding. He inhaled the muggy river air slowly, savoring the smell. He was listening to the boat. "But not tonight. Tonight I become the Truth."

He turned and walked back inside, stepping around the body of Lawrence Smith. He'd have him lugged back into the freezer soon enough.

Dixie Mist chewed her lower lip. Her father? He was inside? It couldn't be true. Not if he was okay. And that poor man up there was dead. But he couldn't have been dead for three years—he'd been walking around. She'd seen him. He'd opened the big door.

She inched up the ramp and then paused. Was it a trap? But what would that crazy Mr. One Hand in the dirty white coat want with her? He wasn't paying her any mind at all.

There were men's voices inside. And she could see the lights on a boat flashing through the pylons beneath the factory. A long rattling echo told her that another big door had been thrown open somewhere.

Two laughing men in shirtsleeves suddenly stepped into view, and Dixie caught her breath. One had a tightly shaved head. The other wore a cap. Both had tattoos of their own bones traced onto their bare arms. Both were barefoot. And they moved strangely—fluidly, like bored cats. They were clearly aware that she was watching them, but they also clearly didn't care.

One of them jerked the body up off the ground and slung it easily over his shoulder. Still laughing, the two walked away.

Dixie exhaled. No one was paying any attention. She could hear someone shouting about unloading the boat and someone else complaining about the time.

She couldn't walk away. Not without looking inside. One Hand had talked about her father. And he had known who she was. He had to know where she lived.

Dixie Mist walked slowly up the ramp, into brighter and brighter light, into her father's old factory.

When she stepped inside, she saw three men working an old timber crane, hauling something up through a hatch in the floor. One Hand was with them, his straggly black hair dangling in his face, the silver knob on his cane pressed against his lips.

The room was cluttered. There were bookshelves everywhere. Near the middle of the room was a large table covered with papers. Worn couches and deep chairs were scattered around without design. Her father's old work radio hung from a hook. She saw the old familiar ladders and tight spiral stairs her father had let her climb up through the holes in the ceiling. A regiment of oversize clear lightbulbs—each as big as a pumpkin—dangled in tight rows from the beamed ceiling. The timber walls and plank floors glistened in the light—the long, hard work of Dixie's father. She'd watched him sand these timbers, and she'd watched him lacquer them over and over again until they'd been sufficiently reborn.

Dixie's heart was pounding, but she wasn't afraid. Not anymore. Her ringing ears, her grinding molars—this was anger. These men had stolen everything.

"Where is he?" Her voice was louder than she'd expected it to be, but the men didn't flinch. They kept hauling on their rope. A large crate was rising through the floor. Tattooed arms shone beneath sweat.

"Hey!" Dixie yelled. "Where's my father? This place is ours!"

The men swung the wooden boom away from the hole as the crate banged onto the floor.

Little Dixie stormed forward. "You! One Hand! Tell me where he is *right now*!" She grabbed at his cane.

The man snarled. The back of his hand slammed into her face. The cane lashed across her chest and sent her sprawling.

Dixie gasped in pain, trying to breathe, trying not to cry. Her mouth was filling with blood.

The men opened the crate.

Dixie found herself staring at four scrawny olive-colored limbs and a pile of tangled black rope. The rope pile rose slowly, and she was looking into a filthy female face. The rope was hair; there was more of it than Dixie had ever seen on a person before. Two huge eyes peered out from beneath the pile. They had whites as clear and bright as polished porcelain, and they were studying Dixie.

"So . . . ," said Phoenix. He clicked open the silver knob. The black tooth swallowed light in his hand.

The eyes blinked in surprise. And then the crate exploded.

Wooden shards flew in every direction. The scrawny figure launched through the air toward a surprised Phoenix. Arms and legs coiled around him, and ropes of hair did the same, constricting and slithering like snakes, pinning his arms to his sides, winding tight around his neck.

The tattooed men jumped forward, grabbing wrists and ankles and fighting to unwind hair. While they did, Phoenix began to sputter and laugh, and when the snaking hair had been unwound from his neck, he managed to speak.

"Pythia, doll, you're not thinking. I can't be crushed. I can't be killed. Not in this cloak, and not with the Reaper's Blade in my hand." He looked up at his men. "Give her the shot."

Instantly, the rest of the hair uncoiled. The hands released, and the shape dropped to the floor and retreated into a corner.

"It knows English?" one of the men asked.

"*She*," said Phoenix, "knows every tongue there ever was and ever could be." He glanced back at Dixie. "Now lock that one up. She'll be useful."

Dixie blinked, tearing her eyes off the strange shape in the corner, suddenly remembering where she was. She rolled over and jumped to her feet to run, but big hands caught her up into the air and she was thrown over a shoulder like the dead man had been.

She kicked. She punched. She screamed and tried to bite. And as she bounced away, two wide eyes in the corner met her own. They watched her go.

eleven

THE PROPHET DANIEL

DANIEL SMITH FELT VERY, VERY ALIVE. The first *very* came from the long bleeding cut down his left shin, carved there by the metal-capped spike on the shoe of one of his opponents. The bone was throbbing, and the torn skin felt more burnt than cut. Blood was sponging into his sock.

The second *very* came from his ribs. The last hit he'd taken should have broken several of them. One year ago, it would have broken all of them. But one year ago, Daniel Smith would not have been playing rugby or even thinking about rugby. He would have been thinking about how to feed Cyrus and Antigone, and whether Cyrus needed to see a therapist, and how he would never be able to afford one.

Now his ribs were humming, his shin was screaming, his lungs were heaving, and he couldn't stop smiling as he stood on the sidelines, chewing on his mouth guard, watching the scrum out on the field. Navy-and-gold rugby shirts pressed against the red-and-white of his own university. Even that was still weird to him—*his* university. He had left his brother and sister in strange but apparently safe hands and had gone off to college. His first two semesters had been amazing, and he'd even managed to get back to Ashtown to see his siblings and his mother twice. Now he was finishing summer classes to make up for lost time, but he'd be back on that strange Estate soon enough, after classes ended and the next rugby tournament wrapped up.

For the first time since his father had died, life felt like it was working—especially with this new body. Getting the body had been horrible. Being kidnapped and wired up by that crazy, twitching cripple in his dirty white coat, having a psychotic invade his mind, all of that had been a great deal less than pleasant.

Dan shivered. Then he clenched his fists, slurped on one end of his mouth guard, and flexed his shoulders, feeling the explosive tension in his muscles. Psychotic or not, the man had done good work. Dan was taller. He was thicker and faster and a great deal healthier. He could hit and be hit harder than he'd ever thought his body could withstand—in high school he'd sprained an ankle in gym class at least once a month. Last match, he'd quit bothering to even tape his wrists, and the coach had pulled him out of the game to lecture him about how to soften an impact so he wouldn't get injured.

Dan pulled out his mouth guard, spat in the grass, and

smiled. He didn't want to soften an impact. He wanted to reach his absolute maximum, to find the limits of this new body, to discover just how much pain it could take. It bruised and bled and split and swelled, but it never broke. There were times when Dan actually felt almost grateful that Phoenix had grabbed him. If it weren't for his eyes, he would be.

His eyes had been blue. Now they were a deep chocolaty brown. He didn't care too much about the color, and his vision was sharper than ever. He cared about what they saw, and how sometimes what they saw wasn't really there.

Sometimes it was just glimpses of the past that would rush in. Sometimes he felt like he was seeing the present, but from somewhere else—somewhere close or distant, but through borrowed eyes. And sometimes, weirdest of all, he wondered if he was seeing the future.

He couldn't be. He knew that. It was impossible. But then it would happen again. Whatever he was looking at would disappear and his eyes—his brain—would fritz. Memories or moments or scenes would crowd out his vision, and they wouldn't let go until they wanted to. The Archer Motel with renovations completed. The old California house being built almost two centuries ago. The same house ancient and rotten and leaning with empty windows. The day Cyrus had been born on the cliff top along the coast.

The longest vision had lasted two minutes. All of them had to do with beginnings or endings. Births. Deaths. Rebirths. Most seemed to connect to Cyrus. Some to Antigone.

From the sideline, Dan blinked and whooped at his team. He didn't like thinking about it. And while he blamed his eyes, he knew his brain was the real culprit. Phoenix had crossed his wires somewhere in there, and occasionally his physical eyes would shut down and some subconscious and usually morbid corner of his brain hijacked his vision for a little while.

"Yo, Ben! Shad! Get in there at wing!"

Dan looked up. His coach was yelling at him, at the one they all called Ben Shad. Rupert Greeves had wanted Dan hidden and had given him all the documents he'd needed to become a new person. Not that anyone would have recognized Ben Shad off of Daniel Smith's old driver's license anyway.

Dan ran onto the pitch, fitting in his mouth guard as he went. Opposing players saw the substitution and called it out, adjusting strategy. They'd seen his last match, and Daniel grinned at their recognition. Adrenaline filled every bit of him, from his toenails to his hacked-off dirty-blond hair. The referee tucked his whistle into his mouth, impatient to start play, as Daniel raced to his position.

He wasn't that abnormal. He wasn't superhuman. He wasn't yoked with oversize muscle the way some of the players were. But when he collided with them, he felt like a stone that couldn't be stopped. They felt like wet clay.

The scrum was long and slow—a raft of red-and-white bodies with arms linked over shoulders, heads pressing against another human raft of gold and blue. Daniel danced on the edge of the mass, and then the ball was kicked back. They'd won possession. His teammate, the center, scooped it up and raced to the left. Dan raced with him, trailing well outside and just behind him, ready for the pitch when it came.

And there it was, floating in the air, a simple thing to grab if angry men weren't racing toward him with thoughts of murder.

Dan's jaw clamped down, and his teeth bit straight through his rubber mouth guard. He snatched the ball out of the air and jumped to the inside as a body dove toward him. Another, and he jumped back outside, toward the left sideline.

He ran.

The turf was soft. His whirring cleats chewed it like chocolate. A big man was bearing down on him. Dan could already see the end of the field, and the long route he'd have to take to get there. He could see the cuts he would—and could—make. The big man would be an easy side step. Dan braced himself to plant. He could already see it happening . . . and then he couldn't.

What Dan could see was a graveyard. And he had

become Cyrus. The big man was suddenly much bigger and bearded and his hands had six fingers.

Dan heard the hit. He felt the ball float out of his hands. He landed on his back with an impossible weight on top of him. He was still Cyrus and he was in the bottom of a grave, pinned beneath loose dirt. Antigone was looking down at him. Phoenix was beside her in his dirty white coat. He opened his mouth and spoke, but the voice wasn't his. It belonged to a woman—high and quiet, lilting like a lullaby: "The seventy weeks will soon be passed. One comes on the wing of abominations, and there shall be no end to war. He shall be called the Desolation, and when he casts his shadow, even dragons shrink in fear."

Antigone and Phoenix were swallowed up as a tall shadow stepped into view at the foot of the grave.

Pain exploded in Daniel's chest. His heart stopped.

Cyrus squirmed beneath the weight of the dirt. His stomach collapsed, and his ribs sighed and popped. Why were Antigone and Phoenix just standing there staring down at him? Why did Phoenix sound like a woman? Cyrus tried to shout at Antigone, but his mouth filled with dirt as soon as he opened it. He tried to squirm, but the loose earth had him well pinned. It was chewing him, swallowing him slowly deeper into the grave.

And then there was no sister. No Phoenix. There was

simply a shadow. The shadow became a shape, and the shape became a man. The man's chest was bare, and beneath his skin there was a circular red dragon—like the dragons on the men he'd dreamed, the men whose heads were on his patch.

The man's powerful limbs were hairless and glistened like polished stone. His hair was black with curl, but short. His jaw and nose and brow were hard and smooth. His black eyes were craters, scarred with old anger.

The man looked like a photograph of a statue that had hung in the art room at Cyrus's old school. Cyrus swallowed. It was weird to notice that right now. It didn't matter. This man was no statue. He was very, very alive.

The man stared at Cyrus, and Cyrus stared back from the bottom of his grave. The man's long upper lip curled slowly, and he smiled.

"*Loquere, serpens,*" the man said quietly.

Cyrus spat earth and grunted. He couldn't reply.

Suddenly, a thin girl with a huge tangle of ropes for hair jumped down into the grave and stood on top of Cyrus, holding a stack of dry leaves in the crook of one arm. Mumbling and rocking in place, she began writing fiery letters on the leaves with her finger. She threw the leaves into the air one at a time, and one at a time they burned into ash and rained down on Cyrus, sprinkling in his eyes, floating up his nose.

His eyes should have been burning. He should have been sneezing. Instead, down at the other end of the grave, his feet began to tickle. Horribly.

Cyrus spat out dirt and swallowed mud. "Stop it!" he yelled at the girl in his grave. "Stop tickling!"

Rupert Greeves appeared beside the statue man. He was also bare-chested, and he was dripping wet. But his arms were striped with old scars. His chest carried a snarled nest of them. Cyrus realized that the statue man had no scars. Not one. He couldn't even see any freckles.

"Rupe!" Cyrus begged. He tried to kick, but his legs wouldn't move. "Make her stop! She's tickling. Please! I swear I'll do the book training things."

"I'm busy," Rupert said. "Swimming."

Cyrus spasmed and twitched beneath the dirt, but the tickling only grew. The girl on his chest looked down at him.

"Cy?" Her voice was Antigone's. "Rus! Calm down and hold still!"

And then she slapped him.

Panting, Cyrus opened his eyes. He was lying flat on his back with sweat running down into his eyes and ears. Antigone was hunched over him.

"You slapped me," Cyrus said. And then he jerked and writhed. The tickling hadn't stopped. "Tigs! What's going on?" His limbs weren't moving—not well, at least. He levered up his head and looked down. He was strapped onto what looked like a dirty cot, and Arachne was seated on a stool between his tortured feet. She looked up at him with her wide icy eyes.

Both of his feet were covered with spiders. Rows of spiders marched across the tops and back around the bottoms, dragging silk lines as little gangs of weavers followed. Spiders lapped his toes. Spiders were strapping a loose toenail back down. Spiders were nipping at flaps of torn skin.

Cyrus screamed. Or he would have if Antigone hadn't shoved a sock into his mouth first. She leaned over, eyeball to eyeball.

"Cyrus Lawrence Smith, get a grip. Seriously. Your feet are really torn up. She's working on them. Stare at the ceiling or something, but stop kicking. It'll take longer, you might hurt some of them, and you might make them scared enough to bite."

Cyrus yelled a muffled death threat through the sock. He'd yelled the same one in a dentist office more than a year ago as Antigone had begged the hygienist to knock him out. For fillings. And this was a lot worse than fillings.

Antigone looked down at Arachne. "Okay, fine. Knock him out again."

Cyrus watched as a pair of larger brown spiders marched around his ankles. He could see their clustered eyes, their twitching fangs. He could feel their fuzzy abdomens dragging across his skin. Something else was marching up his neck. Arachne was humming.

Cyrus shook his head. He tried to spit out the sock. Something sharp pinched him hard behind his ear. He'd been bitten. And then the room began to spin.

Antigone tugged the sock out of his mouth. "Gosh, you're embarrassing sometimes."

"Tigs," Cyrus said. "Tigger. Don't let statue man . . . needs a shirt. Speak, snake!"

Daniel Smith opened his eyes, and a ceiling came slowly into focus. There were cords and tracks and lights up there. Somewhere, something was beeping.

"He shall be called the Desolation," he mumbled. He had no control of his own voice. "Seventy weeks. Seventy."

"Mr. Shad?" A woman leaned into view. Daniel's mumbling stopped. His head cleared. "Welcome back," the woman said. "You've had a close call. Your heart—"

"I know," said Daniel. "Is there a phone in here?" He looked into the nurse's worried eyes. She was young and wearing blue scrubs. She was probably nice, but he didn't care. Cyrus was in trouble.

"Mr. Shad, I'd be happy to call any relatives for you," she said. "Right now, you really shouldn't—"

Daniel sat up, threw his legs over the side of the bed,

and stood up in his hospital gown. The emergency number Rupert had given him was on a card in his wallet, which would be in his pants, which he'd put in his bag when he'd changed into his uniform before the game. He looked around. His bag was on a chair beside the bed.

"Mr. Shad," the nurse said. "Please. Lie back down!"

While the nurse yelled for help, Daniel ripped open his bag and pulled out his jeans. His wallet was still in the hip pocket, and Rupert's card slid right out.

Two orderlies hurried into the room as Daniel grabbed a phone off his nightstand. Through a tall window beside the door, he could see his coach and a cluster of worried teammates.

"Mr. Shad!" the nurse yelled. "You had a heart attack. You were dead an hour ago. Please lie down!"

Daniel grabbed the phone and sat on the edge of his bed. "That better?" he asked. He began to dial. The orderlies watched him, unsure of what to do. A moment later, he heard ringing. He flashed a grin at the nurse. Six rings. Eight. Ten. Fifteen. At nineteen rings, a loudly breathing man picked up but said nothing.

Daniel cleared his throat. "I need to speak with Rupert Greeves."

"Who is this?"

"The brother of your brother." It was what Rupert had told him to say.

"Name?"

"Ben Shad."

A long pause. The orderlies crept closer. Daniel eyed them. He didn't think they'd do anything rough. After all, he'd had a heart attack. But they might try to sedate him. He looked at the back of his hand, where the IV tube was taped down. If they tried to stick the needle in the IV bag, he'd tear the tube out.

He could hear papers rustling through the phone.

"You're Daniel Smith? Brother to Cyrus and Antigone Smith?"

"That's correct," Daniel said. "And I need to speak with Mr. Greeves immediately. It's serious."

The phone banged down on a desk. It always did. Daniel knew that he'd be waiting for a while now. Rupert wouldn't be immediately available, and Ashtown was a big place.

Just to make the nurse happy, Daniel swung his legs up onto the bed and leaned back into his pillows. She hurried forward and slid a stethoscope down his gown against his chest.

"Ah, Daniel Smith." The voice in his ear wasn't Rupert's. It was Australian. Daniel sat back up.

"Who is this?" he asked. "I need to speak with Rupert Greeves."

"Can't be done, I'm afraid," the voice said. "Rupert's off adventuring—more fox than hound this time around.

Not sure we'll be seeing him again. My name is Bellamy Cook, and I've been hoping to have a word with you."

"Why? What happened?"

"I would rather speak in person, but this will have to do. First, the estate of the late William Skelton, of which you are currently an indirect beneficiary, is being seized by the Order. Ill-gotten and piratical gains, as it turns out, cannot be passed along legally."

The nurse was holding out her hand for the phone. Daniel turned his head away. "I don't understand."

"Simple enough, really. Skelton was a thief, and his heirs cannot benefit from his thievery. And the documentation of his estate is a little spotty. We'll be sending representatives out to look over the paperwork on your end. They should be there tomorrow."

"Paperwork? Mr. Cook, I don't have paperwork."

"Who pays your tuition? Your rent?"

"They just get paid, all right? When will Rupert be back?"

The Australian voice laughed. "Mr. Smith, Rupert Greeves is on the run. With the dragons on his trail, he'll be a lucky man if he outlasts the new moon. Sadly, Cyrus and Antigone are with him. I expect they'll share his grave. A great loss to the Order. We grieve. Unfortunately, our hands are tied. Political issues."

"What?" Daniel jumped back to his feet. The orderlies spread out, surrounding him.

His coach loomed in the doorway. "Ben," he said, hands raised. "Settle down now."

"Listen to me!" Daniel yelled into the phone. "I don't know who you are, and I don't care. I will come for anyone who touches my brother or my sister, do you understand me? Do you know what I can do?"

Bellamy sighed. "I've read the file. Phoenix reworked you. My condolences. I have some unofficial experience with those types of modifications. Ox strength today, exploding heart tomorrow. Best of luck to you, and to your brother and sister, wherever they may be."

The phone clicked off.

An orderly lunged forward with a syringe, and Daniel smashed the handset into the man's face. He was limp when he hit the floor. The second orderly backed away.

"I'm sorry," he said to the nurse. "I'm sorry. I appreciate what you're doing, but my family's in trouble."

He jerked out his IV, grabbed his bag, and looked at his coach blocking the doorway.

"Shad," his coach said with wide eyes. "Son . . ."

Dan slipped into his shoes. "My name is Daniel Smith. I'm not sure I'll make the next tournament." He threw the IV stand through the window beside the door and followed the spray of glass out into the hall.

Bellamy Cook leaned back in his chair and drummed his fingers on the Brendan's ancient desk. That went well, he thought. Now the boy would run, and they would follow. Daniel was more likely than anyone to hear from his brother and sister. He looked up at Phillip, his freshly hired secretary—short, wire-thin, with round glasses perched on a needle-sharp nose, he was more dangerous with a knife than any man Bellamy had ever seen.

"Anything?" Bellamy asked.

"No, sir," said Phillip, sniffing. "The estate is disappointing. A small cash account. Dues paid. The rooms. Nothing else."

Bellamy massaged his eyebrows. "The snake lawyer is lying. William Skelton was richer than some countries."

"Yes, sir," said Phillip. "I'm sure he would be lying . . . if we could find him."

The new Brendan sighed and examined the back of his hand. He could see the pale ghosts of the tattoos that had once been etched beneath his tan skin. Bones.

"Sir?" Phillip asked.

"What about the books? In Skelton's rooms? Weren't there books?"

"Thousands," said Phillip. "But every volume appears to be from a different library collection. All stolen or very, very late. Not one with any apparent value."

"Find the lawyer," Bellamy said. "And bring him to me."

The paneled door slammed behind Phillip, leaving

Bellamy Cook alone with his thoughts. Bellamy understood money. Wars cost. Winning wars cost more. But voiding the treaties was a dangerous game.

For the Sages, it had made a simple kind of sense, at least in the short term. They had been sitting on a volcano. Now they were sitting several miles from that volcano. The eruption would reach them, but not just yet. But for Phoenix?

The transmortals were like wolves. One at a time, with powers bound by the Order, they'd been easy to hunt. Easy to control and even kill. But now they were swarming into a pack, forming around the strongest of them, the one who had never bent beneath the chains of a treaty. The one Bellamy hadn't even been sure existed.

But Phoenix had wanted them unbound. Phoenix had wanted them to reengage with the nations of men. He had wanted turmoil. And when the time was right, Phoenix would crack his dark whip. Chaos and fear would birth new treaties—for the nations, for transmortals, but never again for the Order of Brendan.

Bellamy remembered the last time he'd looked into Phoenix's eyes, and felt that man's thoughts wandering around inside his own mind, the whispered threats he couldn't shake. Clenching his fists, he listened to his knuckles crack.

He needed those Smith children *now*, before the

transmortals got to them and any clues to Skelton's hoardings slipped out of reach.

At least the dragons were free and the Order was broken and limping. Phoenix had asked him to sow the wind, and he had. Soon they would reap the whirlwind.

twelve

NOVA

CYRUS SHIFTED on his boulder perch and shut his watering eyes against the cold wind. The lumpy stone under him was digging into his rear, but he didn't bother to move to another. His bare arms were bristling with goose bumps; he wrapped them tight around his knees.

Beneath him, the ocean growled at the base of a tall cliff, and a clatter of rolling rocks sucked out with every wave. It sounded like California. It smelled like California. The salt in the air and the cold and the crash and the clatter—it had been too long since he'd sat beside the sea.

The last time had been a long goodbye. The house had been sold; the red station wagon had been loaded. His sleeping mother had already been flown away. Dan had given him an hour on the cliff. He had spent it staring out at the island where his father had been shot, and down at the waves that had taken his body. Antigone had spent the same hour just fifty yards away, sitting on her own rock, where her brothers couldn't see her cry.

Cyrus opened his eyes again and looked down at

the cold, frothing waves. He had a familiar stone in his chest—a collapsing stone, a black hole growing smaller and smaller even as it grew heavier. His father was gone. His mother might never wake up again. And then this ache would be forever. He hated this feeling, and the fact that things he loved brought it on—the sea, the salt, the taste of old memories. The stone inside him slid down behind his ribs and into his gut. He could've thrown up. His ribs wanted to shake—a sob was bubbling up from that sinking stone. But if he let it come, he wasn't sure it would ever stop.

Cyrus Smith wiped his eyes and stared out at the small boat bobbing in the waves. He could see Nolan perched in the bow, watching the water. And then Rupert Greeves erupted through the surface, grabbed the side of the boat, heaved himself in, and peeled a black squid off his face. The water must have been frigid. He wasn't sure how Rupert could survive as many dives as he had already taken.

"Hey."

Cyrus swung around, suddenly grateful his eyes were dry. Diana Boone dropped onto the rock next to him and tossed him his jacket. She was wearing one of hers. Wool peeked up around her neck at the collar. Her hair was folded on top of her head. Freckles dotted her profile.

"Thanks," Cyrus said. He swung the jacket on.

Boxing monkey, black ship, three heads. He felt warmer immediately. "Leather really cuts the wind, doesn't it?"

"It does," said Diana. "But that's not cow leather. That's goatskin. Old school."

Cyrus studied Rupert. The big man was talking to Nolan. A moment later, he grabbed a new squid from a bucket and went back over the side.

"He brought squid," Cyrus said.

Diana laughed. "He ordered squid. And dragonflies. The Livingstones brought them. And a lot of other things, too. Apparently we're rallying here. I don't know for how long."

Cyrus looked down at his feet, tightly socked in spider silk. He wiggled his toes.

"That was really embarrassing back there."

Diana smiled. "Which part? You got pretty sick in the plane before Arachne knocked you out. Rupe was flying low and fast."

"Oh, gosh," Cyrus said. "I don't even remember that. I was thinking of the whole spider on the feet thing. In my defense, I was having a nightmare."

Diana was nervously popping her knuckles. "In your defense, I think anybody waking up with spiders all over their feet would have screamed." She glanced at him. "Maybe not as high as you did, but still . . ."

Cyrus groaned. The ache in his chest was dissipating.

"Where are we, by the way? As soon as I woke up, I got out of that little shed."

Diana didn't answer. She seemed lost, staring into the sky-racing clouds.

"Di?"

She jerked. "Sorry. The shed? That shed is our bunkhouse. We're on an island southeast of Nova Scotia."

Cyrus nodded, then asked, "What's going on? I mean, with you. Are you okay?"

Diana sighed. "I'm nervous," she said. "And not about all this. Oh, I know, the transmortals are going crazy and they've dropped the paper dragons and they want to kill you and Tigs and Rupe and Phoenix. And Phoenix is out there somewhere with the tooth doing psycho things to people, and the O of B is falling apart as fast as it possibly can, and we're on the run. But that's just adventure, I guess. Or something like it."

"So . . . what then?" Cyrus asked. Diana looked back out to sea. Nolan was boating toward the cliff.

"My parents," she finally said. "They're coming here. My mom and dad." She glanced at Cyrus. "My dad's intense. He was Avengel before Rupe, and the stuff he's done and seen . . . he never talked to me about it, but my older brothers did. I don't think I've seen my dad smile since I was a kid. Even Jeb shuts up around him. They usually keep to the wilds, but now Rupe says they're coming here, and I'm all eaten up with nerves."

Cyrus had no idea what to say. He didn't understand. Diana looked away.

"Silly, right? And then I feel horrible that I'm nervous. I do want to see them. I do. It's just nothing has ever impressed my dad. Nothing I've done has ever made him happy. You think I'm awful?"

Cyrus shook his head. But how excited would he be if he could see his father again? If he could see his mother smile and walk and laugh, if he could feel her arms around him? His eyes were hot just at the thought.

"Yes, I am," Diana said. "You know why I've always liked you and your sister? No parents. You were on your own. Like me. But it wasn't your fault. It *is* my fault. I've always been running away."

"Maybe stop," said Cyrus. "Running."

"Cy!"

Cyrus turned around. Antigone was picking her way toward the cliff edge between gray boulders and towering fir trees. The red-winged blackbird was gliding from branch to branch behind her. Cyrus smiled and clicked his tongue at the bird. She warbled back.

"How are the feet?" Antigone asked.

"Cold," said Cyrus. "Kinda numb. Silky."

Antigone burst out laughing. "I can't believe how much you screamed. Even after Arachne knocked you out again, though then it was more like you were gargling."

"Har, har," Cyrus said. "Like you would have done better."

"True. But the thing is, Rus-Rus"—Antigone slid onto the rock beside him, nearly knocking him off—"when I scream like a girl, at least I am, actually, a girl."

Diana laughed. Cyrus looked down at the water. The boat was gone.

"Any idea what we're doing here?" he asked.

"Rupe will tell us soon enough," Antigone said. She stood up again. "He'll beat us back in the boat. I was supposed to get you for dinner."

Cyrus lowered his silk-socked feet to the rough ground. Diana and Antigone were both in boots.

"Who's cooking?" Diana asked. "Not Jax or Dennis, I hope."

"Alan Livingstone," Antigone said. "And he's using the biggest pan I've ever seen."

Cyrus watched his feet as he walked. He could feel the rough edges of stone, but they were somehow softened.

He placed his foot on a sharp stick and tested it with his weight. Even in his canvas shoes, he would have felt a little pain. Instead, the point of the stick bent and snapped beneath him. And the weave was watertight, too. When he squelched across wet moss, the water beaded up on his feet and slid away. Inside, his feet were dry.

His spider socks might have looked like ballet shoes, but they were as tough as combat boots.

"Oh, that's a good smell," Diana said.

Cyrus looked up and sniffed. Eggs. Cheese. Sausage. Mushrooms. Maybe bacon. And he could hear the sizzling. Up ahead, between two broken-down bunkhouses, Dennis and Jax and Arachne were sitting on old logs, watching Big Alan Livingstone work a massive skillet over a fire. He looked back over his shoulder and grinned inside his blond beard. His left nostril had two little stitches where it met his cheek. His sons, George and Silas, were slicing onions and peppers and meat over the pan, while their father snow-plowed it all around with a long spatula.

Cyrus dropped onto a log and watched the big man work. Rupert had wanted the Sages to name Alan as the Brendan. It was hard to imagine the Brendan being this kind of guy, his nostril stitched on, cheerfully scrambling eggs for a bunch of kids. Of course, maybe that's why Rupert had wanted him. He was big and dangerous, but he was jolly.

"Mouths wanted!" Alan boomed. "Too much wealth in that pan for just the six of us!" He began to hum. "Chicken gifts and udder gold . . . Silas, grab the peri peri. In my bag. Left side."

Silas hurried away.

"You three, grab a log," Alan said. "Coming off hot, and hotter soon enough."

Rupert and Nolan came through the trees on the other

side of the campfire. Rupert was bare-chested and toweling off as he walked. Cyrus couldn't help staring at his scars. They were as stark as they had been in his dream.

"Will these eggs light my belly on fire?" Rupert asked, smiling.

"Only on the inside, Rupert Greeves," Alan said. "Just like your mama used to make."

"Cheers, mate," Rupert said, sitting down. "It's been too long." He looked at Cyrus. "How are your feet?"

"Good," said Cyrus. He smiled at Arachne. "Great, actually. Thanks. Sorry I lost it."

Arachne didn't smile back. "The Angel Skin will be much harder. You will have to be still."

Cyrus nodded, not knowing what she was talking about and not much caring to find out. Silas was dusting red powder all over the eggs while his father stirred it in. George was assembling a stack of wooden platters and forks.

When the platters were passed around, heavy with eggs and cheese and bacon shards and diced sausage, Cyrus dug in without another thought in his head. It was spicy but not scorching, and warmth spread through his limbs as he ate. Platters were reloaded until Alan's bathtub pan was empty of all but the shrapnel of the fried meal. Nolan sat on the ground beside it, picking out egg shards one at a time.

Rupert dropped his platter on the pine needles and slid down beside it, leaning his back against the log.

"Right," he said. "Cyrus, we let this settle, and then we dive."

Silas Livingstone was rubbing his scarred eyebrow. George was splayed out beside him. "Find what you were looking for?" Silas asked. His father shot him a look. "Mr. Greeves," Silas added quickly.

"Not yet," Rupert said, "I need a little time, and a few dives. We'll move again soon."

"I think we should lie low," Diana said. "And this is as good a place as any. Let the transmortals and Phoenix go at it. When the dust settles, we can fight the weakened survivor."

Rupert pulled a knife from his boot and peeled a long strip of bark off a stick.

"Miss Diana Boone, you give the same advice your father did. And it's good advice. He was born a trapper, and that means patience. But hanging back and waiting in ambush has its own risks. The dust might not settle how we'd like." He studied the stick in his hand. "What if the *Ordo* and Phoenix come to terms? Imagine Gilgamesh and Phoenix on the same side."

"Gil wouldn't do that," Arachne said. "He hates wizards and flesh changers." She hadn't eaten anything. Her spider bag was empty on her lap. Cyrus wondered how many of them were feasting in bushes all around him right now.

Nolan laughed and lobbed a pinecone into the low

fire. "You haven't known him long, have you? A wizard and a flesh changer is exactly what old Gilgamesh of Uruk is." He began to pick at a scratch on his forearm. Getting his nails in deep, he peeled the skin off like a wet sock. It reached his wrist, then he tugged it off his hand and his fingers, and was then holding a long, translucent glove of human skin. He let it float toward the fire. "Gil knows how to sling a curse."

"You stole from him," Arachne said. "He could have done worse."

Nolan cocked his head and sent her a glare.

"Ho, now," Alan said. "Old stories, old wounds, no need to claw them now. What Gil does, he does, but Rupe is right. If the *Ordo* can't stomp out Phoenix, they'll find a truce."

"Can I ask a question?" Antigone asked. "Something I've wondered."

Everyone looked at her.

"If there are teams, why are Nolan and Arachne on ours?" She hurried to explain. "I mean, I like you both. But I don't understand. You're transmortals. The O of B made a whole bunch of rules that all the other transmortals hated. Now they got rid of them, but you're still with us. Why? Just 'cause you're nice and they're not, or what?"

Nolan sat up slowly, smiling. Then he began to laugh.

Arachne scrunched up her face. "The others don't

understand, either," she said. Her eyes widened, flashing ice. "But some of them are quite nice."

"To you," Nolan mumbled.

"So . . . ," Cyrus said. "What's the answer?"

Arachne sighed. "We—neither of us—ever wanted the change. Maybe we would have, but we weren't given the choice. It just happened. It was done to us." She looked at Nolan. "Gilgamesh dove for the fruit of life at the bottom of the Persian Gulf. Nolan was the starving son of a fisherman who found him floating."

Nolan stirred the pine needles on the ground beside him. "I ate because I was hungry. Because I thought he was dead. Why would I let a dead man's fruit go to waste? When he woke, he couldn't kill me, though he tried. He gave me my curse."

Cyrus studied the pale boy from the Polygon. Nolan looked up at him, and his eyes were heavy and more worn than ever.

"And you," Antigone said to Arachne shyly. "There was a story we read in school about you. The book said you were in a weaving contest with Minerva, and when she couldn't beat you, she smashed your loom and turned you into a spider."

Arachne's face softened and her eyes drifted away, focusing on something only she could see. "Ovid lied in that poem. I never wanted that contest. Minerva was one of the undying, part demon, part witch. I had only the gift of sight and a little magic in my fingers. She wagered her life against mine and bound us with terrible spells. I had no choice but to weave. But she had cursed my loom—the frame split, and the threads could not hold my weave.

"Desperate for my life, I cast prayers into the sky, to the one who wove the world. And my prayers were heard. For the first time, spiders came to me. They were my loom and my silk, and as I wove, holy power flowed through me, a touch reserved for creatures outside this world. What I wove shimmered like a pond at dawn, and in it a sun rose and set, and men and women moved as if alive. I wove them voices of holiness to curse Minerva and her kind, and to sing of the beauty that once was in the world and that would come again like morning."

Arachne looked up. "That day, Minerva died. Now I never can. And from the moment the judges—kings and priests and wizards—looked on my tapestry, I was hunted. Men searched me out for charms, cloaks, strength, and healing, for beauty and power. For centuries I would hide, but they would always find me. When the Order bound me, I found protection. Often I have sheltered in Brendan's Estates."

She glanced at Nolan. "We two still feel like mortals, like death was stolen from us. We are like you, the dying. Not like Gil or the Vlads or Radu or Semiramis or even Ponce—those who fought against their own mortality."

George Livingstone adjusted his short blond bulk on the ground. "So . . . you want to die?"

Arachne nodded. Her ancient blue eyes were lightless and still. And then, slowly, a sun rose within them. She smiled at George. "Just not today. See, I am like every other mortal."

Nolan climbed to his feet, watching loose pine needles slide off his trousers. His face and body still belonged to a boy, but to Cyrus, he seemed as burdened as the oldest man. When he spoke, his voice was low. "There are things on the other side of death that we may never see. Thirsts we may never quench. Tastes these mouths cannot consume. But down here, under the sun, there is nothing new."

For a moment, the group was silent, listening to the wind rasp through needled trees. But with it, there came a distant drone.

Every head turned. A plane.

"The Boones are here," Rupert said.

Cyrus looked at Diana. She raised her eyebrows and exhaled. He smiled at her.

Rupert rose to his feet. "Cyrus, it's time to dive. Arachne, if you wouldn't mind starting on Antigone?"

Arachne nodded, stood, and whistled into the brush.

"What?" Antigone asked. "Start what?"

Cyrus laughed, following Rupert into the trees. "Whatever you do, Tigs, don't scream like a girl."

Walking through the trees, stride for stride with Rupert, Cyrus glanced at his Keeper. Nolan was trailing behind them.

"So," said Cyrus. "You didn't really answer the question back there." He ducked under a long branch straggling with bearded moss. "If we can't wait until the dust settles"—he hopped a rock—"and you don't want Phoenix and the *Ordo* to become allies"—he switched to Rupert's other side—"then what are we going to do?"

Rupert arched an eyebrow and scratched his jaw while he walked. They broke free of the trees and stood at the top of the gray sea-stained cliff. Rupert began descending on a narrow, winding goat path.

"Besides diving in freezing-cold water off an island somewhere near Nova Scotia!" Cyrus yelled after him. "That's the obvious first step."

"Sun Tzu!" Rupert yelled back over his shoulder. "*The Art of War!* I told you to read it a year ago."

"Well, yeah," Cyrus said, following. "And I even started, but the first couple pages weren't that interesting." He began feeling his way down the path, carefully dragging one hand on the cliff face.

Rupert laughed, and his voice echoed off the cliff walls around them. The boat was just visible below, sheltered in a little harbor of black water. "If you had read and understood the book, you might have some suggestions for me right now. As it is"—he glanced back up the path with a grin—"you're just baggage."

"Don't feel bad," Nolan said behind Cyrus. "Sun Tzu is a friend of Gil's. Extreme dirtbag."

Rupert slid to a stop on a tiny gravel beach beside the boat. Cyrus staggered out beside him.

"So I'm baggage," Cyrus said. "Fine. Now can you just answer the question?"

Rupert kicked off his boots and tugged off his shirt before wading into the frigid water in his trousers. With water lapping around his thighs, he grabbed the boat's edge and leaned in, pulling two squid buckets toward the side.

"We are smaller," said Rupert, and he nodded for Cyrus to follow him. "We are mobile, but not to a degree that provides any advantage. We must establish communication, supply lines, and concentration of attack—which is the great difficulty, given that we face two stronger forces on two separate fronts, and in the O of B and its new Brendan we have a point of soft treachery, or at least vulnerability, in our rear."

Cyrus's spider socks weren't going anywhere, but he dropped his leather jacket by Rupert's boots and pulled off his shirt. His skin immediately tightened in the cold. Rupert was waiting. Cyrus exhaled, bit his lip, and then felt his way into the water. His muscles knotted into rocks. His feet became lifeless dough. The water's bite was so sharp, Cyrus couldn't even feel the wetness of it. He felt only needles and knives.

With his shirt still on, Nolan waded after Cyrus, unaffected by the cold. Cyrus staggered slowly forward, chattering, and Rupert extended a squid bucket toward him.

"Our best hope is surprise," Rupert said. "And that is why we are here. This place and this moment are what Arachne prepared you for, and why I made you risk the water cube—though all too briefly. We are here to do what our enemies will fear but also least expect."

"What'sssstt?" Cyrus managed. The water was up to his hips. He dipped his hand in the bucket and felt a squid latch on.

Rupert smiled. Cyrus raised the squid to his face.

"Red means dead," said Rupert. Cyrus glanced at the beak he was already raising to his mouth. Three red speckles the size of pinpricks dotted the tip of the writhing squid's black beak. "You can't breathe hydrogen."

Cyrus puffed breath onto the dark creature and dropped it back in the bucket. "Jeeps," he said. "That was close. Why would you even bring those?"

"They switch genders. In any group, half are male and half female at any time. Always check the beak, even if you've taken off an animal and are putting the same one back on." Rupert pulled out a squid for himself and offered one to Nolan. Nolan shook his head. "Now tell me this, Cyrus Smith," Rupert said, sorting through the tentacles. "What is the one thing the transmortals would not expect the Avengel of Ashtown to do?"

Cyrus pulled out another squid and squinted at it. He wasn't sure.

"Open the Burials," said Nolan.

Rupert nodded. "The Burials. And what is the only Burial they themselves would fear to open? The Burial of the man who beheaded their fearful dragons."

"John Smith?" Cyrus said. "Seriously? The actual John Smith?" For a moment, he'd forgotten the cold.

Nolan shivered.

Rupert's face split into a wide grin. "The Captain. Do you have your Solomon Keys?"

Cyrus's free hand shot up to his neck. Two keys—one silver, one gold—safely invisible on his tiny snake. "Yeah," he said. "The Burial is right here?"

Rupert plucked three pairs of old goggles out of the boat, tossing one to Nolan and one to Cyrus. "I hope it's right here. I've already searched all but two other coves on this island." Rupert fit the squid onto his face, pulled on his goggles, grabbed a spotlight out of the boat, and began to wade into deeper water.

"Go on," Nolan said to Cyrus. His transmortal skin was as pale as ice. "I don't need one of those creatures. Don't need to breathe when it comes right down to it, and I prefer lung burn to squid face."

Cyrus checked the squid's beak for red dots, and then slid the thing over his face. The beak clicked inside his mouth, trying to nip his tongue, but he'd arranged it right. The tentacles latched tight around the back of his head. He tugged on his goggles, careful not to pinch any of the tentacles, and then slid out into the frigid water.

His ribs froze on contact. Inside them, his lungs tried to shrink. He was going to die of cold, he was sure.

Rupert dove all the way under the surface. The squid bubbled into Cyrus's mouth, but he couldn't make himself inhale. He could maybe last thirty seconds underwater at this temperature. A minute? He tucked and dove.

The squid spat more bubbles, and this time he caught them. Nolan, a pale ghost, came alongside him.

And then the bottom dropped away over a jagged stone shelf, and Cyrus dove straight down, and down, and down. Far below him, the bottom was glowing orange. Rupert's crisp silhouette swam in front of it.

The water was growing warmer.

Dan bumped up the driveway and killed his headlights. For a moment, he stared at the windows of the old house. It had been a couple of weeks since he'd been there, and he couldn't remember how he'd left the curtains. Or whether the screen door had been latched. It was swinging in the wind right now.

Why was he so nervous? The man on the phone had

said someone would come. And he'd known about Dan's heart. How? Rupert hadn't known. The nurses at Ashtown hadn't known. They'd tested it and everything else. Of course, they hadn't known about his "eyes," either.

Because he hadn't told them . . .

The moon was high and bright. If someone was inside, they would be able to see out, but Dan wasn't going to be able to see in. And there was stuff in there he wanted.

Daniel reached under his seat and pulled out a short baseball bat. Then he opened his door as quietly as he could and left it open behind him as he crept toward the house.

A light flicked on in the kitchen and Daniel froze, clenching and reclenching the handle of the bat. He waited a moment, and then he raced forward bent at the waist and ducked beneath the kitchen window. Even over the crash of the distant ocean, he could hear voices. Glass shattered.

Daniel slid up against the kitchen door. He had a decision to make. Run, hide, maybe never come back . . . or go inside and face whatever was waiting for him.

He'd abandoned this house before. He wasn't going to do it again. He slid his key into the lock, held his breath, and said a prayer. With a crash, he exploded inside with his bat raised.

John Horace Lawney VII choked on his toast. Someone tall and freckled looked up from where he was crouching on the floor. He had a short, thick rifle on his back, a large revolver on his hip, and a dustpan in his hand. He had been sweeping up the ruins of a coffee cup.

Horace thumped his chest and hacked up a lump of bread.

"Finally," he said, dabbing at the corners of his watering eyes. "Your dormitory was being watched, so we came here." He swallowed and smacked his lips. "Mr. Rupert Greeves requests your presence immediately."

Daniel lowered his bat. "I was just at my dorm. No one was there. What's going on?"

Horace and the kid with the dustpan exchanged a look. The kid jumped up, flicked off the kitchen lights, and hurried to the window, unslinging his rifle as he went. He peeked through the curtains.

"There's a van," he said. "Out on the cliff. No headlights." He turned to Dan. "You were followed."

Horace picked up an open jar of jam and a small hunk of bread and tucked them under his arm. He glanced at his pocket watch and sighed, then looked at Daniel over his half-moon glasses.

He nodded at the kitchen door. "Off we go, then."

⊰ thirteen ⊱

RIP

CYRUS SWAM DEEPER, trying to stay on Rupert's heels. The water wasn't just warm anymore; it was hot. He felt like he was scuba diving in a Jacuzzi. On one side, black cliffs descended out of sight; on the other, he could see nothing but blue. Beneath him, on what must have been the bottom, lava flickered orange and heat ripples warped the water. In places where the cold water of the open ocean collided with the heat, swirls appeared like straws, belching up heat and sucking down cold. Rupert had already pulled him away from two.

The squid belched air, but not much. Cyrus was worried for it. It might actually cook right on his face. Of course, he might cook, too.

Rupert paused, drifting on rising heat, and looked back at Cyrus. Tentacles glistened across his jaw and ears, and the black squid on his face wobbled like the short trunk snout of a California elephant seal. That, plus the goggles, made him look more than a little alien. Rupert pointed into a large dark cave in the cliff, and

Cyrus swam forward. As he entered, his body jerked with a sudden shock—the water in the cave was cold. Rupert and Nolan slid in after him. Rupert pointed at his own squid, and then floated back against the wall. A rest stop? Apparently Rupert didn't want his squid cooked, either.

After a moment, Cyrus's mouth almost exploded with a blast of cold, bubbling air. He let most of it stream out of his nose, and then he filled his lungs. Rupert was doing the same. Nolan grimaced, still holding his breath. He looked like he was in pain.

Rupert held up one finger. Cyrus braced himself, and the stiff beak clicked against his tongue. Two fingers. Three. Rupert kicked out of the hole and Cyrus followed. Heat flashed around him. Nolan passed him quickly, his skin peeling and trailing as he went.

Down and down into the rippling heat, Rupert dove beside the black cliff. Cyrus wanted to scream, to close his eyes and float away. To cook and be done. And then Rupert turned into a narrow side tunnel. Nolan and Cyrus followed.

Darkness. And cold. The light faded as the temperature dropped. And then Rupert's spotlight flashed on and flickered back over Nolan's body and into Cyrus's face. They were in a cavern the size of a large living room, and it was lined with mussels.

Rupert floated in the center, running his spotlight around the cavern. There was one smooth stone on the otherwise jagged mussel wall. Cyrus swam toward it, blinking.

It was shaped like a headstone and skimmed with olive sea silt, though not one barnacle or mussel had adhered to its face. The squid on Cyrus's face bubbled as he ran his hand up and down the stone. Scum swirled into the water, leaving behind a long inscription. With Rupert spotting the light over his shoulder, Cyrus traced the words with his fingertips. At the top, he immediately recognized the Tri-Dracul crest of the Smiths.

RIP

CAPTAIN JOHN SMITH
SOMETIME GOVERNOUR OF VIRGINIA
BLOOD AVENGER OF THE ORDER OF BRENDAN
WHO BURIED HIS BODIE THE 21ST OF JUNE 1631
HERE LYES ONE CONQUERED,
THAT HATH CONQUERED KINGS,
AND DID DIVIDE FROM DRACULS THREE
THEIR HEADS AND LIVES IN CHIVALRY.
BUT WHAT AVILS HIS CONQUESTS, NOW HE LYES
INTERR'D IN EARTH,
A PREY TO WORMS AND FLYES?
O MAY HIS SOUL IN SWEET ELYSIUM SLEEP,
UNTIL THE KEEPER THAT ALL SOULS DOTH KEEP,
RETURN TO JUDGEMENT, AND AFTER THENCE,
WITH ANGELS MAKE HIS RECOMPENSE.
WAKE HIM NOT, LEST HE WAKE.

Cyrus looked at Rupert with wide eyes. Rupert nodded and tapped at his throat, where Cyrus kept Patricia and her keys. Nolan floated forward and pointed to the *him* in *Wake him not.* Cyrus blasted bubbles out of his nose, and then focused on the spot. The *i* was actually a keyhole.

His throat tightened. The squid shifted a little, regripping his face and curling a tentacle around his ear. Cyrus had entered a Burial before, and it hadn't been pleasant. He didn't see how being related to the occupant would make it any nicer.

But Rupert knew what he was doing. Hopefully. Cyrus reached up and slid Patricia off his neck. The keys, suddenly visible, dropped through the water into his hand, and silver Patricia coiled around his wrist, swallowed her tail, and disappeared. In the water, the strange Solomon Keys had taken their natural shape, which he had first seen in the Polygon when he'd plunged them into the cold showers. The gold key was long and heavy, with a triangle at its head, a circle in the middle, and a square at the foot. It was clearly too big for the hole. Cyrus fingered the smaller silver one—simple, slender, smooth, and sharp, like a miniature corkscrewing scimitar. Trying not to think about what he was doing, he slid it into the hole, and he turned it.

Silence. And then grinding as the inscribed slab fell slowly forward through the water. Cyrus jerked out the key and kicked away. The cave echoed like the inside of a drum when the slab hit the bottom, but Cyrus didn't notice. He was staring at the hole in the stone wall, a square tunnel. Something was floating out of it. Seaweed? It was uncurling out of the darkness, slowly drifting through the water and groping toward them. Nolan bubbled and retreated.

A tangle floated in front of Cyrus. He touched it, rubbing it between his fingers. It was hair. Four hundred years' worth of hair.

Rupert drew a knife and kicked toward the hole.

Dixie Mist pressed her ear against the dusty wall, listening as voices approached. The wall smelled like barn and tobacco. She shifted and tried her other ear.

She'd popped awake at 4:29 a.m. and gotten right to work. The rope knots had finally ground their way off her thin wrists and over her hands; she'd only lost a little skin. After that, the ankles had been easy. Now she was completely free of the thick post the men had lashed her to . . . but she was still stuck in this tiny room.

The voices were muffled, but she recognized the musical tone that belonged to One Hand. She had been stored a long way from the front door and the refinished part of the factory. While she'd worked on the knots in the darkness, the only sounds had been scratching rats, her own strained breathing, and the pylons creaking in the river beneath her. But now the men were close. Doors were rattling open on rusty sliders. How many prisoners were there? Were the men talking to her father? If they were, he wasn't talking back. She would recognize his voice, even through walls.

She ran her hands along the rough wood. She knew the factory well, but this was a part her father had placed firmly off-limits. At this end of the building, the floors were rotten. The previous owner had even lost a worker.

The floors.

Dixie dropped to her knees and began to crawl away from the wall, feeling the floor, hoping to find some weakness. Planks sighed and old nails yawned, but the boards were strong and rot-free. She reached the far wall and sighed.

"Who's there?" The whisper was right in front of her, through a crack in the planks. "You're too big to be a rat. Are you a rat?"

Dixie stared at the wall, but the darkness was too thick for human eyes.

"Who are you?" she whispered.

"I asked you first."

A boy's voice. She held her breath for a moment, thinking.

"Dixie," she said.

"I'm Oliver," said the boy. "You don't sound tied up."

"I'm not," Dixie said. "I was, but not anymore."

"I'm really tied up," Oliver whispered. "They didn't even lock my door. Do you have a window?"

"No." Dixie wished she did. She would already be out.

"Of course not," Oliver said. "Your room is farther in. I have a window." He paused. "There's a moon."

"You can see?"

"Not well. I can't move my head much. I'm stuck looking up."

Dixie stood. He had a window, and his door was unlocked. She only had to get through one wall. She ran her hands across the planks until she found a knothole in the pine. She wormed her fingers through and then tugged. The board barely bent at all. The wood was tough.

"There's a trapdoor in the ceiling," Oliver said. "By a giant lightbulb. Do you have a giant lightbulb?"

A trapdoor . . .

Outside, down the hall, a heavy sliding door slammed. One Hand was shouting at someone. Dixie held her breath and listened.

"They're both dead!" One Hand bellowed. "Is that what you wanted? I want one dead, one alive. Do you understand?" One Hand's last words sounded odd, shifting into an animal-like roar. Wood smashed.

Whoever was out there, Dixie knew they'd never hear her over the noise. She could be as loud as she wanted.

Slapping at the walls, she raced around the dark room, feeling for holds. If she could find a way to climb . . .

A metal light switch dug into her arm. She flipped it on.

A giant lightbulb sputtered to life in the ceiling above her. She blinked and looked around. Just two feet farther down the wall, nailed flush up against it, there was a plank barn ladder. A small trapdoor was set in the ceiling above it.

More wood was smashing outside. Someone, some creature, was snarling. Dixie flipped the light back off and scaled the ladder. Her head thumped against the trap; she scrambled through it and up into the ceiling.

Above the ceiling was something like a hayloft, maybe fifty yards square. Flakes of ancient tobacco cracked beneath her, and moonlight filtered through a hundred holes above her. Dixie crawled quickly toward the boy's ceiling. Off to her left, wood exploded up and she yelped, jerking away in surprise. Pieces of the ceiling scattered through the rafters. Yellow electric light blazed up through the hole.

She had to hurry. Sweeping the floor with her hands, she found the boy's trapdoor, tugged it open, and looked down into a room painted with moonlight that flowed through a small window. She didn't bother with the ladder this time; the ceiling wasn't that high. Reaching through the opening in the ceiling, she found the thick wire that ran to the big lightbulb. Grabbing on to it, she swung down into the room and then dropped.

A floorboard snapped beneath her right foot, which punched through into air. Pulling her leg back through, she staggered forward and bumped into a table.

"Careful," the boy whispered. His arms and legs were strapped with leather to a heavy wooden chair, and the chair was lying on its back, strapped onto a table. His hair was brown and long, straggling and uncut. His skin was pale, even where it was freckled.

"Try the window," Oliver said, twisting his head toward the moonlight. "There's no point in braving the halls when he's like this."

"Who? One Hand?" Dixie raced over to the window. It was small, four little panes, but it had a crank handle and hinges. She twisted hard and pushed on the wooden frame. The hinges snapped and the window dropped, spinning, fifty feet down into the moving river. She heard the glass shatter on the surface.

She ran back to the boy and got to work on the leather straps that held him in the chair.

"The window's not going to work," she said.

"One Hand," the boy said quietly. "He's my uncle. Great-uncle, actually. I guess he does just have one hand, thanks to the Smiths."

Dixie freed the boy's arms and moved down to his legs.

"It's not going well," Oliver said. "He said it would have happened already."

"What would happen?" Dixie asked. The straps on his legs were sticking.

"He would raise the dead."

The boy might be delirious, but he was free. Dixie staggered back, breathing hard, as he swung his legs off the chair and sat up slowly.

"Why?" Dixie asked. "Why would anyone want to do that?"

Oliver seemed dizzy, perched on the edge of the table. His eyes were shaded with dark rings, and his cheeks were sucked tight against his teeth. He wasn't healthy, but he didn't look mean. Or dangerous. "He's making new people from old ones," Oliver said. He looked up. "But they always die. He's waiting to change me until that's fixed. I'm tired of waiting." He closed his eyes and opened them again slowly. "You really should leave."

"You're coming with me," Dixie said, pulling him off the table. The boy obviously needed a hospital. He was a lot taller than she was—long arms, long legs, wide shoulders, but all bone and no muscle. The way he wobbled on his feet, she wondered how long it had been since he'd walked.

She moved toward the door. "Help me find my father. Then we'll leave."

The door wasn't locked. The hallway outside was long and very dimly lit. One Hand was gone now. The factory was silent.

Dixie looked back at the boy. "I'm in charge," she said. The boy looked surprised, but he nodded. She grabbed his hand and stepped out into the hallway.

"Careful," the boy whispered. "He's nuts right now. He took his coat off."

"One Hand?" Dixie asked.

"People call him Phoenix," Oliver whispered, "but not when he's like this. Right now, he's Mr. Ashes. His real name is Edwin."

Dixie led the boy past three open sliding doors. Then they came to one that had a chain and padlock around the handle.

She put her ear against it. Nothing. She cupped her hands against it and whispered as loud as she dared: "Alfred Mist!" She waited. "Daddy?"

Nothing.

"He wants my body," Oliver said. "I'm a Laughlin, too, and the same blood will help him switch. Every Laughlin has died but me. He's old. He needs a young body. . . ." Oliver held up two fingers and grinned. "With two hands."

"Quiet," Dixie said. The boy looked pale, almost ready to pass out. And he was babbling.

"Right," said Oliver. "Sorry."

The hallway echoed suddenly with the sound of more splintering wood and shouting.

"Oop," said the boy. "Trouble." Then he sat down.

"No!" Dixie grabbed his hands, but he was heavy for a skeleton. Still, she wasn't going to leave anyone here, not even a crazy boy. "I'm in charge, remember?"

The boy nodded like he'd forgotten, then stood up. Dixie gripped his wrist and hustled him down the hall. At the end, the hallway opened into what had once been a big rolling room, where her father had said the slave women and then the free women who were treated like slaves had rolled the cigars.

There were lights there. And voices. Dixie pushed Oliver into a nearby dark room and told him to wait quietly. Then she crept down the dim hallway. Nearing the end, she pressed herself against the wall and slid on until she could see into the room.

The bright old rolling room wasn't recognizable. Against the far wall, metal boxes the size of coffins were stacked like bricks, all the way to the ceiling. But every box had a long glass door in its side, frosted over with frozen condensation. And they were humming with electricity. Not just boxes—freezers. And Dixie could see the shapes of bodies behind the glass. Cords were everywhere, mostly running up into the ceiling. In front of the freezers, there was a table covered with strange tools. Where she could see the side walls, the wooden planks were battered and smashed. She couldn't see it, but she knew that, off to her right, there was a big loading door that overlooked the river. Front and center, in a small clear glass pool not much bigger than the one Dixie had played in with a garden hose when she was little, there were two bodies lying beside each other under shallow water. They both had pale skin. One was covered with bone tattoos.

Dixie held her breath, clinging even tighter to the shadows. Beside the pool was the girl with the rope hair. She was on her face with her knees tucked up under her chest and her arms folded in. Her hair was wound tight around her whole body, hiding her face, shielding her ribs, her neck, her sides. She looked like a turtle, or a rolled-up armadillo.

An ape-shaped man hobbled out from behind the wall of freezers. His hair was white and ragged. His shoulders were broad, his eyes were pure black, and he leaned one huge fist on the floor as he went. The monster's other hand was missing. Dixie blinked in surprise. Somehow, this was the same man. Snarling, he smacked the long-haired girl with his arm stump. She tumbled across the floor and stopped, not fifteen feet from Dixie.

One Hand followed slowly. He seemed tired, exhausted in his anger. He paused at the pool and studied the bodies. Then, leaning on his stump, he reached into the water and pulled out his silver-handled cane. A black tooth like a shark's stuck out of the top like an arrowhead. Water dripped off of it.

Curling his lips, One Hand looked at the rope-haired girl. He hobbled forward, raising the cane like a spear.

"Boss! Wait!" A tattooed man hurried into view. He was holding One Hand's dirty lab coat. "It took us forever to find the oracle. She's here. We'll get her to talk." He nodded at the freezer. "We've got plenty of bodies. We can keep trying. But if you kill her . . ."

One Hand wheeled around, staring at his coat. The man held it out. "Put it back on, boss. You'll figure this out."

"I hate the coat," One Hand snarled. His voice was thick and slow.

"I know, boss, but you need it. Just for a little while. Till you get this figured. It will help. Please, boss."

Oliver stepped into the hallway mouth beside Dixie.

"He won't get it figured," Oliver called into the room. "Not ever. Not in time. He's crazy. And he only has one hand. Ha!"

In a flash, Dixie snatched Oliver by the hand and dragged him into the room toward the old loading door. One Hand leapt forward with his cane raised. The man with the tattoos drew a long knife.

And then the girl with the rope hair was on One Hand's back, her coils lashed around his neck. A moment later, the ape had thrown her across the room, but a moment was all Dixie needed. She slammed into the big wooden door, her hands gripped old, cold iron, and she jerked with all the strength she had. The big sliding door hopped open on freshly oiled rails. Ducking under a tattooed arm, she grabbed Oliver by the front of his shirt and tumbled them both out into the air above the river.

While Oliver screamed, Dixie twisted and pointed her feet down at the water's glossy back, and at two surprised tattooed men sitting in a boat below.

fourteen

YESTERHAIR

CYRUS GROANED and tried to sink into his canvas cot. He never wanted to see hair again. The world could go bald as far as he was concerned. His skin was still burning from swimming through lava water, and he had suction puckers on his cheeks and ears and the back of his neck. Antigone said it looked like he'd been making out with a squid, which, when he thought about it, was exactly what he'd been doing. For hours. The taste in his mouth was worse than the marks on his face.

Just last night, he'd been swimming through an endless cloud of human hair with a squid on his face, in a tomb tunnel lined with mussel and barnacle razors, and walls that closed in and in and in until there was barely room for Rupert's spotlight. Whatever charm had kept the shellfish from growing on the headstone slab, it hadn't been nearly as effective in the tunnel behind it. But even after the mussels and hair had closed the tunnel off, Rupert had kept hacking through it for another hour before they'd retreated for the day. And that last hour had truly been the most wretched hour of the year.

Cyrus had discovered a phobia he'd never even thought to have—the fear of being trapped in a tiny underwater hole, tangled up in ancient hair and breathing squid burps while being pinched by mussels and kicked in the head by a big man who was smashing shellfish with a knife and filling the water with seafood gore. And it hadn't helped that Nolan's skin had been floating around, too.

Cyrus's palms were raw from tearing out mussels, and his knuckles looked like he'd been punching rocks. He wanted to be asleep, but Alan Livingstone's voice was booming out by the morning campfire.

He shifted uncomfortably on the narrow cot. Antigone was on the cot beside him. Her black hair was loose, smeared all over her pillow like it wanted to grow for four hundred years and fill an entire stinking underwater cave. He should shave it off now.

Antigone rustled an arm out from under her blanket. "Never want to see another spider again," she mumbled into her pillow.

Cyrus stared at his sister's arm. Antigone had spent her evening being woven into a web shirt—Angel Skin—by Arachne's army. A sleeve ran all the way down to her wrist and was snug to her skin. The pale weave was so invisibly tight and the surface so smooth, the shirt seemed more like liquid than something woven. It wasn't exactly white, and it wasn't silver—at least not in a metallic way. To Cyrus's eyes, it looked like liquid pearl.

Cyrus wiggled his toes inside his magic socks. They'd held up perfectly against the sharp shells. And now his sister had a whole shirt of the stuff—but a much tougher version, according to Arachne.

Antigone moaned. "Seriously, Cy. All spiders, from now on, dead on sight."

Cyrus stretched out his hand quietly and brushed his sister's neck with the tip of one finger. She twisted and slapped at Cyrus's finger. His cot tipped and he fell onto the floor, laughing. Antigone took a swing at him with her pillow.

Rupert Greeves ducked through the doorway and paused, eyebrows up.

"My vile brother," Antigone said, pillow raised, "seems to think he's funny."

"I am funny," Cyrus said. And he kicked over Antigone's cot, dumping her against the wall.

Rupert laughed. "I'll let someone else sort this out."

He stepped aside as Dan ducked into the room.

Cyrus jumped to his feet, but Antigone was a step ahead of him, flinging her arms around her older brother's neck. Dan squeezed her with one hand and slapped Cyrus's shoulder with the other. The blackbird swooped in over Dan's shoulder and circled around the low ceiling.

"Cy, man, you're tall," Dan said. He clasped Cyrus's hand as Antigone stepped back. "It hasn't even been that long. Tigs, your hair's longer. I like it."

Dan's eyes narrowed, focusing on Cyrus's cheeks. "What happened to your face? You fight with a dart gun or an octopus?"

Cyrus laughed. "Something like that. How'd you get here?"

Rupert kicked around a cot, and he and Dan sat down. The bird settled on Antigone's shoulder as Horace stepped into the room. He smiled at Cyrus and Antigone with tight lips and adjusted his glasses.

Dan's eyes were on the bird. "Horace and Jeb Boone came to get me. Just in time, too. I don't really understand who was after me, but we flew all night to get here. How have you two been? We haven't talked since Cyrus started training for some kind of race."

Horace cleared his throat and said, "Family is, of course, wonderful. Three cheers for family, et cetera. At another time, we could even peruse old photo albums and speak of cousins; unfortunately, we really do have urgent business to attend to."

Antigone scowled at the lawyer, but Rupert nodded. "He's right. Jeb had to take a fairly direct course to get here, and he thinks someone might have marked his plane at the first refueling." He looked at Cyrus. "Sorry, Cy, but your Angel Skin is going to have to wait. I need you down in the cave with me. We don't have much time."

Alan Livingstone filled the door with his shadow, his thick arms resting on the lintel. "Rupe . . ."

Rupert nodded back at him. "Everyone else get loaded and ready to go. Cyrus, come with me."

"Wait," Dan said, standing back up. "Rupert, there's something I wanted to tell you. It's strange, I know, but I had this . . . dream." Hesitating, he looked at his little brother. "Cyrus was in a grave. And then I saw a man with a red circle dragon on his chest. Tall. Short black hair. Looked like a statue. He said something, but I didn't understand."

Cyrus stared at his brother in surprise. Rupert was staring, too.

"He said, 'Speak, snake,' in Latin," Cyrus said. "But that was in *my* dream."

It was Dan's turn to be surprised. "In the grave, there was a girl with the longest hair I've ever seen, and she was writing on leaves with fire, and they . . ." Suddenly, Dan's pupils shrank to nothing. His eyes twitched and faded to blue, and he wobbled on his feet. Rupert caught him before he fell.

"One comes," Dan whispered, "on the wing of abominations, and there shall be no end to war. He shall be called the Desolation, and where he casts his shadow, even dragons shrink in fear."

Dan's eyes darkened again, and he looked around the silent room and sighed. "There's something I should tell you," he said quietly. "Something I should have told you a long time ago, back when it started."

Cyrus waded out into the cold water behind Rupert Greeves. He had his goggles on his forehead and a squid in his hand, waiting till the last possible moment to put it on his face. The laughter of the morning was gone—visions were one thing, but his brother's heart had actually stopped?

Rupert had grown angry, but not at Dan—his tenderness to Dan had made Antigone sob. But when he'd been walking through the trees, silent, with his eyes on the sky and the ground and the sea, Cyrus had known he was following a man ready to kill.

Rupert was up to his waist. The spotlight hung over his dark bare shoulder, and two long knives were tucked into a belt at the small of his back. He raised his squid.

"Rupe!" Cyrus yelled at his Keeper, hurrying to catch up. "Wait!"

Rupert paused, holding his squid under the water. When Cyrus reached him, the frigid sea had tightened his bare stomach so much, he could barely breathe.

"The man in the dream . . . ," Cyrus said.

"Radu Bey," said Rupert. "The last Dracul."

Cyrus nodded. "And Phoenix. I know we have to fight, but what do we do about Dan's heart?"

The cold didn't seem to affect Rupert, but the question did. He looked at the gray sky, bulking up with clouds. His voice was quiet.

"Dan's heart does not change the battlefield. It changes the stakes. It reminds us of all that we—and those we love—stand to lose in this storm. It gives us anger and grief. It deepens our resolve." He looked at Cyrus. "Do you know the story of David and the Philistine?"

Cyrus exhaled, managing to keep his jaw from chattering. "You mean Goliath? David used a sling and hit him with a rock."

Rupert nodded. "Soon, Cyrus, we will face giants." He looked Cyrus in the eye. "I cannot be David. But perhaps, if almighty grace permits, I can be the stone. I am here, tossed by the river, rounded and smoothed by hardship. I am ready to be placed in a sling and thrown."

Cyrus swallowed hard.

"You and I are here together, Cyrus Smith." Rupert studied him. "When your father and I were young, we were just like you are now—hungry for the physical tests, never reading what we were told. I am proud to be your Keeper." He gripped Cyrus by the shoulder with thick iron fingers. "Your father is proud of you, Cyrus, proud of his blood and bone. Of that I am sure, as sure as I am of anything in this world." He grinned. "Sun Tzu will come in time, little bruv." He turned back out toward the sea. "Before we freeze, yeah?"

Rupert raised his dripping squid and pulled down his goggles. Cyrus did the same. He'd forgotten the cold. He'd forgotten his worry. He didn't even notice the slimy beak taste or the pinch of the suction cups on his already raw skin. Together, he and his Keeper dove.

This time, now that he knew where he was going, the dive didn't feel so long. They ducked into the cool hole to let the squid rest from the heat, and then pushed on into the cave. The floor was covered with mussel shells torn out the night before and swirls of hair they had hacked away.

Rupert handed one of his long knives to Cyrus, and then led the way into the narrow tomb tunnel.

For an hour or more, Cyrus hung behind Rupert, collecting mussels that the big man pushed back between his legs and kicking them back down the tunnel toward the cave. The hacked-off hair had to be shuttled all the way back.

Finally, Rupert back swam out of the tunnel, handed off the spotlight, and gestured for Cyrus to lead.

Cyrus adjusted his squid mask and bubbled a sigh out his nose. Then he swam into the dark, barnacled mouth. Inside, there was only room for small kicks. With the spotlight in front of him, he used the long knife in his other hand to claw the bottom and pull himself forward through the scattered mussel carnage.

Finally, he reached the blocked end of the tunnel. There were shells beneath him, shells on every side, and shells in front of him—a living barricade, with nesting brown hair creeping out through every crack. The hair was like a guide. Dig toward the hair, and he would know he wasn't drifting off course.

Cyrus set the spotlight on the floor and immediately got to work with the knife, careful to nurse on his squid's sporadic bubbling, and just as careful not to exhale through his mouth during the exertion.

These mussels were big and brittle, and many of them were dead, their shells empty and hanging open. He made it a foot, and then two, letting the rubble sink before shoving it back to Rupert with his feet. He nicked his knuckles and thumped his head, and with every mussel that fell, more hair floated free, ghosting in front of his face.

And then he reached the end. Not the end of the tunnel, but the end of the shellfish. He tugged a whole block free and sent it slowly rolling behind him. It was like a line had been drawn in the tunnel that the creatures had refused to cross.

Cyrus swallowed hard and picked up his spotlight. Darkness. And hair. Swamping, curling, floating centuries of hair.

He held his knife and the spotlight in front of him and flutter-kicked forward. He burrowed through the hair, and it dragged across his skin like fine seaweed, tickling his arms and his face, sending shivers down his back. The walls of the tunnel were tight, and he felt like he was swimming through more hair than water. And then the tunnel ended and he floated out into a dark chamber. In the wider space, the hair billowed like smoke. Cyrus clawed his way through it, shoving it aside as he drifted up, swinging the spotlight all around.

The chamber was maybe twenty feet across, and the ceiling rose into a dark stone vault at least fifteen feet high. The hair was thicker below Cyrus and around his legs. By the entrance, Rupert was gathering armfuls of it in a dense wad, creating a few clearer patches of water. Cyrus kicked further up, and then studied the room below him, tracing every visible corner with the spotlight.

Below him, in the eye of the slow storm of hair, was the body of a man, floating just above a stone table. His face was calm but creased with scars where it wasn't hidden by his beard. His limbs were chained to cannonballs, and the heavy chains kept him floating only inches above the slab. He wore a breastplate that had tarnished black, and a long blue coat with blackened metal buttons. Tall boots had been removed and tucked beneath his floating legs. Long corkscrewing fingernails dangled from his hands, bent against the floor, and ran up the walls. More nails twisted and tangled up from his toes.

Cyrus focused on the man's face. It was like looking at an uncle, or a cousin to his father that he had never known. It could even be his father, if his father had lived to see another decade. The man had his father's brow, a slightly larger version of his father's nose. The same shoulders.

Leaving a floating hill of hair behind, Rupert swam up beside Cyrus. After a moment, he nudged Cyrus, and the two of them descended.

Cyrus floated directly above his sleeping ancestor, face to face with him. Rupert pointed at Cyrus's knife, and then gathered the man's beard together with both hands, pinching it tight like a rope four inches below the jaw. Cyrus set the spotlight on the Captain's chest, then sawed through the coarse hair in a straight line just above Rupert's hands. When the knife broke through, Rupert began to wind the beard hair around his forearm like a garden hose and swam toward a corner, dragging and collecting hair as he went.

Cyrus gathered up the man's hair at his scalp. He hacked one thick fistful, and then another as Rupert wound away the first. Six fistfuls and he was done. A minute or two later, and Rupert had it all crudely mounded in a corner and pinned beneath stones.

Rupert pointed Cyrus toward the fingernails, while

he went to the toes. The nails were soft in the water, and his knife slid through them easily just above each fingertip. One at a time, ten-foot-long corkscrew nails fell from the sleeper's hands and feet and sank to the bottom.

Captain John Smith drifted quietly above his stone bed, free of his hair but still in his chains. Beneath him, on the bed, Cyrus saw a long silver saber—naked, but untarnished and unrusted.

Rupert gestured at Cyrus's neck, and then at the cannonballs that secured the Captain's chains. Cyrus handed the spotlight to Rupert and slid Patricia off his neck, catching the keys as they sank. Then he moved to the cannonball and chain that held the Captain's right hand. Like the sword, the metal of the chain wasn't rusted or even badly tarnished, but he couldn't find a keyhole on the wrist manacle. He traced the chain down to the cannonball on the floor, and then he froze.

It wasn't a cannonball. It was a head. Black, metallic to the touch, and bearded. Engraved in the forehead, there was a name:

VLAD II

Beneath the name, there was a keyhole. Cyrus ran his hands around the head. There were two little hinges in the iron hair on the back. He looked up. Rupert was staring at the ball chained to the Captain's right ankle.

Cyrus floated over to see. It was another head, but this one was beardless.

VLAD IV

Cyrus swam over the top of the table, already knowing what he would find. The Captain's left arm was anchored by a third head, this one with a long, droopy mustache.

VLAD III
TEPES

The left leg was chained not to a head but to a black iron block. The block was labeled:

RADU BEY

Cyrus looked at Rupert and held up his keys. Should he open them?

Rupert was kicking from iron head to iron head to iron head, and then back to the plain block. He appeared to be thinking, and Cyrus could understand why. There was something dangerous here, something truly unnerving about the idea of unlocking the heads—even more than the idea of Cyrus's undead ancestor floating in this cavern for centuries.

Cyrus looked at the unrusted metals, at the unrotten clothes and the man's unrotten flesh, as he waited for his Keeper's decision. Finally, Rupert nodded at Cyrus.

Cyrus chose his little silver key and started with the black block on the left leg. It was the least unnerving of the four. He fingered the keyhole beneath the name.

And then the water quivered with sound waves. The chamber walls shook, and rocks dribbled down from the ceiling.

The walls shook again, and Cyrus watched, horrified, as Rupert bubbled in surprise and the squid unlatched from his face. Rupert snatched the gliding squid, peered through the tentacles at the beak, and then gargled frustration.

"Do it!" Rupert bellowed, geysering bubbles. He kicked toward the tunnel, gliding through the water in a race to get to the surface before he ran out of air. A moment later, he was gone.

Cyrus couldn't move. How far away was the surface? Could Rupert make it? What had just happened? An earthquake?

Cyrus looked at the body of his ancestor, and then back at the tunnel mouth. He was supposed to do this. It was up to him. Cyrus slid the silver key into the hole in the iron block and waited for a moment.

The walls didn't shake. The water didn't quiver.

Cyrus turned the key, and the block fell open. A

small gold ring that had been hidden inside the block floated to the floor. The heavy chain links connecting the block and the Captain's ankle clacked open one by one, settling slowly into a pile.

Beside Cyrus's head, the Captain's toes splayed.

Antigone raced toward the cliff, jumping logs and kicking through bushes, her bag bouncing on her back. The Boones and the Livingstones and Jax and Dennis and Nolan and Dan were in the planes, but she wasn't leaving. Not without Cyrus.

"Tigs!"

She looked back. Dan was chasing her. Behind him, the forest was burning.

"We have to get Cyrus!" she yelled.

"I know!" Dan yelled. He was gaining fast. She'd never seen him run like this. "I'll get him! Where were they diving?"

Two planes roared overhead. Four shapes tumbled out of their bellies, but they weren't bombs this time. They had glider wings, but Antigone could see human legs dangling beneath them. Two were heading toward the harbor where the planes were anchored. The other two were coming in her direction. She heard gunfire, and then spiraling white balls of fire dropped from the gliders like brimstone. She'd seen fire like that before—these were Phoenix's men.

One of the balls was growing larger, swirling toward them like a falling sun.

"Dan!" Too late. The fireball splintered in the treetops and exploded. Antigone staggered as searing heat, burning branches, and shattered timbers fell all around them. Dan was on the ground. Antigone turned back, virtually blind from the afterimage and deaf from the explosion.

Something heavy clamped onto the back of her neck and spun her around. She was looking at a hairy chest, and then at the snarling face and fiery cow-size eyes of Gilgamesh of Uruk.

Gil laughed, his breath hot and rotten, and then another fireball crackled past. Gil looked to the sky. Something had caught his attention. Throwing Antigone to the ground, he unslung a heavy horn bow from his woolen shoulder.

She blinked, struggling for breath. There were other shapes, too. Tall shapes all around her.

Gil drew the thickest arrow Antigone had ever seen and nocked it. He drew the string back to his thick snake lips and raised his bow to the sky. She didn't understand the words he murmured, but she saw the crackle of light that danced around the arrow point and heard the hum that buzzed along the waiting string.

Antigone followed Gil's aim. One of the gliders was swinging around to attack.

Gilgamesh let fly.

He'd already lowered the bow and turned back, laughing, before the tumble of wings and flame and legs fell from the sky. He drew a second arrow, eyeing Antigone.

"Little Smithling!" he boomed. "Your life is forfeit to the dragons, not to that bastard Phoenix!"

Gil's companions came forward, lifted Antigone off the ground, and flung her high into the air. Gil raised his bow.

The arrow struck like lightning, too fast for pain, too fast for sight. It slammed into her chest just above her heart and threw her against a tree trunk. She should have hung there, pierced and dying on a tree, a cursed Smith on a spit. Instead, she fell, tumbling through branches, and then bounced on the earth. The arrow shaft broke beneath her.

She couldn't breathe, and her mouth was pooling with blood. She could see it dribbling on the moss. She spat and coughed, and twisting slowly, she tried to crawl away. Six banana fingers closed around her arm and lifted her into the air.

Her leather jacket and safari shirt were torn where the arrow had struck. Gil shoved a finger into the hole and touched the smooth pearly surface of the undamaged Angel Skin beneath.

Antigone closed her eyes and drifted into a place without pain. She could hear timber burning and wind rushing through the trees, and then Gil filling the forest with an angry roar.

"Arachne!"

Cyrus worked on the metal head chained to Captain Smith's right foot, the gold ring that had fallen out of the iron block now rattling on his thumb.

Clean-shaven Vlad IV had a keyhole in his forehead, but it was full of grit. Cyrus punched at it with the tip of his knife, and then tried the silver key again. Frustrated, he rolled the head onto its face and shook it. Sand and gravel trickled down. He set the head back down and tried again. The key slipped in, and he turned it.

The metal head fell open and a brown human skull rolled out into the water, slowly losing its lower jaw as it did. As had happened with the iron block, the chain links opened and rattled down, and the Captain's right foot seemed to wake.

Trying hard to ignore the skull rocking gently on the cave floor, Cyrus swam up to the Captain's right hand. Vlad II. The key worked easily, and a second brown skull rolled out as the iron head opened and the chains fell off.

Cyrus wanted very much to be done. To get whatever was about to happen over with. He pushed up and swam across the Captain's chest, only able to make himself glance quickly at the sleeper's face before diving down to the final head. What would he do if the man didn't wake up? Drag his body to the surface?

VLAD III
TEPES

As Cyrus slid the key into the iron forehead, silver flashed through the water and a saber blade pressed up against his throat.

He couldn't move. The squid bubbled and he couldn't even inhale. He could feel the razor edge slowly parting his skin. A small cloud of blood floated up around his face.

"Not that one."

The words were bubbled, but Cyrus understood. He slowly pulled out the key.

fifteen

SMOOTH STONES

DAN KNEW he was seeing the present. The dream was fluid, and he drifted through it easily.

There was a pretty young black girl strapped into a chair. She was bruised and damp, and her chin rested on her chest. Beside her, in another chair, was a damp boy with a broken nose and a swollen eye and long straggly brown hair. Dan knew him. His name was Oliver, and he was the sullen boy Antigone had tried to befriend in their Polygoners club. Dan could see the anger in him, the bitterness inside, planted long ago and growing.

Dan drifted through wall after wall. He found a man in a pink shirt chained to a bed. And then another chained man, big and dark-skinned like the girl. Dan could see the fatherhood on him while he slept, the worry and the love he wore all over his soul.

In other rooms there were guards. Some slept and some were waking. They were rotten inside, dying, but on the outside he could see their strengths, stolen and molded and stitched together from other men. When he looked at some of them, he could see only tattoo bones floating in the air around emptiness, and he knew that these had already cheated death.

And then he found the freezers. Behind each door, he saw a relic of pain, bodies broken but laid in cold unrest, seeds unplanted, souls and flesh unhonored.

And limping in front of the coffin freezers, he saw the man called Phoenix. To Daniel's eyes, he looked to be made only of ash, held together by the weave of his white coat. Daniel felt anger swell inside him, and his anger bloomed into hate for the ash man who had broken his eyes and undone his heart.

"Daniel."

The voice was his father's.

"Daniel?"

There was a freezer near the bottom of a stack, beside a clear glass pool. He saw the tall body lying on its back. He looked past the frosted glass and saw the face and the puckered holes in the chest where flying lead had done its violence.

"I see you," Daniel said. "He has you? Why are you here?"

"Dan, son, I am not here."

"I see your body. He stole it."

"Yes, he stole it. But that is not my body anymore. There is more of me in you than in that cold and broken bonehouse where I once lived. That is ash where my fire once burned. My fire burns brighter now, and in flesh that will not decay. Look at him."

Phoenix was preparing the shallow pool, emptying vials into the water.

"He clings to *his* ash until he can steal another's. He wants to mold slaves that will call him god, men and women who will take up and lay down their souls at his word. He wants to call me back, to make that frozen body new and chain me up inside. But I pity him, Dan. Can you pity a destroyer?"

"No," said Daniel. "I can't."

"You will," his father said. "In the end."

"Am I dead?" Daniel asked.

"You are dying," said his father.

"But why?" Daniel asked. "Why do I have to?"

"Because you are flesh, and flesh is grass. It burns and is consumed. But your fire will not go out."

"What will I die of?"

And then his father laughed, a laugh Daniel had not heard in years, a laugh he had never really heard, because this laugh was bigger and richer and deeper than any that had ever echoed in the chest of that body in the freezer.

"Son," his father said. "Run faithfully to the end, and like all good men, you will die of having lived."

The room went dark. Daniel was drifting away. His father's voice followed him, fading: "When you see your mother, your sister, your brother, there you see a part of me—of who I will always be. Help your brother understand."

"Wait, Dreamer." The whisper was female. Daniel was back in the room with the freezers, looking at a wide-eyed girl crouched in a corner. He had seen her before, in his dream of Cyrus and the grave. Her hair was like a mound of ropes, too big and too heavy for her body. Her arms and legs were chained to the wall, and she was looking straight into Daniel's soul and he into hers. She was a tangle of loss and sorrow and slavery. But somewhere in it all, he saw pride. When she spoke, her mouth didn't move.

"Bridle your eyes and ride them. The Phoenix is ready. He has found the dark road. The seventy weeks begin. Mark this place." She blew on Daniel and he passed up through the roof, looking down at the huge building. He could still hear her whisper. "Mark this nest where he will hatch his young. Mark the muddy river. Bring the Desolation."

Daniel opened his eyes. His face was pressed deep into moss, and he'd been snotting all over it. A heavy limb pinned down his head, and something larger was on his legs, digging into his back. Everything around him smelled burnt. Even the moss was smoking.

He shifted beneath the weight and realized that he had found his limits—his body truly hurt.

• • •

Cyrus sat shivering on the gravel beach. The shallow slice on his throat stung with salt, and his teeth were chattering. If Patricia had been around his neck instead of his wrist when the Captain had raised his blade, she probably would have tried to take his arm off. She was back around Cyrus's neck now, once again carrying the keys.

Captain John Smith paced on the beach, water squelching out of his high boots. He held the iron head of Vlad III on his left hip—the only head Cyrus hadn't opened—and had coiled the iron chain around his forearm. His naked saber was in his right hand, and his eyes were on the sea. Cyrus's eyes were on the sea as well. There was no sign of Rupert anywhere, and they'd been out of the water for at least twenty minutes. He'd hoped Rupert would be waiting. He'd been afraid that Rupert would be floating.

The Captain spun on his heel and pointed his sword at Cyrus. His beard was lopped off in an uneven square and his hair was a wild mane of jagged lengths. His brown eyes glowed with anger.

"Fool, fool, fool!" He chewed the word like toffee, his voice as thick and sticky as syrup.

"You said that already," Cyrus said. "And before you ask again, no, I'm not sure what exact move we were planning next."

"I see no we. I see a thee." The Captain strode

forward and spat. "And ye, lad, haven't the feel nor the timbre of a Smith—waking a Lord of the Order and a Knight of the Queen without cause." He turned away, letting his eyes sail back across the sea to the horizon. Cyrus watched the man's ancient battered hands clench and flex at the sight.

"Aye," the man said. "But the world is yet grand and worth the waking, and the sea remains my true queen, fool though ye be."

"I'm going to look for the others." Cyrus stood up slowly. "I need to change my clothes."

"Sit!" the Captain bellowed. Water shook out of his beard. His eyes were alive with fire as he pointed his sword at the wet rocks under Cyrus. "Down, trespasser, or I'll loose your head from your cursed bones!"

Cyrus squinted at him. "What is it with you and heads? Listen to me: The current Avengel told me to wake you up, okay? He was hoping you'd help us fight the transmortals, that you'd be on our team. And I had to cut your nasty hair and hack off your sicktastic fingernails. So I'd appreciate it if you would stop yelling at me."

Cyrus raised his hand to the slice on his throat. It felt like a nasty paper cut. "And this hurts, by the way. You didn't have to cut me."

The Captain snorted and shook back his hair. He held up the face of Vlad III. "Young gutterblud, count it blessed providence that I did."

Cyrus circled around the Captain to the little boat that still held his coat and his bag.

"Better your head roll free," the Captain continued, "than this chain be loosed."

"Stop it!" Cyrus yelled. He tugged his shirt out of his bag. Shivering, he pulled it on. "Enough with the heads!"

"Cy!"

Cyrus looked up. Dan was leaning over the cliff's edge. He was filthy and favoring one leg, and his shoulders were smoking.

"Is that him?" Dan hooded his eyes. "Where's Rupe? The planes had to leave, and some massive guy with a beard grabbed Antigone. We have to go!"

"Antigone . . ."

"Gone, Cyrus! He took her."

The world spun, and Cyrus felt his knees sag. The Captain was yelling something and pointing his sword at Dan. Cyrus slid to the ground and leaned against the boat. Without Rupert, where would they even start? They were on an island. The planes had left. Antigone . . . no. He shook his head. A massive guy with a beard?

Gil.

The Captain was looking down at him, forehead creased, eyes questioning. Cyrus realized that he'd said the name out loud.

"Gilgamesh," he said. "It had to have been Gilgamesh. He took my sister."

The Captain's brows collided. "Gilgamesh? He wouldn't lay a Persian finger on any lady of the Order. I bound his treaty charms myself."

"The treaties have been voided," Cyrus said. "He's in the *Ordo Draconis* now."

The Captain's mouth fell open, his solid beard thumping against his metal chest. "Daft damnation! Voided? Does the Brendan know? Have the Keepers mustered? Who leads these dragons against us?" He turned and strode down the beach. "The kings . . . Christendom . . . old alliances must needs prove strong. The Maltese. Prester John."

The Captain paused, stared for a moment at the iron head on his hip, and then turned around. "The dragons rekindling . . . you were right to wake me. Has Ashtown Keep held firm? Have the Burials been opened?"

"Only yours," said Cyrus.

The Captain nodded. "Well, there's some hope in that. Who leads these—"

The rumble of jet engines rolled across the water. The Captain tensed. Dan limped quickly down the cliff's goat track. Cyrus looked at the horizon. A plane was heading toward them, flying low and fast.

The Captain hopped onto a boulder and faced the plane. He let Vlad III drop and dangle from his left wrist. His sword spun and flashed in his right, and then stopped, poised and ready.

He glanced back at Cyrus. "Cover, fools, or burn."

Cyrus looked back at his brother. "Theirs?" he asked. "Or ours?"

Dan was squinting. "That's the Boones' plane," he finally said as the plane touched down, hundreds of yards out from where Cyrus and Rupert had been diving, sending up two long plumes of sea behind its wings as it cruised toward the little cove.

The Captain watched with narrow eyes as the plane turned sideways at the harbor mouth and let its two jet engines whine. It was longer than Gil's plane and had a sleeker silver body. On the side, just beneath the cockpit, there was a gold rampant lion holding a musket.

A side door slid open and Diana leaned out, scanning the beach and then the cliff. She looked at Cyrus. "Antigone? Rupe?" she mouthed.

Cyrus cupped his hands. "Gone!"

Diana shook her head. She couldn't hear. She beckoned them to come. Cyrus threw on his coat and grabbed his bag. Then he and his brother pushed the boat off the beach and splashed into the shallows.

"Come on!" Cyrus yelled to the Captain, still perched on his boulder.

"What is this wizardry?" the Captain cried, his eyes wide in wonder.

Cyrus and Dan teetered and rocked the little boat as they tried to climb in at the same time. The Captain jumped down and splashed into the water.

"Get in!" the Captain yelled. "Before ye shame the sea!"

He tumbled Cyrus in over the side and Dan behind him, and then Vlad thumped against the bottom. Gripping the square stern, the Captain whooped and drove the boat forward, churning through the water with high splashing knees. And as he did, he began to chant: "Dead men sink, and dead men sail, ho for the bottle and the bonehouse! Ho for the bottle and my lady so lovely, ho for the Queen's Virginia!"

Somehow, while the boat glided out, the Captain vaulted over Cyrus, flinging a waterfall from his coat as he dropped onto a bench. Then he struck out with the two wooden oars for the waiting jet.

Diana was still in the door with her mouth open and her eyebrows up.

"Cyrus!" Daniel sat up. "Seriously, where's Rupe? We can't leave without him. I think I know where Phoenix is."

Cyrus turned back to his brother. "What? How?"

"And he has Dad!" Dan shouted. "Phoenix has his body in a freezer!"

Dan continued shouting, but there was nothing else to hear. The jet engines swallowed it all.

His father . . . he was supposed to be in the sea. His

body was in a freezer? With Phoenix? Why? Why would Phoenix keep a body—

The tooth. The Reaper's Blade. *The Resurrection Stone . . .*

Cyrus felt sick. The Captain turned the boat and slid it up beside the plane. Diana reached down. Cyrus grabbed her hand and was pulled into the crowded plane. Everyone was in there. Everyone but Antigone and Rupert.

Dan followed, but the Captain balked at the door. Finally, with shoulders hunched in worry, Diana and Alan dragged him inside, while Nolan shut and sealed the door. As the plane began to turn, the Captain spread his legs, grabbed at the walls, and began to bellow a prayer. Cyrus barely noticed.

"Cy!" Diana yelled. "Cy! What's going on?"

The plane accelerated, and Cyrus collapsed onto the floor. Exhaustion and horror washed over him. He needed to throw up. He rolled slowly onto his knees and began to crawl over legs and feet toward the rear of the plane. He wanted a corner, someplace dark where he could pass out or die. His arms wobbled, and his chest shook.

Cyrus Smith dropped onto his face, clawed at the tight carpet, and shut his eyes. Diana sat down beside him. He felt her fingers check his pulse. Dan lowered himself to the floor on the other side. Cyrus heard his brother's voice and felt his hand on his back, but he couldn't open his eyes. Not yet. Not for a long time. Deep inside, deeper than anger or fear, inside his gut, inside his bones, his soul was shaking.

The plane flew. And flew. Cyrus slept and he woke and he slept again. But he didn't move. Hours passed, and the world around Cyrus slowly became still. And when the sun began to set in the windows and the whole cabin glowed with fire, Cyrus rolled onto his back. The plane was descending. He didn't care where. He stared at the ceiling and wondered how he could throw a stone at a giant and a monster at the same time, when he didn't know where they were, and he had no stone.

Phoenix sat back in a rickety chair and surveyed his preparations by the light of a single lamp on the floor beside him. For months, he and his men had worked only in deep darkness and quiet morning light. But today had been different. Today had been the final day of preparation. Tonight would be the final night. He massaged his stump and pressed the cool silver head of his cane to his lips, listening to his freezers hum.

His men were exhausted. They had done good work. Five pools had been prepared. Five wombs. By tomorrow night, each pool would have given birth nine times, and he would have forty-five sons . . . if all survived. Which they wouldn't. He expected some chaff. And those that survived would be tested more quickly than he had planned.

By tomorrow night, he himself would be reborn. He ground his itching stump against his chair and sucked on the end of his cane. No more frail legs. No cursed white coat. No missing hand.

Pythia was sleeping in the corner. Her secrets had not been told easily. She was bound to prophecy, to word the mysteries into oracles—that much was part of her ancient curse. But she would not speak. She scrawled her answers on leaves and pages, burning them, flinging them, scattering them as fast as she wrote. He had punished her, but it did not matter. Kings and priests and devils had punished her before. Tonight, perhaps, he would end her curse forever.

His mind wandered back over the trails of his quest, the quest of a lifetime. He, Edwin Laughlin, would father a new race. So many years had passed; so many hurdles had been cleared. He had mastered metamorphosis—mortal and bestial. But the sons and daughters he truly wanted could not be made to last. Human souls were more combative. Hearts burst and souls fled, and he could never call them back. Hundreds of perfect creations had been shaped, only to be given to the grave.

He had needed the Reaper's Blade, the cold Resurrection Stone. But even with it in hand, he had struggled for a year. Now the oracle had scrawled her riddles, but he had solved them. His final hurdle approached.

Phoenix smiled and kissed his cane. The world would never again be mundane.

In the end, the secret of resurrection had been a simple one. He could not conjure up a soul, but he could make fair trade, and now he knew how. A soul for a soul, a life for a life. But it must also be a life in kind. Innocent for innocent. Child for child. Killer for killer.

This would be no failed crop. Let his children's hearts explode. He could raise the dead.

Phoenix flipped open the head of his cane and ran a cold finger along the edge of the colder tooth. It would be time for his own great change. . . .

A new body and more. He would absorb the life of a transmortal. As for his children, they would be the first fathers of a new race. But at some point, years from now, perhaps, he would still need many to die. There would be even greater crops to replace them.

Three dark and dusty rooms had been filled with unconscious convicts in jumpsuits and shackles—and soon a statewide manhunt would end happily when they were all found dead and floating in the river. Phoenix scanned his humming freezers. The convicts would work for his own men, but he wondered how the trade would fare with his frozen trophies. How many of Brendan's children carried bloodguilt or had been thieves? He yawned. Soon he would know.

Phoenix leaned farther back in his chair and closed

his eyes. When the sun was down and the darkness was thick, he would rise and till his flesh garden. His great labor would begin.

In the corner, Pythia opened her eyes and watched the man made of ash while he slept. She could see his future, his past, and his end.

She drew two leaves from a threadbare sleeve. On one, she traced a fiery number with her finger: *70.* She watched the leaf shrivel and burn, and then she blew the ash toward the pools.

On the other, she wrote a name.

sixteen

THE THRONE ROOM OF RADU BEY

ANTIGONE'S RIBS HURT when she breathed, and the hard floor wasn't helping. Her face was stuck to it. For a moment, she couldn't remember anything. And then, in a flash, she could feel herself floating in the air, and she could see Gil's arrow, and her ribs suddenly began to hurt much worse.

Antigone slowly peeled her cheek off the floor and looked around. She was in a huge room that was open to the sky on two sides—two blackened stone walls butted together in one corner, but the other two walls were missing. No windows. No posts. Nothing but blue sky and the barely rising sun. The ceiling was dark, beamed with charred and splitting timbers.

Antigone saw no doors and no stairs. The floor was slab stone, dusty gray around the edges. In the center of the room, thirty feet in front of her, the stone was polished and worn down into a shallow bowl. In the very center, where the floor was most worn, there was a small reed bed mat, a pillow, and a single tightly rolled blanket. The air above the mat shimmered a little, like it was hot, but she was tired and she was hurting. Something was probably wrong with her eyes.

Antigone slid onto her knees.

Just behind her, Rupert Greeves was sprawled face-down on the floor.

Antigone yelped and scrambled to her feet. "Rupe!"

She grabbed his shoulder and shook him. He was limp. As she struggled to roll him over, he groaned and opened his eyes.

"Sit up, Rupert," she said. "Talk to me."

Rupert shut his eyes again, but worked his way slowly upright and put a hand on his head.

"*Bonum diem.*" The voice trickled smoothly across the floor behind Antigone.

She spun around. A man was sitting cross-legged on the mat in the center of the room, where a moment before there had been only a shimmer. He had short curly black hair and a strong hairless face. He was wearing a loose white robe, open wide enough that she could see a band of red scales on his chest.

On the floor in front of him were a small pitcher and a dark brown loaf of bread. The man tore off a piece of the bread with long fingers, dipped it in the pitcher, and ate it. His jaw moved, but his face was still. Poised to strike. His cheeks were gaunt and his eyes were black, but not by color—black because no light escaped them, because they consumed reflection.

When Antigone looked into those eyes, she thought of gun barrels.

"*Bonum diem,*" he said again, and Antigone's mind turned to Latin. Morning greeting.

"*Salve,*" she said.

"*Brevi te devorabo,*" he said, chewing.

Antigone blinked. She, uh, well . . .

"English," Rupert said loudly. He used one hand to shield his eyes against the sunrise pouring in where there should have been a wall and glared at the man in the middle of the room. "What do you want with us?"

"*Non loquor—*"

"No Latin," Rupert said.

The man tore off another bite, dipped it in the pitcher, and slid it into his mouth. He chewed slowly. When he had swallowed, he set down the loaf and uncrossed his legs. His limbs were as thick as Gil's but without the hair, and without the strange giantish proportions.

"Do you know who I am?" he asked. His accent was slight, but Antigone heard it—like music in another room, or the smell of a spice she'd never tasted. It made her think of the vanished countries and swallowed-up kingdoms described in the muddy middle of her old history books.

Rupert smiled. "I know some of what you have done."

The man's chest inflated slowly. Sharp, cold air rushed in through the open walls. His robe snapped, and his voice rode the gust. It spun and swirled around the room and was everywhere at once. "I am Radu Bey, son of the moon and the sea. When I sing, the tides change their course. When I speak, the moon kneels. I have swallowed kings and drunk the blood of harems. Where I step, stone shivers; where I stride, mountains flee. I have devoured children and felled forests and sucked the marrow of nations. I am Radu Bey. Gods fear me."

The wind died, and Antigone shivered. Rupert groaned, closed one eye, and knuckle-massaged his temple.

"I believe you," he said. "And I'd wager it all began at your father's knee. Did he teach you to be cruel to kittens?"

Antigone looked at her Keeper in surprise, and then back at the polished man. Radu's gaunt cheeks had tightened. "You would like to die now?" he asked. "You desire your destruction?"

Rupert rose to his feet. Antigone watched her Keeper walk slowly toward the man on the mat.

"Spit out my skull when you're done, Dracul." Rupert dropped to the floor ten feet from Radu Bey, and then stretched out his long legs. "Or tell me why we're here."

"Your Order is dead," Radu said.

"Ill, yes," said Rupert. "Rotten, surely. But the O of B isn't yet in the grave."

Antigone looked around the room. Where had the big man come from? How had they come in? She stood up and moved cautiously toward the closest missing wall. Radu's eyes followed her, but his words were for Rupert.

"Your new Brendan is a puppet."

"A puppet on *your* finger, I suspect," said Rupert. "Bellamy might have been a good man once, if briefly, but no more."

"Not my finger," Radu said. "Bellamy Cook is well sworn to the man called Phoenix and has been for years, even before William Skelton turned his dark heart back to the Order."

Antigone was nearing the edge of the floor and she still couldn't see anything but sky.

"*You* put Bellamy in that office," Rupert said. "Not Phoenix. With your riots and your violence and your threats. The treatied transmortals put him there. Why?"

Radu smiled and his front teeth were slightly gapped. "Why?" he asked playfully. "Why would I support a man who would free my people when they are being hunted, who would shatter the chains that have bound their strengths and anchored them to mortal masters for centuries? Blood Avenger, you tell me why. Even now my people are retesting their potency."

"They have always had their strengths," Rupert said. "We did not strip them."

"You bound them." Radu's lip curled. "Arachne

could weave, but never the Angel Skin that little Smith now wears, nor another Odyssean Cloak. Gilgamesh could not lose his physical strength, but his ancient charms were powerless. Koschei, Hannibal, Semiramis—what choice did they have? The treatied immortals were marked, and then tracked like toothless wolves whenever they struggled against their bonds. Some were Buried, and some destroyed; only a few were strong enough to remain free."

"Meaning you?" Rupert said. "Free? For centuries we've believed that John Smith ended you—that you were dead or Buried or both. If you were free, why are you only whispering now?"

"Whispering! I whisper like a storm whispers, like the quaking earth whispers. I have heard my people groaning, and now they are free. The tide is rising, mortal. Your old walls cannot hold."

"And can you hold?" Rupert asked. "Against the Order and against Phoenix?"

Antigone had reached the edge. She looked down into a wall of cold air rushing straight up past her face. Beneath her, she could see clouds and a distant airplane, like a minnow swimming through the bottom of the sky. Farther down, through the clouds, she could see an island city, bristling with towers. She looked up. Above her, the sky's blue was deeper and darker, and in its very center it was black. And in that circle of blackness, there were more stars than she had ever seen at night.

"Rupe . . . ," she said. The voice of Radu Bey drowned her out.

"Phoenix is this century's fool. He wants a war. And now he shall have one. You are here so that my eyes can lock with yours when I, the last Dracul, extend my hand to the Children of Brendan. Give over the maps to the Burials. Release your prisoners and your relics. Renounce the charter of Ashtown. If you do this, your Order shall continue on as it does now, as a society of wealthy travelers. Keep your aeroplanes and your sailing ships, but give over the Keepers' keys. Brendan, too, must follow in the shadow of the dragon."

"Rupe!" Antigone said. She tore her eyes off the sky and backed away from the edge.

"Refuse," Radu said, "and the life of every member shall be extinguished. We will throw down the stones of Ashtown and every other Estate, and we will give your bodies to the flames."

Rupert waited a moment, and then he sighed. "That's it? That's your offer? Total extinction, or total subservience?" He sighed and looked at Antigone. "What is it?"

Antigone looked into Radu's gun-barrel eyes, and then back at Rupert. "I think we're in a Burial. Right now. Or something like one. But totally opposite. A sky Burial. Do they have those?"

Rupert turned back to Radu Bey. For a moment, they were motionless. Then Rupert looked around at the worn floor. He smiled.

"Are you chained?" he asked.

Radu Bey sprung forward. His fist connected with Rupert's face and sent him spinning across the floor. Cold wind roared through the empty walls and swept Antigone off her feet.

Rupert scrambled onto his hands and knees. He spat blood out on the floor and smiled.

"Do they know?" he yelled, laughing. "The dragons follow a man still bound?" He stood slowly.

Radu Bey was on his feet. Four chains, invisible before, ran from his wrists and ankles through a hole in the floor beside his mat. His face flushed. "The liar Smith gave me these chains. Then he minted his own treaty with me, beyond the boundaries of his Brendan. He swore that if I taught him how to take my brother's head, I would walk the earth as unbound as he. We bonded the oath with talismans, and I gave him what he sought. He took two heads more, and then the deceiver Buried himself!" Radu tore his robe from his shoulders and let it dangle at his waist. His chest and ribs were knotted with muscle beneath a red circular dragon. He reeled his chains up through the floor. Three came through with shattered links, but the fourth grew taut and held.

Radu Bey let the taut chain fall back through; the

other three dangled in his hands. Roaring, he ran at Rupert. The first chain lashed out and Rupert ducked, snatching it out of the air and letting the links wrap around his arm. He tried to pull Radu off balance but was too late. The big man had already swung his double whip, and the combined chains wound around Rupert and slammed him to the ground.

Antigone slid away. There had been a way into this place; there had to be a way out. Balancing against the wind, she raced along the edge while Rupert yelled in pain behind her. She found no ropes, no ladders. Nothing up or down. She reached the corner and the beginning of the first solid wall. She pressed herself up against it and tried to grope around outside the stone, but the wall was too thick.

The floor shook beneath her, and she turned. Behind her, Rupert spun through the air, slammed onto the floor, and tumbled toward the edge. There was no time to think. Antigone took two strides and dove. She hit Rupert in the side as he slid. His head and shoulders stuck out into the wind. She grabbed on to his collar and heaved her whole weight onto the back of his legs.

Rupert grabbed at the edge and pushed himself—and her—back into the room.

Together, gasping, they turned.

Radu Bey held his one unbroken chain between his hands and spread his thick legs to brace himself. He wound his wrists up in the links, inflated his lungs, and then pulled. Sweat poured off his face and down his huge shoulders. His body shook and every muscle shivered beneath glistening skin. The dragon on his chest flushed with blood and inflated, pulsing, swelling slowly into limbs and scales and wings. And then, as Antigone watched, the red dragon began to writhe.

Lifting his face, Radu Bey shouted. Lightning lashed in through the open walls and struck the linked chain between his hands. Thunder rocked the room. Antigone tucked and curled into a ball as bolt after bolt cracked through the room. She was deaf. Her eyes burned with white light, and the stone floor smoked around her.

The lightning stopped. Thunder rolled away.

Stillness.

Antigone blinked. Her fillings throbbed in her mouth, and her ears were ringing. She watched Radu drop the unbroken chain and pick up the others. His chest was heaving, and the blood dragon still twisted beneath his skin. Rupert lifted Antigone to her feet.

Leftover electricity danced down the chains and Radu stepped forward, dragging three crackling metal serpents, prepared to strike.

Rupert grabbed Antigone's hand.

Radu Bey looked into her eyes and raised his chains.

"A little Smith blood," he said, "is better than none at all."

The chains whipped forward, and Rupert pulled Antigone back. He pulled her off the edge. Together they fell, down into the sky. Lightning flashed above them.

Antigone could feel the scream in her throat as she fell, but she heard nothing.

Instead of piercing clouds, she slammed against a wooden floor. Her limp body bounced and thumped back down, landing in a tangle with Rupert's legs.

Perched on a pole high above her, there was a room with only two walls. She wondered why. Above that, she could see huge steel beams holding up a distant roof.

Gil's enormous face slid into view.

"Don't . . . like you," Antigone said quietly, and the world went dim. She was already far away, dreaming that she was a bird, and that a red-winged blackbird was teaching her how to glide.

Cyrus stretched, kicking bare feet across crisp cool sheets. He opened his eyes and blinked. He was on a bottom bunk. Through a window beside his bed shone the rosy light of a predawn sky.

Little Jax was sitting on a stool in front of another bunk bed, with a piece of toast on his knees. Cyrus squinted at him.

"Dennis is still asleep, too." Jax took a bite, chewing quickly. "I'm worried about the zoo. The Cryptos can do without, but the others will be tough to feed correctly. I did leave instructions."

"Where are we?" Cyrus asked. The room had thick carpet and maps and antlers on the wood-paneled walls. Blankets were rumpled on the other bed, but it was empty.

"Kentucky," Jax said. "But I don't know what part. Somewhere in the mountains. We got in late." He managed to fold the rest of the bread into his cheek. "You left my squid in the North Atlantic. Do you want breakfast?"

Cyrus sat all the way up and swung his legs to the floor. He was wearing a clean white shirt and a pair of blue shorts; they weren't his. Someone knuckle-knocked on the bedroom door. Before he could answer, Diana was in the room. Her hair was wet and pulled back in a tight braid. Her face shone like it had been freshly scrubbed.

"You're awake. Good. My dad's been complaining about late sleepers for the last hour, but I made him leave you for a while."

Cyrus raised his eyebrows and opened his mouth, trying to widen his eyes by stretching his face. "What time is it?"

"Six forty-seven in the a.m.," Diana said. "Big Alan had to carry you in from the plane. You should come out now. They're talking."

Six forty-seven was too early. And Cyrus didn't even

know who "they" were. "Where's Tigs?" he asked. "Is she up?"

Jax stopped chewing. Diana bit her lip. She sat down on the bed beside Cyrus, clenched her knees, and looked at him.

She didn't need to say anything. It was all in her eyes. The last twenty-four hours flooded over Cyrus. His sister was gone. His Keeper was gone. His brother was having heart attacks and visions.

Phoenix had his father's body.

"I'm really, really sorry," Jax said. Cyrus looked at James Axelrotter, the little zookeeper. The boy's face was sagging. He meant what he said; after all, he'd lost most of his own family a long time ago. But it didn't help. Cyrus nodded and stood up. He wasn't going to lose his family. He wasn't going to be the last Smith standing.

"Let's go," he said.

The hallway outside the bedroom surprised him. For starters, it was fifteen feet wide and at least forty long. And quiet. He followed Diana over polished slate floors in the dim light. The walls were heavy with art and trophies and skins and old rifle racks.

They turned a corner and walked into a great room the size of a gym. Cyrus crossed bear rugs as he walked beneath a full-size cloth airplane, hanging from peeled log rafters thirty feet above him. Couches and chairs surrounded a river-rock fireplace bigger than his old room in the Archer. The floor was littered with blankets and pillows as if people had slept here. Rough log beams framed floor-to-ceiling windows overlooking a meadow that ran down to a glassy black lake. Deer were nosing through the meadow, and two long docks stuck out into the water. Boats were lashed to one; the other led to a massive floating plane hangar. Cyrus stopped and stared. Beyond it all, he saw a blue-green mountain range and a glowing horizon. As he watched, the sun crept above the mountains, painting the forested hilltops with morning gold.

"Cy!"

Cyrus turned his back on the morning. Diana was waiting for him, ready to descend a flight of stairs wider than a mobile home.

"This is your house?" Cyrus whispered. He couldn't help it. "Seriously? You said your parents lived in the wilds."

Diana laughed. "Well, this isn't the city."

Cyrus looked around. "It's like a log palace."

"Logs, yes. What did you expect? But don't say *palace* around my dad. And don't say *rich*, either. He hates rich people."

Cyrus reached the stairs and began to follow her down. "Hates rich people? That doesn't make any sense. You're now officially the richest people I know. You're the *only* rich people I know."

Diana glanced back at him. "You know plenty; you just haven't left Ashtown and seen them at home. Besides, if dining hall gossip is true—and it always is—you Smiths are the richest people *I* know."

"Yeah, right," Cyrus said.

At the bottom of the stairs was a slate and maple kitchen the size of a restaurant. Off to Cyrus's left, there were stone counters and wooden cabinets and a fridge the size of a car, and a large sizzling stove beneath a polished metal hood. The far wall was made of glass doors that had all been thrown open to a terrace, the sunrise, and the breeze. Sitting in front of the windows was a rough-hewn table big enough for fifty. It was lined with picnic benches currently dotted with breakfasters. Only Nolan and Arachne were missing. And the Captain . . .

Right in the middle, Horace had a napkin tucked into his shirt and was surrounded by eggs and bacon and sausage. Jax passed Cyrus and hurried over to a jar of jam and a stack of toast at an empty spot on the bench beside the lawyer. George and Silas were across from Horace and working on omelets. Huddled around one end of the table, Dan and Alan and Jeb sat with emptied plates pushed away, their arms crossed on the table and intent looks on their faces. Between them, at the head, leaning back in the only chair, there was a tall, wiry man with dark brown hair, combed with a sharp part. His face was hard and worn, with grimace lines around his eyes and deep creases in his cheeks.

Dan was trying to tell him something, but the man seemed more interested in mining his very white teeth with a toothpick.

Standing beside the stove, a tall woman with silver in her long red braid was wiping her hands on her apron. Her face was dotted with sun freckles, just like her daughter's. When she caught sight of Cyrus, her green eyes flashed a moment of pity before dousing him with warmth. She hurried over.

"Cyrus, honey," she said. "I'm so happy we could have you here, though I wish it were under happier circumstances. I'm Sadie, and you just tell me what you need." She swallowed him in a hug, and her arms were soft but strong. The smell of breakfast hung all over her, but especially cinnamon. She released him and turned to the table. "Boone, you have another guest to meet."

Everyone looked up. The man at the end studied Cyrus. Cyrus couldn't even see his eyes inside his hard-creased squint.

"We met," the man said. "In my plane."

"Sorry," Cyrus said. "I don't remember much."

"You were busy rubbing your sad all over my floor."

"Pa!" Diana said.

Cyrus flushed. The table was silent. No one even chewed.

"He's a boy, Robert," Sadie said. She threw an arm around Cyrus and steered him toward a bar stool near the stove. "Can I get you some biscuits and gravy? French toast? Oatmeal? What would go down best right now?"

"Thank you, but I'm really not hungry," Cyrus said. Sadie released him, and Cyrus turned back around, focusing on the table.

"Mr. Boone." He said it loudly, like the words were something to throw. His heart was racing, and his cheeks were hot. "I need to borrow your plane."

Robert Boone lowered his toothpick and waited a moment. "Son," he finally said. "I wouldn't loan you my horse."

"Well, that's lucky," Cyrus said. "Because I don't need your horse. I need your plane."

"Pa," Diana started. "I think—"

Robert Boone raised his hand. "And what do you think you could do with my plane?"

"I'm going to go find Gilgamesh and get my sister back."

Robert Boone drummed his fingers on the table. "In my plane?"

"Yes."

Dan leaned in over the table. "Sir . . . we really need the help. I was trying to tell you—"

"Daniel Smith, you're still breathing. You're here.

You're fed. I've given you help. Now, you're not in the Order, so I don't expect you to know this, but we don't hold truck with dreaming or visions or sightseeing in your sleep—whatever you might call it."

"Didn't used to be that way, Bobby Boone," said Sadie quietly. "And you know it."

"No, ma'am," her husband said. "But the Order outgrew that dabbling and a lot of other nonsense, too."

Diana moved toward the table. "Pa, you have to try something. Rupert and Antigone are both missing."

Her father looked up. "Diana Boone, I am aware. And while I appreciate my daughter telling me what I *have* to do, you might wanna save your speeches till you've spent more than one night under my roof in the year."

"Pa . . . ," said Jeb.

Alan Livingstone cleared his throat and rapped his knuckles on the table politely. The room grew quiet. His voice was smooth, but there was disappointment in it. "Robert, Sadie, my sons and I appreciate your assistance and your hospitality. However, we have a search waiting for us, and an Avengel to support. I apologize, but I must request the loan of a number of tools, some materials, and a flight back to Nova Scotia, where we will attempt to repair our own plane, which is currently floating damaged in a harbor."

Robert Boone chewed his lip, and then he nodded.

"No," said Cyrus. Dan was shaking his head, too.

"I'm sorry, but no. We don't have time. All the way back, and then plane repairs?"

"In my dream," Dan began, "Phoenix—"

Robert Boone burst out laughing.

"Hey!" Cyrus yelled. He snatched up a bowl and banged it on the table. It smashed in his hand, and glass skittered down between the loaded dishes and onto the floor.

Cyrus leaned his hands against the table, careful to avoid the glass. "Mr. Boone, you can loan me your plane, and I will use it to find my sister and my Keeper, Rupert Greeves. Then I will find Phoenix, and I will kill him and get back the tooth and my father's body. I will not be careful with your plane. I do not care what happens to your plane unless it stops flying while I still need it. And if you don't loan me your plane, I will go down to the lake right now, and I will steal it."

"Finally!" Horace said. "Some initiative!" He pulled his napkin from his shirt, dabbed at his mouth, and stood up. "Shall we go, then?"

Cyrus was staring at Robert Boone, and Robert Boone was staring back—or Cyrus assumed he was. He could have been asleep behind the creases around his eyes.

"Sorry about the bowl, Mrs. Boone," Cyrus said.

"Perfectly fine, honey," Sadie said behind him. "Break one over his head if you need to."

"Well?" said Cyrus.

Robert Boone smirked. "You got the blood, kid. But you gonna fly this plane yourself?"

"If I have to," Cyrus said. "But I'm pretty sure everyone is coming with me. Jeb can fly it, if he wants."

"Am I invited on this warpath?"

"Do you have another plane?" said Cyrus. "We might need two."

"All right, little chief," said Mr. Boone. "You got me. Where to?"

Cyrus opened his mouth, but he didn't have an answer. He looked at his brother.

"I'm not sure about the Gil guy," Dan said. "Just Phoenix, and that's a little general, locationwise."

Cyrus looked around the kitchen, his eyes drifting out of focus. His mind was racing. No, it was tumbling down a flight of stairs completely out of control. Where would they go? Rupert would know, but . . . maybe Diana would . . . Dan? Could Dan be in charge? He shook his head at the thought. He needed Antigone. He needed to talk all of this through with her. Even if he could just see her . . . He blinked in surprise. He *could* see her.

The Quick Water. Antigone had said his half was in his pack. If she was alive, Antigone would have hers. She'd remember. But there was a good chance Gil would have taken it from her. So maybe he couldn't see Antigone, but he could see the man who had taken her. Would that help? Would he even be able to tell where Gil was? No, but . . .

The kitchen returned to focus. Even Rupert had gone looking for help.

"Where's the Captain?" Cyrus asked. "Are Nolan and Arachne here?"

Sadie handed Cyrus a fat slice of cold apple pie on a plate. "Boone wanted the transmortals to eat in their rooms," she said. "And you need to eat something, too, honey."

"Hey, now," Boone said, raising his hands. "Under the circumstances, transmortals won't be dining at my table for some time, even if . . ."

Cyrus was already walking toward the stairs, wolfing the pie. Diana was right behind him. Dan jumped off his bench and jogged to catch up. When they were gone, Robert Boone looked around the room. He nudged Jeb.

"Little hard on him, Pa," Jeb said. "Given what he's going through."

"Hard?" Boone asked. "Nah. I like that kid. Born to trouble. Hard is what he'll be when he's passed through this valley he's in. Hard . . . or dead."

seventeen

EVERY WHICH WAY

CYRUS REACHED the bedroom door and stopped. There was a padlock on the handle.

"Wow," Diana said. "Sorry. I'll try to find the key."

"Don't worry about it," said Cyrus. He was already slipping Patricia off his neck. A moment later, the padlock was off and he'd thrown the door open. Nolan and Arachne looked up from the carpeted floor inside. Nolan was eating scrambled eggs; Arachne hadn't touched her plate. She was sitting primly with her legs crossed and her spider bag in her lap.

"Where's the Captain?" Cyrus asked.

Nolan nodded at another door. "Bathroom," he said. "Been in there awhile."

Cyrus crossed to the door and knocked hard.

"Hey!" He gripped the handle. "John Smith! We need to talk." Cyrus pushed and the door swung in. Steam billowed as Cyrus stepped inside.

Captain John Smith was sprawled on the floor. He was on his side, bare-chested, and his shirt was dangling over a towel rack like he'd washed it and set it out to dry. His breastplate was in the dry bathtub and glistening gold—a tube of metal polish sat on the edge of the tub beside blackened rags. His coat was on the floor as well, and the buttons gleamed.

The Captain had his chained left hand hooked into the toilet bowl. Steam was rising up around his wrist, and his chest was heaving. The chain ran down to where iron Vlad III was leering on the floor.

Cyrus jumped forward, and Dan and Diana followed. Together they rolled the limp Captain onto his back and fished his hand out of the steaming toilet. His eyes were shut tight, and his skin was slick with sweat. The chain was hot around his wrist, and his skin was badly blistered.

"Bloody heat," the Captain muttered into his beard. "Bastard nighly molt his last shackle."

"I don't know what you're talking about. Are you okay?" Cyrus asked. "Can you stand?"

"Can I stand? Child, away!" the Captain shouted. He pushed Cyrus back, then grabbed the toilet bowl and the sink and heaved himself to his feet. Vlad rolled behind him. Above his wide belt, his belly and chest were thick with hair except in a sharp bald triangle over his heart—there, his flushed skin visibly quaked with his pulse. He rolled his head slowly, moaning, his chest hair clinging to his square beard like straggling Velcro.

"I have a plan," Cyrus said. "Sort of. But I need help. Have you read Sun Tzu?"

The Captain squinted. Centuries-old lines jutted out from the corners of his brown eyes—eyes that had hardened long ago, staring at the sea and sun. "A right tick, that one. A blood-suckling eel."

"I mean, you were a general or something, right? You planned battles?"

"Admiral," the Captain said. He seemed to have oiled his square beard and slimed his mustache into heavy curling loops at both ends. Cyrus looked at the counter around the sink. Two small bottles of hair conditioner were empty and missing their caps. Cyrus opened his mouth, but clicked it back shut. It didn't matter what the man did with hair conditioner. Not right now.

"Grab your shirt and get out here," Cyrus said, backing through the door. "I need a strategy."

"A stratagem?" the Captain asked. "Aye. That you do."

John Smith snatched his shirt off the towel rack and picked his gold breastplate up out of the tub. "From plotter's clay, the plotter's hands shall soon beget a plot unseen. Lead me to thy plottery wheel! Ha!"

"Um . . . ," said Cyrus. "Well, just come out here."

Dennis and Jax and Horace had come into the room and joined the others, sitting on the floor. Cyrus paced as the Captain worked himself back into his shirt—he had sliced the left sleeve open in order to get Vlad through it. When he had the shirt on, he let the chain dangle, and Vlad rested on the floor. Then he began buffing the breastplate in his hands.

"Okay," said Cyrus. "We have to find a way to deal with Phoenix and Gil at the same time."

"That sounds nightmarish," Nolan said.

"How many regenerations has this Phoenix seen?" the Captain asked. "Has anyone glimpsed him? Do we ken his scale and his heft?"

Everyone stared at the Captain.

"Not a real Phoenix," said Nolan. "A man called Phoenix."

The Captain seemed befuddled. "Is he transmortaled then? Undead? Undying?"

Arachne looked up. "He has the cloak, John. And has worn it for many years."

"The Odyssean Cloak!" The Captain sputtered his lips into his slick mustache. "That cursed cloth, and from your hands, weaver!"

"It served you well," Arachne said quietly.

" 'Well,' you say? Devils have treated me with better love."

"I could not weave it as I was told," Arachne said. "Things would have been much worse if I had."

"Wait," Cyrus said. "You wove the Odyssean Cloak? The white coat Phoenix wears?"

"Who else could?" Arachne asked. "Odysseus demanded that I weave him a cloth that would make him stronger than any man and more cunning than the craftiest serpent, that would give him immortality like the gods, but an immortality which he could shrug off when he finally wished to die. He began killing my spiders until I let him bind me with his oath. I did as I swore, but not the way he desired."

Dennis Gilly's eyes were wide. "At Ashtown! When Phoenix took off his coat, he became a beast! We all saw him."

Arachne nodded. "The cloak bonds to its master. When it is worn, a man is clever and cunning and unable to die—though he is as strong or weak as he was when he put it on. When it is taken off, he loses all cunning but becomes as powerful as one of the ancient apes."

"So get his coat off," Horace said. "And then shoot him."

Arachne shook her head. "He has worn it too long. His only life is in the cloth. The cloak must be destroyed. Burn it, and he will burn."

Cyrus nodded. He knew that already. He and his sister had burned one arm off the coat on a kitchen stove in Ashtown. Phoenix had lost his hand.

John Smith finally sat down. "That cloak was my undoing, too, alas, and shame to my folly. I donned it to gain cunning in my war with the dragons. I did not know I would become a beast when I laid it down."

Dennis's eyes sparkled with unhidden awe. "That's why you were Buried?"

"One part to the blend of my damnation." The Captain sighed. "I wore it too long. Once I learned that I could not shed the cloak and remain a man, I asked Arachne to unweave a corner for me, and I bound it into myself, above my lifeblood, forever." He pulled open his shirt, revealing the bald triangular scar above his heart. Then he flicked his shirt closed again and began to buckle on his breastplate. "Undying, wily as the serpent, desperate for victory, I broke the oath of a Blood Avenger—I knelt beneath dark sorceries." The Captain stared down at his breastplate. "Better that I still slept entombed."

"Dark sorceries?" Jax asked.

The room waited in silence. Horace cleared his throat. "Technically, Captain, you have never been convicted of any wrongdoing."

The Captain snorted. "God Almighty, lawyer, I covenanted with the serpents. I need no jury to speak. By the thinnest chance, three Keepers encaged the great Radu Bey while hunting another. When I arrived, they had all been killed, but he was not yet free. And I saw how I could end myself and the dragons. I soul-bonded myself to him as a brother. I gave him my very hearts-blood for his spell and swore he would be as unchained as

I, if only he betrayed but one Dracul—his hated brother, the Impaler."

John Smith raised the iron head by its chain. His jaw was set, and his hard eyes angry. "I found the Vlads where Radu promised. And I professed my transmortality and begged to be slave-bound to their *Ordo.*" The Captain drew his sword, and everyone in the room inched back from the flashing steel. "With this ancient blade, gift of the dragon gods of their fathers, they pricked their bloods. They spoke the spells to make me thrall—a Smith as slave to play their fool. And they passed the bloody blade to me, to plunge into my heart.

"But I was already twinned to Radu; my hands could wield the Dracul blade with Dracul power just as they could. With it, I took their heads. And I gave their bodies to a witch's black flames in a secret place." He looked directly at Cyrus, and Cyrus couldn't help squirming. His throat had tightened while he listened, and the stinging in the cut on his throat reawakened.

"Blood can ne'er be unspilt; oaths can ne'er be unbroken," the Captain said. "My soul was stained. I'd accrued guilt enow. Radu was Buried on a pillar in a cave. And I, as much dragon as he, sent myself into the sea, as anchor to his freedom."

"*Sic semper draconis,*" Cyrus said quietly. "Thus always to dragons."

For a moment, the room watched the Captain in

silence. He sheathed his sword, then coiled Vlad's chain around his forearm and tucked the iron head into the crook of his arm.

Cyrus looked down and saw that his knee was bouncing. He had his plan. He had the whats and the whys and almost all the hows.

The door opened and Alan Livingstone eased his blond bulk into the room. George and Silas slipped in behind him and stood at his sides. Alan sniffed with his stitched nostril and then scratched his beard. "Is this the council of war?" he asked.

Horace tucked his thumbs into his vest. "A confession, more like. Our friend, the Captain, has himself a heavy conscience."

The Livingstones all looked confused, but Cyrus didn't try to explain. He moved right into his plan.

"Okay," Cyrus said. "I'm going to contact Gil."

"How?" Dennis asked.

"He probably has Antigone's Quick Water. I'll hold up messages or something. I'll figure it out. But I'm going to tell him that if he gives us Antigone—and Rupert, if he has him—he can take Phoenix and do whatever he wants to him. I'll even tell him where Phoenix is—as much as Dan knows."

"Lad," said the Captain. "That's a steep gamble. This Phoenix holds the tooth. If the dragons take it, the world sinks in a worse slough. But if we take it, e'en the dragons can die and rot. Then ho for a war that can be won, for victory and new treaties writ in dragon blood. We must go for the tooth above all else, even Avengels and sisters."

"I know," said Cyrus. "But we race them. We get there first. We beat Phoenix and get the tooth. And then, like the Captain and like Arachne, we keep our promise, just not how the transmortals expect. We give them Phoenix but no tooth."

"It all sounds so easy," Nolan said.

"Phoenix won't roll over," said Alan. "I won't say it's a bad idea, but he'll have men and defenses. We'll be betting everything on our little band to win a race and then a battle, and with little time for preparations."

The Captain pointed at the gold ring on Cyrus's thumb—the ring that had tumbled from the Radu Bey block when he'd unlocked the Captain. Cyrus looked down at it. He'd forgotten he had it on.

"You hold the blood talisman of Radu Bey," the Captain said. "Charmed gold. I kept it sealed and hid. Now that it's out, he'll trace his own scent easy enow. No need to race. Lead and let them trail behind. Gil and his hounds will be baying at these doors if we wait."

Cyrus inhaled slowly and looked around the room, waiting for objections. His eyes settled on Dan. His older brother looked nervous. Dan crossed his arms, then nodded.

"Right," said Cyrus. "That's what we'll do. I need my

Quick Water." He faced Arachne. "Will you help me talk to Gil?"

Arachne rose and moved quietly toward Cyrus.

"As for taking Phoenix," Big Alan said, "have you any thoughts to that? We have guns in the planes and in this house, but not much else."

Robert Boone stepped in from the hall and leaned against the jamb. Jeb was behind him. "That's not all we have, Brother Elephant." He picked at his teeth with his toothpick, then looked around the room. When his eyes passed over Diana, he smiled. "My name's not Boone by any kind of accident. My pappy could snare a ghost in high mountain wind using nothing but twine and moonshine. I think we might be able to do something about old Phoenix." He looked at Cyrus. "Not saying I care for the plan. The dragons will want the Reaper's Blade, not Phoenix. And that's not a trade I can allow, two souls on the block or twenty."

Cyrus clenched his jaw. He knew they couldn't give the tooth to the *Ordo*, not for anything. Of course he knew that.

"Maxi wanted the tooth, too," Cyrus said quietly. "He wanted me to trade it for Dan." Flashes of memory tumbled through his head. Rupert fallen. Nolan fallen. Fire. Maxi's grinning face and nothing but a key ring in his own hand and the cold dark tooth jutting out between his knuckles.

Adrenaline whispered through his body, and on his neck, Patricia sensed it. She slithered slightly, tightening. Cyrus could still feel his final lunge, the crunch of bone. He could still see the keys dangling against Maxi's dying face.

"I didn't make any trades," Cyrus said quietly.

"No," Boone said. "No, you didn't. But just so we're clear, I'd rather see the underside of my own tombstone than have that tooth go to the likes of Radu Bey." He looked from face to face. "I hope that's what sets those in this room apart from Bellamy bloody Cook and the cowards and compromisers of Ashtown—a willingness to die rather than bow and scrape before the darkness."

Captain John Smith rumbled a long amen in his chest.

"The Order can rot," Boone muttered. "If this doesn't destroy it, maybe we will after. It's just another institution that's tried to master free men."

The Captain's rumble stopped and he eyed Boone.

"The O of B is still real, Pa," said Diana. "Our oaths are real. We're still in it, and if Rupe's alive, he's still Avengel; not even the Brendan can remove him while he's in the field."

Captain John Smith drew himself up, facing Boone. "Sir, the ants serve queens. Hornets defend a hive. Wolves hail a chieftain, and the great apes bend to their silver king. The tides to moon, the moon to earth, the earth to sun. Man hath the divine seal, but even he must be mastered."

Boone smiled with tight lips, wry eyes sparkling. "Well then, I stand corrected."

Cyrus jumped in. "You all can argue more later. We need guns. And whatever Mr. Boone might need to trap Phoenix. Dan can tell you what the place looks like. Mr. Boone, Mr. Livingstone, I'm sure you'll come up with a plan, but make sure the Captain likes it."

"But don't mind me." Nolan sighed. "I can hate it."

Cyrus backed toward the door, and Arachne followed him. Alan Livingstone and Robert Boone were eyeing each other like two dogs at a park, deciding if they were friends.

"How long till we're ready to fly?" Cyrus asked.

"Thirty," Boone said. "Maybe sooner. I keep the birds ready."

Cyrus nodded. "Okay. Thirty minutes. Oh, and Jax and Dennis," said Cyrus. "You're staying here."

Relief washed over Jax, but Dennis flushed embarrassment. Cyrus ducked quickly out of the room before there could be another discussion.

Arachne crossed her legs and set down her spider bag. Cyrus had already shut the bedroom door. He grabbed his bag from beside his bunk and sat on the floor across from the wide, icy blue eyes.

"It is hard for you right now," Arachne said.

Cyrus inflated his cheeks. "Yeah, it is." He set a little oilcloth pouch in front of Arachne. "I'm doing my best. Now you do yours and maybe we will get Rupert and Antigone back."

"If you rush at Phoenix," Arachne said quietly, "he will be unready." She looked down at the pouch. "What *exactly* do you want me to do?"

Cyrus stared into her cold blue eyes. "Try to find out . . . from the room, or from Gil's face . . . if my sister is . . ."

"Dead?"

Cyrus nodded. "And Rupert, if Gil took him. If he has either of them and they're still alive, then make Gil our offer. Do you need a paper and pen?"

Arachne shook her head, unlaced the pouch, and let the Quick Water roll out and wobble on her palm. Cyrus and Antigone had found it by accident in one of Ashtown's African collections. When divided in half, each ball looked out of the other, regardless of distance. Antigone and Diana had used it to find Cyrus when the treacherous Ashtown cook, Big Ben Sterling, had tied him up in one of the kitchen pantries. Now Cyrus hoped it would be just as useful.

The small ball of liquid fungus behaved a lot like mercury, but instead of being silver, it was clear. It quivered and wobbled on Arachne's palm. She traced the surface with one fingertip, then looked up at Cyrus, surprised.

"This is real," she said. "I expected a Victorian imitation. This is wild-grown. African."

Cyrus shrugged. He didn't know what that meant or why it mattered, but Arachne seemed encouraged. She was humming.

When Cyrus had used the Quick Water, he had simply held the ball up to his face and stared into it, seeing whatever was in range of Antigone's half, bent and warped by the shape of the sphere. But Arachne placed the blob on the carpet in front of her and dragged her fingers through it, separating it into strands. Then she separated those strands again. As she did, the strands tried to bead up into balls, but her fingers forced them back down and stretched them out, like noodles made of water, and then even thinner. Like threads. After a quick hiss through her teeth, Arachne's spiders marched through the carpet to help. With her small servants lining her fingertips, Arachne began to weave.

Cyrus watched as the Quick Water became a cloth. The cloth became a clear sheet of liquid glass. Arachne leaned over it and peered through.

Still looking down, she raised one hand into a slice of morning sunlight that was pouring in through the window. She smiled at Cyrus, then twisted her fingers. Beams of light flashed down from her fingers like she was holding a dozen tiny mirrors, pouring through her water window in the floor.

After a moment, she spoke.

Antigone opened her eyes. Her body ached and her head felt like a gong, still vibrating from her fall. She was upright, but a little off the ground, pinned to a brick wall. Thick leather straps held her arms and legs tight.

Antigone blinked slowly and looked up. The ceiling was stadium-height, six or seven stories up at least, and paned windows lined the walls just beneath it, letting in a waterfall of morning light. She could actually see birds up there, slowly circling perches.

Down at her level, rows of freestanding bookshelves ran all the way out of her blurry focus. Some held spines, and some scrolls. There were chairs. And tables. And more shelves. And partition walls. And art. And statues.

Halfway between floor and ceiling, there was a room mounted on a towering stone column. It was missing two of its walls, and it was smoking.

She'd fallen from that? No wonder she hurt all over. She tugged at the leather straps that held her to the wall. Strange, having straps like this in a library—if that's what this place was.

Where was Rupert? There were empty straps next to hers and sticky blood on the floor beneath them.

"Rupe?" Her voice echoed a little. When the echo

died, she heard nothing but the muffled sound of feathered wings and her own breathing.

"Rupe!" She screamed the name long and hard, half expecting a librarian to appear to shush her. At least, she expected *someone* to appear. No one did.

There was a table, no more than fifteen feet in front of her, tucked into the shadow of a two-story shelf. She squinted at it. Her leather jacket and her bag were on one end. The contents of her bag had been spread across the table—some clothes, the little box with the Chinese lantern globe that Skelton had left them. A knife. Canvas shoes. Hair bandanas. The oilcloth pouch with her half of the Quick Water. The mouth of the bag was open; she could just see the shimmery curve of the strange African fungus. She stared at it, hoping that Cyrus was looking.

As she inhaled to yell again, an old man shuffled out from behind a shelf and stood in front of her. He had a bulbous nose, a bald head, and eyebrows in need of a lawn mower. A straggly beard covered his cheeks and chin. He was wearing a child's hooded sweatshirt with a zipper, baggy corduroy trousers rolled up around his ankles, and red wool socks that had been forced into flip-flops. Across his chest, his sweatshirt excitedly announced a single word.

Soccer!

Scrunching his face as he examined Antigone, he tugged at loose white hairs on his throat.

"I'm Antigone Smith," Antigone said. "Who are you?"

The old man began to rustle through her belongings on the table.

"Hey!" She tugged at her straps. "Stop touching my stuff!"

The man found a dry granola bar in her bag, took a bite, and dropped into a chair. Grinning and chewing, he mumbled something in another language.

"What is that?" Antigone asked. "Greek? English would be awesome. Could we use English, please?"

"Shouldn't do it. Not these things. Not here," the man said. His accent was rich. "Don't like it. No." He studied the granola bar and took another bite.

"What things?" Antigone asked. "What are you talking about?"

He pointed at her. "You." He gestured at her straps. "This." His eyes sank to the blood on the floor. "That."

Antigone followed his eyes to the sticky puddle and then looked back up. "Where is he? Is Gil here?"

"Gil." The old man snorted the name. "Gil, Gil, Gil. Doesn't listen." He pointed the granola stub at the room high on the column. "That one is chained. Chained up tight. For now."

The man squeezed the last piece of the bar into his cheek and looked back at her bag, hopeful.

"That was my last one," Antigone said. "Please, talk to me. Who are you?"

The man went back to pulling at the hair on his throat. "Mentor," he said.

"Okay . . . ," Antigone said. "I don't know what you mean."

"Mentor," the man said again, tapping his chest cheerfully. "My name. I'm Mentor."

"Mentor? Really? Like . . . will you be my mentor?"

"Exactly. Correct. Me," the man said. "A name, and my name, and mentoring is named for me." He tapped the side of his nose and waggled his eyebrows.

Antigone tried to catch any glimpse of a joke in the man's eyes, but he seemed serious enough. He also seemed homeless and behind on his meds.

"So you're one of the transmortals?" Antigone asked. "You're in the *Ordo Draconis*?"

"*Ordo*. Or-do? Or-don't!" He laughed. "Or-die. The dragons do their dragooning." Mentor tapped his nose, then yawned slowly. "Dragons for the young. Steam and fire and fits. Too much for Mentor. Too much too muching. And Gil."

Mentor grew serious and looked around secretively. Then he whispered the name again and nodded importantly. "Gil. Doesn't care about books, Antigone. Nor the bottles sleeping in the cellars. Sleepy cellars. That's where Mentor sleeps. With the bottles." He touched his nose and yawned again. Antigone fought back a yawn of her own.

Mentor nodded at the tall stone column, capped with

the two-walled bedroom. "Fits, fits, fits. Fits and thunder. And dragons. And wolves and heroes. The old world, Antigone Smith." He leaned forward. "Put to bed, Antigone Smith. It was. Tucked into tombs and corners under cobblestones and cobblewebs. Brendan's children sang the lullaby. Lulla-bye-bye."

The old man slid out of his chair and walked toward her, scratching at his *Soccer!* "Dragons sleep, Antigone Smith. They sleep long." He was close enough for her to smell his breath—a smell like dirt and mushrooms and wine. The old man touched his nose again. "But they wake. They do. And when they do, listen to Mentor, listen. Do what needs doing."

"I'm listening," Antigone said. "What needs doing?"

Mentor hissed a whisper into her face. "When the chains break, when the dragons wake . . . *run*."

A door slammed. High above, pigeons fluttered. Mentor spun and raced away in his socks and flip-flops, disappearing between the shelves. Antigone waited. She could hear heavy feet. Many feet.

"Hey!" she yelled.

She listened. The feet were approaching.

"Gil!" she shouted. "If you hurt him . . ."

Gilgamesh of Uruk stepped into view between the rows of shelves. There were others behind him in the shadows. The bloody body of Rupert Greeves—gripped by the back of his shirt—dangled from Gil's right hand.

As he approached, Antigone could see the patches on Rupert's shoulders. His shirt was on inside out, and blood was soaking through it.

Antigone couldn't speak. Her eyes welled up as Gil dropped Rupert at her feet, and she chewed back a sob. Rupert was motionless. She couldn't see the rise and fall of breathing.

"*If* I hurt him?" Gil asked, grinning.

Light flashed on the table behind Gil. All the transmortals turned.

The Quick Water was moving.

eighteen

IN THE BONEHOUSE

ANTIGONE WATCHED THE QUICK WATER roll out of the pouch. She watched it twist and spin itself into a hundred strings. The strings wove themselves together and flattened until they had formed a glistening sheet like a pool on the tabletop.

Sunlight erupted out of the Quick Water, casting a vertical pillar of gold straight up through the dusty air to the distant ceiling.

"Gilgamesh?" The voice was female, but strange, almost metallic. The pool rippled as the center rose from the table, forming a tent, and then a balloon, and then the fluid statue of a head and neck—the miniature glassy face of Arachne, alive with sunlight.

While Antigone watched, liquid Arachne looked around the room, at her, at Rupert's body, at the pillar room of Radu Bey, and finally, at Gil, painting him with light.

"Gilgamesh," the water girl said again. "What have you done?"

Gilgamesh hooded his eyes against the sunlight and moved closer to the table.

"The dragons have the same question for you, Arachne," Gil said. "You shielded the Smiths in Ashtown, you strengthened the weave of their sinews, and then, when the treaties were voided and the world became ours, you fled with our enemies." He snorted. "You've woven Angel Skin for the girl, and you question me? Radu has sealed your treason on the pillar beneath his throne room."

"His throne room is a cell," Arachne said. "It is justice. Ask Radu what oath I have broken. Ask the dragon what pledged allegiance I have betrayed. Gilgamesh, you are a good man. You could *be* a good man."

Gil's ribs heaved as he laughed. Pigeons rustled high above in the rafters. "A *man*? Did a man strike off the head of Khumbaba? Did a man best Enkidu? Did Inanna fall in love with a mere man?"

"I do not know what you are anymore," Arachne said. "Men die to become their true selves. Wine and life cannot remain bottled forever. They sour." She paused. "Have you?"

On the floor at Antigone's feet, Rupert groaned. His hand flexed and moved. Relief flooded through Antigone, and she tugged forward, wishing she could reach him.

"I know where you are, Arachne," Gil said. "The

Smith boy carries Radu's ring. I stood in the throne room and looked down on you from the sky. We will come, little weaver. It will be best if you are not with the children of Brendan when we arrive."

Gilgamesh stepped forward and raised his hand to crush the liquid head.

"Wait!" Arachne said. "Gil, your war is with Phoenix. The Smiths are nothing more than an old grudge. They do not hold the tooth. We can show you where Phoenix is. Cyrus carries the ring. We will lead you there."

"Why would you do this?" Gil asked.

"Phoenix is an enemy to all. We will lead you to his lair, and you may do what you will with him, but give us Rupert and the girl . . . alive and well."

Gil looked down at Rupert and then at Antigone. He scratched at the hair high up on his cheek, and then turned toward Radu's pillar room. Finally, he nodded.

"Fine," Gil said. "We leave as soon as you've shown us where the dog is hiding. Go quickly, or the log mansion in the mountains burns along with the forest around it."

"Bring them," Arachne said. "The girl and Greeves. When you come."

Gil nodded again.

"And, Gilgamesh, I—"

Gil slapped the Quick Water flat with his wide hand. It splashed up through his six fingers, found itself in the air, and slapped down onto the table, quivering and quaking, a glowing sphere once more. Gil rolled it into its oilcloth pouch, cinched it tight, and pocketed it.

The other transmortals stepped out of the shadows. A man almost as large as Gil moved to the front. He had a red beard down his chest and a long, thick braid down his back. When he spoke, his voice was deep and wild—part growl, part waterfall.

"The dragon has his plans, Gilgamesh. We cannot take these two along."

"We won't," Gil said. He nudged Rupert with his toe. "Strap him up. Then we wait. The little spider will show us Phoenix."

Antigone bit her lip as Red Beard lifted Rupert off the ground and slammed him against the brick wall. A slender, worn-looking woman with silver hair stepped forward and cinched the straps tight around his arms and legs.

Red Beard looked into Rupert's face. "You'll give us the maps, Avengel," he said. "And the Burials will empty."

Leaving Rupert, Red Beard sniffed at Antigone. He bent slowly, lowering his face to hers. Antigone held her breath, trying not to smell. His eyes were swampy green. He raised a hand to her face and rubbed the back of it against her cheek—it was covered with red hair as thick as pig bristles.

Antigone jerked and turned her head. Red Beard

grabbed the top of her head and twisted her face toward him. He smiled, baring two teeth in his huge lower jaw that were unnaturally long. But they were blunt, more like tusks, not fangs.

"Strange," he said, "a pretty little Smith wearing Angel Skin. Unfit for devils."

"Enkidu . . . ," Gil said.

"You had your play, Gilgamesh," Enkidu said. "I shall have mine." He drew a long knife from his belt. "We test the spider's weave."

Antigone's heart pounded. She wanted to spit in his face, to scream. But her throat clamped shut. She felt the tip of the knife creep into her stomach, barely muted by the Angel Skin.

"Enkidu!" Gil boomed. "We spend her later. Come!"

The huge redheaded pig grunted, then backed away. He and the rest of the transmortals followed Gil through the shelves and into shadow.

"Well done," Rupert said quietly.

Antigone turned her head, surprised. Rupert was looking at her. His face was swollen and bloody. Patches of his beard had been torn out. But he was smiling.

He looked around the huge room and up at the pillar. "I've heard tales of Radu's room," he said. He spat blood on the floor. "From my Keeper, the Avengel before Robert Boone. This pillar was originally in the caves of Slovenia. But we are not in Slovenia now."

"How do you know?" Antigone asked. "I wasn't conscious when they brought us here, were you?"

"I know, as you will learn to," Rupert said, straining against his straps. "From the tilt of the earth beneath my feet and the pull of true north on my bones."

"Rupe, do you think . . . the others . . . ?"

Rupert Greeves relaxed in his bonds. "I don't know," he said. "And I did not know that John Smith had so deeply bonded himself with Radu Bey. I made a terrible mistake in going to wake him. He had four chains in his Burial, as Radu did in his. Three are now broken."

He shook his head. "I was a fool. I told Cyrus to loose all four when they were all that still bound the last Dracul."

"Wait," Antigone said. "John Smith was chained up, too? And Cyrus was supposed to unlock them?"

Rupert nodded. "And he must have unlocked three. Radu still wears one chain."

"But that's good," Antigone said. "Or better than it could be." She nodded up at the room. "He's still stuck in there."

Antigone swallowed hard and leaned her head back against the bricks. "What are we going to do?"

"This is the valley of the shadow of death," Rupert said quietly. He smiled slightly. "We will fear no evil."

"Valiant! Valley, valley, valiant." The scrawny old man shuffled back into view. He sat down at the table, then pulled up the hood on his sweatshirt and cinched it tight around his face. "I will listen to your speeches."

Rupert leaned his head forward, squinting beneath his bloody brows. "Who are you?" he asked.

"He says his name is Mentor," Antigone said. "He stole a granola bar out of my backpack."

The old man winked and clicked his tongue. "My belly borrowed it," he said. "Sorrowful poor, my belly. Always borrowing." His hood-puckered face grinned. "Borrowing and sorrowing."

Dixie Mist opened her eyes in the darkness of her new cell. She hadn't slept more than a few exhausted minutes all night. Her wrists and ankles were raw from twisting in the bonds that strapped her tight into her chair. She'd read about people who could dislocate their joints to slip free of cuffs and ropes and chains.

Turned out, she wasn't one of those people.

The noise had kept her awake. All night, there had been footsteps and shouts. Sometimes a scream and sometimes laughter. Sometimes snatches of music. There had even been applause—cheering. She couldn't imagine what anyone would cheer for in this place. Nothing good, she was sure. Nothing good at all.

Men had carried Oliver away in his chair hours and hours ago.

Though there were no windows in her room, she knew

the sun was up. Her body had anticipated her old alarm clock. She'd even imagined its ring. It felt like a whole world had passed since she'd last heard that clock. Like maybe, somehow, she wasn't Dixie Mist at all. She was someone else in a very different life, a life gone wrong.

Hours had passed since then. Boots were thumping down the hall outside her door, but she closed her eyes and tried to ignore them. She tried to picture her mother's face. It was hard. The more she had stared at her mother's photo, the more the photo was all she'd been able to recall. She wished she'd known, back when she'd had her mother, that she would need to remember everything, that memory would be all she would have. She would have done nothing but stare at her mother every minute of every day, stamping memories with her mother's smile, her eyes, her hair, her voice, her smell. . . .

Smell. In a rush, Dixie remembered. She could see her mother slapping flour off her apron after rolling piecrust. She could smell her perfume—she was going out with Daddy soon—mixing with the cinnamon and lemon that she'd put on the apples Dixie had helped her slice. She could see her mother smile as she pulled back her hair; she could see the little lines at the corners of her bright bayou-emerald eyes, and the light catching those long gold earrings against her dark perfect neck. Her daddy came into the room, and she could hear her mama begin to sing. . . .

The heavy door rattled open. Light filled the room, and Dixie was back in the world gone wrong.

Two men stepped in, shadows against the lit doorway.

"What's he want with this little swamp rabbit?"

"Does it matter?"

Tattooed arms picked up her chair and carried her out into the hall. Lined up in a neat row along the wall were unconscious men in orange jumpsuits.

The tattooed men carried Dixie into the old cigar-rolling room with the freezers and the bodies and the girl with the rope hair.

The freezers had been pushed back; their electric cords ran up into the ceiling in bundles. Five shallow glass pools had been arranged on the floor like the five dots on dice.

The men set Dixie down against one wall, then backed away to the other side of the room, where many more tattooed men were waiting. Some of them looked normal, like hard old truck drivers or swamp loggers—like some of her daddy's friends. But some were different. They were taller and leaner, the muscles on their bare arms netted with strangely symmetrical veins. Small flaps of skin like fish gills fluttered on the sides of their necks. All of the changed men were dripping wet.

Behind them, beside the wide track door she had jumped out of with Oliver, was a jumbled pile of bodies in orange jumpsuits. Two men began throwing the bodies into the river below.

Oliver. Where was Oliver?

She looked back at the pools. Four of the pools held a tattooed body; the center pool held Oliver, floating with his eyes shut and his arms extended, his face barely breaking the surface of the water. His ribs were rising and falling slowly as he breathed.

One Hand hobbled out from behind the freezers. His dirty white coat was dripping. His black hair was slick wet, clinging to his face. His eyes were glittering with excitement. His one hand leaned against his bamboo cane. Hanging over his stump was a bundle of loose thin wires attached to long needles.

Dixie watched as he set the needle wires down beside Oliver's pool, then hobbled to a bench against the wall, making sure to circle far around the chained Pythia as he went. She was facing a corner, wrapped tightly in her hair.

On the bench there sat an old-style record player. One Hand lowered the machine's playing arm onto a record that was already in place and spinning. The sounds of an orchestra jumped from the speaker, filling the room.

One Hand swayed cheerfully as he limped back to Oliver's pool. He knelt beside it and began to insert the needles into Oliver's pale flesh. He worked several in at every joint, then placed others in lines along his limbs and torso.

When all the needles were satisfactory, Phoenix muttered to himself, and the thin wires attached to the needles uncurled and stood up straight, five feet tall, swaying and twisting in the air like swamp grass in the breeze.

One Hand moved to the other bodies, setting needles, humming, conducting the music with his stump.

When all the needles were set and the room was full of the strange, swaying wires, Phoenix shut his eyes and stretched out his good arm, running his hand slowly across the tops of the wires, whispering as he did. The water in the pools began to seethe, bubbling cold, and the bodies in the pools began to twitch. Dixie watched as Oliver's skin boiled and rolled. His muscles knotted and bulged like exploding tumors. His joints unhinged and folded backward.

Dixie shut her eyes and tucked her chin against her chest. She thought about her mother, about her father's laugh and the sound of the odd songs he'd sing while he worked, the whir of his saw and the crack of his hammer, anything but the loud music and the bodies splashing and thumping and One Hand's terrible whispered groaning.

Dixie couldn't say how much time passed. She sent her mind racing elsewhere and elsewhen. She spent whole days with her parents, whole weeks at her grandmother's.

She hopped through summers, and the life spans of two pets. She rearranged her rooms in three different houses. Until finally, she noticed that the room around her had grown still.

The music had stopped, but she could hear the record player still turning. One Hand was breathing hard. Sniffing.

Feet moved past her, and finally, she opened her eyes.

The wires and needles had been collected and carried away. The bodies they had been connected to had changed. Tattooed arms had lengthened. Necks were gilled. Muscles bulged strangely. Joints and limbs were bent akimbo. Men who before had looked like floating sleepers now looked dead and violently broken. Oliver was the least changed, but still his back was twisted. One of his legs was hanging over the side of his pool and bent sharply back at the knee.

Tattooed men were dragging four of the unconscious jumpsuited bodies into the room from the hallway. Each was laid beside a pool, with one hand flung over the edge and into the water. Only Oliver did not receive one.

One Hand hobbled from pool to pool, prodding the convicts' submerged hands with his cane.

"Pythia!" he shouted, pausing beside one. "Oracle! Is he like enough? Is he a killer?"

Dixie looked at the mass of hair in the corner. The

hair didn't move, but a single leaf fluttered up into the air. Dixie saw a symbol burning on the leaf before it turned to ash and dusted out of the air.

The smell of the fiery leaf made her think of fall, of her father's old burn barrel, of watching football with him on the back porch and yelling at the men in the wrong-color shirts on some faraway field, picture flickering on their little screen.

One Hand nodded, and a tattooed man stepped forward. He took the convict's wet hand and laid it on top of the floating hand of the broken body in the pool. Then he stepped away.

One Hand began to speak words that Dixie couldn't understand. These were not whispers. They grew louder and louder, and as they did, he opened the silver head of his bamboo cane, revealing a sharp black point. He turned the cane around like it was a spear.

"Come on, Roger!" one of the tattooed men shouted from the side.

With a quick thrust and a sharp word, One Hand speared the two hands together. Blood leaked through the pool as the watchers fell silent.

The big jumpsuited body jolted, and the body in the pool stretched slowly. Joints straightened as the watchers burst into cheers. One Hand withdrew his spear, and the man called Roger rose from the water. His symmetrical veins ballooned. The gills on the side of his neck fluttered. He nodded at One Hand and then joined his fellows, clasping his bloody hand with theirs.

Dixie couldn't help watching the next three. Two of them rose just like Roger had, to the excitement of his comrades. Only one remained broken and motionless. When the cane spear was withdrawn, he and the convict were both dead.

Finally, only Oliver remained. One Hand turned and smiled at Dixie. Men approached her chair, and in a flood she realized what was happening.

She was for Oliver. Her hand would be pierced to his.

When she began to scream, a rag was shoved into her mouth. The men unstrapped one of her arms and carried her whole chair to the pool, where they tipped it onto its back. A hand closed around her wrist and forced it into the pool.

She stared at the ceiling and the giant lightbulbs her father had so carefully collected, the wiring he had so carefully run through the rafters. At a burning leaf floating through the air. And then another. And then a whole flock. Ash snowed down on her, and she closed her eyes.

"I don't believe you!" One Hand was saying. "Child for child, innocent for innocent. You're telling lies, sweet Pythia. If only you hadn't been raised in a cave, you would know that lies are unacceptable."

"Never," a girl's voice said. "Lie."

"Ah," said One Hand. "The savage little oracle can

speak after all." One Hand loomed above Dixie, massaging his bamboo cane, his eyes on Pythia in the corner. "As you're now consulting more thoroughly, I should explain that this is only the first phase for this particular boy. He is meant to die three times tonight, and in the third resurrection, his flesh shall become mine." He paused. "Is that why you lie? Is that what you hope to prevent?"

A leaf floated by.

"No leaves!" One Hand screamed. "No more! Shape your oracle with a tongue!"

Dixie's heartbeat was pounding in her head, but she could still hear the girl's quiet, simple voice as it grew to fill the room.

"Pierce her, pierce him. Soul with soul, they bird away, smoke float, river rush, twain flee forever. Truth escapes. The boy is no innocent."

One Hand raised his cane to his lips, then looked down at Dixie. His wet hair bent around his eyes and clung to his jaw and his thin, stretched neck.

In his eyes, Dixie saw death.

He turned away. "Find me the youngest convict!" he yelled. "Not a killer. A thief, perhaps."

The tattooed man holding Dixie's wrist in the water restrapped her arm to her chair, lifted her up, and carried her back to the wall, where she was set down out of the way.

• • •

Phoenix slid the cane's silver cap over the tooth and kissed it. He looked at his remaining men. Three more cycles before the task was complete. The thought poured exhaustion into his bones. He was cracking, flying apart with the strain. Without the coat, the forces flowing through him, through the tooth, would have splattered his ash all over the walls.

His mind . . . only the ancient charms in the white weave were keeping him clever now. The time would soon come when he must shed the coat. And then . . . would the beast do what he commanded? Would it complete the task ungoverned? Or would he be completely mad? He shut his eyes and doused the tiny flame of fear that had sparked within him. There had always been risk, and it had always been worth taking.

He looked at his new regiment of sons. Thirty new lives in thirty new bodies, with hearts that would never explode . . . unless he spoke the word. And when he'd managed to collect enough transmortals, the greatest among his sons would be rewarded further, with unending life in his service.

Two more cycles of his men, and then one or two from the freezers before his final work on Oliver. That's all the strength he could risk before the struggle with the transmortals. His unchanged men would die when the transmortals came. Enkidu would bring them after midnight, as he and Phoenix had agreed. The trap would be sprung, Enkidu would have his payment, and Phoenix would have the first of many pet dragons.

There wasn't much time, but there was enough. His new crop would rest and be prepared. By midnight, the snares would be set.

Unless the transmortals found him sooner. Even a few hours early, and . . . Phoenix shook his head, shedding the thought. No. They wouldn't. If another of the transmortals had tracked him, the dragons would have descended on him already. Ponce had no summoning magic, and the other transmortals he'd captured were all dead and at the bottom of the river from his testing with the tooth. He looked at Pythia, once again hair-shrouded in the corner. What could she do besides conjure leaves and write in flame? She could see the future, but she could not summon. Could she? Even if so, she had never been allied to the Great Dracul.

"Pythia! Oracle! When will the dragons come? No leaves. Speech."

Pythia's hair stirred and slithered as the girl stood. Her eyes were fierce, her voice stone.

"Seventy weeks. Dragons will fear the one called Desolation."

Phoenix laughed as four more of his men lay down in the pools around Oliver. There were fear and resolution in their blinking eyes. They were prepared to die and rise again.

"Seventy weeks is rather generous," Phoenix said. "And Desolation is rather harsh. If I destroy, it is as a farmer tills a field. I sow men and reap gods."

Phoenix pointed his cane at one of the floating men and shook his head. Surprised, the man jumped up, dripping. Phoenix pointed at the freezers.

"It is time for a specialty," he said. He ground his cane into his itching stump. "Bring me the Smith."

nineteen

DRACUL

ANTIGONE'S SHOULDERS WERE KILLING HER. Once again, she tried to shift her weight, bending her legs as far as her straps would allow and then straightening them again. She slid her arms against the leather at her wrists over and over and then exhaled frustration.

Rupert was asleep, his head hanging. Mentor had disappeared, she had seen nothing of Gil and the transmortals, and her mind wouldn't stop running laps. Were the transmortals really off chasing Cyrus? He wouldn't lead them to Phoenix. He couldn't. No one had a clue where Phoenix was. What was Cyrus planning? Knowing her brother, something crazy and borderline stupid. She hoped the older people were keeping him sane. And safe. They had to be. That had been her job for the last three years, and she wasn't there to do it. Cyrus had better realize that Gil would never honor the trade. Of course, whatever his plan was, Cyrus would be welching, too. And that meant that Gil would come back angry. . . .

At least Cyrus was alive. For now. But how long would she be?

Up in the pillared room, quiet light flickered. Antigone groaned. She was hungry. She was exhausted and in pain and she needed to go to the bathroom.

"Rupe?" Antigone said. "Rupe!"

Rupert opened his eyes and looked at her. Despite all the blood soaked into his shirt, the patch with the flying chess knight shone perfectly silver on his shoulder.

Antigone squirmed, scraping her back against the bricks. "We can't be here. When Gil gets back, I don't think we'll be alive for long."

Rupert's bloody lips smiled slightly. "I do not think today is our day to die. You saw Arachne in the Quick Water. Our friends and your brothers are out there. And now they have seen us. They know we are alive."

An orange flame billowed slowly from the side of the pillar room. Antigone and Rupert looked up at the crawling flash.

"What's he doing?" Antigone asked.

"The same thing we are," Rupert said. He jerked his arms hard against the straps. "Straining at his bonds. And like us, he will need help if he's going to break free."

The flame died and pigeons slowly resettled in their roosts. Coming from high in the rafters, Antigone heard the call of a red-winged blackbird. She squinted up at the distant windows.

"Down here!" she yelled. Before the echo died, a shape was fluttering through a slice of window light. When the bird landed on top of the nearest bookshelf, Antigone could finally see the red feathers on her wings.

Antigone laughed as the bird belted a triumphant call. She hopped off the shelf and glided to Antigone's shoulder. Singing angry threats to unseen enemies, the bird hopped down Antigone's arm and pecked at the leather strap on her wrist.

Rupert watched with his brows down. "How much have you thought about that bird?"

"What do you mean?" Antigone asked.

"You know what I mean," said Rupert. His voice was low. "You and Cyrus must have talked about it. You call it 'she' when the plumage is male. You've never trained it, and yet it's always around one of the two of you. Was it ever at the motel?"

Antigone shook her head. She licked her dry lips. She and Cyrus hadn't talked about it. Not much, at least. Some. A little. Enough. But when Arachne had knocked them out back in Skelton's rooms, and they had both heard their mother's voice, and she had talked about watching them . . .

"You'd be crazy not to wonder," Rupert said. He watched the worried bird flutter to Antigone's other arm and squawk irritation at the toughness of the leather. "When did she show up at Ashtown?"

Antigone didn't want to talk about it. Not that part.

Rupert's voice lowered. "Before or after Phoenix?"

"At the same time," Antigone said quietly. "Well, maybe. Cyrus saw a red-winged blackbird in a cage in Phoenix's plane with Mom and Dan after the crash in the lake. But it might not have been this one."

"Really?" asked Rupert. "And after that night . . ."

". . . the bird has always been around," Antigone finished. The bird hopped up onto her head and then flew back to its shelf perch. It turned in place, surveying the room. "Can we not talk about it?" she asked. "Sometimes it's nice and I like to think that she really is watching, that she really sees how hard I've studied and how fast Cyrus runs, and sometimes it just makes me want to cry, and sometimes it makes me think I'm all the way crazy. I don't like thinking that she's—that my mom . . . that Phoenix might have . . ."

Rupert's eyes were on the blackbird, but she fluttered away.

"Tell me a story," Antigone said. She twisted as far toward Rupert as she could. "Please. Tell me one about my dad."

Rupert laughed. "A father story? Now?"

"Do you have something better to do?" Antigone asked. "We could be killed any time, and I have to go to the bathroom, and I feel like I'm going to start crying and I'm not going to be able to stop. Unless you're planning our escape, I think you can tell me a story. If you don't, you're just going to fall back to sleep and leave me here worrying about absolutely everything all by myself."

Rupert leaned his head back against the brick wall and looked up at the distant ceiling. "A Lawrence Smith story . . . and one that makes him out to be the soundest of role models for his daughter." He smiled. "And with a little bird that might be listening in, too. Not the easiest task, Antigone Smith."

"Oh, come on. Tell me about how he met my mom. You've told us a little bit about that already."

"Lovely," Rupert said. "A mother story now as well? Fine. Brilliant. It's as good a tale as any, though I shouldn't be the one to tell it."

"Tough," said Antigone. "They can't, so you will."

Rupert cleared his throat. "The last trek of Lawrence Smith, it is. Right. Picture your father, but younger. In fact, picture Cyrus, only a little taller, blond, and heftier in the shoulders and chest."

"Dan looks more like Dad than Cy does."

Rupert tried to shrug. "Sure. But your father's aura, his attitude, his mouthiness, his stubbornness—that's all Cyrus." He smiled. "And you too. But you control it better than either of them.

"The two of us set out for northern Brazil because those jungles had swallowed more of the Order's bodies than any other. And because winter was settling in at

Ashtown and other members were scattering for distant homes to pass the holidays. We had no family but each other, and no desire to share dry turkey in the dining hall.

"Lawrence had read stories about a network of valleys tangled through the jungle mountains. We tracked down an old Keeper in Africa—Alan Livingstone's father, an even bigger elephant than he, called Sir Curtis by everyone who knew him. He had been in the region as a lad, and he told us all the drunken campfire tales he'd heard from natives and traders alike. Hidden villages were said to be built into the cliffs of those jungle valleys, and in the central valley there was supposed to be a city like those long ago destroyed in Peru and still hidden in parts of Mexico. The rumors were not especially unique—the valleys were charmed, the city was cursed, no one who entered was ever seen again, untold wealth, impossible danger—the kind of stories men tell themselves both to frighten and entice the minds of young explorers. Alan Livingstone wanted to join us, but his father had other plans for him. It was years before I saw him again.

"Your father and I packed one heavy backpack each, chartered a nearly broken-down plane, and parachuted into the deepest valley we could spot from the air, not too far north of the Brazilian border." Rupert looked at Antigone. "Still awake? Still interested?"

Antigone laughed. "No . . . not at all. Please stop. I've only tried to get you to tell this story for a whole year."

"Well, the next part is long and boring. That's why I asked. It was the rainy season, and we walked through that jungle for six weeks, tromping beside every flooded stream and river and valley and gulch we could find. It was horrible and long, but all I really remember is the hunger. We ate bark and birds, and every beetle we could find. Fruit was hard to come by, which surprised us both. Finally, we even ate a half dozen fat newts we caught in fast rapids, praying that they weren't as toxic as most of their kind, hoping we would wake up alive in the morning. We did wake up, but deathly ill. Would you like to know how ill?"

"Not really," Antigone said. "Skipping, skipping, skipping—you threw up, you felt better, and then . . ."

"We didn't feel better," Rupert said. "We just didn't want to die there. We made an embarrassingly terrible raft—shameful construction—and we pushed out onto the fast river, curious if we would die at the first waterfall.

"We shot rapid after rapid and lost a little of our raft each time. And then we hit the real waterfall. It hurled us over a cliff, but we only fell part of the way. We landed in a churning, cauldronlike pool high on the cliff face. Both of us managed to clutch onto rocks. The raft shattered and scattered.

"The water spilled out again and dropped out of sight—down and down and down. Later, when we were at the distant bottom, we actually stood directly beneath that torrent and it was like standing in a quiet rain. The water fell so far that most of it vaporized in the drop and wafted through that broad lush valley, painting even the cliff walls green with moss."

"But what happened at the top?" Antigone asked. "In the cauldron? How did you get down?"

Rupert laughed. "In the cauldron we were attacked by dragonflies. Huge dragonflies, and not just in the air. We were in their breeding pool. While mothers with heads as big as grapefruit slashed at us, ripping at our faces and shoulders and scalps, dragonfly nymphs the size of footballs attacked our legs beneath the water's surface. They had jaws like bulldogs."

He stopped and shut his eyes.

"And . . . ," Antigone said. "This is no place to stop talking. Come on, Rupe. How'd you get down?"

"We were lowered," Rupert said. "Believe it or not, we had stumbled upon the legendary valley and had ridden our raft right over the waterfall into its well-defended gate. Tall brown men with shorn heads and bronze weapons appeared on the cliffs around the fall and snared us in nets. A few of them laughed, but most acted as if they were sorting rubbish. They hauled us out of that cauldron like fish.

"They lowered us all the way to the valley floor, where more of their people waited for us. An older woman pressed a small green viper against my neck. The bite felt like fire, and within seconds, I was asleep. Your father fought and managed to cut himself out of the net. I don't know how long he lasted."

Someone coughed in Antigone's ear. She whirled in surprise. Mentor was standing on her other side. He winked and clicked his tongue.

"The Captain's daughter, eh?" he asked. "Daughter to the Beheader? Heads and heads, chop, chop?" He hacked at his own neck with his hand, then stuck out his tongue. Antigone looked at Rupert, but he was studying the old man's face. And he saw something he liked.

"That she is," Rupert said, smiling. "The Captain's distant daughter. Did you know him?"

The blackbird swooped out of a shadow and landed on Antigone's shoulder.

"All's right then," Mentor said. He tapped his nose. "Captain Smith, he found me when no one cared. Old Mentor. Sought counsel—my own counsel—right where I slept." He winked. "In the Angel. Londontown's taverny Angel. Had a bench for my roof. Oh, Mentor's bench and he sat on it and I said my wisdom from beneath like a prophet and he gave me coin like it was Christmas." He sniffed. "And it were." He widened his eyes. "Christmas. When the Captain sought old Mentor."

He smiled, as if his whole tale had made complete and perfect sense. "The Captain," he said again. Then he reached up and undid the leather strap on Antigone's arm. It dropped stiffly to her side, firing pain through her creaking shoulder. She rolled it slowly as Mentor moved to her other arm, then crouched to undo the straps at her ankles.

Antigone dropped awkwardly to the floor and Mentor backed away. He tapped the side of his nose and winked.

"Christmas. In summer," he said. Then he added, "They're gone. The beasties. Off to fight and hack and hew."

He blew Antigone a kiss, turned, and hurried away between the shelves.

Antigone tugged Rupert's straps loose. "You're not getting out of it," she said.

"Getting out of what?" Rupert asked.

His first arm swung free, and he groaned.

"The story," she said. "You're telling all of it. And soon."

Rupert smiled as he stepped down from the wall. He pointed at the room perched on the pillar. "I hate to say it, but I have to go back up there."

Antigone looked at her Keeper like he was crazy. "That's not funny, Rupe."

"I know," Rupert said. "Gil stole your Quick Water or I would use it instead. But wherever he and the others are heading, wherever he believes your brother to be, they saw it from up in that room. I have to know where we're running, and what we're running into."

"In case you've forgotten," Antigone said, "there's a transmortal in that room who doesn't like you very much."

Rupert nodded. "Mentor said he was asleep."

Antigone looked around the empty rows. "Seriously? That guy? You're just going to trust him? What if he's wrong?"

"Then we run," said Rupert simply. "And we don't stop." He swept Antigone's remaining possessions into her pack and tossed it to her. Then he turned and began to limp through the rows of shelves toward the room and the stone pillar it rested on. Antigone hurried after him.

Crossing that sprawling building was like wandering through a badly organized library on top of a badly organized museum, intermingled with a village or two and an extremely well-organized junkyard. The place was as big as a blimp hangar, dimly lit, and crisscrossed with tall bookshelves, overflowing storage containers, tidy collections, and even small houses. They passed three helicopters in a row, all partially assembled, and after that, a cottage with metal siding and lights on in the windows.

A woman ducked inside as they approached, and they heard children's voices as they passed.

"They have kids?" Antigone whispered. "And they live in here on purpose?"

"They're not normal people," Rupert said. "My coin over yours, that woman and her children are mortal and she cannot remember when she first wandered into this place. Transmortals lead a very lonely existence. The more men and women die around them, the lonelier they grow. Sometimes they're driven mad, or they simply deteriorate, like Mentor. Some, like Nolan, seek the stillness of dark isolation, but never too far from the noise of mortal life. Some seek the companionship of the other undying, like Gil and Enkidu." He glanced up at the pillar. "But the darkest of the strong ones—half-gin and blood sorcerers, and the Dracul chief among them—they are like lightless dying stars. They have a deep gravity that pulls pain and hurt and oppression into orbit around them, even when unseen. It always happens," Rupert said angrily. "Victims, worshippers, and slaves gather around a destroyer, fearful but devoted."

Antigone could see three more crude cottages with glowing windows up ahead, and one truck camper without a truck. Hushed voices floated past, carrying from another row.

"Weird," she whispered. "These people want to be here?"

"They were drawn," Rupert said quietly, "like flecked metal to a magnet. The dark undying must be Buried deep. Encase one in stone, and within a year, broken and twisted people will be dancing around it at midnight. Strap Radu Bey to an anchor and toss him into a volcano, and it wouldn't be more than a generation before bloody muttering priests would be tossing in virgins after him."

Antigone kept her head on a swivel as she followed Rupert. The strange hush of the place was even more disturbing to her than the little houses. She could hear birds rustling far above. The snatch of a word, lost in echo. A small crash in the distance. The bark of a dog barely louder than her own breathing.

And then, from behind her, came the sounds of a bicycle. She turned just as a boy wheeled into their lane and shot past, staring at them with wide eyes. Rupert nodded at the boy's back.

"Exhibit A," he said. "Most likely, his mother found this place by accident, but would now die gladly if it meant her son would be empowered to serve her new Dracul god. I've seen it before."

Antigone felt sick as she watched the boy pedal away. When he looked back over his shoulder at her, she waved.

They were close now. Rupert led Antigone around one more corner, and the stone pillar rose up ahead of them. It had the uneven skin of a stalagmite, and around its base was a crudely built circular platform, like a stage, covered in loose wooden planks. She felt suddenly grateful to whoever had decided to build the thing. That's where she and Rupert had bounced, and without it, she probably wouldn't be alive—or at least not walking. The lower third of the pillar was covered with disordered carvings—crude portraits, and scrawled words in alphabets Antigone didn't recognize, and in some alphabets she did. She saw Latin and Greek and Arabic, and in many places, names with dates, and in others, two simple initials together inside a heart. She almost laughed, curious how long people had been doing that. Probably as long as there had been sharp objects to scratch with. There was probably an *A* + *E* in the Garden of Eden.

She looked up. The stone underside of the balancing room was at least thirty feet above the platform. "How did you know we would be okay when you jumped?" she asked.

"I didn't," Rupert said. "I hoped. If I'd known it was that high, I wouldn't have. Come on, then. No point in waiting." He scrambled onto the platform and walked toward an old rusty spiral stair that wound up to one of the room's corners.

Antigone climbed behind Rupert, sometimes pausing to let the stairs' shaking lessen. The blackbird had already fluttered to the top.

Antigone couldn't imagine Gilgamesh and the Red Beard pig climbing at the same time. If some of the treads hadn't already held Rupert, she wouldn't have trusted them at all.

They moved as quietly as they could, but rusty screws whined, and treads popped and sighed. As they neared the top, Antigone could see that the two solid walls of the room joined in the corner they were climbing toward.

"Psst!" she heard from below.

She looked down. The boy on the bicycle was at the bottom of the stairs.

"That's not smart," he said. "He'll eat you. He ate my sister."

Rupert leaned over the handrail. "Ate?" he whispered.

The boy nodded. "He picked me, and ate her. I hate him."

"Did your mother bring you here?" Rupert asked.

The boy nodded. "She won't leave."

"Where's your father?"

"He's in prison."

"Would you like to leave?"

The boy nodded.

"Then wait right there," Rupert whispered. "We'll only be a minute."

The top of the stairs dead-ended in a little metal landing jutting out from the joined stone corner.

Rupert rested his hands on the stone. Antigone's heartbeat was tap-dancing on her eardrums. She didn't like this. Not at all. The bird hopped onto her shoulder and shifted from one leg to the other.

"Stay right here," Rupert whispered, and he pulled.

The wall split along the seam of the corner as two

thick stone doors swung smoothly toward them, leaving the corner gapped wide.

Antigone's dancing heart stopped.

In the center of the room, coiled in the worn circle in the stone floor, there was a dragon.

The dragon was sleeping. Its scales had an oily sheen and were the color of dried blood. Two stumps protruded from its shoulders where wings might once have been. Its thick, spiny tail twisted away to the open corner of the room and ended in a bulbous cluster of black spines. They were smoking. On top of its head, two curly horns twisted back into a black mane, and on its snout was a shorter horn, bent back like a scythe. A single intact chain bound the dragon's foreleg. Three shattered chains trailed across the floor from its other limbs.

Antigone couldn't move. She wanted to run or close her eyes or even scream. Instead, she bit her lower lip hard. The bird was frozen on her shoulder. Together, they watched Rupert Greeves limp quietly into the room.

He turned and moved out of view, walking toward one of the empty walls.

No. Antigone's panic unlocked her limbs. Rupert couldn't do this alone. She stepped into the doorway, and then just inside the room.

The room's empty walls were full of sky, sun and clouds and blue. Rupert reached the end of the stone wall. Steadying himself by resting a hand on it, he peered down into the abyss. After only a moment, he lifted his head and continued on, limping along the edge of the floor toward the other open wall. When he reached the empty corner, he carefully circled around the tail, which rasped on the stone floor as it swished.

Antigone watched the dragon's sealed eye. She watched the slowly moving tail.

Rupert reached the other end of the room and looked down, his bloodied shirt rippling in the wind.

The dragon was going to wake up. Antigone knew it. And as she watched, the great eyelid flickered, then slid open. A golden eye rolled in its socket. If it saw Rupert, he was dead.

Without thinking, Antigone yelled. "Hey!"

The dragon leapt to its feet. Crouched on all fours, it sniffed at her like a wolf the size of a whale. It lashed its tail, just missing knocking Rupert over the edge.

"Where's Rupert?" Antigone asked, making it up as she went along. "What did you do with him?" She locked her eyes on the dragon's face, without even a glance at her Keeper, trapped on the other side of the beast.

The dragon yawned like a crocodile, his jaw popping like snapping branches, flashing white fangs and a slender yellow tongue mottled black. There was enough room in there for Antigone to lie down.

The beast slid forward, but Antigone didn't move. The chain cinched tight around the scaled foreleg, and the dragon stopped, only feet away from Antigone, its black claws clacking at the very edge of the worn circle. It puffed hot breath from its nostrils, rustling Antigone's hair. It smelled like rotting apples. She didn't see any smoke, but maybe she wasn't supposed to.

Rupert was creeping along the edge of the floor toward the nearest solid wall.

"If you can't speak, turn back into a man," Antigone said. "Then tell me where he is." She tried to glare into its eyes, but they were far apart. And huge.

I can speak.

Oh, crap, Antigone thought. The voice was in her head.

Yes. You know where he is. You will tell me. . . .

With only a moment to act, Antigone looked to the empty side of the room—where Rupert wasn't—and shouted, "Rupe, jump!"

The dragon whirled one way while Rupert raced forward from the other. At the same time, the dragon's tail cracked like a whip. The blackbird lifted off from Antigone's shoulder as she ducked, and the tail sailed over her head, clattering down the stairs behind her.

Thinking only of Rupert, Antigone stepped under the tail and stood back up. That was her mistake.

Metal stair treads and the handrail were shredded as the dragon snapped its tail back into the room. The spines slammed into Antigone's back and pinned her to the landing. She screamed as they tore through her pack and into her ribs.

Rupert leapt over the tail, crashed onto the stairs, and grabbed Antigone's ankles.

The dragon swung back to the door and roared, its mouth wide. It cracked and lashed its tail as it tried to reel Antigone into the room and closer to its snapping jaws.

The spines dug deeper into Antigone's back, and her screaming died. She couldn't breathe. Her lungs were pierced, collapsing. The blackbird swooped into the room and attacked the dragon's head, pecking and clawing at its eyes. The dragon recoiled. Snapping at the air, it released Antigone and pulled its tail back into the room. Antigone tumbled through the door and into her Keeper's arms.

Rupert let go of Antigone and crawled over the top of her to slam the doors.

Gasping for air, Antigone writhed on the steel landing. Her lungs wouldn't expand. Rupert flipped her over and pulled up the back of her shredded safari shirt.

"Breathe," he said. "Breathe. It will pass. Breathe."

Antigone clenched her teeth tight. "Mom," she said. "Mom."

"Breathe," Rupert said, pressing his hand down hard on her back. The blackbird landed on the floor in front of Antigone's face and screamed worry.

Antigone shut her eyes, and she breathed.

Her back felt pierced; she felt skewered and torn. But as she breathed, as her lungs filled, the panic faded. Rupert pressed down hard, and it was like the deep gouges rose up to meet his palm.

"What," Antigone grunted, "are you doing?" She still hurt, but the pain seemed to be all in the pressure of Rupert's hands.

Beyond the closed stone doors, the dragon was raging. Out of the corners of her eyes, she could see flashing flame trail away beneath the high rafters. The whole pillared room shook. The stairs rocked beneath her.

Screws were squealing. Popping.

"It isn't me," Rupert said. "I'm not doing anything. Thank Arachne, her ten thousand spiders, and the power in her weaver's fingers."

He lifted Antigone and sat her up with her back to the stone. The wire landing shook and rocked beneath them.

"How are you feeling?" Rupert said.

Antigone shook her head. "It felt like I was being ripped apart."

"You were," said Rupert. "And yet you weren't. Angel Skin cannot be pierced by normal weapons, and apparently not by a dragon, either. But if a blow is too strong to turn away, the weave retreats into the wound with the blade, and then heals as it reemerges."

Rupert smiled. "Antigone Smith, you were brilliant in there. Amazing. Thank you. I owe you my life. And if possible, Radu Bey now hates Smiths even more than he already did."

He looked down the shaking, damaged stairs. "I saw what I needed to see. Phoenix is in an old factory on the Mississippi. I can guess the latitude close enough for low flying. Our people are already there and circling, in what looked like two of the Boones' planes. Gilgamesh can't be too far behind. It's time for us to go. Can you walk, or should I carry you?"

Antigone grabbed for the flimsy handrail, but Rupert pulled her to her feet before she could get it. She closed her eyes, a little dizzy on her feet.

Rupert gripped Antigone's wrist and led her down the stairs, helping her where the treads were torn or missing. The room above them was quiet. The boy on the bicycle watched from below. The stairs wobbled beneath their bouncing weight.

They were almost halfway down when the dragon's tail lashed out of the open wall toward the stairs. Fire blasted out of the smoking spines and smacked into the metal landing, knocking it loose.

Antigone pushed Rupert in the back. Metal screamed as the whole staircase began to fall, tipping to the side.

Around. Around. Around. Rupert was faster. He reached the bottom and rolled free. Antigone vaulted over the handrail, dropped the last eight feet, and rolled on impact.

Wobbling and bending like a damaged spring, the stairs fell to the floor, smashing through crates and shelves and cottages.

The boy was still perched on his bicycle.

"C'mon," he said. "I know a way out." He began to pedal away.

Antigone groaned and stood. "We're not really running after him, are we?"

"Yes, we are," Rupert said. And he began to jog, limping as he went.

It wasn't a long run, but long enough for Antigone to get a stitch in her side. This time they passed more people in the rows, gazing up at the pillared room. Wild-eyed whispering men and cowering women, dozens of children, and even more dogs. They watched the bicyclist and Rupert and Antigone as they jogged past, and then they looked back at the room on the pillar with worry in their eyes.

"I'm leaving!" the boy on the bicycle shouted. "Don't tell my mother."

The other children joined them, and the dogs couldn't help themselves. By the time the boy had led them to a towering wall and an inset flight of stairs, they'd become a parade.

The worried voices of mothers called after them, but

only a few children turned back. Surrounded by shouts and laughter and barking, Antigone and Rupert climbed the long flight of stone stairs. The boy carried his bicycle up beside them. At the top, they looked back over the tremendous room, a Burial that had been discovered but whose prisoner could not be freed, surrounded by servants and junk and treasure hidden in shadow. It made Antigone think of some old Eastern potentate, entombed with his wives and animals and thousands of servants doomed to die just because he had. Entombed and then forgotten.

The boy led them down an enclosed hallway to another stair. And then another. The last stair was narrow and long and wooden and unlit. To Antigone, it felt like a mine shaft.

Some of the children stopped at the bottom, but most didn't hesitate. They climbed and laughed and shouted, reveling in the parade and the sound of marching feet. The flood of them pushed Antigone up, and extra hands even helped with the bicycle.

At the top, they reached a simple wooden door.

Rupert tried the knob. Then he stepped back and kicked it.

The door smashed open into the back of a janitor's closet. Plaster exploded into the little room as shelves fell. Brooms and buckets tumbled to the floor. Rupert and Antigone led the children through the rubble to a metal door on the other side of the closet. It was locked, but on the inside. Antigone unlocked it, pulled it open, and a sudden surge of children forced her through.

She was standing in the middle of a wax museum, crowded with tourists. The boy with the bicycle stepped past her and set his bike down on the red carpet.

"Goodbye," he said, and he pedaled away. A family with cameras jumped out of his way.

The rush of children flooded after him. Security guards began to shout.

"C'mon, then," Rupert said. He took Antigone's hand and led her, still limping, in the other direction.

People stared at his bloody shirt and battered face. They stared at the girl in the tattered shirt with the glistening pearl skin underneath. They stared, and they stepped out of the way.

Rupert and Antigone rode down an escalator and walked through a massive glistening lobby crowded with wax statues and lines and concessions. They pushed through glass doors and stepped onto a hot sidewalk beside the biggest, busiest street Antigone had ever seen.

Buildings on both sides scraped the sky.

"Where are we?" she asked.

"New York City," Rupert said. "Could be better, could be worse." He grabbed a man passing by and talking on a cell phone. "Beg pardon, bruv," he said, pulling a small gold coin from a pocket on his leg. "This is worth about five hundred of your dollars . . . could you spare the phone?"

The man took the coin, and his eyes widened in surprise. "This is Spanish," he said. "It's worth a lot more than five. Where did you get it?"

Rupert shrugged, already punching in numbers. He turned away, pressing the phone to his ear.

The stranger studied Antigone. "Are you two okay?"

Antigone nodded. "Better now."

"That's an interesting shirt," he said, pointing awkwardly at her stomach. "The, uh, the under-one."

Antigone looked down. Her buttons had blown off, and her shirt was mostly open. In the sunlight, she could see shapes woven into the perfect silk, white on white, silver on silver—her protectors. A bull with a man's head and tremendous wings. A snake with six wings. A regal-looking woman with young trees growing in her hands.

The shapes were moving.

"Thanks," said Antigone. She smiled and closed her tattered safari shirt.

"Liv?" Rupert said. "Pick up, it's Rupe. Pick up— Liv! No, don't start. Listen, I'm in the city, and I desperately need to not be." He looked at Antigone and smiled. "Forty-Second Street. I need a run down south. Immediately. Still flying that tiltrotor?"

"Would you sell it?" the stranger asked Antigone. "The shirt?"

"What?" Antigone asked. "No!"

"Not Brooklyn," Rupert was saying. "Deep south. Louisiana south. Right." He nodded into the phone, clicked it off, and tossed it back to the stranger.

"Thanks, mate. Tigs?" Wincing and biting his lip, he began to stride down the sidewalk. Antigone jogged to keep up.

"See that building?" Rupert was pointing to a glistening glass tower taller than anything Antigone had ever seen, but still not the tallest one she could see now. "We have ten minutes to get to the top," he said. "That's when our ride will be there, and she won't be able to wait."

twenty

TO WAR

PRESSING HIS HEAD against the window of the plane, Cyrus looked down at the massive factory as they made another pass over it. The two planes had circled the decrepit factory more times than he wanted to count—blazing in low, past the roofline, over the swamp sweltering in the afternoon sun, and always swinging back up and around for another pass.

Cyrus twisted Radu Bey's heavy gold ring around his knuckle. His stomach was in his throat. Antigone was alive. Rupert was alive. Arachne had seen them both. If he managed to capture Phoenix, they might stay that way. If he didn't . . .

He looked around the cabin. Jeb and Diana were up in the cockpit. Nolan was leaning against the seat in front of him, pale arms crossed and head down. The two Livingstone boys were whispering to each other—Silas was rubbing his scarred eyebrow with the butt of a knife, and George was checking the chambers on a battered old revolver. Dennis—the porter had insisted on coming—

was watching them both from across the aisle and fidgeting with his bowler hat.

Across the aisle from Cyrus, Captain John Smith was humming loudly, with his eyes glued to his window and iron Vlad on his lap, resting against the Captain's polished gold breastplate. Horace was in front of him, winding his pocket watch and shaking it by his ear. He was wearing two borrowed six-shooters on a belt, and a blunderbuss lay across his knees. Beside him, Arachne sat with her spider bag in her lap. She had no weapons, and Cyrus had no idea why she'd wanted to come. But she hadn't listened to anyone who had suggested that she stay behind with Jax and Mrs. Boone any more than she'd considered Mr. Boone's offer to give her a gun.

Dan was in the front, his arms above the cockpit door, talking to Jeb and Diana. Cyrus didn't think his brother looked like someone with a heart problem—if people with heart problems even had a look. He looked ready for the Olympics. Even relaxed, his arms had muscles like oak roots just beneath the skin. A boxer? A wrestler? Something the opposite of sickly, at least.

The other plane had already landed downstream and out of sight. Alan Livingstone and Robert Boone had flown it alone, and they would set their trap alone. Cyrus was nervous about that. Rupert had said that Robert Boone was one to hang back and wait in ambush, and that's exactly the plan that Boone had insisted on. At the first sign of trouble, Phoenix always ran—that's what Boone had said, and Cyrus knew he was right. And now he would run into a trap. But Cyrus was still worried. He would have been more comfortable creeping in quietly, rather than trying to spook Phoenix on purpose.

Jeb and Diana turned the plane out of a final circle and started their descent toward the river, just upstream of the wooden factory on its forest of pylons. There were no real roads to and from the place, and no trucks or cars visible from the air. Not one person had so much as set foot outside the factory, but the big loading door overlooking the river that had been open when they arrived was shut now. And beneath it there were two boats tied to the factory pylons, and one seaplane.

After a few passes, Robert Boone had told Jeb over the radio that the river was the only route they needed to close.

Nolan sat up, stretching.

Dan was walking back down the aisle. He dropped into the seat beside Cyrus.

Cyrus's chest was tight. His whole body was tight. His knee was bouncing. He yawned slowly—he couldn't help it. His nerves were pretending to relax. "What will we do if Phoenix doesn't run?"

"Our best, little brother." Dan slapped his knee. "We'll get him. And we'll get Antigone. She'll make it, okay?"

"Did you dream that?" Cyrus looked into his brother's strangely dark eyes. "Or are you just saying it?"

Dan shook his head. "I believe it. But, Cyrus, there's something else. Dad . . ."

"I know," said Cyrus. "You told me Dad's down there. I don't want to think about it." Cyrus looked back out his window. The trees were rising. He couldn't see the river. The plane tipped and he shut his eyes, swallowing down a throatful of sick. Cold sweat beaded up on his face. He could see the old kitchen door closing behind his father. His last real glimpse.

"What if Phoenix . . . what if before we get there . . ." Cyrus breathed, trying to quiet his queasy stomach. He looked at his brother. "What if Dad's already alive again?"

Dan shook his head. "We can't let it happen," he said quietly. "It would be evil, and Dad would hate it."

"Even if Phoenix brought him back," Cyrus said, "he wouldn't be bad. He couldn't be."

"*He* wouldn't," Dan said. "But his coming back would be. His body would be a cage, and Phoenix could make it do horrible things with him stuck inside it. That's what I think, anyway."

The plane touched the water. Cyrus rocked forward as they slowed.

Dan gripped his brother's shoulder. "We miss him, Cy. But we shouldn't want him back, not like that."

Cyrus nodded, but he wasn't sure. The plane had

completely stopped, and he wanted to throw up more than ever.

The Captain stood up and punched the ceiling. "Ho, I've had enough of this sky machining. Open the ark."

Jeb came back into the cabin and threw open a side door. Together, he and Diana slid three heavy waterproof cases down the aisle and out into the water. Then they looked at Cyrus. Nolan looked at Cyrus, his ancient eyes curious. Arachne and Horace and Dennis looked at Cyrus.

Cyrus shut his eyes. He felt Dan's hands between his shoulder blades and exhaled. He opened his eyes.

"Right," he said. "Dennis and Horace and Arachne, stay with the plane. If Phoenix tries to escape upstream . . . well, your job is to make sure he doesn't. We have to send him downstream to Boone and Alan."

"Aye, aye," said Horace, saluting.

Jeb opened a black case, revealing a fat tube and leather-coated rockets branded with different symbols—smoke, fire, lightning. "These will stop the plane or the boats," he said. "If he gets out, burn that cloak. Remember, bullets are no good against Phoenix."

"Can that be a hand-cannon?" the Captain asked. Vlad was resting on his left hip.

"It rests on the shoulder," said Jeb. "Or you can rig at the waist, too."

The Captain rubbed his gold breastplate. "Perchance

you have another?" he asked. He beamed when Jeb nodded.

"The rest of us are going in," Cyrus said. "We don't have to kill or capture anybody; we just have to spook them into the boats. Remember to stay behind the Captain and Nolan."

Nolan leaned against the back of a seat and split half a smile. "For the record, we do feel pain. We just don't die."

"Yeah, well, we do both," said Jeb. "Let's get going."

"Right," said Cyrus. A wave of dizziness rippled through him. He was going to throw up. Now it was just a question of where. Gagging, swallowing, his jaw clamped shut, Cyrus pushed past the Captain and staggered down the aisle past Horace and Nolan, Dennis and Diana.

At the door, Jeb stepped out of the way. Cyrus dove into the river, breaking through the warm, slick surface and kicking deeper, to where the water was cool. There, out of the light and out of sight, he threw up his nervousness in a cloud.

He surfaced, spitting, beside one of the floating cases. A cluster of faces watched him from the door of the plane. He didn't say anything. Instead, he grabbed the case and began swimming it toward the bank.

No more thinking.

Phoenix stood beside the shallow pools, leaning heavily on his cane. Only two of the five still held bodies.

Around his feet, the floor was slick with water. Sweat rolled down his nose as he pushed his wet hair out of his face with his stump. In the last hour, he had finished six more of his own men.

He could barely stand.

At his feet, Oliver, the last of the Laughlins, floated in the center pool. While his men had only needed a single cycle to meet Phoenix's needs, more was planned for his nephew. Like the men, Oliver had died under the first pulsing barrage from the needles and wires. Like the others, he had been brought back—a young convict had worked well enough in the end. Unlike the others, more needles and wires had been attached to the new Oliver, this time focusing on the head. Oliver's mind had needed . . . expanding. Now Oliver was floating peacefully—young, strong, pale, dead—ready to wake again. Now Phoenix needed a transmortal.

Not Ponce. Phoenix would use the pink-shirted Spaniard only as a last resort. He needed someone stronger. Someone who would arrive later.

The two planes roared overhead again, dust snowing down from the shaken rafters. The factory doors had been closed and bolted after the planes' first pass. The necessary windows had been sealed. All but two of his men had scattered to their defensive positions.

Phoenix wasn't worried. These planes did not belong to the dragons.

Sniffing, ignoring the wobbling weariness in his knees, Phoenix hobbled away from Oliver to the only other pool that held a body.

Lawrence Smith. Phoenix had always planned to graft the Smith line into his new humanity. They were forever defiant, trusting themselves and their own blood before they listened to the winds of the world or the word of the Brendan or the vote of the Keepers. As a man, Lawrence had needed so few improvements. But mortal mankind itself was still in need of so many.

Long ago, Harriet and Circe Smith, Lawrence's sisters, had stubbornly died rather than serve Phoenix. And Lawrence himself had turned away from the Order and its enemies completely. He had walked away from everything, from his history, from his blood, from his friends, from the treasures accumulated by generations of Smiths—all for a girl with eyes like jungle shade. And in that, he had acted like a true Smith. Like the Captain had acted when he'd Buried himself. Like dozens of others had acted before him. Smiths always seemed to be turning their backs on something, and frequently everything.

Phoenix was surprised by the chuckle that sprung from his own throat.

Now Lawrence Smith would turn his back on death.

Phoenix studied the floating man with his icy skin and bullet-puckered chest. Even a once great Explorer of the Order of Brendan could be struck down by a few flying shards of metal—bullets from a gun—and then swallowed by the cold water of the Pacific. The soul fled the body so easily. It was a flaw that could be mended.

The third convict Phoenix had tried to use now lay dead beside Lawrence's pool—dead as quickly as the others, and there weren't many more. It was a puzzle. Lawrence had been friends with Skelton. He'd had rogues for friends planet-wide. A convict should have been sufficient.

Phoenix couldn't change a corpse. He needed Lawrence alive before he could make any improvements. And of course, the improvements would kill him again. So Phoenix needed two human batteries before Lawrence would become the Lawrence he wanted. He had one, but if he used him now, he might not be able to find another. Why go to the trouble of bringing Lawrence back and improving him, only to shove him back into a freezer?

Frustrated, Phoenix slapped at the water in the pool with the end of his cane. The splash spattered onto his hand and wrist, and for a moment, he was surprised at how cool the water had become. Lawrence's body was thawing.

Phoenix beckoned to the two men who had stayed with him, both freshly born into bestial speed and bestial strength. One was curiously fingering the gills on the side of his neck.

"Get rid of this body," Phoenix said, kicking the dead convict at his feet. "Bring me Alfred Mist."

The men jumped forward and picked up the body. Phoenix turned to the little Mist girl, asleep in her chair in the corner, head lolling. Pythia was on the floor beside her.

The little girl would want to see her father die. Phoenix hobbled over and raised his cane to wake her, then paused. Waking her would just mean more kicking and screaming. He lowered his cane. The girl didn't need to see anything.

Antigone pressed a cold glass bottle of soda against her split lower lip. She was in the cabin of an old airplane that reminded her of the lobby of the Archer Motel.

The five seats in the cabin were cream leather, cracked with time. Behind her, there was a little bathroom with a carpeted wall and a mirror dotted with gold fleck. In front of her, past a little metal Coke cooler full of drinks, Rupert Greeves sat in the copilot's chair wearing a headset. He was arguing with Liv, the crazy old woman with the long white scarf and long, caramel-colored coat flying the plane. It was incredibly hot in the cabin. Antigone didn't understand how the lady could stand to be in her coat. It had one patch on its shoulder—a green shield with a woman riding a jumping dolphin stitched in white thread.

It was hard to say what the strangest part of the day had been. It should have been the dragon, or seeing the moving shapes that Arachne had woven into her shirt. But the strangest part had actually been racing through New York City with Rupert. After a year at Ashtown, Antigone had almost forgotten that she belonged in this world, the one with taxicabs and skyscrapers and hot dog vendors and telephones and overflowing trash cans.

No one had paid any attention to them when they'd been jogging along the sidewalks. That changed when they entered the tall glass building. The lobby was large, marble, and lined with bookshelves behind glass. The only way to get to the elevators had been over the turnstiles and past the security guards.

Rupert hadn't even hesitated. While people in suits yelled *sir! sir! sir!* he'd hopped the barrier and boarded an elevator, Antigone right behind him. Three floors up, Rupert switched elevators. Three more, and they took the fire stairs up the next four. Sweating and breathing hard, they'd stepped out onto a floor with a small crowd of frustrated people complaining that the elevators had stopped working.

Rupert and Antigone had followed them back into the fire stairs and up to a floor with a bridge to another elevator lobby. And as if their bloody and torn clothing hadn't made them conspicuous enough already, the amused and cheerful red-winged blackbird spent the whole time singing on Antigone's shoulder.

Just thinking about it made Antigone start sweating again. They'd shot up floors, and then had to take the fire stairs again, and then shot up more floors. They'd forced their way into another set of offices and past another set of security guards, and then into a residential block, and finally through a door that had set off alarms as they entered someone's extremely nice penthouse. A man in a very nice suit was having lunch with some fragile-looking bony women—he was the only one eating.

Rupert had politely said hello, and then pushed past the lunch party out onto the balcony. From there, they'd climbed to a bigger balcony that led to a helicopter pad and one fat security guard, the one that had elbowed her in the face and split her lip.

A strange plane, with a propeller above each wing, had been descending like a helicopter. After they'd boarded and taken off, the propellers had swung down in front of the wings.

The heat in the cabin was stifling. Antigone stood and stretched, then moved forward to the cockpit door. The blackbird was perched on the dash, looking out the windshield.

"Liv, listen to me, love," Rupert said. His face was slick with sweat. "I need speed. I need it."

"What is this tone?" the old woman asked. "Where is the young Rupert who was content to enjoy the air and a soda?"

Antigone glanced at the controls. They were at 11,000 feet, flying almost 300 miles per hour. Pretty fast.

"There are times to fly like a grandmother," Rupert said. "This isn't one of them."

"I am not a grandmother," Liv said. Her voice was accented. She glanced back at Antigone and smiled. Her face was creased, but thin and younger-looking than Antigone had expected. Her teeth were impossibly white, and her eyes were a very Nordic blue, ready to freeze. "I fly like an affectionate aunt."

"There are too many miles to make up," said Rupert. "Fly like an affectionate banshee. I know what Thor did to these Rolls-Royce engines before he died."

"Um," Antigone said. "Could we turn on some air-conditioning?"

"Heat is healthy," Liv said. "It stimulates memory and the flow of the bloods." She looked at Rupert, smiling slightly. Then she unbuckled and slid out from behind the controls. "It also stimulates odor in men." She patted Rupert's shoulder. "Fly my plane as you like, Rupert Greeves. Play at banshee with my Thor's old toy."

Rupert had already taken the controls.

"Air-conditioning?" Antigone said again.

Rupert nodded, flipping switches.

Antigone went back to her seat. The old woman sat down across from her. She was surprisingly tall—almost Rupert's height. She stretched out a pair of very long legs that ended in worn knee-high boots.

The whining pitch of the engines shifted. The plane was accelerating.

"So," said Liv. She smiled with pursed lips, and then crossed her long legs at the knee. "Antigone Smith, is it? And we're having trouble with the dragons, yes?" She raised her eyebrows and pushed back her gray-blond hair. "It all seems so primitive. One would think the Order could simply move on from such . . . earthy . . . conflicts."

Antigone cocked her head, listening to the woman's accent. She didn't recognize it.

"Where are you from?" she asked.

Liv laughed. "Norway, once upon the times. But my Thor loved New York. He left and died. I stayed." She studied the back of her hand. "The Order, for me, is only memory. I haven't set foot on an Estate in years. But I pay the dues." She smiled. "I'm sentimental. But really, all those Explorers milling about training, and for what? At least the medievals had a mission, dreadful as it now seems to modern minds. Still, it was something. Young

Rupe has that in him. He's terribly . . . what is it?" She held up her hands on either side of her eyes. "Tunnel-visioned? Blinkered? But I admire his simplicity. He finds importance in his work."

Liv glanced over her shoulder at the cockpit, then leaned toward Antigone as if she were going to tell her a secret. "When he was younger, I wanted him to call me Auntie Liv." Liv laughed. "The stubborn boy never would! My Thor had some of the same primitive fire—boys, yes? I couldn't get it out of them. Thor took Rupert in and oversaw some of his training after his dear parents passed. When I think of what that boy could have achieved outside the Order . . ."

"What Rupert does is very important," Antigone said. Her voice was low, almost gruff.

"Ah," said Liv. "Yes, you would think that, dear one. You're young, and you're a Smith. I'd almost forgotten it. The fight, the mission, the fanatic is in your blood."

Antigone bit her lip and winced from the pain. She stood, bracing herself as the plane shook, then nodded at the cockpit.

"Do you mind if I go up?"

Liv smiled and shook her head. "Go. Sit with your Keeper and plan your wars. I had a long morning in the stables. I will nap." Her smile was genuine. Antigone felt as if the woman truly liked her, but she also felt more than a little pitied . . . and not for the right reasons.

While Liv reclined, Antigone moved through the narrow doorway and slid into the empty pilot's chair. The plane was bouncing hard, tearing through a stretch of rough air. The controls weren't like in any of the little planes she had flown. They weren't even like Gil's plane. She twisted open her soda bottle and set it in a cup holder. Then she slid on a headset.

Rupert flashed her a smile. His voice crackled quietly in her ears.

"What do you think of Auntie Liv?"

Antigone grimaced and stuck out her tongue. "Nice, though," she added quickly.

Rupert nodded. Antigone scanned the dials. She could hear the low chatter of pilots and air-traffic controllers in the headphones, and wondered how anyone knew whom it was they were talking to. There were a lot more voices than when she cruised around at low altitude over Lake Michigan.

The needle was kissing six hundred miles per hour. They were really hauling, and it felt like it, too. She looked out her side window and back at the big turboprop engine.

"How long till we get there?" she asked.

"Ninety minutes," Rupert said. "Seventy-five, hopefully. I need a little more altitude, and then I'll push this Boop harder."

"Where are we now?" Antigone asked.

A loud voice chirped in her headphones. "This is Andrews Tower. You are entering regulated airspace. Identify and redirect. Repeat. You are entering regulated airspace. Identify and redirect."

"Washington, D.C.," Rupert said to Antigone. "Cross all your fingers and your toes." He held down a switch in front of him. "Andrews Tower, this is Brendan-Zed-one-one-eight. We are clear of your traffic and passing through."

Antigone looked at Rupert and waited. She didn't have long to wait.

"Andrews Tower to Brendan-Zed-one-one-eight, you are not cleared to pass through. Repeat, you are not cleared to pass through. Redirect now. Be advised, we will engage."

Rupert squinted, rubbed his eyes, pinched the bridge of his nose.

Despite her headphones, Antigone heard a sudden roar even louder than their own engines. To their left, a needle-nosed fighter ripped through the cloud layer and leveled off just off their wing. Beyond it, another jet rose.

"That was quick," Rupert said. He pushed the switch back down. "Brendan-Zed-one-one-eight to Andrews Tower. Note: Red-Zed on board, Red-Zed, Adams-Jefferson-Madison, one-eight-one-two. Advise."

Antigone looked from the jets to Rupert and back to

the jets. All the distant pilot chatter in her headphones was gone—the airspace was silent. She wondered how many other pilots were listening in. She waited, and waited, expecting some missile to suddenly smash them out of the sky. Finally, the tower responded, but the voice was now a woman's.

"Andrews Tower to Brendan-Zed-one-one-eight, you are cleared to continue on. Good luck, Red-Zed. Over."

"Thank you, Andrews," Rupert said. "Cheers." Outside of Antigone's window, the closer pilot waved, and then the two jets banked hard, disappearing into the clouds.

"What just happened?" Antigone asked.

"We cut five minutes off our flight time," Rupert said. He laughed. "You can thank the Marquis de Lafayette. After he poured himself into the War for Independence, he wasn't about to let the O of B support the British in 1812—and the fools would have, too. But Lafayette prevailed upon the Keepers, and the Order tipped battles in New Orleans and Baltimore in America's favor. In exchange, a grateful President Madison signed a treaty with the Order. Relations have been cautiously maintained ever since."

Antigone looked out her window. "And they know all that? Down there? Because of something that happened back in 1812, we get to fly where we want?"

Rupert grinned. "Oh, no. All that woman in the

tower knows is that we have the necessary security clearance."

The bird hopped off the dash and onto Antigone's shoulder. She looked at her Keeper. "Where *exactly* are we going?"

Rupert's jaw flexed and his brows lowered slowly.

"To war," he said. "And that's as exact as I can be."

twenty-one

CIGARS

CYRUS EXAMINED the factory from the shelter of the trees. It had five large entrances on this side, and more small ones than he wanted to count. Somewhere in there was his father's body and Phoenix and the tooth. In a minute, Cyrus would be in there, too. He hoped Phoenix was already preparing to escape down the river, but not really. Cyrus surprised himself—he wanted to see him. He wanted to face him, and he wanted to fight.

Cyrus had taken a revolver from one of the three cases they'd carried up from the river. It rested in a holster on his right hip. Nolan, even paler in the sun, had two long knives tucked into sheaths at the small of his back. Beside him, the Captain was standing with his face tipped back, savoring the sun with his eyes closed. He had Vlad on his left hip, just above his sword hilt. A short grenade launcher like the one from the plane was slung over his right shoulder. The leather football-looking rounds were belted around the black tube.

"We have to make sure he doesn't come this way,"

Jeb was saying. "We should split up and push into all the doors at once."

Diana shook her head. "I don't think so. We don't know what we're up against in there."

"A lot of guys with tattoos," Dan said.

Jeb pointed at the closest door. "If we all push in at the same door, they can escape out the other doors and into the bayou. We need them to go into the river."

Cyrus tried to assess the situation. Too little sleep, he thought. *Doesn't matter.* Too little training. *Maybe. But also doesn't matter. You're here now. This is really happening. Think.*

The Livingstone brothers carried short, antique-looking double-barrel shotguns with pistol grips. On their belts, they each had a bag full of shells, a thick bladed knife, and a small club. The sun cast a gnarled shadow beneath Silas's eyebrow scar that made him look a lot older.

Cyrus waved at the factory. "What do you two think?"

George glanced at his older brother, then stepped forward. "Leave your two best marksmen out here, centered on the building. They can cover any attempted escape in this direction, or any attempt to circle around and surprise you from the rear. Then divide in two, and send a team in on each end and work toward the center. Hopefully, that will press them into retreating on the river."

Silas and Jeb were nodding. Diana shrugged.

"Who are our best marksmen?" Cyrus asked.

The argument was short. Everyone knew the Boones were the best shots in the Order. But Diana didn't want to be left outside. Eventually, Jeb quieted his sister's objections.

"Ridiculous," Diana muttered.

"Okay. Teams," Cyrus said. "Nolan leads one, the Captain leads the other. Smiths go with the Captain. Livingstones go with Nolan. Arachne . . ." He looked around. "Arachne?"

"Cy . . ." Diana was pointing. While they'd been talking, Arachne had quietly drifted away from the group. Now she was walking up one of the factory's ramps. She didn't try the large sliding door. Instead, she tried a smaller door beside it, pulled it open, and stepped inside.

"Treachery," the Captain said. "Transmortal treachery!"

"No," said Cyrus, shaking his head. "I don't know what it is, but it's not that." He looked around at the group. "Everyone ready."

"No," said the Captain. "You're a Smith, lad, and are Kept by the Brendan's Blood Avenger. Ye need a blade leading this parade." He unbelted his sword, the sword from his own tomb that had parted the skin on Cyrus's neck with just a touch. "You're worthy enow to smite with this, Smithling." He wrapped the belt around Cyrus's middle and cinched it tight. The scabbard dangled most of the way down his leg. The Captain grinned. "War! Can ye hear the blood drums beating in thine ears? Can ye feel the prickling lightning in thy limbs? Come! Let us send this Phoenix back to his ash."

Turning suddenly, with Vlad crooked in one arm and his new hand-cannon in the other, he began to run toward the far end of the factory. Dan and Cyrus ran after him, revolvers in hand. Cyrus fell behind as the sword clattered and kicked against his legs and darted between his shins. Finally, still running, he switched the revolver to his left hand and drew the long blade, letting the scabbard bounce limp.

The blade was light. Lighter than the sabers he trained with in Ashtown, even though the blade was longer and thicker. The hilt felt familiar enough, but the steel looked samurai. As the sun glanced off it, he saw the ghost of an image—scaled, long, reptilian.

The sword was sharp; that's all that mattered. And it felt good in his hand. He hoped he wouldn't have to use it.

When the Captain reached the farthest ramp, Cyrus was with him. Breathing hard, he made his way up, glancing toward the other end as he did. Nolan and the Livingstones were in position and waiting. Jeb and Diana were centered, lying in the grass with rifles extended. There was no reason to wait, no reason to start thinking again, to start worrying about . . .

Cyrus stopped his mind.

The big sliding door was chained. He slid his new blade down behind the rusted links and jerked down. Surprised, he watched the iron split and tumble loose. The sword was a lot more than sharp. Grabbing the door handle, he tugged. The door rattled along its rails, revealing . . . darkness. Dust trickled out into the sun. Cyrus inched forward, blade raised.

A tiny flame flickered to life in the darkness. Shadows moved inside the room and a roiling fireball suddenly swirled toward Cyrus. With a yell, the Captain jumped to the front and the fireball shattered around him. Cyrus dropped to the ground in his shadow.

Somewhere distant, Cyrus heard Nolan shouting. And gunfire. As the fireball died, Cyrus scrambled backward, raising his revolver. Dan had sheltered against the factory wall, beside the door. The Captain stood inside the doorway, legs spread, armor glowing with heat, hair smoking. Bellowing like a bull, he swung Vlad from the chain on his left wrist like a medieval mace. From his right hip, he fired his first grenade into the dark room.

Lightning flashed inside and thunder shook the ramp under Cyrus's feet. The Captain and Cyrus tumbled backward.

Dazed, Cyrus rose to his feet, clutching the sword in

front of him. Dan was halfway down the ramp, shaking his head and trying to stand, his back to the door. There were bodies just inside the doorway—Cyrus could see tattoos beneath scorched skin.

Cyrus heard Diana shouting over the sound of rifles firing and a more distant explosion. Glancing down the length of the factory, he could see that the far end was burning. In the center, shapes were flooding out of the building, parting, and racing toward the ends.

This didn't look like running away. The Polygoners were being surrounded. But that didn't matter. Not just yet.

Tall men, lean and tattooed, stepped out of the doorway. In the sunlight, their skin was tinged green. Cyrus had faced creatures like this once before, but never so many. Six, seven stepped onto the ramp. Some carried the four-barreled fire-belching guns that had burned down the Archer. Others carried something smaller—pistols with short belts of darts dangling beneath the barrels.

The man in front raised his dart gun and pointed at Dan's back. Cyrus didn't hear himself yelling as he ran forward. Dan twisted and flipped to the side in a way the old Dan would never have been able to do. The dart punched into the wooden ramp where Dan had just been.

Cyrus heard a roar from behind him and felt the trailing heat of the Captain's second grenade as it passed over his shoulder, plowing through the air toward the tattooed men. They parted like cats, like vapor, and the grenade disappeared into the room behind them. A moment later, the world shook again. Thick black smoke billowed out the door, engulfing Phoenix's men.

Swinging his sword and shouting, Cyrus plunged into it.

His blade sliced into something, and he heard a scream. Smoke burned his throat and eyes as he pressed on, blindly executing the thrusts and slashes of a training routine.

Someone grabbed his blade and pulled him forward. A hand clamped onto his throat. Cyrus raised his revolver and fired blind.

He tripped over his falling attacker, and then collided with a wall. Holding his breath, smoke tears streaming down his face, he followed the wall until he found a door.

Somewhere ahead of him was a prize he was willing to die for. Cyrus went through the door.

Dennis Gilly sat in the open door of the plane beside John Horace Lawney VII and gnawed his fingernails. The blunderbuss sat across Dennis's legs; Horace wouldn't let him touch the Boones' launcher.

There had been no movement on the river side of the factory. The windows were still shuttered. The doors were still closed. The boats and the plane were still lashed to the pylons.

But from the other side of the factory . . .

"Do you think they're okay?" Dennis asked Horace. "We should have gone with them."

"No use thinking," Horace said. "Hope. Pray. Don't think."

Smoke was climbing into the sky from both ends of the huge structure. There had been explosions. Rifles were cracking. And then, over it all, Dennis heard the roar of jet engines.

Horace and Dennis looked upriver. The plane was coming in low, rippling the surface of the water as it passed. It looked like a wide single wing, with two snarling jet intakes fixed close together beneath the cockpit.

Dennis had seen the plane before, when it had dropped paper dragons on Ashtown.

As they watched, the plane rose and banked hard over the length of the factory. Four shapes dropped from its bomb-bay doors, one after the other. They punched through the roof, spaced evenly from one end of the factory to the other. But nothing exploded.

Diana Boone backed into the trees beside her brother, loading and firing as fast as she could. Nolan and the Livingstones were facing fewer than before, thanks to Jeb's sharp eye. But there were still too many.

On Diana's side, Dan and the Captain were fighting back to back, holding the ramp. The Captain was swinging the iron head and launching grenades. Dan was firing one of the enemy flame guns. Together, they were a swirl of flame and smoke and whirling chain. Diana didn't have many clear shots that didn't also risk them.

"Di!"

She twisted back toward her brother's side, rifle raised and ready. He was pointing at the sky.

The transmortals' single-wing jet was banking over the factory. Four figures dropped from the plane, crashing through the roof like boulders.

The tattooed men saw it, too. On both ends, they raced back toward the center doors. They ran like two-legged cheetahs, fast and agile. Diana only got three shots off before they were back through the doors, managing to drop only one.

Suddenly, it was quiet. One of the Livingstones was on the ground; the other was on his knees beside him. Nolan faced the door. They hadn't managed to set one foot inside.

At the other end, the Captain and Dan were entering the smoking doorway.

"Dad was wrong," Jeb said. "Phoenix isn't running. He's holed up a bloody army. We need to get everyone out of here. Now!"

"Help Nolan!" Diana yelled. Reloading as she ran, she sprinted toward the door where first Cyrus, and now his brother and the Captain had disappeared.

◆ ◆ ◆

Cyrus crept down a dark hallway. He could hear fighting outside, and occasionally pounding feet on planks, but he hadn't encountered anyone, only rooms full of archaic machines and dust.

At the next hall, he turned, hopefully in the right direction. *Mazecraft.* The word sprang into his head. There were techniques for this kind of searching, but they were locked up in books. And not even his Solomon Keys had helped him open those.

With sword and gun raised, he peered into every doorway he came to. His skin was hot and blistered from the fireball that had hit the Captain. Around his neck, Patricia was nervous, constantly shifting her cool body.

The snake heard the noise first, tightening and growing still. A jet. Cyrus paused as the plane roared over the roof, rattling the walls around him.

Twenty feet down the hall, the ceiling exploded as something punched through it and slammed into the floor like a wrecking ball.

Dust billowed toward Cyrus as he staggered back into a doorway. He watched as the shape picked itself up and stood.

Cyrus tightened his grip on his sword handle. Gil? No. A transmortal he hadn't seen before. This one had a braided beard and long red hair. He drew a wide blade from a scabbard over his shoulder.

A stampede of feet rattled on planks. Cyrus stepped all the way back into the empty room as tattooed men passed by with dart guns raised.

But there was no fight. When Cyrus peered back into the hall, the tattooed men were leading the transmortal the other way. They were on the same team.

Phoenix paced excitedly, limping in circles. The Smiths had found him, and not just the boy and his brother, but the father of them all—the Captain himself.

Phoenix ignored Alfred Mist on the floor. He ignored Dixie as she tried to rock herself free of her chair. He had lost men, yes; he could feel them dying even now—his children. But they were proving to be as strong as he had hoped, and he would make so many more.

Phoenix looked down at Oliver's body, floating in the center pool. There were transmortals aplenty now—Nolan, Arachne, John Smith. Gilgamesh, when he arrived. Even Enkidu—traitors deserved to be betrayed. But the Captain? What a wonderful, delectable choice!

The two men that had stayed with him fidgeted nervously. Their eyes were distant, like dogs listening to the faraway whisper of a siren. Their nostrils flared, sniffing at battle air.

There wasn't much time now. Phoenix limped over to the sleeping form of Alfred Mist, lying beside Lawrence

Smith in his pool. The girl squealed, and Pythia rattled her chains. Leaves floated over his head, but he paid no mind.

"Like for like," he said aloud. "Father for father. Soon, perhaps, it may be Smith for Smith."

Tucking his cane under his arm, Phoenix placed Lawrence's cold wet hand on the edge of the pool. He raised Alfred's heavy arm and placed his hand on top of Lawrence's, black on top of white. Straightening, he opened the top of his cane and braced himself for the pulse, the burn, and the weakness he would feel when the tooth, the Reaper's Blade, pinned flesh to flesh. He began to chant.

Gilgamesh exploded through the ceiling like a cannonball, crushing an empty pool and sending a flood of water swirling across the room.

Phoenix staggered back, the water washing around his ankles.

Gil was already rolling to his feet.

"Edwin Laughlin!" he boomed. "I'll take your head and feed it to my magpies. You think I can't tear that cloak off your glass bones? You think I can't gut the pathetic beast you'll become?"

"Now!" Phoenix yelled, bouncing in place. "Now!"

His two men stepped forward, dart guns raised. Gil laughed as a shower of darts feathered his chest. Then, raising his fist, he collapsed.

• • •

Cyrus followed the tattooed men and the red-haired transmortal to a large, well-lit room. The far wall was stacked high with freezers, and bundled electrical cords ran up into the ceiling. There was a gaping hole in the ceiling where sunlight was flooding in.

From a hall on the other side of the room, Cyrus could hear fighting. Near the center of the room, the red-bearded transmortal stood beside Phoenix, looking down at Gil's body, which was covered with darts. At least ten of the tattooed men were in the room, guns in hand, eyes on Gil.

On the floor were four pools of water. A fifth had been smashed. There were bodies everywhere. The largest pile was by a big sliding door on the river side of the room, and they were all in orange jumpsuits. A large black man lay by one of the pools, and in that pool and one other, bodies were floating.

"Oh, Gilgamesh," Phoenix drawled. "Did you forget that I possess the tooth? Did you think I could not potion a paralysis for you?"

Behind Phoenix was a girl tied up in a chair. In the corner next to the girl, something moved. It was another girl, swallowed by her own hair. With a shock of recognition, Cyrus realized it was the girl he'd seen in his dream about being in a grave.

Some of Phoenix's tattooed men were lugging Gil

toward a pool in the center of the room, one of the pools with a body in it. Careful to stay in the shadows just outside the room's entrance, Cyrus stood on tiptoe, peering down into the pool. He could just make out the face.

Oliver? How? Was the boy dead?

He looked into the other pool and froze. He could see his father's profile, a face he had last glimpsed in the rain three years ago, laughing. His father was floating in water like Cyrus had always pictured him, except it wasn't the cold water of the Pacific. His hand was up the pool's edge, under the black man's.

"Go!" Phoenix was laughing, yelling at his men. "I have everything else I need; now get me the Smiths! All the Smiths!"

"Aye, here's the heart of the fight." The whisper tickled Cyrus's ear, and he jerked back in surprise.

The Captain and Dan were pressed against the wall behind him. The Captain's beard was burnt and melted into smoking lumps. His face was black with ash and blisters. Dan was bruised and singed, but otherwise looked fine.

The Captain loaded his last leather missile into his tube. Cyrus shook his head. "There are innocent people in there, people they've captured."

Captain John Smith didn't answer as four of the tattooed men jogged around the corner. The Captain smacked the first one in the face with Vlad. The next two dropped as a rifle cracked behind them in the hall, pierced by the same bullet. Diana joined them, sliding another round into her rifle chamber.

The last tattooed man retreated into the room.

"Board! Over the side, lads!" the Captain yelled, leaping into the room and whirling Vlad above his head. Dan and Cyrus followed.

Red Beard rushed forward as the tattooed men showered the Captain with darts. They glanced off his breastplate, snagged in his beard, and pinged off his spinning chain. Then one punched into his thigh, and another into his cheek.

Red Beard caught Vlad in his hands as the Captain collapsed. He lobbed the iron head over a rafter, caught it when it came back down, and wrapped it around the Captain's neck, letting him dangle.

Dan charged him, only to be kicked across the room. He slammed against the freezers and slumped to the ground.

Sword and revolver raised, Cyrus turned in place with Diana beside him. They were surrounded by men who crouched like wolves, gill slits on their necks flapping in excitement. Phoenix began to laugh.

Arachne stepped out of the other hallway, opposite Cyrus.

"Phoenix!" she yelled. She didn't wait for an answer. As Phoenix turned, she lobbed her heavy spider bag at the one-armed man in his white coat. Phoenix raised his cane, and the bag burst around it. Ten thousand spiders spilled out onto him, coating his shoulders, his face, his chest, his arms.

Behind Arachne, tattooed men stepped out of the hall. They were dragging Nolan and Jeb and both Livingstone boys with them, along with two heavy transmortals Cyrus didn't recognize. One of the men pointed a dart gun at Arachne. She didn't flinch as a dart punched into her shoulder. Slowly, she slumped to the floor.

Phoenix was twisting in place, slapping at himself with his one hand. Two of his men helped, scraping off hundreds of the tiny creatures and stomping through them on the floor. When the spiders had been cleared from Phoenix's face and hands and hair—hundreds still clung to his coat—he pushed his men away and picked up his cane. He hobbled over to where his men had dropped Jeb to the floor, spun his cane around, and placed the tip of the tooth against the base of Jeb's neck.

"Miss Boone," he said. "The rifle?"

Angry tears streamed over Diana's freckles. She dropped her gun.

Phoenix hobbled forward and stopped beside the pool with Cyrus's father in it.

"Mr. Smith," he said, and looked at Dan, who was back on his feet, held at gunpoint over by the freezers.

"Mr. Smith." He turned to the paralyzed and dangling Captain.

Finally, he turned to Cyrus. "Mr. Smith. I fear there's been some misunderstanding between us. All I plan to do is raise your father from the dead. And you hope to stop me?"

"It's vile," Dan said. "You would make him your—"

"Enough, Daniel," Phoenix said, brushing at a spider that had crawled onto his neck. "I know your thoughts. I've wandered them. I want your brother's." He studied Cyrus. "Your father would walk again, talk again." He flipped his cane and rested the tooth on the pair of hands stacked on the edge of the pool. "Would you like to hear his voice?"

Behind Phoenix, the girl tied in the chair shook and struggled.

As Cyrus stared at Phoenix, anger pricking at his eyes, he could see motion all over Phoenix's white coat. Spiders. Hundreds had survived and they were hard at work. Suddenly, Cyrus understood what Arachne had in mind. The surviving weavers were picking apart the coat at the hem, on the left shoulder, in the joint of the right arm. Ancient threads were quietly fraying—the Odysean Cloak was being unwoven.

Cyrus had to stall, to give them time to work. "What would he be like?" Cyrus asked.

"Cy!" Daniel yelled.

"Evil, like you?" Cyrus asked. "Or would he be free?"

Phoenix chuckled. "We can find out together, Cyrus Smith," he said. "I'll give you a father, and you can give me that Dracul sword."

"Or?" Cyrus asked.

Phoenix grinned, but Cyrus noticed that his face was sagging, graying even while Cyrus watched.

"Let's not discuss 'or,'" said Phoenix. "There's no need for threats. I'd like to think the Smiths could be my friends. Who else is there? The Order?" He laughed. "The dragons? Who else but me?" He pointed at Dan. "Look at your brother. Look at what he has become. With the tooth, his heart need not plague and fail him. It can be mended."

"I'd rather die," Dan said.

"And so you will," said Phoenix. "Unless the Smiths ally to me. And why not? The Smiths could be the backbone of a new, better people."

Despite himself, Cyrus felt the tug of the offer. He felt Phoenix's thoughts trying to wander into his own. Of course he wanted his brother's heart to be whole. And for his father . . . But what Phoenix promised was an illusion, and he knew it.

Cyrus shut out Phoenix's voice. He pushed away all that might be and focused on what was. Time was kind to him. It slowed while his mind raced. Phoenix was smiling, drawling his offers and promises and threats, still unaware of his spider assassins. Two tattooed men on Dan, four on Jeb and Nolan and Arachne, five on Cyrus and Diana. The red-bearded transmortal had his sword drawn and was sneering at the hanging Captain. Cyrus's father was dead in a pool with a black man's hand resting on top of his own. Oliver was dead in a pool with his hand beneath Gil's. And Gil's hand was starting to move. Cyrus blinked. Gil had a whole chestful of paralyzing darts. His eyes slipped back to the Captain. Only two darts in him; a third unused, tangled in his molten beard. And the grenade launcher, with one last shell, still dangled from his shoulder. The Captain's eyes blinked in his bulging, flushed face. The corner of his mouth twitched up.

"Fine," Cyrus blurted. Phoenix paused midsentence and leaned forward on his cane, breathless, gray.

"Bring back my father," Cyrus said. "And heal my brother. Smiths safe. But that goes for *all* the Smiths. Do what you want to the Order. They never cared about us." He tossed his revolver to the floor and flipped his sword around, gripping it carefully by the blade. Cyrus stepped forward, drifting closer to where the Captain hung from Vlad's chain. The tattooed men in front of him lifted their weapons.

"Why, Mr. Cyrus," Phoenix purred. "I *am* pleased. Let him pass."

The tattooed men drew aside, and Cyrus stepped

around a pool, even closer to the Captain. As he walked, he began to extend the hilt of his sword toward Phoenix.

Behind him, Diana gasped. "Cyrus, no!"

Dan's face was red with anger. "Cyrus, what are you doing?" he shouted.

Enkidu sneered as Cyrus approached. He reached up and patted the Captain's head. "Aren't you proud?" he said. His speech was strange and guttural.

Cyrus inhaled slowly as he moved. Now was the moment. *Now,* he told himself. The Captain was in reach. *Now!* He wasn't sure what he was waiting for. And then he heard it. They all did.

Another airplane.

Cyrus snatched the dart from the Captain's beard and lunged toward Enkidu. The tip plunged into his chest, and the red giant staggered backward.

Dan didn't miss his moment. He bowled into the two men in front of him, crashing with them into one of the empty pools.

Diana dropped to the floor and came up with her rifle, firing.

As Enkidu fell, Cyrus flipped his sword, snatched the hilt, and swung the dragon blade at the Captain's chain.

The links exploded, stinging Cyrus with shrapnel, but the Captain was ready. As he fell, he raised his launcher and fired.

The river-side wall exploded out in flame. Tattooed

men flew. Phoenix tumbled, and the concussion sent everyone else sprawling.

"River!" Phoenix screamed. "To the river!" But he crawled for the pools.

Cyrus rose to his knees. He'd lost the sword. On Phoenix's command, the surviving tattooed men retreated, scrambling through the burning wreckage. Diana fired after them as they leapt through the gaping fiery hole and dove to the water below. Phoenix was kneeling in the pool on top of Cyrus's father. He was raising his cane above the pair of hands.

Cyrus rushed forward, splashing through the nearest pool and diving for his father. As the stab fell, Cyrus landed on his father's cold body, knocking the two hands apart. Phoenix cursed as the Dragon's Tooth scraped across the edge of the pool.

Twisting onto his back in the chilly water, Cyrus kicked Phoenix in the chest and sent him tumbling. A piece of the cloak fell away as Phoenix hit the floor, and a cloud of ash rose.

Cyrus watched understanding bloom in Phoenix's eyes. Desperate with panic, he crawled toward Oliver's pool, trailing ash as he went, his coat finally unraveling beneath the small army still clinging to his back.

His stumped arm fell away in a cloud. His feet were gone in puffs.

He slithered across Gil's darted chest toward Oliver.

The big transmortal's hairy hand still rested on top of Oliver's.

Gil's eyes were rolling frantically. His fingers curled, but he couldn't move his hand.

Cyrus jumped across Gil and grabbed Phoenix's coat. It came apart in tatters in his hands. Snarling, Phoenix morphed into Mr. Ashes, but with the magic of the coat gone from the world, the beast was weak. He slid into the pool, rolled onto Oliver, and slashed at Cyrus with the tooth.

As Cyrus stepped back, he kicked Gil's huge six-fingered hand away from the side of the pool.

But Mr. Ashes smiled. Even as his body slowly dissolved into ash, muddying the pool, he spun the cane around and placed the tip against his heart.

"Laughlin for Laughlin," he whispered. With the last of his beastly strength, he plunged the tooth-cane all the way through his chest and into Oliver's. The bamboo snapped, and his body collapsed into ash and sank into the water around Oliver's body.

The river-side wall was fire. Wood crackled and burned. Diana ran to her brother where he lay collapsed on the floor. Nolan was beginning to move, and the Captain had managed to sit up.

Cyrus and Dan stood over the body of Oliver Laughlin. The tooth was buried in his chest, bamboo sticking out from between his ribs.

Then Oliver opened his eyes.

Cyrus and Dan stepped back as the boy sat up and tore the tooth free. His eyes were dark. Gills fluttered on his neck.

"Smiths," he said quietly. The voice was Oliver's, but now it drawled. He looked down at Gil and over at Enkidu. "Would you like me to end these dragons for you before I go?"

"Oliver?" Cyrus said.

In a flash, Oliver lunged forward, slashing at Cyrus's neck. Cyrus threw up his arm and took the cut across the wrist. Oliver was already running for the burning hole. Dan and Cyrus chased after him.

Oliver jumped. Two steps later, side by side, the Smiths both did the same. Across from the door, hovering in the air above the river, there was another airplane.

Antigone was in the pilot's seat. Rupert was beside her.

As Cyrus tucked into his dive, he stopped caring about the tooth, about Oliver and Phoenix and Gil and the *Ordo* bloody *Draconis.* He felt free, light enough to fly, even while falling like a stone. And when the water pounded his skull like a hammer, when his left eardrum broke and blood gushed from his nose, he kicked up, and broke the surface laughing.

twenty-two

WAKE

ROBERT BOONE WOULDN'T STOP offering explanations, which meant, in his own way, that he was apologizing.

"Phoenix always was a runner," he said, standing at an oversize flame grill on his patio, sipping iced tea, overlooking his black mountain lake. "And that's the truth, as Rupe can testify. Always a runner. Didn't figure him to stand and fight like that." He shook his head and exhaled something that was part relief and part embarrassment. "Sent my kids in there. My girl. Can't believe it."

"Pa, it's okay," Diana said, putting her arm around her father's waist. "We're alive."

"Don't let him off easy, Di!" Sadie yelled from the open kitchen.

Boone shook his head. "Shoulda been me in there."

But nobody was listening. Meat was coming off the grill, and everyone was happy to be alive. Mostly.

The small basement cellar was cool. Jars of jam and jars of apple sauce and jugs of moonshine lined the shelves.

Between the shelves, lying on the cold concrete floor, there was a pine box six and a half feet long.

Cyrus sat on one side. Antigone and Daniel sat on the other.

Three memories shared a single past. Wordlessly, they wandered the same coast, the same house, they looked into the same eyes and listened to the same laughter. The same man and the same strong arms swept them up off their feet and slung them over the same broad shoulders. The same games. The same jokes and stories and tasks. The same woman smiling the same smile from the safety of an embrace they could all still feel.

Antigone didn't bother to wipe her eyes.

Finally, Dan slid one arm around Antigone's shoulder and stretched the other across the box for Cyrus. Cyrus clasped it.

And then they spoke—those three souls sprung from two. What they said to each other in that cellar, they never shared with anyone, and they never said again. They never needed to. The words were etched deep, down in the heartwood and in the roots they shared.

Later, Dan and Cyrus and Antigone sat together, their backs against a stone wall and their feet stretched out in the meadow grass. They had come up into the sun, but in some way, they were still gathered around that simple pine box in the Boones' coolest cellar.

And they always would be.

The others came by one at a time. The first was Arachne.

She sat down in the grass with her bag in her lap. She had mended the rips, but the bag was much smaller now, and Cyrus could see the grief in her impossible eyes. It was strange, grieving for spiders, but Cyrus understood. Finally, Arachne spoke.

"Daniel, your heart . . . ," she said. "I can't fix it. No one can. Not all the way. But I can make it stronger."

"How strong?" Antigone asked. She tugged at the pearl silk visible at her waist. "This strong?"

Arachne smiled. "No. But strong enough for years of drumming."

"How many years?" Cyrus asked.

Arachne's smile faded. "Not many," she said sadly. "Sixty. Seventy, maybe."

Dan laughed. "Deal. That's old enough for me."

"By the way," Antigone said. "How do I get this Angel Skin off?"

Arachne raised her eyebrows. "You don't. It is skin. It will grow into yours, and its charms will seep into your soul."

Antigone blinked. Cyrus and Dan stared. Then Arachne giggled like a girl who had been terribly funny. "I'll show you later," she said. "When we're alone."

Little Dixie Mist was the second to come by. Sadie

Boone had insisted that she and her father stay with them as long as they liked. Cyrus thought they might like for a very long time. Alfred was thin, weak, and underfed. He'd spent the flight to Kentucky with Dixie on his lap and tears on his cheeks, rocking in place, whispering in his little girl's ear.

Cyrus hadn't been able to watch.

Now Dixie sat down cross-legged at Cyrus's feet, blocking his view of the lake. Her brown eyes were very serious.

"Your name is Cyrus Smith," she said simply.

Cyrus nodded.

"The man in the pool," Dixie said, "the man One Hand was going to bring back, he was your father."

Cyrus nodded again. It was easier than talking about it.

"We thought he was lost in the ocean," Antigone said. "But Phoenix—One Hand—had his body the whole time."

It was Dixie's turn to nod. She did so very seriously. "The girl, Diana, told me. One Hand was a devil. I'm glad you killed him."

Cyrus didn't correct her.

"You could have had your father back," Dixie said, "but you chose mine instead." Her cheeks were wet.

"Not really back," Cyrus said. His throat was tight. He bit back his words and looked at the sky, at the distant mountains, kissed by the sunset.

Then little Dixie's arms were around his neck, and his chest was shaking, no matter how hard he fought it. He sniffed and blinked and wiped his face, but it did no good. And then Antigone's head leaned onto his shoulder, and Daniel's hand grabbed his knee.

Dixie held on tight. When Cyrus exhaled and his body calmed, she let go, smiled at him, and bounced away, back to her living father.

Looking up, Cyrus saw Rupert Greeves standing beside him, his big arms crossed. Cyrus wiped his face again and blew out a long, level breath. "Embarrassing," he said.

Rupert shook his head. "Cyrus Smith, there's not a thing embarrassing about it."

And Cyrus sat and sat, with his sister leaning on him and his brother beside them. And as the sun dropped and night fell and the Kentucky stars spun across the sky, Boone lit a fire, and Sadie brought out blankets even though the night was warm, and Jax worried about his animals, and Dennis wondered aloud what Hillary Drake might be doing, and Alan Livingstone told stories about Africa, and George winced when he laughed because of his burns, and Silas tried to explain exactly what had happened on their end of the factory, and Alfred and Dixie Mist paid no mind to anyone. Neither did Horace. He was eating.

Robert Boone apologized some more, and everyone

knew he wouldn't have felt so badly if he'd actually managed to catch Oliver, who was now Phoenix. He explained that men with gills are hard to catch when you're expecting men in boats. The trap was wrong. No one really wanted to hear him explain.

For a while, Diana sat with the Smiths. She didn't say much, but what she did say was nice. And Nolan sat with them for a while, peeling his skin. What he said wasn't nice at all, and was all about how he hoped Cyrus would start training for real now and maybe read a book—not that it would do any good. But it was nice to hear him say it, and Cyrus couldn't help laughing at the grouch who lived in the Polygon.

And finally, when the voices and the fire were drifting toward sleep, Cyrus looked at his sister, and then at his brother.

"Something's missing," he said.

"Mom," said Antigone. "I know."

"Rupert says we can't go back to Ashtown yet," Dan said. "But we'll see her soon."

Cyrus looked around. "Where's the bird?" he asked.

Antigone sighed. "It freaked out," she said.

"It?" Cyrus asked. "Not she?"

Antigone nodded. "It was at the factory. We were hovering over the river, watching Horace blow up a boat and wondering what was happening, when that fireball blew out the side of the building. A minute later, the bird went nuts, flapping around the cockpit, scared of me, scared of Rupert, scared of everything. When we landed and opened the door, it took off."

Eventually, Sadie showed all of her guests to their rooms. Everyone except Cyrus. Diana took him to the Captain. They found him in the basement.

Gilgamesh was sitting on a couch with his head in his hands. His wrists and ankles were heavily chained. Enkidu and two other transmortals had been immobilized in another room. Arachne was sitting beside Gil, holding her bag. Ponce, the skinny Spaniard in the dirty pink shirt, sat on her other side.

Pythia was in the corner, half hiding in her hair, half listening to Nolan and smiling as he demonstrated the use of scissors on his own messy crop.

The Captain, still in his breastplate and filthy clothes, still with his blackened face and charred beard, was pacing. The sword was back in its sheath on his belt.

As soon as he saw Cyrus, he stopped and cleared his throat.

"Now, Gilgamesh," he said.

Gil looked up at Cyrus with his huge cow eyes, his thick purple lips, and the short beard that climbed his cheekbones.

"I'm sorry," Gil said.

Cyrus shook his head. "Not interested. I just wanted to find the Captain."

"Not interested?" the Captain asked. "Become interested, lad. Ye've received the apology of a gentleman."

"He threatened my mom," Cyrus said. "And he tried to murder me and my sister more than once in the last week. I'm not interested in anything Gilgamesh of Uruk has to say. Ever."

Gil's head sagged. The Captain nodded. "Fair is as fares due, Gillie lad. You've a debt owed. Without this lad, ye'd have been ox slaughtered, your life given to another, your carcass left as char for hungering flame."

To Cyrus, he said, "Do ye still hold the golden ring of Radu?"

Cyrus shook his head. "I lost it in the river. That's what I wanted to tell you. And also, about your chain . . . I didn't realize what it was for. Maybe I should have, but I didn't. I'm sorry I broke it. Cutting you down seemed like a good idea."

The Captain lowered his brows and eyed Cyrus, his left hand resting on the hilt of his sword.

"Fret not, son of Smiths," he said finally. "'Twas done, and done with vigor. Sorrow wins no wars. Now I play at jailer and nursemaid for your Avengel, but soon I shall be loosed upon the world. I'll be hunting dragons. Perhaps you'll join me."

Diana laughed. Cyrus shrugged. "Maybe. That will

be up to my Keeper. And thanks. I didn't mean to make things worse."

He turned to leave with Diana, but the man in the pink shirt stood up and held out his hand. When Cyrus shook it, he said, "Ponce de León, your friend and servant, Señor Cyrus, since the day Maxi was made to depart the earth with a tooth in his temple." He sank back into the couch, smiling. "And my thanks, señor, for your courage today, as well. But of course, the sweet Arachne was my guardian angel. She gave me a spider to keep watch." He crossed his legs and slapped his knee. "When I was taken, I knew she would come. She assembled quite the rescue, yes?"

Ponce slid his arm around Arachne's shoulder.

"Don't touch her," Gilgamesh growled, and Ponce's hand jumped back into his lap.

Arachne smiled.

The house slept, but Cyrus went back up to the patio. Rupert had invited him to a council of war first thing in the morning, and Horace had asked Cyrus if they could discuss Skelton's hidden holdings, but Cyrus's mind was elsewhere. He sat in a chair and stared at the stars and the fireflies and lost himself in memories of his father.

Diana curled up beneath an ancient Boone quilt in a chair just at his feet, and she fell asleep.

Cyrus pulled Patricia from his neck and let her cold

body wind around his hands and through his fingers, and he plucked her tail from her mouth so often that she gave up and coiled in his palm, content to glow.

North and east, in the bright flashing city where Liv had wearily gone to bed without so much as a massage or a shower, complaining loudly to her servants about fanatics, a man stepped onto a sidewalk.

He was tall, very tall, and his robe dangled loosely over his belt, and a dragon the color of old blood was curled on his chest. Broken chains hung from his wrists and ankles.

Barefoot, he walked the bustling streets of New York City with long, easy strides. Some tourists looked at him in fright and hurried away. Others raised their cameras. Still others felt drawn to him. They wanted to follow him and be where he was, and be what he wanted them to be, even if it killed them.

And Radu Bey marveled at the works of man and laughed, because he knew they would be his.

On Forty-First Street, he threw a policeman from his horse and jumped into the saddle.

He rode toward the brightest lights.

North and west, on the shores of Lake Michigan, Ashtown was quiet in the darkness.

In a hospital room with white walls, where a curtain

slowly stroked the back of a lake breeze and a ceiling fan ticked quietly in the darkness, there was a woman on a bed, breathing low, wet breaths.

The breathing stopped. The curtain floated. The fan ticked. And then the woman's ribs quaked with a long, long breath, like she was inhaling her own soul.

Because she was.

Katie Smith's eyes opened, and she looked around the room.

Gratitude

Jim T. for trekking
Knox A. for devouring
Aaron R. for stomping
Sisters for insisting
Parents for believing
Rory for waiting
Lovely

⚜ About the Author ⚜

N. D. WILSON is the bestselling author of the 100 Cupboards series and *Leepike Ridge.* Once, in the fourth grade, he split his buddy's arrow while shooting at a mattress from twenty yards. Now he writes at the top of a tall, skinny house, where he lives with a blue-eyed girl he stole from the ocean, their five young explorers, two tortoises, and one snake. For more information, please visit AshtownBurials.com.